Nights of Blood Wine

Nights of Blood Wine
Lush Dark Tales of Vampires ... and Others

Freda Warrington

First Published in 2017 by Telos Publishing Ltd,
5A Church Road, Shortlands, Bromley, Kent BR2 0HP, United Kingdom.

www.telos.co.uk

Telos Publishing Ltd values feedback. Please e-mail us with any comments
you may have about this book to: feedback@telos.co.uk

ISBN: 978-1-84583-951-2

Nights of Blood Wine © 2017 Freda Warrington

Cover Art © Martin Baines
Cover Design: David J Howe

The moral right of the author has been asserted.

British Library Cataloguing in Publication Data. A catalogue record for this
book is available from the British Library.

Contents

Author's Note

The first part of this collection contains ten vampire stories all based on the 'Blood Wine' world of my novels, *A Taste of Blood Wine*, *A Dance in Blood Velvet*, *The Dark Blood of Poppies* and *The Dark Arts of Blood*. Six have appeared in previous publications, four are brand new. You will find familiar characters, such as Karl, Charlotte, Stefan and Violette, amid newer faces. Some stories are self-contained, while others – for example *The Ghost Who Looks Like You* – weave in and out of the existing novels, extending the characters' stories into the past, present, and even the future.

They can be enjoyed whether or not you have read the novels.

The second section, 'Other Tales', contains five further pieces: a 'journal' extract that became part of my 1997 novel, *Dracula the Undead* – a sequel that was written to commemorate the first publication of *Dracula* in 1897, and went on to win the Dracula Society's Best Gothic Novel Award – followed by three stories loosely based on my *Aetherial Tales* series, *Elfland*, *Midsummer Night* and *Grail of the Summer Stars*. *Elfland* won the Romantic Times Award for Best Fantasy Novel, while the American Library Association named *Midsummer Night* among its Top Ten Books of the Year.

Finally there is a story, *Ruins and Bright Towers*, written in honour of the late, much-missed Tanith Lee from the 2015 anthology, *Night's Nieces*, published by Immanion Press in loving tribute to Tanith.

Part One: Blood Wine Tales

Shadows on the Wall

France, 1925

Whatever a respectable solicitor should be doing, he should most definitely not be hiding among the wisteria on a narrow balcony and spying, like a common voyeur, upon his client in bed with a lover.

Jean Paul Beauchene – thirty years old, but often told he looked like a fresh-faced undergraduate still – was a solicitor of considerable experience. He'd recently taken over the firm's special clients when the senior partner, Victor Lalande, had died at the age of seventy-nine. This select group had particular requirements, legal needs that were not always entirely legal, and, of course, absolute discretion. Jean Paul was determined to look after them with the same calm, professional dedication as his respected predecessor. After all, Victor had spent years training him.

But … without his mentor, the job was harder than he'd anticipated. And much stranger. That was why some irrational impulse had compelled him to come here – the most stupid exploit of his life – and here he stood now, trembling from the exertion of climbing up the trellis, shivering with nerves.

The bedroom was in a remote chateau. The room's colours were all faded blue, aqua and old gold, the furnishings lush with embroidery and tassels, every piece of furniture a riot of rococo embellishment. How cosy and luxurious the room looked, warm in the low amber light of oil lamps. The drapes of blue velvet were held back by twisted gold rope. The lace curtains behind them were draped more loosely, partly obscuring the scene, kissing the panes where they clung to a mist of condensation.

The bedroom was thus made foggy, framed by filmy layers like an old photograph. But he saw clearly the great four-poster bed that dominated the room. The canopy was a lavish tapestry of pastoral scenes. Carved gold-leaf cherubs cavorted around the posts. The embroidered bedcover had been thrown back to reveal white sheets and lace-edged pillows.

And on the bed – on the bed lay his most valuable and enigmatic client, Karl Alexander von Wultendorf. Presently shedding his last piece of clothing, a white shirt. It pooled on the rug with a scattering of other garments: dark trousers and jacket, a tie, a dress of peachy-gold lace, translucent wisps that were slips and stockings.

Jean Paul had never before seen his female companion.

In fact, he had never seen Karl with anyone. Their meetings had always taken place after dark, in secret, sometimes in the office and sometimes in a hotel room or some rented apartment. Often it had been just Victor and Karl, behind a closed door, but occasionally Jean Paul had sat in. Learning.

A few weeks ago, Karl had written to express his sorrow at Victor's death. He also instructed Jean Paul to carry out the purchase of a property in Switzerland, a remote and ramshackle dwelling that had stood empty for some years. A strange choice. But Karl insisted that he and his wife wished to buy the place.

Wife? Jean Paul had been startled. Karl had never before mentioned a wife. Victor had told him that Karl was solitary by nature. This was new. So, Karl had fallen in love, and his lover was not a secret passing fancy but a soul companion to be officially acknowledged – at least to those he trusted.

And those he trusted should not be spying upon him …

Beauchene put that thought aside.

The woman was breath-taking. The sheets were thrown back so he could see every inch of her. Slender, not too thin, but sleek. Ivory skin burnished by lamplight. Her hair flowed in ripples and cascades over her shoulders, changing colour as she moved. Blonde and corn and russet, now darkening to brown, now shining again like spun sunlight. How he envied Karl, finding such a rare and sweet beauty. But Karl was an arrestingly handsome man, with dark hair that was red-tinged like glowing coals, a quality of absolute stillness and astonishing eyes that held you in thrall: the eyes of a panther. Naturally he would find a jewel.

The solicitor envied them both, as they ran eager hands over each other's bodies and shared long deep kisses. He caught his breath to see the woman lift one knee and Karl, with exquisite slowness, aligning his hips with hers, accepting her warm, hungry invitation and sliding … sliding inside her. Deep inside that gorgeous rose.

Jean Paul was now so close to the glass balcony doors that his breath clouded the pane. He started back, terrified of being noticed. Yet he couldn't stop watching, any more than they could pause in their urgent journey.

Transfixed, he stood there.

Oh God, he thought. Sweat ran down his face. Heat swelled in his groin but the stirring was drowned by fear. He shouldn't be here. He was terrified – of being discovered, or of something worse he couldn't even name.

He saw the woman throw her head back in pleasure. Her mouth was open, eyes closed. Even through the glass her heard her cries, saw her whole gilded-ivory body undulating with spasms of ecstasy. Saw Karl moving with her. The way his limbs tightened, every muscle rigid, arms straining, frozen for a moment like an athlete chiselled from stone – then relaxing, going with her, deep inside her, losing himself … both of them, joined and lost in each other.

Karl's mouth went down to Charlotte's throat. She convulsed again.

When the dark head rose, there was blood – on her neck, and on his lips. Not much, but there – a few thick crimson drops like garnets. They were both panting for breath, eyes fixed on each other. Then she reared up – made Beauchene think of a striking cobra – and bit Karl on the shoulder. He saw her teeth go right into the flesh. Her *fangs*.

They seemed almost to fight each other – clinging tight, like two predators in a death grip. Straining hard against each other, climaxing again and again, as if they would never stop. Karl rolled over, lifting Charlotte above him. She arched up and backwards, her head falling back and her hair streaming, riding him like a princess mounted upon an eager horse. Now the blood streaked his shoulder and escaped onto the pillow and sheets. Drops fell from her tongue onto his chest. She bent and lapped it up.

And they were both laughing.

All the blood, and yet they laughed!

He'd never seen such perverse joy. God, such wild abandon. The way they were wrapped up in each other, welded together in their amber cocoon of lust and torn flesh, creating their own unholy paradise … Jean Paul's too-quick breathing made him turn faint. He clung to the balcony rail. He should never have witnessed this, and now he could never unsee it.

But … this had answered his most pressing question, at least.

Just how long had Victor Lalande been dealing with Karl's legal affairs, before Jean Paul had even joined the firm? He had no idea, but the records went back well into the nineteenth century. He had once asked the older solicitor if perhaps they pertained to Karl's father, even to his grandfather, but Lalande had responded with a quiet, fierce warning.

'Ask no such questions. Ask no questions of him at all, ever. All you need to know is that he requires the utmost discretion. Do precisely as he instructs you, and he'll reward you well, as he always has me. But *no questions*. Do not even think them.'

Victor grew old, while Karl stayed the same.

You should not be here, said his conscience as he stood watching the lovers in their lazy, contented afterglow. *What is wrong with you? What are you thinking?*

Jean Paul dared not give any shape to the answer. He took a flask of brandy from his coat pocket and swallowed a sip. His hands were shaking.

Inside the bedroom, the woman stirred in the tangle of sheets, sat up draped in her shimmering mermaid hair, and looked towards the window.

She said something he couldn't catch, but the meaning was plain. She'd seen or sensed a presence on the balcony. Karl got up – stark naked, as graceful as a Greek statue come to life – and then it seemed they were both staring straight at him, their eyes lit from inside.

He panicked. Hitched himself over the balcony, fell twelve feet to the garden below where a dense, leafy bank of shrubs saved him like a prickly mattress. Above, the light vanished as someone closed the curtains.

'I thought I heard something. Sensed someone,' said Charlotte. She'd become a vampire barely three months earlier. Their only choice after that had been to flee her family and leave England altogether.

'So did I,' said Karl. 'But we were both distracted. There's nothing there now.'

'They always take me by surprise, these impressions that filter in from nowhere. It's like having extra senses. I think a human is right beside me when they are two rooms away. It's wondrous, but it still startles me. When will I get used to it?'

Karl returned to the bed and sat beside her, playing with her hair. Charlotte had been in his world such a short time, but now he couldn't imagine his world without her. He had done the thing he'd sworn never to do – created another vampire – so that they could stay together. And that meant they'd left behind a trail of death and sorrow in order to share this all-consuming love. But Karl was not inclined to feel guilt. Not for long, anyway.

He did, however, take Charlotte's well-being more seriously than anything else in the world.

'And when will I get used to no longer being alone?' he said. 'Everything is strange and new for both of us. And quite wonderful.'

'Paradise,' she said, resting her cheek on his hand. 'A novelty for you, to think of buying an actual house? A home. *Our* home.'

'Well, I promised I would not take you to live in a mausoleum. I have no taste for tombs, beloved.'

'I'd happily live in a tomb with you.' Charlotte smiled. 'I rather like *this* place.'

'Yes, a pleasant chateau to rent for a while. Alas, not for sale, and anyway too close to civilisation. It's desirable for us … to vanish.'

'I shall love a chalet in the mountain wilderness just as much,' she said. 'When is Monsieur Beauchene coming?'

'Tomorrow evening, at seven. I always meet such people after dark.'

'Why? To unsettle them?'

'To keep matters as secret as possible. However, if they are a little nervous, that's no bad thing. It makes them more eager to please. But remember the rules …'

'His blood is out of bounds. Karl, really, you can trust me. I won't touch him, I promise. What is he like?'

'A pleasant young man. I don't know him well: I mostly dealt with

Victor, his mentor. He's a hard man to replace, but Beauchene seems decent. Handsome, fair-haired, very earnest. Quite shy, especially in female company.'

'I like him already,' Charlotte said. 'I'll try not to terrify him. Was it the chateau gardener, do you think?'

'What?'

'Watching us from outside. He must be more agile than he looks, to clamber up the vines. I hope he thought the effort was worth it. Disgraceful old man.'

'Dearest, it was most likely just an owl,' said Karl.

Back at his modest apartment in Paris, Jean Paul took off his damp coat, hat and gloves, removed his wet shoes, lit an oil lamp. He'd driven his car to the chateau, but walked the last rural half-mile so that Karl and his bride wouldn't hear his approach. Then done the same in reverse, pushing though wet foliage and hurrying along the road beneath dripping trees. The fall from the balcony had shaken him. Every shadow made him jump, and the night was full of shadows. Finally he had reached home, shaking with cold and nervous exhaustion.

He poured himself a brandy. Sitting down in an armchair, he carefully cleaned the raindrops and smears from his spectacles with a soft cloth. He concentrated hard on the task so as not to think of anything else. Outside the rain fell into the dark wet streets, discouraging revellers and muffling the skeins of noise that drifted from theatres, jazz clubs and restaurants nearby.

All his life he'd been studious and correct in his behaviour. Averse to risk. His exploit tonight was completely out of character, and yet …

A scratching noise at the window.

Now a fluttering sound, like wind ruffling through the ivy, or some animal seeking a firmer purchase on the vines as it climbed the outside wall.

Tap tap tap.

Jean Paul drained his glass and went to the windows. He saw the black shape clinging below the window ledge, reaching up with one hand to claw at the pane. The street was blurred, dark like an abyss full of wind and water. Nothing else existed.

No, Jean Paul whispered to himself in a kind of slow-rising panic. *No no no.*

Now the thing was climbing higher, the inky head rising inch by inch until it was level with his. The featureless face stared in at him. He was caught there in a state of utter terror, seeing his own face reflected dimly as if superimposed on that of the night creature. And yet he found his hands rising, fumbling with the latch.

The window was barely a palm's width open when the shape came slithering into the room, as soft and fluid as a jet-black altar cloth.

At first it was a pool spread on the carpet, then it rose upright into a wavering form: not solid but a gap, a door onto the terrifying abyss of night. Then it spoke.

'Here you are, Jean Paul.'

It was a man's voice, low and smoky. The man-shaped nothingness became three-dimensional, a sudden switch like an optical illusion. Jean Paul caught the hint of facial features. Eyes. His heart dropped with fear, only to rise again, fluttering upwards with horrible excitement and anxiety.

The intruder moved into the dim lamplight. He was young, good-looking, with tousled dark hair and a sardonic half-smile. Jean Paul knew him – in a way – but had not expected to see him again. But then, he never did.

'Antoine.'

'Aren't you going to invite me in properly?'

'You must leave,' Jean Paul whispered. 'The concierge ...'

'Damn the concierge. She can't keep me out. Are you not happy to see me again?'

'No, I don't want this ...'

'And yet you let me in. You always let me in. Oh, there is blood on your face! You're covered in scratches, my friend. You've had an accident?'

'Yes. I tripped, it's nothing.'

The half-stranger raised his hand and ran his thumb down one of the lacerations on Jean Paul's cheek. He licked the smear of blood from the tip, then ran that thumb-pad across Jean Paul's lips. His eyes gleamed, drawing his prey into his power ... panther eyes, just like those of Karl von Wultendorf. Exactly like Karl.

Jean Paul felt himself falling. It was a terrible feeling, guilt-laden and dirty, but laced with the promise of bliss, like an addiction to opium.

Oh God, he thought. *No. Not again.*

'Yes,' he said out loud. 'God, yes. I always let you in.'

Jean Paul began trembling again as he approached the chateau, this time for his official meeting with Karl. He drove his small Citroen right up to the doors. The sun was setting, a great red globe dropping and dissolving into the cloudy horizon. A breeze made everything flutter around him. Grape vines and wisteria. He glanced up at the balcony where the dangling purple blooms had helped to conceal him the previous night. A chill of guilt, horror and excitement rushed through him.

'Monsieur Beauchene,' Karl greeted him, and led him through to a dimly-lit salon. The woman he'd seen last night was there, as formal and elegant as a young duchess ... he hoped he was not blushing. In the centre was a small round table with three chairs, ready for them to conduct their business. 'Charlotte, allow me to introduce Jean Paul Beauchene ...'

'Madame.'

The feel of her hand in his was like a cold waterfall. Like Karl she was beautiful, but in her own way, all shades of rose and sunset gold. An aura surrounded her. Sequins gleamed on her elegant low-waisted dress. Her hair was moulded in soft, fashionable waves, clasped at the nape of her neck – but last night, he had seen her hair unbound, rippling over her shoulders, trailing over Karl's naked chest like flame.

Now she was like a different woman; dignified and reserved, even shy, although he wasn't even sure that *shy* was the right word. Reserved, not because she was nervous, but because she was cautious, self-contained, observant.

'I understand that congratulations are in order, sir.' Jean Paul's voice almost failed. 'A new bride!'

He saw Charlotte look sideways at Karl. Her profile was heart-rendingly pretty. 'Do you always introduce your new brides to your solicitor?' she said.

Karl gave her a speaking look, eyebrows slightly raised. They smiled at each other, sharing some private joke. Jean Paul cleared his throat.

'Er, one and only bride, of course. Forgive me. Congratulations.'

'Thank you,' said Karl, expressionless.

'Do sit down,' Charlotte said with more warmth. She looked so human, and yet he knew ... 'Would you like some tea?'

'No, Madame, thank you.' He pulled a sheaf of papers from his briefcase, nearly dropped them but managed to capture them before they slid through his fingers into chaos. As he squared the papers into a neat pile on the table, Karl put his hand on top of Jean Paul's. The touch made him freeze.

'Before we begin,' Karl said, 'I wish to say how very sad I was to hear of Monsieur Lalande's death. My deepest condolences. He will be greatly missed.'

Jean Paul nodded, swallowed. 'Yes, indeed. Thank you. His were very great shoes to fill, and I can't hope ... but I shall do my utmost to serve you as he did before me.'

'You know your work inside out. If the documents are in order, that will suffice,' said Karl.

Jean Paul began to talk through the technicalities, aware he was talking too fast, all the time trying to blot out his intrusive thoughts. Images of this proper, beautifully dressed couple naked and in disarray ... the blood ... sharp fangs piercing flesh, whirling faintness ... the terrible gaping black abyss ... Karl's eyes. Glowing panther eyes like fiery moons. Tried to stop himself thinking, *I know what you are. I know what you are. I know ...*

'There's no need to explain every point of law,' Karl said, smiling now.

'Show me where to sign.'

'And you are happy to proceed with the completion of this purchase? I understand the chalet, although it stands in an area of unsurpassed beauty, is in some disrepair ...'

'Yes, we are happy,' Karl answered. 'Carpenters and builders can be found. Let us worry about that.'

'As you wish, sir.'

Karl signed the document with one of the false identities he used for such transactions. If anyone chose to investigate who owned a remote chalet high in the foothills of the Swiss Alps, the trail would wind through unknown names and businesses, through a maze of false trails to nowhere. Thus non-human beings lived in the human world, leaving no imprint.

Karl passed a wallet of fine black leather to him. A large amount of cash – several times what a human would pay for the same service – in a discreet and elegant package. Their business was over. Yet Jean Paul sat there sweating, not knowing what to say. He was light-headed. This felt all wrong and unfinished, yet he did not know how to finish it.

'Monsieur Beauchene, are you well?' said Charlotte. 'You look pale.'

Jean Paul became aware that he was swallowing too often. The more he tried to control his trembling, the worse it got. 'Quite well, Madame, thank you.'

'Please, let me pour you a brandy.'

'Thank you, that's most kind, but I should be on my way now. I'll be in touch in due course. I bid you good evening, Monsieur, Madame.'

He got up fast, clumsy as he repacked his briefcase.

'Oh, there's no hurry, is there?' said Charlotte. Her voice was warm, her whole demeanour so alluring ... 'We've barely met.'

'Forgive me, I don't wish to be rude, but I really must ...'

'I'll fetch your coat and hat.'

Jean Paul followed her, but he stopped in the doorway, hesitating. Karl was in the salon, Charlotte near the front door. Their aura wove webs of terror over him, an irrational feeling that if they decided to keep him here, there was nothing he could do to escape. Yet their eyes were full of concern. Glowing, unhuman, yet kind.

He snatched a breath. He had to tell someone, and who could he ask but them? He was desperate for help, advice. The words gathered on his tongue but would not come out. There was no one else he could turn to, yet he dared not trust them. Shame overwhelmed him.

'Jean Paul?' Karl said softly. 'Is something wrong? You have turned quite grey. If there is a problem, you can tell us.'

'Yes, you seem upset. Do come back in and let me pour you that brandy,' said Charlotte.

At that point his nerve failed. 'Thank you.' He gave a small bow, pushed his spectacles up his nose with a shaking hand. 'Madame, Monsieur, it's nothing. A slight head-cold, this damp weather ... I bid you good evening.'

And he strode across the hall, snatched his coat and hat from Charlotte with rude haste, and dashed out into the night.

'Well?' said Charlotte. She and Karl sat in chairs by the fireplace, facing each other. 'I wish he had stayed to talk. He looked dreadful.'

'I want him to be Victor. Dry, emotionless, focussed entirely upon business. But he is not Victor, and that's a difficulty. We cannot deal with a solicitor who is in any way ... unstable.'

'Karl, my beloved darling, aren't you being a little callous? All humans have their flaws. He might be heart-broken, or unwell. That doesn't mean he can't do his job.'

'I don't wish to be callous, but in these matters we need his expertise, not his private troubles. Unfortunately, this is serious, because I believe his difficulties are with us.'

'You mean that he ... knows what we are?'

'Victor knew, but was ever the soul of discretion. Jean Paul knows, and cannot cope with the knowledge. He's unsettled. He feels he's in danger, and that may lead him to do something rash.'

'Such as what?'

'Something more likely to harm himself than us. I suspect ...' Karl shook his head. He watched the way the fire-glow danced on Charlotte's hair, on her sunset dress and her smooth arms. 'I shall have to pay him a visit.'

'Not to frighten him? Promise you won't cause him any distress. I like him.'

'I can't promise. It's not my intention to alarm him. But Charlotte, *liebling*, you realise ... You know he was the one on the balcony last night, spying upon us? I was not sure at the time, but when Jean Paul arrived this evening, I recognised his aura. It was him.'

'Oh,' she said. Her eyes widened. '*Oh.*'

Karl went alone into the streets of Paris, seeking the signature of a vampire – a subtle thing like a sliver of cold glass pressing into his mind, an icicle amid the hot bustle of humans. Past night clubs and theatres he went, searching for the little ice-breath amid the crowds pouring from cabarets. Clouds of cigarette smoke and alcohol-tainted human breath washed over him, along with the deep pulse of so many rushing heartbeats ... but he ignored temptation.

Nothing.

Then the obvious struck him. With a dull sense of dread, he made his way to the offices of *Lalande & Beauchene, Solicitors.*

Inside, the musty old rooms panelled with dark wood were deserted. The smell was of cigar smoke, leather, and old books. He saw Victor everywhere, could not believe he was gone. Karl felt a very human sense of sorrow. He missed the old man who had dealt with his clandestine legal affairs for years. Dry, strait-laced and humourless, Victor had nonetheless proved utterly reliable. A friend.

Still, Karl had no time to linger or mourn. Quickly he found Jean Paul's home address in a desk drawer.

He lived in a modest *arrondissement*, a slightly seedy area not far from the *Moulin Rouge.* In time he would grow wealthier, if he applied himself wholeheartedly to doing business for his particular clients – but not, Karl thought, if he cannot shape himself into another Victor Lalande.

The thought of having to discard Beauchene and search for another advisor of Victor's skill dismayed him. It could take months, years.

Karl soon found the grand old building, divided into many small apartments, and there he entered the Crystal Ring in order to pass through the walls. Jean Paul's was on an upper storey; Karl caught the signature of his aura, a cool pale grey-and-blonde outline, like the man himself.

And something else, a cold black sliver of obsidian …

Entering Jean Paul's bedroom, he saw only pale hands and feet on the bedcover. The rest of him was covered by what seemed to be a black cloak. A moving cloak made of absolute darkness.

Karl seized the shadow. He thought his hands might go straight through but they did not. He felt solid shoulders in his grip. Then he groped upwards with one hand, along the vampire's neck and chin until he found the place where its mouth was fastened on Jean Paul's throat. A lot of struggling began beneath him, but he focussed entirely on prising the jaws open – easing the fangs out of the flesh so that the victim's throat would not be torn.

He heard the jaw crack. The vampire uttered a noise of pain and rage. Then Karl hauled him upwards and backwards, off Jean Paul, and flung him down onto the floorboards.

The solicitor – embarrassingly attired only in his undergarments – lay flopped on the bed, gasping. His eyes were sightless with confusion. But he was alive. Still alive.

Meanwhile the dark vampire was rising to his feet and lunging away, trying to flee into the Crystal Ring.

Karl leapt after him and held him in place.

In that second he knew himself to be much stronger and older than this vampire. This was a stranger, and quite young, inexperienced – no danger to Karl, but still a very great danger to any human.

'Who are you?' said Karl, holding on to the angry, struggling intruder.

'Show yourself. I will take your blood, if I must.'

At that threat, the stranger went still. The strange inky fog that cloaked him faded away to reveal a man who looked only in his twenties, handsome but jaded, like any man to be found smoking and drinking and leering at a burlesque show. Almost human, but for his savage display of teeth and the blood slicking his lips.

'Karl,' Jean Paul's voice came weakly from the bed.

'How long has this creature been visiting you?'

'Don't know. Few months.'

'Has he a name?'

'Antoine Matisse.'

'Is this not some breach of etiquette?' the vampire Antoine growled. He rubbed at his chin. 'I think you have broken my jaw. We do not interfere with each other's prey. How dare you?'

'You have been preying upon a human who is valuable to me, Antoine.'

'So? I prey on all sorts. Do you own him?'

'In a way. I certainly intend to protect him.'

'Well, he's rather dear to me also.' Antoine's fangs retracted but he still looked furious. 'Anyway, what business is it of yours? Who are you?'

'Someone who will destroy you unless you leave him alone.'

Antoine began a mocking snort of laughter, cut off as Karl grabbed him by the throat and slammed him against the bedroom wall behind him. 'Now I am asking politely, as a courtesy between our kind, that you leave him alone.'

Antoine made a defiant face. 'I can't. I won't. He is special to me.'

'Perhaps my name will help you make a decision. I am Karl Alexander, also called Karl von Wultendorf.'

At that, all the younger vampire's defiance bled away. The fresh blood reddening his cheeks drained to white. He looked … awe-struck, if anything.

'Jesus,' Antoine gasped. '*You are the vampire that killed Kristian.*'

'News travels fast. Yes, I killed him.'

'Such news travels like lightning. You slew the tyrant. I would like to shake your hand, if you would desist from trying to choke me.'

Karl pressed harder. The contours of Antoine's face made a subtle transition from pained shock to terror. He tried to speak, but only *agh* noises came out.

'You will leave Monsieur Beauchene alone. He will never see you again. You will never seek him out again. If ever I hear of you preying upon him, or even *near* him, I will find you. Do you promise?'

When Antoine nodded – as best he could in Karl's grip – and rasped out, 'Yes, I promise,' Karl let go and watched him slide down the wall to his knees.

'Drink my blood to seal the vow,' said Karl, and put his wrist to the hapless Antoine's lips. 'You're an idiot, but perhaps not beyond hope.'

'Karl?' Jean Paul was on his feet, now wrapped in a dressing gown. He looked ghastly.

'Go into the parlour and wait for me.'

Then Karl took his wrist from the other vampire's mouth and pulled the wilting Antoine to his feet. 'Leave.' He marched Antoine to the apartment's front door, opened it and pushed him outside into the stairwell. 'Use the conventional way out.'

'I wish to offer my sincere regret,' Antoine said unexpectedly. 'I should not have encroached on your … territory. We need not be enemies, Karl, need we? I feel I could learn much from you. Now, damn it, I shall have to find a new solicitor.'

'Get out,' said Karl.

Back in the parlour, he brought Jean Paul a glass of red wine and sat him on the small hard couch. Outside, a cold breeze ruffled the ivy. Street lights created flickering patterns in the darkness, ever-moving sinister shadows.

Karl closed the window and the curtains, sat down beside Jean Paul in this small room of dim browns and reds. The typical lodgings of a bachelor.

'How did you know?' said Jean Paul, subdued.

'I suspected,' said Karl. 'You showed signs that are familiar to me. A greyish pallor, a particular type of nervousness … irrational behaviour that is out of character.'

He meant the balcony incident, as Jean Paul obviously guessed. 'Yes,' he said, wincing. 'I have not been in my right mind at all.'

'So, Antoine was one of your clients?'

Beauchene nodded miserably. 'Victor had several unconventional clients, as you know.'

'But there has to be trust. There are certain humans we do not exploit. Antoine should have known that.'

'He began to … visit me. I didn't know how to stop him.' Jean Paul was quiet for a while. Without his spectacles, his face looked naked and very young. 'Once you see, you can't unsee. I do not think I can do this job, Karl.'

A week later, Jean Paul was at the chateau again. He had not meant to come back. He was too embarrassed, too afraid, so acutely aware of how close he'd come to death. As he stood outside looking up at the handsome building with its small wrought-iron balconies, a thrill of dread went through him. He almost turned back to his car, but the door opened and Charlotte was there, so lovely, so welcoming.

'I wish to apologise.' He stood in the hallway with his hat in his hands, turning it round and round by the brim.

'For what?' said Karl.

'May we speak in private?'

Charlotte and Karl exchanged a glance, then she went upstairs and Karl led him into the salon and closed the door. Jean Paul sat down and huddled by the fire, still in his coat, while Karl stayed on his feet.

'You look somewhat better,' Karl said. 'He kept his word?'

'Yes. I want to say thank you, and to apologise. You saved my life. But I have behaved abominably … his visits … I should have known better than to have any contact with a client outside work, but I didn't know how to make it stop. You see, I never knew the exact nature of Victor's clients until I met Antoine. After that, I suspected everyone.'

'As you said: once you've seen, you cannot unsee.'

'Exactly. And his attentions … I went mad for a while. Did something perfectly unforgivable. I became obsessed with discovering if you were also, like Antoine, something not human. I did not expect to witness … but that's beside the point. I should not have been spying upon you *at all*. It was utterly reprehensible. You'd be quite right to dismiss me …'

'No need to say any more,' said Karl. 'I'm sure it won't happen again.'

'Of course not, but … perhaps you, as another man, can accept my apology for seeing what I should not have seen, but Charlotte, Madame Alexander – how can she ever possibly forgive?'

'She can, believe me. I won't embarrass either of you by asking her to say as much to your face, but I assure you, Jean Paul – she knows more than you ever will of the madness induced by vampires.'

'I am so sorry.'

He was still shivering, despite the flames' heat.

Patiently Karl said, 'Is there something else? I can see you are still troubled. You have a choice: you could see the doctor for your nerves, perhaps move to a different city and work for normal clients. Forget all this – if you can. Or learn to live with the darkness. It's up to you.'

'Yes, I know. It's not that. Oh, damn it!' Jean Paul gave a grunt of frustration, then forced out the truth. 'It's Antoine.'

'You said he had not come back. And he won't, I promise.'

'And that's the trouble. I – don't know how I can live without him.' The words rushed out. 'This is so shaming! I dream of him. I sit up in bed in the dead of night, waking violently from nightmares. I weep for no reason. I stare out of my window, waiting for the dark shape of his head to appear. It's sick, it's appalling. I – it's not as if I even have a predilection for men, I love women, I dream of being contentedly married one day, but this … It's as if my heart is being torn out of my chest. I feel – I feel exactly like an abandoned lover. Broken. And I am so ashamed.'

Jean Paul subsided, drained. Karl did not look at all shocked by the outburst. He leaned down and rested a hand on Jean Paul's forearm, calming him.

'No, there's no need for shame. The vampire's bite can cause a kind of addiction, if it is repeated. It's what we do. Personally, I try to avoid such a circumstance, but other vampires might not care. They might prey upon a single victim on purpose, and eventually leave them dead, or feeling as you do now. It's not your fault.'

'What shall I do?'

'As I said, you have a choice. The trouble with running away is that the nightmares may well follow you. You will always be their slave. But if you stay and embrace the darkness, as Victor did – I can't promise it will be easy. But I can help you.'

Jean Paul swallowed hard. He was still terrified for his very soul. To let Karl down, though, or to let *Victor* down – that would be worse. Unthinkable.

'Help me,' he said. 'I wish to stay. Please help me.'

'You are certain? This will not be pleasant.'

'I'm certain.'

'Very well.'

Karl emitted a very faint sigh. He paused, then a change came over him, as if he'd made a decision and passed into a different, terrifying state of consciousness, devoid of emotion like a cobra.

He bent towards Jean Paul. This was not as it had been with Antoine, quick and lustful. Karl's approach was something altogether more disturbing, slower, more profound. Mesmeric. Mystical, terrible, transformative on a level so deep it could not be defined.

His eyes were soft and completely hypnotic, like two moons the colour of honey, with two discs of infinite black space at the centre. Jean Paul was lost in his gaze. He went still, stopped breathing altogether as Karl bent down and bit neatly into his neck.

Of blood Karl did not take much. He sipped economically, keeping Jean Paul in place with a thumb pressed to his forehead. The room rotated gently around them, like a carousel coming to rest, all its blurred golden lights gradually settling. Time paused. Then it began to move again, second by second. Karl licked clean the wounds he had made and drew away. Soon the marks would heal, leaving only the faintest silvery scars.

'Forget all this now, Jean Paul. In the deep layers of your subconscious, in the back of your mind, you will always remember, and know full well, that your clients are different and particular in their needs. But no word of it will ever come to your lips. No doubts will ever cloud your intellect. Be at peace now. Wake, and be at peace with what you know.'

Then Karl released the pressure of his thumb on the solicitor's forehead and sat back.

Jean Paul opened his eyes and looked around the room, bewildered.

'What was I saying? Forgive me, I quite lost track of our conversation. Please tell me I didn't fall asleep.'

'Perhaps for a moment or two,' Karl said with a smile. 'It is late.'

Hurriedly he got up, swaying. 'I should bid you goodnight. I did not mean to outstay my welcome.'

'You haven't, not at all. Don't forget your hat,' said Karl, escorting him to the front door. 'Do have a safe journey home, Monsieur Beauchene. Thank you.'

Charlotte was on the bottom stair. Beauchene bowed and tipped his hat to them both as he left. 'Thank you for your continued business, Monsieur and Madame Alexander. Anything else I can do for you, at any time ... I'm always ready to help.'

The front door closed, wafting the scent of night flowers into the hall. Karl turned to Charlotte and took her hands. He sighed.

'You altered his memory in some way.' Her voice was softly disapproving.

'Helped him accept, so he doesn't go mad.'

'You know I heard every word that passed between you?'

'Then you heard that he gave consent.'

'Karl, you fed from him. *Really.* His blood is out of bounds, you told me. Let us never feed upon those we know, you said.'

'Sometimes there have to be exceptions. Yes, it is against my principles to interfere with human lives ... And you know that I've fallen short of those ideals more often than I care to admit. That is why I laid the choice before him. When we need to deal with such matters, legal matters, in the human world, it's vital we have solicitors of the utmost reliability and discretion. And often, in fact almost always, we have to ... coach them in this way.'

'Subdue them,' she said. 'Bend them to our will.'

'Yes, because - however long it may take - in the end they always see what we are. And then they grow frightened, and start making rash mistakes. So I had to break his link with Antoine. I had to detach him from his shame and fear and self-doubt so that he can *function.* We need someone steady and mature, who knows what we are but turns a blind eye. Someone we can trust.'

'Of course. Karl, I appreciate that. This *is* a different life.'

'Do you think my old solicitor, Victor, was always the wise soul of discretion on whom I came to rely so completely? No. All those years ago ... Victor was young, enthusiastic, bright, even more nervy and impressionable than our new man. So of course I had to accustom him to the darkness. As with old Victor Lalande ... so with Jean Paul. *Now* he is ours.'

The Fall of the House of Blackwater

Note: Sebastian Pierse is also a major player in The Dark Blood of Poppies, *and his experience here takes place before the novel begins – setting the scene, in a way.*

She enters the room, luminous by the light of the candle she carries. In the darkness beyond her curtained bed, I wait unseen. No one ever sees me until I want them to; I'm less than a whisper, a dream. The bedroom is cavernous. Its heart glows orange from the fire banked in the grate, but this weak radiance cannot reach the massed black shadows around it.

She is luscious, barely eighteen. Her hair falls like honey over the white shoulders of her nightdress. She's quite short, slightly plump; completely desirable. Her eyes are darkest violet, her mouth so deep a red it looks almost purple, like a ripe plum. Her name is Elizabeth.

She's the only surviving child of her parents and they've arranged a marriage for her, so I've learned, to some cousin who will come here to live and thus secure the future of the family estate and fortune … A respectable Christian marriage, designed to provide mutual wealth, a place in society, a new dynasty … all that stuff. I don't care for the dry details.

She's a virgin, trembling on the chasm lip of marriage. That's all we need to know.

She sets down the candle beside her bed and climbs in. Clutching the sheets around her chin, she stares with those enormous pansy-petal eyes at her future. A pulse ticks in her temple. Can she sense me watching?

A maid bustles in, causing me to draw back with a faint hiss of annoyance. This young, freckly intruder chatters as she pokes the fire, then wipes her hands on her apron and fusses with the bed-covers even as my prey sits prettily against the pillows, waiting for her to leave. The maid brushes dangerously close to me as I draw back behind the heavy bed-curtains. She has no idea I'm there, inches from her. She says things like, 'Ah, it's soon you'll be married! You look like a child still. Before you know it, your own children will be running around the place, and you a grand lady!'

The girl smiles enigmatically.

At last the maid is gone, taking her bustling energy with her. The fire fades to a red sulk. Elizabeth bends towards the candle, her lips pouting to blow it out – then she hesitates. Looking over her shoulder, she asks, 'Who's there?' She speaks lightly, as if she feels foolish at her own sudden fear.

If ever someone introduces himself to you by saying, 'Don't be afraid,' my advice is to run, run like the wind! Why would a stranger anticipate fear, unless it was they who posed a danger? Yet that is what I say. I even speak her name.

'Elizabeth. Don't be afraid.'

She startles, clutching the bed covers to her chin. Her eyes are pools of astonished innocence. I catch her warm scent; soap and rosewater, with a hint of smooth female musk beneath. She's terrified – not in a make-a-screaming-rush-for-the-door sense, but in the deeper way that turns the victim deathly still. Yet there's fascination in her gaze. Before she acts, she needs to know what I am. And that's the space I have to work in.

'How did you get in?' she whispers. 'Who are you?'

'A ghost,' I reply. I move just enough to let her see me. Her lips open. I glimpse myself in the looking-glass on her dressing table – it's a myth that we cast no reflection – and I see what she must see; a high, curved cheekbone, shapely nose and jaw, long black lashes. Pallid features a sculptor might have chiselled with idealistic fingers, shaded by hair that is dark, formless and too long. My eyes are deceptive; they're the green-brown of hazel nuts and they look gentle, pensive. They tell you nothing about my character.

'Just a shade, fair child,' I tell her gently. 'I need your help. Would you help me?'

There's so much history in this house, Blackwater Hall. I should know, for I built it.

Eight years the construction took me, and in 1704 the Hall was finished, standing magnificent beside the River Blackwater amid the rich landscape of County Waterford. My wife Mary was weeks from giving birth. Years, it had taken us to conceive a child! Now all my dreams were close to fruition. Soon we would be leaving the decrepit tower of my Norman and Anglo-Irish ancestors and moving into the new mansion, a place grand enough to befit our heirs. Such struggles I'd had to keep my estate from the hands of the conquering English! I even changed faith from Catholic to Protestant to save it from confiscation – and yet it slipped from my hands anyway. All gone in one terrible night.

Perhaps this was divine punishment. To me, it meant little to betray my religion, since I never was devout. All I cared about was keeping my lands – not out of greed, but passion. I loved my birthright so deeply; I valued it even above my immortal soul. Some say Irish Catholicism is only one step away from paganism, that the faerie folk were never destroyed, only assimilated into the new faith and given the names of saints so the people could still worship without heresy. I believe in those darker, older gods; devouring black mother Callee and her ilk. They never went away, only vanished into sea and stone, tree and sky. And that dreadful night, three of them came to wreak vengeance. Three ancient gods with burnished skins and writhing hair and terrible golden eyes.

They took me, and reforged me into what I am.

The trinity who chose me personified that very peculiar delusion some vampires have – that they have become mythological personalities, demi-gods. And who's to say they are wrong? We slip into another reality when we change, a soup of dreams and nightmares that some call the Crystal Ring. It swarms with archetypes born from the human subconscious (and from the subconscious of other beings, too, I don't doubt). Who is to say that the thought-form of a god or an archangel can't take over a newly-made vampire, fusing with a soul that has been broken apart like a raw egg?

I digress.

When I recall my human self, I peer through a veil. I recall Mary as beautiful, a tall fine woman. We loved each other, I thought … I'd been patient with the long time it took her to conceive, as I had with the long construction of the house. Wasn't that enough to prove my devotion? Apparently not, by her standards. Mere days before the house was ready for us, it came to pass that I discovered her in the old tower house in the company of some stuttering, milkweed clerk from Dublin. She was packing, ready to run away with him.

Each time I return to Blackwater Hall and stand once again in the courtyard, the grey walls rising like thunderclouds above me, I relive that night. The yellow ropes of Mary's hair hanging over her breasts, the swell of her belly beneath her clothes as she made her confession. *'The child is not yours, Sebastian. In ten years, you could not give me a child. You care nothing for me – all you love is the house! My lover has come for me and we're leaving.'*

She shrank away then as if I would strike her, but I didn't. Instead, I ran into the courtyard of the new house and screamed my rage at the heavens. The black sky split open, the deluge of rain sent me skidding to the door of a cellar. Somehow I'd gashed my arm in my anguish and blood was dripping from me.

In a few fatal minutes I'd lost everything. I had no wife, no child, so what now was the use of a grand hall? There was wood stacked inside and I meant to set light to it, to burn my dream to its foundations.

The darkness inside the cellar was absolute, but I knew its shape; a long chamber with racks set ready for storage. Only a store-room … yet it felt in that moment like an ancient torture chamber, silent but for the drip of water and the sobbing of the damned. I remember sinking down against the wall in my despair, my last moments of being human …

Then someone shut the door.

They'd been shadowing me for months, years. In retrospect, I felt they'd been watching me all my life. They had marked me as 'special' in some way, prime raw material for vampire-hood. Who knows why they chose this moment? Perhaps it was my anguish that drew them. Or merely the scent of my rain-watered blood.

They were vampires and yet they were angels. I mean that they *believed* they were angels, messengers from a punishing God, something more than mere demons. Simon, a magnificent golden man with extraordinary deep yellow eyes like a cat's. Fyodor, an attenuated male with silvery flesh and snow-white hair. Rasmila (Callee?), a woman with dark brown skin, her hair a fall of blue-black silk.

In that annihilating moment, all my human concerns fell away in a blast of lightning from heaven.

'Sebastian,' they said, their voices mellifluous, amused, and as coldly sonorous as bells. 'Don't be afraid. We have come only for your blood and your soul.'

Only.

I remember how different the world looked, afterwards. Nets of light webbed a clear deep sky; I'd never before seen with such clarity, never dreamed that such crystalline beauty was hidden from mortal eyes. I could see for miles; northwards to the Galtee and Knockmealdown mountains, to the towers of Cahir Castle, the Golden Vale of Tipperary and Cashel of the Kings; closer at hand, my own beloved estate. The stump of the old stone tower was a shadow behind the new house, which appeared a great, pristine mansion like a gold casket swathed in deep blue twilight. Three storeys it has, with tall imposing windows, a pillared portico that soars the height of the frontage. All was wrapped in night-colours I'd never seen before. The air was sweet and icy, like wine.

How unutterably beautiful it was, the home that I built for myself. For us.

And then I walked away.

I left, only because of what I became. What need had I for anything of the mortal world? I needed no wife or child, no home, no land or wealth, none of that. All I needed was blood, and the wonder of my new senses.

I had no intention ever of coming back. And yet ...

Here I am again, unseen in the shadows, a ghost haunting the ruins of my own life.

There are two ways I might proceed with Elizabeth. The road of instant violation and swift death; or the slower path of enthrallment, followed by a wasting decline into madness. Each has its own pleasures, so I am undecided. I live in the moment, watching how the warm light gilds the swell and dip of her breasts, the way her tongue flicks out to make her lips glisten.

'A spirit?' she whispers. And then, 'I know you. I've seen you before.'

This shocks me. No one is meant to see me! Her parents never have, nor their servants nor any of their numerous visitors and relatives. They're aware of me; I am the guilty secret that no one mentions. They shiver and start at shadows, but they don't *see* me. 'When have you seen me, fair one?' I ask very gently.

'When I was a child. You never spoke to me before.'

When last I was here, Elizabeth had indeed been a small child. Her older brother lay dying of a mysterious wasting disease, so crazed by strange ecstatic nightmares that they called the priest to exorcise him ... Ah, memories. She doesn't know that I was responsible. Obviously she glimpsed me, yet never connected my appearance to his death.

'What did you think, when you saw me?'

'I don't know. You were just a face in the shadows. A sad and restless soul with such beautiful eyes.'

'You weren't afraid, then?' I smile in relief. 'You know I'm a friend.'

'Yes,' she murmurs. So, she has some dim memory of me, which has imprinted itself favourably upon her. And thanks to that – after her initial alarm – she's receptive. She sees me, not as a threat, but as someone familiar, fascinating. A lonely, mysterious phantom!

The idea of killing her, swiftly or slowly, loses its appeal. Instead – to win her trust! Her love. There's a novelty.

'You are the ghost of Blackwater Hall,' she says, speaking as decisively as a child.

'Yes.' I laugh softly at that. 'I suppose I am.'

Her eyes grow more intense. 'You're him, aren't you? You're Sebastian Pierse, who murdered his wife and her lover, and then disappeared.'

'And been in torment over it ever since,' I concur. 'She betrayed me most sorely, but I wronged her the more. Now I seek atonement.'

'My parents and grandparents have always feared you,' she whispers. 'They are always looking over their shoulders in the dark. They brought in priests to cleanse the place – but it didn't work, did it?'

I try not to laugh at this, since she's so sincere. I speak with quiet, desperate need. 'Elizabeth, it is the dearest wish of my heart to trouble the household no longer. But I'll never be at peace unless you help me.'

'Help you, how?' She is trembling. We're half in love already. The warm weight of her body so close is driving me mad. 'Should I pray for you?'

'Yes. Let me come to you at night like this, and we'll pray together. A link with the living ...'

'I can't have a man in my room!' she says in a panic. 'I'm to be married.'

'But I'm not a man, I'm a soul in torment. Connection with a living being, that's all I need.'

'All?'

'And a sip of your life-blood.'

She blinks. It doesn't sound much, put like that. She touches my hand, doesn't flinch when I sit beside her. 'You're very solid, for a ghost,' she says.

We talk like this for a long time, a game of thrust and parry that grows ever more intense. There are soft touches between us; my fingertips on her hand, hers on my sleeve. Confidences are shared. She holds nothing back.

I gather she is dreading this marriage to a man older than herself. It is no love match, clearly. As our dialogue strays into more intimate areas, she confesses that she fears the wedding night. 'George will expect me like this – all pure, untried and nervous. But I ... I don't see why I should be lying here ignorant and frightened!'

'You deserve pleasure,' I tell her. 'He will not give you pleasure; you are just a possession to him.'

'How do you know?'

'I can tell, from your words, exactly the sort of man he is. Domineering, certain of his rights. He will have despoiled a hundred women in his time and yet expect his wife to be a perfect innocent. He will use you brutishly.' My outrage is genuine. 'I can't bear to think of him hurting you.'

She chafes her lip with her teeth. I want to bite that rose-pink pillow. I see in her eyes a violet fire of rebellion. At last she asks, 'Will you show me, then? So that when the time comes, I'll know what to expect and I won't be afraid. Will you, Sebastian?'

'Nothing would please me more.' I speak with complete sincerity.

'But he must never know!'

'He won't,' I reassure her. 'It will be our secret. After all, with a ghost, it doesn't count.'

At last I lean in and feel the sweet, fresh warmth of her neck against my mouth. She sighs. I am lost.

When I became a vampire I walked away from Blackwater Hall. I left others to find my wife and her lover in the old stone tower, where I had left them marinating in pools of their own blood. I took a ship to America, like the long wave of Irish emigrants after me, thinking never to return. I put an ocean between myself and the old country; I wanted no more of its shadowy magic, its religions and superstitions, its wars and the endless struggle I'd had, just to hold onto what was mine.

In those early years of my new existence, I was savage and bitter. Yet as time passed, as bitterness faded and I brought the blood-thirst under control, I began to think of the house again.

Some sixty years after I left, I came back. Just curiosity, you understand. I discovered that the scandal of Sebastian Pierse – who'd murdered his wife, her lover and her unborn infant before vanishing – was local legend; a folk-tale told by old men in their cups. My estate had been claimed by the British and awarded to a family of English Protestant settlers. They were decent enough folk, I concede, who looked after the estate well and were fair to the tenants. I'd no argument with the way they ran my affairs.

And yet, they had no right to be there. I owed it to the house and to myself to haunt them a little; to frighten the old men, to feed on the young and strong. To turn a capable wife into a crazed neurotic, to kill a first-born son here, a beloved daughter there. Just to darken their lives once in a while, as the generations came and went.

So every few years I return to Ireland for old times' sake, and listen with pleasure when people say, 'That Blackwater Hall is haunted; it's cursed the family are!' And I slip silently into the house and torment the hapless inhabitants a little more.

I could have killed them all, but I let them stay and survive. Why?

If I were of a more violent disposition, I would have ousted the usurpers long ago. I prefer to play a long and subtle game. How much more sense it makes to let them stay, to enjoy the slow burn of revenge over a century or three.

I tolerate them for the pure pleasure of haunting them.

'Just a sip, just a drop of your lifeblood,' I whisper to Elizabeth in the darkness. 'It must be freely given. Without it, I'll fade from Earth and be dragged into hell.' In the euphoric convulsions of our love-making I draw on her neck as she groans with delight and pain. I resist the urge to take too much; she's too delightful to me, alive. And so she thinks she's saving a poor damned soul from the abyss!

For a while, anyway. By the time she realises the falsehood, she no longer cares.

It helps that I have this supernatural glow of beauty – the honey in the trap – that her new husband lacks. And she has the darkness in her soul that welcomes me, loving the danger and deception of it, loving the sheer sin.

I was right about the husband. He's some remote cousin of hers and his name is George. He's an older man, experienced in the ways of the world to the point of debauchery. He's handsome enough in his way; tall and strong, with a ruggedly arrogant face, thick brown hair, an overpowering sense of arrogant masculine entitlement. (Probably I would have been just like him, had my human life progressed as planned). George has made a fortune from trade in Dublin. He's been everywhere and done everything, and yet he expects as his due a shimmering, untouched maiden on his wedding night! To me, he seems coarse and charmless. There can be no love in this match. Society has shackled her to him, but her hidden self writhes and lashes against it like a serpent.

Elizabeth acts well the part of his new bride. How innocently she glides from church to bridal chamber, trembling and virginal, God-fearing and full of nervous anticipation. How flawlessly she feigns pain and inexperience! Attentive to detail, she even covertly pricks her finger on a pin to fake a few drops of virgin blood (ah, her sweet blood) on the sheets. Drunk on wine, blind in his triumphal lust, the husband suspects nothing.

As he takes her, grunting and oblivious, she looks at me over his shoulder. Her lips part and her eyes shine as she smiles at me, her secret lover in the shadows.

Every girl should have one.

I am standing once again in the courtyard, which still seems to echo with the screams of Mary and her pallid weed of a lover as I tear them apart, feasting on their blood, ripping the still-moving foetus from her womb to suck the tender fluids from it as if from an unborn lamb …

I write about all this as if I still cared, but in truth I don't. When the unholy trinity of vampires came to feed on my blood and grief in the rain – golden Simon, dark Rasmila and pale Fyodor, as white as ectoplasm – I entered a clearer state of consciousness in which human pain no longer tore me. Since I was determined to burn down Blackwater Hall at the time, you could say that they saved the house, my three demon-angels. Should I thank them?

Whenever Elizabeth and George are absent, I walk through the salons as if I own the place. It has an eerie grandeur. There are high ceilings with elaborate plaster decoration, impressive fireplaces surmounted by coats of arms, rows of long windows hung with gorgeous curtains. Exotic rugs sprawl on polished floorboards. Along the walls are the antlered heads of stags, staring out with black marble eyes. And countless dark portraits of ancestors, fixing their painted gazes on mine.

Double doors lead from one great room to the next; here a drawing room that is insistently golden; wallpaper, frames, curtains, the scrolled woodwork of chairs, all gold. There are chairs lush with needlepoint roses, tapestry stools and fire-screens. Too many ornaments; clocks, statuettes, vases, elephants carved of onyx and jade. More paintings, huge mirrors rimmed with gilt.

None of this stuff is mine. Only the shell matters.

These great rooms – which feel so alien to me, even though I commissioned them – fill me with delicious, creeping awe. This place has the feel of a theatre, each room a lavish set waiting endlessly for the actors to arrive. The house creaks. Speaks. Upstairs there are nurseries and playrooms where expensive toys have been played with too little. Alas, the mortality rate of children has been tragically high over the decades – and not all my fault, far from it.

Feeding upon infants is a dull game, after all. True pleasure lies in toying with the adult inhabitants. I goad them, rather as a dog scratches at fleas, to remind them they should not be here.

Some regard the house as ugly. All things decay, of course. Each time I come I see further hints of weathering, paint peeling, rust-marks streaking the render. Perhaps Blackwater Hall is, as some claim, a brute of a place, as desolate as a prison fortress. Well, I don't ask anyone to admire it. It's the mirror of my soul. It is my soul.

In truth, I've no need to reclaim it, because it was never truly taken from me. It can't be taken; it's as if it exists partly in the Crystal Ring, an etheric house that transcends its earthly form. It transcends beauty itself.

If I speak of my house like a lover, it is because I regard it as a lover.

On the surface, Elizabeth is the good wife, attending church, managing her household, pretending to be thrilled when her husband brings her some trinket. She affects ignorance of his gambling, drinking and whoring when he's away in Dublin or in London. Like the dutiful wife she is, she turns a blind eye. But she has a secret.

Me.

Our limbs twine like snow in the moonlight, blood streaking darkly down her throat. Blood on snow. She knows by now that I'm no ghost, that my needs are nothing to do with saving my poor tormented soul – but she's beyond caring. We are both too addicted to this sensual game. When she feels faint, I hold her up and give her dark stout to drink, to strengthen the blood.

She knows that if we keep doing this, it will kill her, yet she cannot stop. Neither of us can. Urgently she welcomes me to her bed, whenever the husband is absent.

Then one night, panting in the aftermath of passion, she cries, 'You must leave me alone, Sebastian.' She pushes me away into the wreckage of bed sheets, her essence still sweet on my tongue. 'I need to have children. Can you give me children?'

I laugh and reply, 'I hardly think so. We both know that I can't.'

Even in life, as I've mentioned, I failed to impregnate my wife. Whatever cold essence now spurts from my member, it is as clear as ice-water and as sterile as *poteen*. There is no life-force in it.

'Then you have to go, and leave me to my husband!'

So I do as she asks – out of curiosity, not compassion. I let her alone for a few years, and children she has. Three rosy daughters and two sons, who suck as greedily upon her breast as ever I have feasted on her neck. The beating urgency of life will always win out against the vampire.

Why did I indulge her? Well, I have patience. Of course the temptation was there, to guzzle the life from those rosy children, from mother and father too, all in one debauched night – but I didn't. What am I, a fox in a flapping hen coop, to go on killing and killing until nothing moves anymore? No.

I was too soft on Elizabeth but, you see, if I'd destroyed her – and it would have been so easy, done in a moment – I'd have destroyed the very conditions that made my existence worthwhile. I was in love, a little. If not with her, then with the situation.

I still had to feed, of course, and so I went away for a while, a fair few years in fact, and found entertainment elsewhere. I might even have lost interest and never gone back at all – but by coincidence, nearly twenty years on, we meet at a ball in Dublin.

Elizabeth greets me with the same sly smile of recognition and, as I bow gallantly, we both know – the game is on again. She is tangibly older, of course – flesh thickening, her stiff layers of corsetry and clothes giving her the grandeur of a duchess. Still a desirable woman, though. She still has the gleam in her violet eyes, once so innocent, now full of shrewdness; knowing and sultry. I still desire her – how not? Her flesh is as plump with blood as ever and the blood as sweet in its promise.

Later, at Blackwater Hall once more, we face each other in her bedchamber, but something is different. The first thing she says to me is, 'Make me a vampire.'

I only look at her. Somewhere deep inside me, dreary horror wells, a kind of tired revulsion.

'That's what I want,' she insists. She clasps my arms, imploring me with luminous eyes. 'Look at you, forever young and powerful, fearing nothing! I want that too!'

'Never.' I tear myself from her. Surely my contempt must pierce her to the heart. 'I couldn't do it, even if I wanted to. It's not a simple process. It takes three vampires to create a new one.' And I explain a little about Rasmila, Fyodor and Simon.

'Then find two others to help you,' she persists, addressing me as if I were some inept boot-boy.

'Don't you understand?' I say patiently. 'The gathering of three means that the change can't happen by accident. It must be planned. Which means that it must be desirable.'

'But it is. I desire it.'

'Desirable to *them*. To me.'

She looks at me as if I've lost my mind. The look makes me angry.

'Who do you think you are, Elizabeth?' I say with cold spite. 'You were never anything to me but blood-filled flesh. What, you think you're worthy of immortality? No, you are not so special. You are no different from any other mortal. A lump of aging flesh.'

Strangely, she doesn't appear to react much. Her eyes narrow a little, but she keeps her burning, wounded anger contained inside her. She doesn't scream or beg. I'm too dismayed at her tiresome request to care about the feelings she is hiding.

Eventually she says, in a surprisingly cutting tone, 'What you're telling me is that you, alone, lack the power to transform me. You can't do it without help. Poor Sebastian.'

I should have killed her for that. Should have done so long before now. I hate it when I let them reach this stage.

I go away then, leaving her standing ghost-like in the centre of the large and shadowy bedroom that, so often, had witnessed our convulsions of ecstasy.

Unbelievable as it may seem, I almost entirely forget she ever made this request. It passes from my mind in the manner of a lover's tiff. Some months later I arrive at the house again, as jaunty as a young suitor who's gone off, got drunk, and returned later utterly oblivious to the fact that his lady friend has been seething with rage all this time.

I can't altogether have forgotten, though, because I feel wary. I don't approach her at once. Instead I haunt stairwells and alcoves for a time, watching the family from a distance. It amuses me to do this, but I'm sure Elizabeth knows I'm around. She's uneasy and over-sensitive, just as she used to be in the old days when I would look at the pale peach column of her neck with such delicious longing.

Actually, I have some vague intention of starting on one of the daughters now. Or maybe a son, for a change. Or all of them. They must be of an age to make it fun.

Alas, it seems I'm too late. Where did the time go? All but one of the offspring appear to have left – farmed out to schools or to relatives in order to become ladies and gentlemen, ready to marry money and enter society – they're out there in the world, but Elizabeth and her husband are still here. Their youngest is about eight, a plain bookish boy who doesn't interest me.

Still, I'm a patient man. I can wait for the son to grow up and come home with a trembling, fresh young wife, or even wait for grandchildren … After all, the house is mine. Generations will come and go but I will always be here, like a curse.

Only something is wrong.

I start to notice changes in Elizabeth. She's lost weight; she looks younger, more slender, her hair restored to its lustrous gold. She's languorous, pleased with herself – as she used to be in the early days with me. The changes aren't just in her, but in her husband George, too. It's as if his coarseness has been fine-polished away, and he no longer strides around like a drunken officer, slapping the furniture with a riding crop. Instead there's a thoughtful quality about him, a shine to his hair and a pale bloom to his skin.

Have I been blind? Isn't it strange, how we don't see what we don't *expect* to see? Some ghastly trick has been played upon me, here in my own house. Voices seem to be whispering and laughing at me from the corners of ceilings. Stags stare at me from black glass eyes. Something is pulling at me, an unseen current whirling me along, rendering me as wide-eyed and vulnerable as Elisabeth on that first night. As if in a trance, I walk into the drawing room and they are sitting in chairs on either side of the fireplace, George and Elizabeth, just as if they have been waiting for me to arrive. They sit perfectly composed, like brother and sister, hands lightly clasped in their laps. They are gazing at me with liquid eyes and their skin glows like candle-flames shining through the thinnest possible shell of wax.

'How did you do it?' My voice almost fails as I speak, emerging hoarse as an old man's.

'We met your angels,' she answers simply. 'Your three angels. They came back. I knew what they were and I persuaded them to transform us.'

I should have remembered. The vampire's kiss, when it does not kill, brings madness. Not always in the form of wilting terror, but sometimes as a kind of megalomania.

'Why? They can't be persuaded. They take only those who are special, chosen. That is what they told me.'

'And it's what they told us, too,' she answers serenely. 'You take yourself too seriously, Sebastian. Perhaps they changed us simply to annoy you.'

'But him?' I point at the husband, who looks back at me. He sits motionless as only vampires can, fixing me with his all-knowing, pitiless gaze. 'That – that coarse, arrogant, drink-raddled merchant?'

'Why would I want to be immortal, without my husband at my side?' she replies, genuinely surprised.

'You hate him, and all he represents!'

'No, I don't. It was your idea, that I hated him, that he maltreated me. Your perception, not reality. I love my husband. Have you no idea of the wonders I've shown him? We are one soul, George and I.'

So, all the arts she learned from me, she has taught him in turn! And far from being suspicious at her knowledge, it turns out he was delighted with it, enthralled! Unbelievable.

And now they are holding hands, and he lifts hers to his mouth, pressing her knuckles to his lips. She laughs, showing the tips of her new fangs.

'What, did you think you alone were the custodian of this delicious dark secret? Selfish, Sebastian. You wouldn't share, so we found another way, and now we don't need you anymore.' And she laughs again. Laughs at me!

So this is what I did.

I went away and dressed myself up as a priest, and I arrived in the nearest village all dishevelled, with a crusading fire in my eye; a man of the cloth, on a mission from God. First I found the local priest and plied him with whisky as I spun my story. Despite his unpromising appearance, he was soon full of holy ardour. He was a fiery fellow, eager to make his mark on the world, to impress his bishop and win the undying admiration of his congregation, or something on those lines. I wound him up and set him spinning.

He gathered the populace, and I spun my story; that Elizabeth and George were undead, that they'd sold their souls to the Devil in exchange for immortality, that I'd been hunting such creatures down across Europe, Britain and Ireland for years in order to bring them the mercy of death. Oh, a rare tale I wove.

I'd come to warn them, to help them purge the evil. Were they with me? Oh yes, by God, they were!

The priest fell in eagerly behind me like a captain behind a general. He took me for the scholar and holy man I purported to be and he wanted to play the hero, scrambling for his share of my glory. Turned out I'd walked into a community already possessed by rumour and fear. Elizabeth and George were young vampires, you see, not yet adept at hiding their tracks. There had been deaths, injuries that set a fair old fire of stories blazing. I'd walked in at the perfect time to become the saviour of the community.

All I had to do was to point and say, 'They're the guilty ones,' and the entire town became a mob, ablaze with righteous vengeance.

They will fight like tigers, I warned, so we'll go in a big band like an army. Some of us will probably die, but that's the risk we must take to be free of this curse.

They don't sleep in coffins, I told them, but they are more dangerous by night and more apt to be off their guard during the day, from the necessity of pretending to be human. Don't bother with a stake to the heart, I said – that will only make them mad. No crosses, either; you'll only waste time while they laugh. Simply hack off their heads, I instructed. Hack the heads and the bodies into pieces, then throw the pieces onto a bonfire.

That should do the trick.

And so it happened that I led a vast, inflamed army to Blackwater Hall – priests and farmers, blacksmiths, washer-women and their big daughters, stomping along with rolled-up sleeves, everyone – and they took Elizabeth and her husband by surprise and overwhelmed them.

Too inexperienced to vanish into the shadows of the Crystal Ring, they fought for their lives with fangs and nails. They fought with all the desperation of mortals – and thus they fell, hacked to pieces.

The mob spared the little boy, who watched as his parents were cut down before his terrified eyes. Had he known what they'd become? How could he not? And yet, I still believe he didn't know. His parents had kept up a front of humanity for his sake, ensuring that he only saw what they wanted him to see.

I still wonder what nightmares haunted him down the rest of his years. At one time I would have been eager to know ... would have sought him out wherever he was, and hidden in the shadows watching the liquid shine of his gaze questing for me in the darkness ...

Strange, I never did. I lost my taste for it, somehow.

In the midst of this carnage, I slipped away.

A column of smoke rose behind me, turning the air bitterly fragrant like autumn – but it was a pyre that burned, not the house itself.

Their children survived. The older ones, I understand, never set foot in Blackwater Hall again. The youngest son, however – once he'd reached an age to make his own choice – lived there until his death; a bachelor. Quite eccentric, quite mad. He never threw anything away, it seems. He filled the place with collections; with animals stuffed rigid under glass domes, with drawers full of fossils and coins, with butterflies pinned in glass cases and huge, ugly beetles impaled on cards. As if, by heaping talismans around himself, he built a great nest in which to hide from the darkness outside.

A grand job he did of tormenting himself; he didn't need any help from me at all.

Some years ago, he died and since then Blackwater Hall has lain empty, a shell loved by no one. And here it remains, falling into slow decline.

Sometimes I still come back.

I view the familiar sweeps of grass, magnificent lone trees, copses, the river gleaming like milk in the vaporous gloom. In the distance, the mountains are soaked in layers of folk-tale and myth, haunted forever by the black goddess Callee. And there it stands, Blackwater Hall; a great mansion, broodingly desolate. The walls are mottled and flaking, as if the place is shedding its skin with age. The windows, fogged like cataracts with dirt, stare indifferently at long-neglected gardens and stables.

I stand outside and gaze at it for hours, watching it decay by slow degrees. I'm filled with the sensation that it was not I who built the house after all, but some greater power acting through me. In darker moments I feel that I have simply been used in order to create a theatre for some great drama that has yet to unfold. In my mind the house is a sighing black tomb, and in place of antlered stags along the walls, there are horned demon heads.

Thus the house remains to this day – its walls grey with neglect, paint cracking, windows netted with cobwebs and dust. Somehow it withstands the vigorous, mindless invasion of life – the nesting of birds and bats, vegetation trying to drag it down with green tendrils. I wander the grand salons and bedrooms, corridors and attic nurseries, where rocking horses stand motionless under the soft, endless fall of dust. The house endures like an ancient castle fortress, tired yet impervious to time.

Was it I who sucked the life from this house? Will it ever be done with its revenge? I wanted the family gone and yet, without them, it is nothing. The house is dead yet here it stands, undead. Blackwater Hall draws me back, I swear, like a jealous lover. I know it is not done with me yet.

One day it may yet spring to life again. Some rich and enterprising young family might take on the Hall and restore it to glory, filling the rooms with fresh colours, with the chat and bustle of their lives, with scents of flowers and cooking; with the vigour of their own throbbing, blood-filled bodies. Children will run laughing and screaming along the endless corridors. Doll's house doors will be opened, gigantic child-faces staring in awe through the windows. Rocking horses will creak into life.

And on that day I will be here, waiting to claim my own.

The Dead Do Not Tempt Us

Note: In The Dark Arts of Blood, *Pierre and Ilona head off on their travels and take no further part in the story. So here is a taste of what they got up to …*

Russia, 1928

'You are arrogant, insufferable, self-centred, vain, ignorant and conceited,' said Ilona. 'Only you could make a long journey seem literally endless. All you think about is your own pleasure.'

Pierre gave a huff of outrage. His breath plumed on the wintry air. 'That's rich, coming from you. My pleasure? You are the one who must have everything her own way. You also are arrogant, selfish, vain and … all the rest. If I'm in the gutter, you're there with me.'

'I carry my vices with style,' she said with a smirk. 'That's the difference.'

'You make a show of despising me, yet you know we're just the same. That must burn.'

'Mm. At least I'm not an idiot.'

'How am I an idiot, to long for a little glamour, grand balls and easy pickings in St. Petersburg?'

'Because that glamour is all gone, dear.' Ilona slipped her hand through his elbow. 'Don't you read the papers? It's Leningrad now. Since the Bolsheviks took over, everything is grey and the aristocrats must flee for their lives, or join the party and pretend they were never aristocrats at all. No more grand balls.'

Pierre swallowed and looked away into the vast dark forest that crawled past on either side as they walked. He remembered the French Revolution's aftermath. The fact that he'd been part of the peasant class did not make the memory any more palatable.

'That's not the point,' he said. 'How does it make me an idiot to dream of romance? The jingle of troika bells. Our sleigh flying through the landscape of a winter folk-tale, with snow swirling around us, forests and mountains on every side. You, wrapped in white furs … the two of us, holding hands, flying through the Russian night …'

'What on earth are you babbling about?'

Pierre sighed. 'I wanted to give you the fairy tale. Yes, we've done nothing but bicker since we left Prague, and we're agreed that this enterprise has been a disaster so far, but I still wanted to give you the fairy tale.'

Ilona went quiet for a few seconds. The only sounds in the wilderness were the crunch of their boots and the whisper of snow falling onto their overcoats. The sun had not quite set, but the forest path already lay deep in blue dusk. Around them the immense landscape rolled on and on into the half-light: wilderness on a scale that made France or Switzerland seem picture-book tiny in comparison. You could imagine, feel the land sweeping onwards through forest and terga and steppe, up towards the Arctic Circle, across the vastness of Siberia and east towards the rim of the Pacific Ocean.

'Well, that is almost ... quite ... sweet,' she said. 'Especially for you, Pierre. But I want to see the real Russia.'

'In all its fresh brutality? That's the sort of thing Karl would do. Haunting battlefields like the Grim Reaper. You take after your father more than I realised.'

She shrugged. 'Perhaps. Once, I would have knocked you down for saying that ... but now, I think Karl is not so terrible a father after all. I must be going soft in the head.'

What a strange couple we make, Pierre thought. *Not even a couple in any conventional sense; just a pair of vampires, thrown together by circumstance.* Pierre, a gleeful predator without conscience, had been Karl's friend, enemy and a thorn in his side for over a century. Ilona – turned by Karl when she reached adulthood because he couldn't bear to lose her to mortality – was even more ruthless than Pierre. Sometimes they were casual lovers, for the hell of it. Much of the time they couldn't stand each other, and did nothing but argue and goad each other ...

But.

Something had happened, a whirlwind named Violette who'd torn them to pieces, leaving them both in their different ways exposed and humiliated and stripped back to their naked essence before she'd shown them how to heal. They'd found themselves doing things they'd never thought possible: horrors such as admitting to terror, weakness, or love. Such soul-deep injury left scars.

That was why they'd decided to go away for a year or so. Away from Violette and all the others. Just the two of them, Pierre and Ilona, who cordially loathed each other but were bonded together like reflections in a distorting mirror.

Pierre knew he'd never get the better of her. She knew it too. She looked like Karl, feminised: beautiful pale face with the bone structure of an angel, softly glowing irresistible eyes, and a core of steel. Unlike Karl, Ilona was cruel and pleasure-addicted. Pierre had that in common with her, but unlike her he was weak-willed, and didn't really care who knew it. He rather gloried in his failings.

'Is this it, then?' he said. 'Just walking until we fall off the edge of the world? We could at least have stolen that broken-down cart and donkey we passed four hours ago.'

'I like the nothingness,' she said dreamily. 'And there'll be something, dear. Victims. The blood fountain of youth to slake our thirst.'

Just her mention of the word, *blood*, was enough to make his fangs tingle in their sockets. He felt his mouth bend into a fierce smile, his eyebrows forming a demonic V. He could even smell blood on the air, a rich savoury smell threading through the numbing cold of the air. Wishful thinking.

'Wait,' said Ilona. 'Look!'

Not wishful thinking.

A small heap of darkness lay on the track ahead. Vampire eyesight saw deep into the invisible spectrum, perceiving colour where humans saw only black and white. Against the snow-glow, he saw a trail of blood spattered like a red comma around the fallen man's head.

His hunger leapt, like a chameleon's tongue. He gripped Ilona's arm.

'Oh. God. What luck. Hadn't realised how hungry I am ...'

He started forward, but she pulled him back. 'Don't pounce on him like an animal! He's alive. Can't you feel his warmth, hear his breathing?'

Even at some distance, the life signs were distinct.

'Of course I can,' Pierre snapped. 'Obviously he's alive. The dead don't tempt us, do they?'

'Well, don't leap in and kill him. I want to know who he is.'

'Why?'

They walked cautiously closer as they spoke.

'Because people don't lie around in the snow unless they've been attacked.' Her eyes glinted beneath the brim of her thick leather hat. 'There's something about him. I'm curious.'

The man groaned as they approached, as if he sensed them but couldn't move.

'Looks like just another peasant in those drab clothes.' Pierre sniffed. 'Still, all the Russians dress like that nowadays. So dull.'

'Doesn't matter,' Ilona said softly. 'They're still people underneath, with their own stories. The real Russia.'

Pierre watched as she bent over the man, swallowing his own blood-thirst as if suppressing a surge of inconvenient lust. The fallen man lay curled on his side, dressed in trousers of rough greyish cloth, boots, a shabby overcoat. His breath was laboured, wheezing. One gloved hand lay outstretched and loose on the snow, as if describing the arc of blood-drops that lay scattered around him.

He looked young. The face was unlined, pale and smooth as the snow.

His hat was askew, revealing a bristle of red-blonde hair. So young, so troubled and in pain. Dying. Ilona investigated all this with rapt care.

Pierre didn't know what had possessed her.

'Well? Is his blood good? Can we take him, or are you going to play doctor all night?'

'Shut up,' she hissed. 'Look at this.'

She showed Pierre the inside of his left wrist between coat sleeve and glove. The skin was a mess of cuts, still welling. That was the source of the blood on the snow. Drops had flown out as he'd collapsed.

'So?'

'He's done this to himself, you idiot. Tried to kill himself.' She bent her head, lapped the crimson fluid from the wrist and stifled a small moan of pleasure. Licked the skin clean, then stopped herself going any further.

The man groaned. The whites of his eyes showed, flickering.

'Hello?' Ilona said gently in Russian. 'Can you hear me? I'm Ilona. What has happened to you?'

'No. Go away. Nothing.'

'He's not made a very good job of it,' said Pierre, squatting down on the other side of him. 'Listen to his heart. Good and strong.'

'Perhaps he does not really want to die.'

'That's bad luck, then.' Pierre ran his tongue over his lips. He needed to feed. Ilona's stalling was an annoyance.

'What's your name?' she asked, holding out a palm to keep Pierre away.

'Vasily.'

Now she drew his head onto her lap and leaned over him as if cradling a sick child. 'And what are you doing out in the snow? Night's falling. It's freezing.'

'Don't care. Let me die. Let me ...' He began to sob, pressing the fingertips of his right hand to his forehead. He shivered.

'Why do you want to die, Vasily?' Ilona held his chin and tilted his head so he was looking straight into her eyes. She had him then. Pierre saw the instant connection, saw the youth's soul melt and flow towards her.

'Why do you care?'

'Do you see anyone else ready and willing to listen, aside from me and my friend? This might be your last chance to be heard. You may as well tell us.'

'Angel,' he whispered, reaching up to touch her cheek.

'Not quite,' said Ilona.

His hand fell. 'You look like her. Like my Katya.'

'Who was she? Dear, tell us quickly, for we need to take you somewhere warm where you may rest and recover.'

'Great God Almighty,' Pierre said under his breath, now convinced there would be no chance to feed tonight. Ilona was on a mission. Somehow she could do that: switch off her appetite when it suited her.

'My wife,' said Vasily. 'That bastard! My father-in-law, Dmitri …' In hesitant, coughed-out words, his tale emerged. A tragedy. A struggling artist, he lived in a nearby farm, so happy with his wife and baby daughter until a sudden cruel fever had killed them both. Since then, it had been just him and his father-in-law, cooped up in mutual grief and hatred. For months the old man had been growing drunker and angrier, while Vasily battled to go on painting. He couldn't make a living. He was depressed, desperate.

'Yesterday we had a big row and the old bastard said he'd reported me to the authorities.' Vasily was sitting up now, propped against Ilona, his head drooping.

'For what?'

'Degeneracy. My paintings don't fit the regime's vision of what art should be. What Stalin wants. There's a purge coming … Artists must paint what the state demands, or we pay the price. But I cannot – cannot work against what's in my heart. What true artist can do that? I won't sell my soul.'

'Quite right too,' said Pierre. He was now rather interested, despite himself. Once, very long ago, he'd dreamed of becoming an artist.

'So old Dmitri says the state police are coming for me. I fled, but I have nowhere to go, not a rouble to my name. I have nothing. No wife or child, no home, not even my art.'

He began to weep again.

'That is a terrible story,' crooned Ilona. 'I quite see why you'd want to end your life. However, I don't think you really want to die. You didn't cut your painting hand, did you?'

'No.'

'So I don't think there's any need for you to die, Vasily dear. First, let us take you somewhere safe.'

'There's nowhere. Only the farm, and I can't go back there.'

'Oh, can't you?' Ilona gave Pierre a burning, meaningful look. 'We'll see about that.'

'I can't – I beg you …'

'Don't worry. Everything will be different now that we're here.'

'What the hell are you doing?' Pierre began, but she tutted.

'And we are going to help you. Aren't we, Pierre?'

The scene looked to Ilona like a painting. The farmhouse resembled a low barn with slatted walls and snow-covered roof, surrounded by broken-down fencing. Behind it were a couple of outbuildings incongruously adorned with onion domes, rickety turrets and spires. A brilliant orange sunset flamed on the horizon. The sky began fading to grey and lemon even as they reached the place, but just for a few moments all the windows reflected flame as if the cottage were on fire. The landscape around it, thick with snow, looked blue, cold and shadowy. So bleak.

Vasily lay over Pierre's shoulder like a sack of cabbages. Rousing, he saw where they were and moaned.

'No, I can't go back in there. I'd rather die than see his ugly old face again.'

'You don't have to,' said Ilona. 'Is there a back door?' He shook his head. 'More than one room inside?'

'Three rooms.'

'Pierre, take him in through the back. Use a window if you must. I'll knock on the front door and … distract the farmer.'

'Then what am I meant to do with him?' Pierre's expression was exasperated, verging on furious.

'Make him warm and comfortable. Bandage his wound. Stay quiet. And *no feeding.*'

Ilona waited until he'd tramped around the side of the building with Vasily hanging over his shoulder before she stepped towards the front door, soundless in the snow. Ten seconds of silence followed her knock. Then came the sound of boots stomping on a wooden floor, someone grunting and breathing heavily like a bear woken from hibernation.

The door opened, releasing a slab of light and the thick stench of animals, smoke, stored vegetables and human sweat. The farmer was dressed in thick dark cloth, baggy breeches with boots to the knee, a shirt with no collar and an ancient waistcoat. He was well into his fifties, with straggling grey hair and a red face. He glared.

'Not another of his tarts! He's not here.'

The man shoved the door towards her face, but she wedged her foot and shoulder in the gap. The door bounced off her, shuddering as if it had hit a wall. His stare widened.

'I'll wait,' she said.

'What?' He lurched back as she pushed her way in. She hooked his gaze with hers: not easy, because he was unsteady and struggling to focus. She reeled him in anyway. Her serene brown velvet eyes caught his red-rimmed pin-point pupils, and her hand rested along his sleeve. He went still, his mouth slack.

'I said I'll wait. May I come in?'

He waved the vessel he was holding, a jug of vodka, she assumed from the sharp medicinal smell. 'Sure. What the hell. You're already in, aren't you?'

The room was a kind of kitchen-cum-parlour with a wooden table, oil lamps burning, a big square stove bellowing heat. Ceiling and walls bristled with wooden pans, implements, strings of vegetables.

Distantly she heard Pierre and Vasily entering a room elsewhere in the cottage, scrambling in through a window judging by the racket they made. But her hearing was sensitive, and the old farmer's was not. He appeared to notice nothing except her.

'My name's Ilona. Yours?'

'As if he didn't tell you.' Dmitri waved at the table, indicating her to sit down on a bench. He sat facing her, swigged from the jug and clumsily slammed it down, pushing it towards her. 'You want a drink?'

She eyed the jug with distaste. 'No, thank you. You seem upset, Dmitri.'

He huffed. 'They say I am *kulak.*'

'What does that mean?'

Dmitri blinked, as if he found Ilona far more fascinating than her question. 'Where are you from? Your accent is strange. You don't look right.'

'Vienna, once. A very long time ago.'

'Vienna? What the devil are you doing here?' His body swayed, giving off sour smells of sweat, farmyard animals, alcohol. His very aura whirled around him like a tornado, messy and uncontrolled. Even the unkempt wisps of his hair and beard danced like white fire. His eyes, though, were still. Fixed on hers. She could make him believe anything. Do anything.

'I like to travel.'

'Into the wastes of hell? Vasily has picked up some crazy strays in his time, but you beat them all.'

'As models?'

A gruff laugh. 'That's what he calls them.'

'I'm not a stray dog,' Ilona said icily. 'Nor am I a "tart". You don't think being an artist's model is a respectable occupation?'

'I don't give a shit what you do,' he growled, leaning towards her. He waved at an inner door, as if indicating some evidence of horror she couldn't see. 'It's what he does. Calls it art! Obscenity. He'll get us arrested. Damn him, damn the very day he met my daughter!'

From her calm centre - the vampire studying the mortal - Ilona watched this man spilling his raging energy and she knew that he was near the end. She put her hand on his and said, 'You're obviously in distress, Dmitri. Please tell me.'

Because he was in her thrall - although he didn't realise it - and because he was drunk, the words came easily from him.

'We were content, my daughter and me, until she met this rogue. She's at market, he's slumming it from Leningrad, looking for pretty girls to paint. The next I know, they're married, and he's moved in! Brought all his paints and canvases, because what he doesn't tell us is he's penniless, he has nowhere else to go, so he'll make my farmhouse his studio! I can refuse my Katya nothing. She loves him. So like a fool I let them stay.' He dropped his head and began to sob. Ilona regarded his falling tears without emotion.

'Last year she had a beautiful baby girl. But a fever came and took them both. So fast! Just like I lost my wife ten years ago … Both times, before it happened, a crow pecked the window. I knew that was a bad omen. Why could not Vasily die, instead of them?'

He wept and drank for quite some time, until he was such a mess that Ilona passed him a cloth to wipe his dripping face. Then he shuddered and sighed and drank again.

'So he does nothing to help on the farm?' she said. 'You don't want him here? Why not ask him to leave?'

'Oh, he's going, all right. The authorities come for me, they're damn well going to come for him first.'

'I don't understand.'

'It's already started. This Stalin, he's coming for people like me. *Kulak.*'

'What does that mean?'

'I am a wealthy landowner, apparently!' Dmitri spread his arms wide and gave a hollow laugh. '*Kulak* is what they call the "rich" farmers. They say we are the class enemies of the poorer peasants. Bloodsuckers, they call us. Vampires, plunderers of the people, profiteers who fatten on famine. Their words, not mine.'

'You don't look very wealthy to me,' she said softly.

'I'm not. But possession of a single cow is too rich for them. Anyway, rumour is that the authorities are coming to take our farms. It's already happening. The OGPU, the state police, they're sweeping towards us like a locust plague, to steal our land and throw us out of our homes.'

'I'm sorry. That is terrible.'

'So, what is the point of living? *He's* the vampire, that good-for-nothing artist I have supported for two years. Let them take him. By the time they come back for me – I'll be dead.'

'Is that what you want?'

'I don't care. It's over. Without my Katya, all is pointless.'

'I am so sorry,' said Ilona, sounding as if she meant it, secretly thinking that it was time to end the encounter. The sounds from the rear of the house had ceased. All was deathly still. Did that mean Pierre had defied her, and fed on Vasily after all?

'Well, I'm not gone yet. May have a few months yet.' Dmitri laughed in a bitter, resigned way. He leaned across the table, breathing fumes into her face. 'Hey, you any good at farmwork? You looking for a husband?'

She laughed coldly. 'I am not going to marry your son-in-law.'

'Not him. Me!'

He roared with laughter. The noise made the wooden walls shake. Something in the atmosphere broke, and Ilona heard footsteps pounding towards the parlour.

Vasily burst through an inner door, wide-eyed with fury.

'The old man dares to laugh at me?' he yelled. Pierre was just behind him in a dark passageway, shrugging helplessly as Ilona glared at him. 'You old bastard! My wife's dead, and you laugh?'

'Hey, you piece of shit. I thought you were gone for good!'

Dmitri rose and stepped over the bench, turning around as he did so. In the same movement he swung the jug at the younger man's head. Stoneware and bone connected with a thud. Vasily went down on one knee. Then his father-in-law kicked him, catching him in the thigh so he toppled over, aiming the next kick at his kidneys. He was a big man. Vasily looked small and defenceless under the attack.

Ilona grabbed the farmer from behind as if he were a child, almost lifted him off his feet. His fists and booted feet flailed comically in the air. Then she snapped his head roughly to one side and bit deep into his neck.

Dmitri sank to the floor and she fell with him. A rushing red ocean washed away reality. Their two heartbeats joined and she spread along the floor with him as he reached out blindly for … help? A vision of heaven?

She was only bringing what he had sought from his vodka. Oblivion.

Ten years later – so it seemed – she opened her eyes to see Vasily on his feet, staring at her. He stepped back, only to collide with Pierre who was right behind him. Pierre glared over his shoulder, his blue eyes on fire with blood-thirst from witnessing her feast.

'What?' said Ilona. She rose, straightening her coat and dishevelled hair. Without haste she licked the blood from her lips. 'Isn't this what you wanted, Vasily? I've set you free. The old man's dead. The farm is yours now, if you want it.'

He went on blinking at her, bewildered. Breathing too fast. She saw all the questions in his eyes – *what are you, what have you done, are you going to kill me too?* – but he couldn't voice them. Didn't need to.

'Since you've dined,' said Pierre, 'May I …?'

His fingers crept spider-like onto Vasily's shoulders. The young man froze.

'Pierre, patience,' said Ilona. 'I want to spare him.'

'Why?' Pierre snarled at her, but he still obeyed. In their battle of wills, she always won. She knew he hated it, yet he kept coming back for more.

'I don't know. Call it one of my whims.'

'You don't understand.' Vasily found his voice at last. He rubbed his forehead, leaving blue and black smears from his fingers. Paint. He'd been … painting? 'I can't live here. The police are coming for me. And the state is going to confiscate the farm in any case. I have nothing left, nothing.'

'When are they coming?'

'I don't know. Tomorrow, probably. Before dawn. If you're going to kill me, do it quickly.'

'No need for that,' Ilona said, meeting Pierre's cold blue gaze.

'Very well,' said Pierre. 'Because I once dreamed of being an artist, I'll give him a chance.' He beckoned. 'But Ilona, you really must come and see this.'

The air was dense with the smell of fresh oil paints, underlain by a revolting rank stench: homemade pigments at best, more likely dead rats. Canvases were propped all around the bedroom, most of them on the floor, a few on easels. The surfaces looked wet in the dancing candlelight, full of jarring colours. The room was full of paintings, as if a mad insomniac had been at work here.

Boris and his comrade looked around the room in a stupor of disgust and contempt. They were OGPU agents, state police, as proud and nonchalant as soldiers in their dark jackets with red collars, blue breeches, their peaked red and blue caps. Pistols by their sides. They looked at each other, then at the supposed art once more. God, that smell. Most of the images were obscene: naked women, contorted in sexual poses. Even the landscapes were wrong, impressionistic, painted with manic fury. The work was not even good. It was grotesque.

Definitely an offence against the state.

'Gods, look at this.' His comrade pulled an easel aside and pressed his hand over his mouth. The farmer's body they'd found in the parlour was fresh, but the corpse in the bed was decaying. A young woman ... Boris flung back the covers. Christ, she had a baby in her arms. Mother and child lay there, slowly mummifying.

That was the source of the stomach-turning smell.

'Well, we have more than a crime of artistic expression here,' said Boris. 'We have murder, and we have the apparent concealment of two deaths.'

His comrade turned for the door, breathing hard while he got the urge to retch under control. Boris, however, was spellbound by the delicious horror of it all. He stared from the two sad corpses to a portrait of a couple. The canvas stood on an easel in the centre of the room, surrounded by a mess of palettes and rags, so new that the paint was still wet. A man with curly brown hair, fierce expression, hypnotic blue eyes spaced a little too wide. Standing close at his side was a woman with an angel's face, dark red hair cut short but soft in the European fashion, plum red lips and dark eyes to swallow you. The brushwork was messy with haste, dancing with dark energy, yet the faces were clear. They both were so beautiful, so sinister. Boris couldn't look away.

'But where's the culprit?' he said.

'Fled, obviously.' His comrade moved beside him, also staring into those mesmeric, painted eyes. Carefully not looking back at the bed. 'He's deranged, dangerous.'

'Can't have been gone long. This looks like he only finished it last night. Look, the brushes are still wet.'

'We'll find him.'

'Not if I find you first,' said a voice from the darkness.

Both agents jumped, turning to stare as the man from the portrait moved out of the shadows. Faster than they could lay hands on their guns, he was on them, all claws and fangs like a ravenous wolf.

The troika flew at breathtaking speed across the snow: three magnificent grey horses drawing their sleigh so fast they seemed to fly along the forest path. The greys' harness was heavily decorated, and a carved wooden arch rose like a bright arc over the central horse, gleaming blue and red and gold like a stained-glass sculpture against the snow-filled sky, or a huge triumphal garland. Ilona was wrapped in thick white furs, Pierre in brown like a bear.

Vasily sat squeezed in between them, his face patched red with cold and white with terror.

In front of them was the hunched back of their driver. His pockets were stuffed with roubles, his mind blank. Amazing what a mixture of money and vampiric glamour could achieve. Even in these austere times, a troika could be had from party officials who'd ousted some aristocrat from his mansion.

Presently they would send Vasily on to a suitable border, where he could slip across and flee to Europe and paint whatever rubbish he wanted, starving romantically in a garret. They had spared his life, she and Pierre, just because they could. Ilona smiled to herself, feeling rather virtuous.

Whether they'd spared his sanity was another matter. Vasily was hardly stable to begin with, and the vampire's kiss brought madness and delusions. Some mortals recovered; others never did. Perhaps he'd stay like this forever: staring, hands trembling as he pushed his paintbrush over the canvas in his garret, obsessively creating portraits of Ilona and Pierre over and over again, as if to exorcise them … Or perhaps he'd remember them with a smile and a dark, secret rush of pleasure.

For now, though, she lost herself in the rush of speed, the racing hoof beats and stinging snow.

'See, I saved the best for you, Pierre,' she said. 'Two soldiers. Your favourite.'

'You did indeed. Five corpses for the authorities to puzzle over! Quite the haul for one night, *cherie*.'

'Monsters,' Vasily whispered. 'You're both insane.'

'Oh, that's fine coming from you,' said Pierre. 'The husband who kept the bodies of his wife and child in his bed?'

'I didn't want them to … I couldn't …' Vasily trailed off, went back into his silent trance.

'Where shall we go, once we've dropped our friend here?' asked Ilona.

'Wherever you wish, my lady,' said Pierre. He was in a very good humour now. 'My troika is at your service.'

'Well, it's been fun so far,' murmured Ilona. 'Thank you for the sleigh ride.'

She bent her face into the young man's neck and took a small delicious sip of his blood. He gasped, pressing his eyes shut. His lips moved as if he were praying.

Carefree, Ilona and Pierre held hands across Vasily's lap, the fur of their thick gloves and coat-sleeves entwined, brown and white. Around them snowflakes swirled and rushed past in great flurries, and the three magnificent grey horses leapt onwards through the snowstorm, pulling their sleigh at wild speed, harness bells jingling.

'My pleasure,' said Pierre. 'I promised you the fairy tale.'

Ultra Silvam

The castle of Ursula, Countess Gerlaszhovsky, stood high in the mountains, perched on an impossible peak and frowning down upon a wilderness of lesser mountains, of rivers and forests. The sun was setting behind the tallest spire, as if the turret wore a blazing crown. Count Gyorgy Vadaszh studied carefully the path he must take to reach her abode. Of course, the way was steeper and more complex than the map would suggest, icy in places, but he was shrewd and careful, his horse surefooted. He turned the hefty black beast and, using his spurs, directed it to begin the ascent.

The Countess was a widow of forty-nine and, according to rumour, no beauty. Her husband, long dead of some wasting disease, had left her childless, but what she did possess in her own right was immense wealth. She held the great castle vaunting over half a country, forests teeming with deer and wild boar, farms and their tenants, jewels and gold and priceless tapestries.

Certainly she must be lonely, Gyorgy thought. No woman should be alone to bear those heavy responsibilities. How could a lone woman be expected to manage such wealth?

He was thirty, the son of a penniless aristocrat who'd bequeathed him a title and nothing else. He was considered handsome, despite the early ravages of drink upon his face and physique. In the city he attracted harlots and dissolute friends who encouraged him to gamble, drink and brawl through the night - but to rich families seeking a noble match for their daughters, he was plainly as appealing as typhoid.

Gyorgy was a pariah, yet he wasn't bitter. Fate had dealt him a poor hand, so no use crying over it. Instead he threw in his cards and tried a different game.

The Countess would be delighted to receive him, said the note delivered in response to his request - his impertinent request - that he pay a social call upon her. He styled himself a friend of her late husband: a claim she could not disprove.

An ageing widow - How grateful she would be for the attentions of a much younger man! A dashing young aristocrat, no less. He was confident of his ability to display an essential balance of virility, mature strength and wisdom.

He intended to fuck her until her eyes rolled in her head. Her looks? The uglier the better. Her gratitude would increase in direct proportion to her hideousness – all the better to send her delirious with astonished joy. And then …

Gyorgy intended to marry her.

His horse was gasping by the time they reached the top of the difficult path, and his backside ached from hours in the saddle. The temperature had dropped. All around him vaunted the castle, enclosing the courtyard with frowning balconies and sheer towers; a brutal edifice of grey-brown stone, sealed by a vast black studded door. The door stood closed, unwelcoming to visitors. The air at this height was lung-freezing. Snow whirled on the wind, dusting the courtyard flags, clotting in his horse's mane.

Behind the massing iron clouds, daylight faded and he saw lights glowing through small stained-glass windows: blue, red and emerald.

Before he had a chance to grasp the eagle-head door knocker, a dishevelled boy with sandy hair came to take his horse. So, someone had been watching for his arrival. A ruffian, this stable lad: he was surly, hollow-cheeked and clad in rags. Surely she could afford a better class of servant? That would be the first thing he would set right, once they were married.

Clearly she was in desperate need of a husband.

'Rub down my horse and put a blanket on him, or he'll catch a chill,' Gyorgy ordered. 'Shall I knock?'

'Uh,' said the stable lad, turning rudely away.

'Vagabond,' Gyorgy said under his breath. He raised a hand to the eagle's head, but one half of the double door was already opening. An equally surly manservant beckoned him in. The man was elderly, corpulent and stooping, with heavy jowls and small clever eyes.

This aged retainer, too, would have to go.

There was also a maid, a skinny milk-pale thing under a floppy white cap. She looked … apathetic. Positively simple. No one else appeared to greet him. Dear God, was this all the staff the Countess had?

The hall itself was more promising: walls plastered and painted white, full of dancing golden light from a surfeit of flaming torches in sconces. He noted a sweeping staircase. The traditional grandiose array of family portraits was displayed along the walls and across the landing above.

'Count Vadaszh?' said the manservant. 'Allow me to take your cloak and hat. Her grace the Countess awaits you.'

Things will be changing here, thought Gyorgy as he pushed his cold outer garments and gloves at the retainer. The maid – really, where were the footmen? – beckoned and led the guest through to a reception room.

Surprisingly, a very grand room. There was a huge carpet of the finest Persian design, a swirl of red and green and indigo – yes, it had seen better days, but must have cost a small fortune when new. Tall golden half-columns along the walls framed paintings and frescoes. There were curtains of luscious red velvet and three extravagant golden chandeliers down the length of the room, dripping with crystal like showers of diamonds. The whole room seemed to run with gold. Seats were arranged in pretty groups, as if the space awaited dozens of guests. Very fine. This was one of the most splendid salons he'd ever seen, and he'd seen a fair few.

He could definitely make something of this place.

Improve the road so that the nobility could ride up here by coach to attend the grand gatherings he would host. He pictured himself holding court in front of that magnificent rose marble fireplace … Caution, though. He must not make the path so easy that an invading force from Russia, Turkey, Hungary or some other greedy nation might stroll up here and take what would soon be his.

The maid announced his arrival. A woman rose from a chair by the fireplace and held out a gracious hand.

'My dear Count Gyorgy, what a pleasure to make your acquaintance.'

'Your grace,' He took her hand, gave a practised click of his heels and bowed.

'Your manners pass the test, sir, but may we be less formal?'

'As informal as you wish, my lady.'

Well – she was not that bad. Average height, thick in the waist, brown hair heavily mingled with silver. Pleasant enough face, though he doubted she had ever been a great beauty. Not enough bone structure to carry off the sagging of age, nose too long. Cheerful brown eyes, flirtatious. She carried herself with impeccable dignity, yet looked as if she'd dressed in the dark. Her gown of blue velvet and gold thread (turning brown) was over-elaborate and a touch too small for her frame. The neckline was crooked, the colours fading. Her décolleté was lavished with the most extravagant necklace of gold and rubies he'd ever seen, so ostentatious he wondered if it was a fake. Really – not unattractive at all. She reminded him of his mother …

Oh God, who was he fooling? She was ghastly.

'What a very fine uniform!' she said. 'Do come in, sit with me here by the fire. Will you take a little plum brandy?'

Her voice, however, was beautiful: velvety, full of teasing sweetness and good cheer. If she had a happy temperament, a compliant disposition – that would go a long way to making her tolerable. If he closed his eyes, listened to her voice and thought of her money, surely he could manage … to perform for her satisfaction.

'How was your journey? The path becomes so icy and treacherous at this time of year …'

'The path, madam, was in good order.'

'I'm so glad to hear it.' Lightly she touched the back of his hand. 'Let us be

Ursula and Gyorgy, at least for this evening.'

'As you command. Ursula.'

'It is so kind of you to call upon me. These days, few will brave the long and perilous journey to my home, alas.' Then she gave him a broad, warm smile, full of kindness. Her teeth were strong and straight, yellowish in the firelight. But there was a black gap. One of her canine teeth was missing. The contrast of the perfect smile and the missing tooth jolted him.

'Jakab, my manservant, will bring wine while we wait for Klara to serve dinner. A modest repast: just some fish soup with lemon, stuffed cabbage rolls, a stew of venison, and then we have some Amandine cake and a lovely *sarlota* in the French charlotte style, with custard and cream. And cheese, of course. We live simply here.'

His stomach growled. He hoped she didn't hear him. 'That sounds like a feast fit for royalty.'

'And after, we could play a hand or two of cards, if it pleases you to do so.'

'I should be delighted.' And he smiled back at her, completely taken with the image of this castle as his.

She leaned forward, revealing an impressive cleavage beneath the weight of rubies that, he saw plainly, were real and as red as blood. 'So, my dear Gyorgy, tell me a little about yourself. Better yet, do tell me all the gossip from the city!'

They passed twenty minutes or so in small talk, sitting in cosy intimacy before the fireplace. The plum brandy was potent, and soon made him relaxed and confident. She laughed at his stories; her laugh was soft and throaty, encouraging him to reveal ever-greater scandals. He chuckled with her. In truth, they did not even talk a great deal. After the first few nervous parries, they fell into a quieter engagement, with occasional silences that felt comfortable. The sort of easy exchange that a married couple might share.

Her eyes shone softly as they shared their idle comments and smiles. Gyorgy was startled to find himself deeply at ease in her company. He leaned forward, paying close and warm attention to comments she was making about some princess she had met in Vienna so many years ago …

Could he endure this – supposing they were to be married? Yes. The exchange was pleasant. Ursula was pleasant. This could work.

And sharper pleasures could always be found elsewhere.

Noises came from the outer hall: doors opening and closing, male voices, boots on the tiled floor. Servants, he assumed. A river of chilly air blew in, making the fire spark and rush up into the chimney.

He made a mental note: find out what type of artisan was best skilled to cure draughts. An additional porch might be needed. Doors repositioned. Expensive improvements, perhaps. But … Ursula would be paying.

'Madam – Ursula, permit me to go and tell Jakab to close that wretched door! No wonder you cling to the fireside. It's unacceptable that you are forced to sit in this cold gale.'

He stood up, but she stood with him.

'Oh, I am used to this draughty place. My other guest is here.'

Other guest? Gyorgy was startled into silence. He had not been warned of any other guest. He'd thought he and Ursula would be quite alone. Damn the intrusion.

He saw, out in the hall, Jakab struggling with a heavy snow-caked cloak and a large fur hat, pools of water forming on the tiles. Then a tall grey-haired man filled the doorway, striding in, practically blustering in, regal in the immaculate uniform of an army general. Rich red jacket festooned with sashes and gold braid and a ridiculous jangling array of medals. White breeches, a sabre following the heavy curve of one thigh, high black boots, the obligatory scar crossing the left cheek of his smug, granite face. He looked like some great over-decorated piece of furniture, more like a king's throne than a man.

Gyorgy, who until now had felt grand, perceived himself as drab in his own blue-grey cavalry officer's attire.

'His Royal Highness, Duke Otto Banfi de Matra,' said Klara. Her meek voice was drowned by the loud, rich bass of the Duke.

'My dear Countess Ursula – my lady–' The Duke gave an extravagant deep bow, seizing both her hands and planting kisses on them before holding them up to his own heart. 'What delight to see your fair face again! It's been too long.'

'Indeed, Otto, it has,' she replied.

They smiled into each other's eyes, oblivious to Gyorgy's silent fury. He felt the blood rising in his face.

'Come, let us all sit by the fire. Jakab, more brandy! Klara, do take yourself to the kitchens and ensure dinner is not late. Duke Otto – allow me to present Count Gyorgy Vadaszh. Gyorgy was acquainted with my late husband. Duke Otto – well, there can be no one in the land who isn't familiar with your name, your great bravery and renown.'

In fact, Gyorgy had never met her husband, the late Count. He'd spun the tale as an excuse to call on her. The Duke, however, was all too familiar.

Then the two men shook hands. Grimacing, Otto said, 'We've met.'

'Oh, you know each other? How splendid! Then this will be a merry evening indeed.' Ursula's lips curved in her teasing smile. 'Gyorgy, Otto is an old and dear friend of mine too. Dinner will be served at precisely eight o'clock. If you will excuse me for a few minutes …? I'll leave the two of you to catch up – upon good times, I trust.'

She swept out, leaving the two men alone, seated opposite each other and glowering. Gyorgy could hear snow pellets clattering across the windows, wave after wave.

'An ill night for riding,' he said.

'Indeed.' Otto leaned back in his chair, booted feet spread wide, fingers poised under his chin. 'The winter closed in fast behind me, but my horse is strong. So, Gyorgy Vadaszh. What brings you here?'

Gyorgy saw the avaricious gleam of the Duke's eyes, and felt violently jealous, protective.

'Paying my respects to the widowed Countess. You?'

'You used to call me "sir", albeit under sufferance. Your manners have not improved, I see.'

Gyorgy sipped his brandy. Some years ago, he had served under the Duke. The man had always terrified him. But – Otto was not Gyorgy's commanding officer any longer. 'I beg your pardon, sir. So, you are a friend of the Countess. It is good that she has found in you such a noble ... father-figure.'

'Ah.' Otto laughed. His cold grey eyes narrowed. He leaned forward, his expression positively murderous. 'Father-figure? You mean to get your little stabs in early.'

Gyorgy managed not to flinch. 'Well, you must be twice her age at least.'

'I am sixty-two, not ninety! You devil. And you are what? Young enough almost to be her son? I know what you are at, young Gyorgy. You're here to court her. It's pitiful.'

'And you're not, old man?'

'Oh, you truly think she would choose you over me?' Otto refilled his own glass and sat back again. 'She trusts me. She respects me. She knows my rank and reputation.'

'Then why hasn't she accepted you already?' Gyorgy maintained a smile, but he felt the blood beating in his ears.

'I have not yet asked her.'

'Or perhaps she is waiting for younger, fresher meat. Someone who doesn't have to pluck the hairs out of his nose. A man who can keep it up in the bedroom.'

'You despicable little shit,' Otto said through grinning teeth. 'Shall I tell her, then, that you have not a penny to your name? That you dare still to wear the uniform of a cavalry officer even through you were expelled in disgrace some years ago for your cowardice? That you have a grand reputation in the city for drinking and whoring – and no doubt that you carry some filthy disease to boot?'

'She will think less of the elderly man who tries to besmirch my reputation. Shall I warn her that her trusted "old friend" desires to marry her – for her wealth?'

Otto scoffed. 'She will marry you over my dead body. You, sir, are a chancer and a parasite.'

Deep in the shadows at the far end of the salon, someone began to play a piano. A Bach prelude, very soft. Gyorgy looked, but could only see the shadowy shape of the instrument and not the pianist.

'But she will be the woman who redeems me,' Gyorgy said, lowering his voice to ensure the pianist would not hear. 'Women cannot resist that. I can make her love me. And I will cherish her.'

'Cherish her gold, more like, until you've gambled it all away.'

Gyorgy shook his head. He and Duke Otto had always loathed each other. Nothing had changed. Now the Duke was past his prime, he should no longer have held any power over Gyorgy, yet he did: the power of his steely character, the sheer unbending force of his will. And that was everything. Gyorgy knew that Otto was going to have his own way, whatever happened.

The knowledge made him furious. He couldn't endure it.

'Perhaps you should leave, old man, before you embarrass yourself.'

'Do I not still cut a rather dashing figure? My wife is long dead, God rest her soul, but I have grown children who would appreciate such an inheritance as this.' Otto waved his hand, indicating the salon, the castle, the land. 'At least my motives are unselfish ones.'

'Unselfish? You already have vast riches and yet you want more. I am the one who has nothing!'

Otto sniffed. 'No one's fault but your own. The choice will be Ursula's, in any case. Do calm yourself, Count Gyorgy.' He leaned forward again with a semblance of amiability. 'Here, I have a suggestion. Since you are penniless, why not come and work for me?'

'What?'

'It's traditional, after all. Wealthier families take impoverished nobles under our wings. Works well for both parties. You might even find yourself working here, since you like the place so much.'

Gyorgy was so enraged he nearly lost the power of speech. The pianist continued his prelude, a slow plangent march. Snow swirled down the chimney, making the logs spit.

Softly he replied, 'So, you want me working here ... doing your duties for you ... not least the duty of fucking your wife?'

'Try that, and I'll drop you over the battlements.'

Gyorgy stood up. He threw his glass at the fireplace, where it smashed. The pianist in the shadows stopped. 'Damn you, sir. If you wish to kill me, let's settle this now! I challenge you to a duel!'

'A duel? You're drunk. And there are procedures ...' Otto spoke with a sort of drawling contempt that enraged Gyorgy further.

'Procedures be damned. Outside. Now.'

'First blood?'

'To the death.'

The courtyard was already deep in snow. The blizzard stung their wine-reddened cheeks, dense with swirling flakes. Every parapet and roof and wall was capped with white fleece. Gyorgy swept his sword out of its scabbard.

The sky had an eerie glow, pregnant with tons of unshed snow. Below the castle, the whole mountainscape was paling as layer fell upon layer, reflecting the sky's gloomy light as if an ice-blue moon illuminated the whole world. Winter suffocated the land.

The cold penetrated his clothing but he was numb, too fired up with righteous anger to feel it. He had a vision: blood spreading bright red on the pristine snow. One man standing, the other falling into the crimson snow, an arm raised in a plea for life. Snowfall veiling them both. Who lived and who died – it didn't matter.

Otto had experience but Gyorgy had youth. He held his sword, held himself *en garde*, felt the edge of Otto's blade slide ever-so-gently along his, as nerve-jangling as a scream.

Then a sliver of light appeared and widened to a wedge, pale yellow on the shadowy whiteness. They were both caught in the judgemental light, as if on stage in some melodrama.

'What in heaven's name do you think you are doing?'

Ursula was in the doorway, wrapped in a fur cloak.

They froze, like eight-year-old boys caught in some mischief by their governess.

'Stop this nonsense immediately. Dinner is served.'

In the dining room – an equally grand chamber that led off the salon – the two men sat on opposite sides of the long table, working their way sulkily through sour soup, stuffed cabbage, venison and all the rest, followed by cheese and creamy *sarlota* and an array of cakes. They eyed each other throughout. Jakab and Klara kept their glasses filled with wine. Ursula sat at the head of the table, watching them. She did not seem at all perturbed by their earlier outrageous behaviour, Gyorgy noted. She was like a school teacher, or a mother superior: displeased but inclined to forgive, once they'd shown themselves to be sufficiently contrite.

'It was foolish,' said Gyorgy at last. 'Entirely my fault. Ursula, my lady, I ask your forgiveness.'

'Forgiven. No harm done,' she said.

In the background, the piano played on. The notes sounded thin and mournful, like a clavichord.

'So, it appears we have a dilemma,' she said at last.

The dining room was intimately lit by the many candles on the table. Ursula looked unexpectedly alluring in this light, gilded, all her wrinkles smoothed away. Her eyes shone with promise. Even the gap where her tooth had fallen out was one more mysterious shadow.

Gyorgy was very drunk by now. He didn't care if the night ended with him dead, married, or in bed with lovely Ursula. All was equal.

'Are you ready to tell me what you were fighting about?'

Both men grunted. They looked at each other, not at her: their prize.

'When winter comes, it does not let up for months,' she went on. 'Neither of you will be going home tonight. Perhaps not for many nights. So you had better make peace. I have had Klara make up beds for you and light fires in your rooms. Unfortunately you may still find your accommodation quite cold and damp. I can only apologise.'

At that, Duke Otto stirred.

'Why do you not close up this place, my lady – Ursula – and come down to spend winter in the more comfortable environs of the city? Think of the balls, the parties! You could stay in Bucharest, Vienna, Paris – wherever you choose. If you stay here a day longer, you'll surely be stranded until the spring thaw. Allow us to aid you: pack all you need, and we'll escort you down the mountain at morning light.'

'It's already too late, Otto dear.' She smiled with closed lips and shook her head. 'I don't care for society. We have endured many winters here, my loyal staff and I. Please, there is no need to concern yourself about us.'

'But we are concerned!' said Gyorgy.

'If you wish to please me, I beg of you – no more talk of duelling. I adjure you both to be courteous to each other or I shall marry neither of you.'

Gyorgy felt his face burning.

'Was there talk of marriage?' Otto spoke archly.

'Was there?' said Ursula. She snapped her fingers and called out, 'Rasvan! Champagne!'

The music stopped in the other room. Gyorgy heard the piano stool scrape back.

'I know I am a fat little widow, of no interest to anyone – except for my estates. I know what you both want. But what do I get out of the arrangement?'

'Companionship,' said Gyorgy. 'A husband to take care of you, to keep your home in good repair, to deal with all the problems of a great estate …'

'A legacy,' said Otto. 'You have no heirs, but my children will take great pride in this castle and pass it down through generations …'

'You are both persuasive.' She plucked a candied cherry from a bowl on the table, dipped it into her wine, and ate it, her full lips closing around the stem. 'You realise that you are not the first. Nor will you be the last.'

'I admire an independent woman,' said Gyorgy. 'However …'

'Any nobleman with a few soldiers in his service,' Otto interrupted, 'might come up here and hold you to siege in your castle. All you own could be taken from you quite easily.'

She went still. 'Are you threatening me, Duke Otto?'

'I'm suggesting that you need the protection of a husband and the men he commands.'

'It sounded like a threat.'

'No. A warning. I can protect you from such dangers.'

'Without love, all that is worthless,' she said, gazing into the middle distance with an unreadable, glowing gaze.

'Love cannot thrive without security,' said Gyorgy. This seemed a very profound statement to him, drenched in wine as he was.

Ursula said nothing. Someone new drifted into the room, a slightly-built young man with strawberry blonde hair to his shoulders. For a moment, the flow of shining coppery hair made Gyorgy think this was a woman dressed as a boy. But no, the sharp face was definitely masculine. He brought a tray bearing a bottle of French champagne and three long-stemmed glasses.

'Ah, my third guest. Duke Otto, Count Gyorgy – allow me to present Rasvan.'

As the new arrival went about the business of placing glasses on the table and opening the champagne, Gyorgy stared. Surely this was not the unkempt stable boy who'd taken his horse? He looked drastically different: his hair full and shining like rose gold, the attire of a nobleman, all white and blue satin, expensively tailored to accentuate his fine lean figure, with cuffs and buttons and brocade. His face was clean, calm and bright – but definitely the face of the stable boy. Dark eyes, nearly black.

Gyorgy was thoroughly confused. This graceful young man and the surly, grubby stable hand were the same person? An accomplished pianist who'd sat in the shadows … watching, eavesdropping? He felt he was going mad. This made no sense.

'I did not know you had a son,' said Otto, plainly irritated by yet another male arrival.

'Not my son. Rasvan is the nephew of a friend.'

'Ah,' said Otto with a clear note of relief. Not that the Countess was likely to consider wedding such a youth, Gyorgy thought. 'A chaperone, naturally.'

'But of course,' she said, and laughed, showing the black gap in her yellowing teeth. Gyorgy felt a little twinge of revulsion. 'Rasvan, how goes the weather?'

'As bad as can be, my lady.' His voice was gentle, deferential.

She got up and pulled aside a curtain to reveal dense flurries billowing past the windows, forming drifts on the window ledge. Chill air poured across the room, making the candle flames waver. She let the heavy curtain drop back into place.

'Now are you not glad you're not both still out there, with the snow mounding over your corpses? Whoever did not die of a sword thrust would surely have died of cold. This winter takes no prisoners. The snow freezes as it falls. The path becomes a waterfall of ice. So make peace with each other, and resign yourselves to my hospitality for a while. Let us drink a toast.'

Rasvan stayed on his feet, like an attentive footman. The other three each took a glass.

'What are we drinking to?' said Gyorgy. The liquid in his glass caught the firelight, dancing and bubbling.

'To your intrepid effort,' she said. 'To the happy future of Castle Gerlaszhovsky.'

'To Countess Ursula,' said Otto. They raised their glasses. Gyorgy sipped, but Otto threw his champagne back in a single gulp.

In the second before he did so, while the pale gold liquid still sparkled and fizzed, Gyorgy saw something bobbing near the bottom of the glass, rising and falling as the bubbles surged around it. Something shiny-smooth, like a piece of yellowish ivory, stained red at one end.

A tooth.

This Gyorgy glimpsed just before Otto knocked back his drink – champagne and tooth together.

Duke Otto lurched, gripping his throat. He made no sound. Gyorgy saw at once that he was choking. He entirely forgot that he'd wanted the man dead an hour ago – now instinct sent him rushing around to the far side of the table. Otto was on his feet, panicking, one hand gripping his throat. His face was red and darkening towards purple. No breath went in, no breath came out.

Gyorgy gripped him and struck him between the shoulder blades. Again, again.

Otto tumbled and hit the carpet. His lips went blue. Froth clung in the corners like drifted snow. He convulsed, then, within a minute, he went still, eyes fixed open.

Afterwards, Gyorgy was not sure what Ursula and Rasvan were doing while Otto panicked and Gyorgy tried to save him. Too shocked to act, or trying to help? It all happened so fast. Suddenly Rasvan was kneeling beside Otto, leaning down until his face nearly touched the Duke's.

'What are you doing?' said Gyorgy. 'Help him!'

Down went Rasvan's head until it seemed to rest between Otto's jaw and collarbone, and his hair covered the neck and the lower part of the Duke's face in waves of gingery silk. Gyorgy had no idea why he was doing this. Time had stopped and he couldn't move.

Faint sounds. A soft crunch, a couple of gentle moans. The Countess stood above them with a bizarrely serene smile.

Then Rasvan raised his head and Gyorgy saw … Blood on the young man's mouth, dripping. Gyorgy's windpipe torn open, a mess of split flesh and cartilage and gore. The vampire spat something into his own hand and held it up between his thumb and forefinger.

The tooth.

Gyorgy turned away, stomach lurching.

'Well, I got the obstruction out of him,' said Rasvan to Ursula. 'Alas, it does not seem to have done him any good.'

'Is there no life left?'

'None, damn it. Forgive me, my lady, but you know I can't feed after the heart has stopped.' Rasvan brought a handkerchief from his pocket and delicately wiped the blood from his mouth, as if he had eaten a particularly bloody piece of steak.

'I know, dear. Such a shame,' said Ursula the same smooth, calm tone. 'Rasvan, have a care! Blood is so hard to remove from the carpet. Just move him onto the floorboards. I'll summon Jakab to put him with the others.'

The others.

A sort of torpor came over Gyorgy. He stared down at the corpse of Duke Otto: the magnificent decorated general, felled like an oak. Rasvan eased him from the Persian carpet to the polished floorboards with effortless strength and a strange tenderness, cradling the heavy grey head as Otto's shocked, dead face blanched from purple to bluish-grey.

'I didn't mean him to die,' Ursula said. 'The tooth was a joke. I only meant to shock him out of his arrogance. Rather a shame. I would never have married him, but I did like him.'

Gyorgy felt he should take action. Draw his sword and strike the head from the vampire and then from the Countess – if only he could move. But all the strength had gone out of him. He felt he was watching a ghastly play. This hellish debacle was nothing to do with him.

'I – I should leave now,' he stammered. 'Yes, yes, I'm going. You will excuse me, madam, my lady Ursula. I have long outstayed my welcome.'

She moved away, crossing the room as if gliding on wheels. He followed, out of the dining room then across the salon and out into the great hall. From the corner of his eye, he saw the manservant Jakab appear from a narrow corridor, heading towards the reception rooms. Meanwhile the maid Klara stood at the foot of the grand stairs, smiling to herself as if she were too simple to understand what had happened – or enjoying every moment. The sight of her empty, joyful face turned him cold.

He had to get out before Jakab reappeared, dragging the corpse of Duke Otto. That was a sight that would surely send him mad.

Countess Ursula pulled open the great front door. A wall of bitter-cold air slammed into him. The wind moaned. Snow whirled in, plastering their clothes and hair, swirling across the floor. Snow filled the night. It half-blocked the doorway, filling the courtyard to waist height.

Even so, he would have run out into it, but the blizzard was so strong it held him inside the building like an iron door.

'Quite impossible,' she said, pushing the door shut with some effort. 'No creature can be outside tonight. Alas, your clothes will be damp. Shake off the snow before it melts. Klara will show you to your room.'

Gyorgy, by now out of his mind, fled blindly. He ran to the far side of the hall and into the corridor from which Jakab had emerged. He went through an ancient door, down a narrow stone stair closed in by dank stone walls. Down and down he went into the darkness, panicking now. Perhaps he should turn back, but he couldn't. Something came behind him: two shuffling footsteps and a bump, repeated over and over again.

He found himself in a cellar, a long wine cellar with a curved ceiling, ill-lit by a couple of candles. He tried not to look, but he saw anyway. On either side were rows of stone biers, and on each bier a corpse. How many? Dozens. Their state of decay grew worse the further he ran until the last few were mere skeletons inside their mildewed garments. Open-jawed skulls stared at him.

At the far end, he burst out of a door and found himself outside. He was on some lower level of the courtyard. The glacial bite of the wind took his breath away. The snowfall was easing now, turning to needles. Thick stalactites of ice hung from the edges of every roof, like frozen cataracts, their opaque white cores as hard as iron and coated in glass. A hard frost sparkled on the snow. To his right he saw a vertiginous view of the steep valley and the endless pallid mountains, a frigid wilderness that held no hope of escape.

His cheeks and fingers were instantly so cold they hurt. He felt the tears freezing in his eyes.

In front of him stood the stable block, lit by golden lamps. He closed his eyes against the bitter cold and ran inside.

The stables were warm. He saw his horse, cosy in a rug, munching hay. Other horses were there in the stalls – he counted eight – and their body heat steamed into the air, mingling with the scent of dung and straw. The stables were a cocoon of life and hope. He still had some wild plan to take his horse and set off through the thick deep snow, hoping the very snow would cushion them against slipping on the treacherous path, protect them from plummeting into a ravine and down onto the merciless rocks until the forest swallowed them ...

No one would miss him. His body and that of his horse would be buried by an avalanche, hidden by mounds of fresh snow until the spring thaw revealed them, months from now, still intact – perfectly preserved by the cold that had killed them.

Then a female voice behind him said, 'You can't leave, Gyorgy. You're a good man: you would not take your horse into this. I'll have Jakab lock all the doors to protect you from making this foolish mistake again. Did I not promise you a card game before we retire? Come back into the castle. Come.'

Her voice was seductive velvet, but he was long past being seduced. Turning to face her, he drew his sword and swept it above his head, ready to strike – to take off her head with one blow.

A strong hand stayed his arm from behind, stopping him with the force of an iron bar. He yelped with pain. Rasvan's supernaturally strong hand kept pulling, wrenching his sword-arm backwards until he felt the shoulder joint tear out of its socket, felt a bone break with a sickening crack.

Gyorgy screamed.

'You are not going anywhere, my dear brave Count Gyorgy,' said Ursula.

The countess lay in bed with her vampire lover. Before dinner he had changed out of his disguise of stable rags and washed his hair. Now he looked like his true self: a lean and lovely work of art, golden-amber hair brushed back from his face and flowing down over his shoulders and naked chest.

His face bore the expression that delighted her daily, a look of sweet teasing affection. His erection was impressive, especially considering he had already pleasured her to the point of exhaustion. She ran her hand down the delicious muscular abdomen and clasped that thick warm stem she loved so well.

'A shame about the older one,' she said. 'I meant to alarm him, not to kill him. I had intended to keep him alive for you, darling Rasvan.'

'Never mind. His blood ... I've tasted better.'

'The younger one should last a while.'

'Oh, you are not going to marry him, then?' Rasvan said, teasing.

She gave a huff of contempt. 'All these men,' she mused, stroking him. 'What eighteen-year-old, untouched beauty of a princess ever received so many proposals as I? I see the adoration in their eyes, but their eyes shine all for my wealth. You notice that tiny wince, when first they set eyes on my person? They try their best to hide it, but how I loathe them for it. That barely-perceptible wince. You see it?'

'Yes, and I could kill them for it. In fact ...' He gave his lazy smile. 'Death is only what they deserve.'

'My teeth are coming loose,' she sighed, fingering the gap where her canine tooth had shockingly fallen out a few days ago. 'I run to fat, my joints ache. I grow old. Diseases begin to afflict me. My body is decaying. I was beautiful once, but I am beautiful no longer.'

'To me, you are beautiful always.' Rasvan rose over her, his ageless face glowing – truly lovely. Tender, as her long-dead husband had never been. 'I love you, Ursula.'

'No, you don't,' she said gently. 'But Rasvan, I don't need you to love me.'

'I would make you immortal if I could. You know that.' He pressed kisses along her throat.

'But I don't want to be immortal, in any case. I want to stay as we are, forever.'

'And it is your warm mortality that I love,' he said, moving his hand gently over her hot voluptuous flesh. 'I don't see any decay. All I see is your sweetness, your human qualities which are divine to me. Your blood.'

'As long as you stay and pleasure me until I am too decrepit to crave such delights any more ... as long as you stay ... Promise that you will hold my hand and kiss me as I die ...'

'Don't, you will make me weep.' There were real tears in his eyes. 'I promise. I could never leave you, my sweet mistress, queen of my heart.' He pressed kisses along her arm from hand to neck, bit and took a small sip from her throat, just enough to make her tense with pain and pleasure. 'I'm yours.'

'Yes, you owe me that much,' she said, smiling, 'since you drank my dear late husband dry. You owe me your heavenly self, Rasvan.'

Ursula lay content in her lover's arms, listening to the brutal wind howling around the turrets of her castle. How the night moaned! She heard ice pellets lashing the window panes, wave after wave, shaking the casements like angry ghosts.

She heard the distant thud of footsteps as poor Count Gyorgy stumbled up and down stairs, along corridors and back again, the fist of his good arm striking the unyielding barriers of doors and windows. His wails of terrified frustration blended with the voice of the storm; the bone-freezing, lethal, glorious winter storm.

The Raven Bound

'Millions long for immortality who don't know what to do with themselves on a rainy Sunday afternoon.' – Susan Ertz

England, 1932

I walk a tightrope above an abyss. The silver line of wire is all that keeps me from a thousand feet of darkness yet I feel no fear. I flit across the rooftops of London like a cat. I lie flat on top of underground trains as they roar through sooty tunnels. I climb the ironwork of the Eiffel Tower and I dance upon the girders at its pinnacle, daring gravity to take me. And all of this is so dull.

Dull, because I can do it.

I move with the lightness and balance of a bird. I never fall, unless I throw myself wantonly at the ground. Then I may break bones, but my bones heal fast. It is not difficult. It will not kill me. All of these wild feats bore me for they hold no challenge, no excitement.

What is a vampire to do?

I see him in a nightclub. He could be my twin, a brooding young man with a lean and handsome face, dark hair hanging in his eyes, lovely miserable pools of shadow. How alone he looks, sitting there oblivious to the crush of bodies, the women glittering with beads and pearls. He is hunched over a glass of whisky and he raises a long, gaunt hand to his mouth, sucking hard on a cigarette stub. Dragging out its last hot rush of poisons.

'May I join you?' I say.

'If you must.' His voice is a bored, English upper-class drawl. I love that.

'There is no free table.' I wave to emphasise the obvious; the club is crowded, a sepia scene in a fog of smoke. 'My name is Antoine Matisse.'

'Rupert Wyndham-Hayes.' He shakes my hand half-heartedly. His cigarette is finished so I offer him another, a slim French one from an elegant case. He accepts. I light it for him – an intimate gesture – and he sits back, blowing smoke in sulky pleasure. 'Over from Paris, one assumes? First visit?'

'I have been here before,' I reply. 'London always draws me back.'

He makes a sneering sound. 'I should prefer to be in Paris. Funny how we always want what we haven't got.'

'What is preventing you from going to Paris, Rupert?'

I look into his eyes. He doesn't seem to notice that I am not smoking. He sees something special in me, a kindred soul, someone who will understand him.

He calls the waiter and orders drinks, although I tip mine into his while he isn't looking. Then his story comes tumbling out. A family seat in the country, a father who is proud and wealthy and mean. Mother long dead. Rupert the only son, the only child, with a vast freight of expectations on his shoulders. But he has disappointed his father in everything.

'All the things he wanted me to be – I can't do it. I was to be a scholar, an officer, a cabinet minister. Worthy of him. Married to some Earl's daughter. That's how he saw me. But I let him down. I tried and failed. Gods, how I tried! Finally something snapped, and I refused to dance to his tune any longer. Now he hates me. Because what I truly am is an artist. The only thing I can do, the only thing I've ever wanted to do, is to paint!'

He takes a fierce drag on his cigarette. His eyes burn with resentment.

'Isn't your father proud that you have this talent?'

'Proud?' he spits. 'He despises me for it! Says I'll end up in the gutter.'

'Why don't you leave?' I speak softly and I am paying more attention to the movement of his tender throat than to his words. 'Go to Montmartre, be an artist. Prove the old man wrong.'

'It's not that easy. There's this girl, Meg …'

'Take her with you.'

'That's just it. I can't. She's the gardener's daughter. My father employs her as a maid. D'you see? Not content with being a failure at everything else, I go and fall in love with a common servant. So now the old man tells me that if I don't give her up and toe the line, he'll disinherit me! And Meg's refusing to see me. Says she's afraid of my father. Damn him!'

I have not been a vampire so very long. I still recall how hopeless such dilemmas seem to humans. 'That's terrible.'

'Vindictive old swine! I'll lose her and I'll be penniless! He can't do this to me!'

'What will you do about it, Rupert?'

He glares down into his whisky. How alluring he looks in his wretchedness. 'I wish the old bastard would die tomorrow. That would solve all my problems. I'd like to kill him!'

'Will you?'

He sighs. 'If only I had the guts! But I haven't.'

So I smile. I rest my hand on his, and he is too numb with whisky to feel the coldness of my fingertips. I have thought of something more interesting to do than just take him outside and drain him.

'I'll do it for you.'

'What?' His eyes grow huge.

I should explain, I am poor. It seems so cheap to go through the pockets of my victims like a petty thief. I do it anyway, but it yields little reward. The wealth I crave, in order to live in the style a vampire deserves, is harder to come by.

'Give me a share of your inheritance and I'll kill him for you. No one will ever link the crime to you. Natural causes, they'll say.'

His breathing gets quicker and quicker. His hands shake. Does he know what I am? Yes and no. Look into our eyes and a veil lifts in your mind and you step into a dream where anything is possible.

'My God,' he says, over and over. 'My God.' And at last, with a wild light in his eyes, 'Yes. Quickly, Antoine, before he has a chance to change his will. Do it!'

I am standing in the garden, looking up at the house.

It's an impressive pile, but ugly. Grey-brown stone, stained and pitted by the weather, squatting in a large, bleak estate. A sweep of gravel leads to a crumbling portico. No flowerbeds to soften the walls, only prickly shrubs. It's tidy enough but no love, no imagination and no money have been lavished upon it for many a cold year.

In the autumn twilight I traverse the lawns to the rear of the house. The gardens, too, are austere and formal, with clipped hedges standing like soldiers on flat stretches of grass. But there are chestnut and elm and beech trees to add sombre grandeur to the landscape. Brown leaves are scattered on the ground. The gardener has raked them into piles and I smell that English autumn scent of bonfires and wet grass.

Somewhere behind the windows of the house sits the father, the rat in his lair, Daniel Wyndham-Hayes.

It's growing dark. Rooks are gathering in the treetops. I am taking my time, savouring the experience, when a figure in a long black overcoat steps out of the blue darkness and comes towards me.

'Antoine, what are you doing?'

It is another vampire. His name is Karl. Perhaps you know him, but if not I shall tell you that Karl is far older than me and thinks he knows everything. Imagine the face of an angel, one who felt as much bliss as guilt when he fell, and still does, every time he strikes. Amber eyes that eat you. Hair the colour of burgundy, which fascinates me: the way it looks black in shadow then turns to crimson fire in the light. That's Karl. He's like a deadly ghost, always warning me not to make the same mistakes he made.

'I am thinking that this house and garden are the manifestation of the owner's soul,' I reply archly. 'Will they change, when he is dead?'

'Don't do this,' Karl says, shaking his head. 'If you single out humans and make something special of them, you'll drive yourself mad.'

'Why should it matter to you, if I am driven mad?'

He puts his hand on my shoulder, and although I have always desired him, I am too irritated with him to respond. 'Because you are young, and you'll only find out for yourself when it is too late. Don't become involved with humans. Keep yourself apart from them.'

'Why?'

'Otherwise they will break your heart,' says Karl.

They think they know it all, the older ones, but they will each tell you something different. You can't listen to them. Give them no encouragement, or they will never shut up.

We stand like a pair of ravens on the grass. Then I am stepping away from him, turning lightly as a dancer to look back at him as I head for the house. 'Go to hell, Karl. I'll do what I like.'

I am inside the house. The corridors are draughty and need a coat of paint. Yet old masters hang on the walls and I finger the gilt frames with excitement. Riches. This seems ironic, that Daniel should collect these grimy old oils for their value and yet consider his own son's potential work valueless.

Following Rupert's instructions, I find the white panelled door of the bedroom, and I go in.

The father is not as I expect.

I stand beside the bed staring down at him. With one hand I press back the bed curtain. I am as still as a snake; if he wakes he will think someone has played a dreadful joke on him, placed a mannequin with glittering eyes and waxen skin there to frighten him. But he sleeps on, alone in this big austere room. Dying embers in the grate give the walls a demonic glow. Like the rest of the house it is clean but threadbare. Daniel is hoarding his wealth. Perhaps he thinks that if he disinherits Rupert, he can take it with him.

Why did I assume he would be old? Rupert is only twenty-three and this man is barely fifty, if that. And he is handsome. He has a strong face like an actor, thick chestnut and silver hair flowing back from a high forehead. His arms are muscular, the hands well-shaped on the bedcover. Even in sleep his face is taut and intelligent. I stand here admiring the aquiline sweep of his nose and the long curves of his eyelids, each with a little fan of wrinkles at the corner.

He will not be easy to kill. I expected a frail old goat in a nightcap. Not this magnificent creature, who is so full of blood and strength, a lion.

I bend over the bed. I am salivating. I touch my tongue to his neck and taste the salt of his skin, the creamy remnant of shaving soap, such a masculine perfume … I am shaking with desire as I press him down with my hands, and bite.

He wakes up and roars.

I try to silence him with my hand in his mouth and he bites me in return! His teeth are lodged there in the fleshy part of my hand but I endure the pain, I don't care about it, all is swept away by the ecstasy of feeding. We lie there, biting each other. His body arches up under mine.

A scratching noise at the door.

We both freeze, like lovers caught in the act. I stop swallowing. Slowly I withdraw my fangs from the wounds. Daniel only gives a faint gasp, though the pain must be excruciating. We look at each other. The door opens, an apparition floats in.

She's wearing a thick white nightgown and she carries a candle that reflects in her eyes. 'Daniel?' she whispers. 'It's midnight ...'

I can tell from her manner that she hasn't come in response to his cry. I doubt she even heard it. No, she comes in like a thief and it's obvious that she is here by appointment. I am partly hidden by the bed curtain so I have a good look at her before she sees me.

She is lovely. Dark brown hair flowing loose over the white gown. Ah, such colours in it, the lovely strands of bronze and red. She has the sweetest face. Dark eyes and brows, a red, surprised bud of a mouth.

She's coming towards the bed. Daniel rasps, 'Meg, no!' and then she sees us, sees the blood on his neck and on my mouth.

The candle falls to the carpet, her hands fly to her face. She is backing towards the door crying, 'Oh God, no! Help! Murder!'

I have to stop her. I launch myself at her, pinning her to the door before she's taken two steps. I'm in a frenzy now, I must have her, I can't stop. I savour his blood still in my mouth as I bite down, and then I am swept away by the taste of Meg flooding over my tongue. Ripe and red and salty and ...

Her head falls back. She clings to me. It is so exquisite that I slow down and draw delicately on her until she presses her body along the whole length of me and I feel her heart pounding and the breath coming out of her in little staccato cries of amazement.

For some reason I can't kill her. My fangs slip out of the wounds they have made and I hold her close as she sighs. I haven't the energy or will to finish it. No, I like her alive. I love the heavy warmth of her body slumping against mine, and her hair soft against my wet red mouth.

We stand like that for a few minutes. Then I feel Daniel touching my shoulder. He has staggered from his bed.

'Who are you?' he whispers. His big hand wanders over my arm, my shoulder blade, my spine. It slides in between me and the woman and lies warm against my ribs. He's resting against my back. The three of us, pressed together.

Well, this is cosy.

I am in the garden again when she finds me. I am pacing back and forth on the grass beneath the cold windows of the mansion with the moon staring down at me, and suddenly there is Charlotte. She steps from the shadow of a hedge to walk at my side.

'It's difficult to leave, isn't it?' she says, slipping her cool hand into mine. 'What are they like, your family?'

'Interesting,' I say. 'Rupert, the son, is in love with the delicious housemaid, Meg. How am I to tell him that Meg slips in regularly to service the father? No wonder Daniel has forbidden Rupert to see her.'

Charlotte utters a soft, sensuous laugh. 'Oh, Antoine, hasn't Karl told you what a mistake it is to ask their names, to become involved in their lives? You know you shouldn't, yet you can't stop. That's always my downfall, too.'

Ah now, Charlotte. She is Karl's lover and her presence is all it takes to reveal the folly of Karl's advice. Don't get involved with humans, he tells me? Hypocrite. For he took Charlotte when she was human, couldn't stop himself, couldn't leave her alone. And who could blame him? There is something of the ice queen and something of the English rose about her. She is the perfect gold-and-porcelain doll with a heart of darkness. She's like a princess who ran away with the gypsies, all tawny silk and bronze lace. But ask which of them is the more dangerous, the more truly a vampire – it is Charlotte.

She is the seducer. She is the lethal one. You will never see Karl coming, he takes you swiftly and is gone before you know what happened, no promises, no apologies. But Charlotte will worship you from afar, and bring you flowers, and run away from you and come back to you, until you are so mad with love for her that you don't know which way to turn. Oh and then she'll turn on you and take you down, our lady viper, and soak your broken body with her tears.

Not that she has done this to me, you understand. But I have watched her in complete admiration.

'Why must it be a downfall?' I ask, annoyed.

'Humans are so alluring, aren't they? You can't go only for one taste. You can't be like Karl, just strike and never look back. You're like me, Antoine. You want to play with them, to get to know them, to love them. Is the pleasure worth the pain? I never quite know. You have to do it again and again, to see if it will be different this time.'

'It's only a game to me. I don't care about them. I'm doing it for money, that's all.'

'Really?' she says. 'Then why couldn't you kill them? Why are you still here?'

Charlotte stands on tiptoe and presses her rosy mouth to mine; and she's gone, in a whisper of silk and lilac.

Behind this hedge I find a kitchen garden, where Meg's father lovingly grows vegetables to feed the household. Ah, now I see. He is a man who despises flowers and prettiness, loves prosaic potatoes and beans – just like his employer. The air is thick with the rot of Brussels sprouts, the scent of wet churned soil and compost. Through a gap I see the cold shine of the greenhouse, and – where the garden meets the servants' area of the house – the tantalising glint of glass in the kitchen door.

When Rupert discovers that I have not killed his father, he is beside himself with rage.

We meet beneath a line of elm trees. The rooks squawk and squabble in the bare branches above us.

'You liar!' Rupert screams. 'You traitor!'

He flies at me, arms flailing like windmills, but I hold him off. He's useless at fighting, as he is at everything. Perhaps he is a useless artist too, merely in love with the idea of brooding and suffering and being misunderstood.

'Why didn't you finish the old devil off? You only wounded him!'

'I was interrupted.'

'What the hell do you mean – interrupted?'

So I tell him. Rupert rages. He paces, he punches trees, he weeps. Finally he turns to me like a man in the grip of a fatal illness, his face white and frail as the skin of a mushroom.

'This is a disaster!' he cries. 'If Meg and my father are lovers, then I have nothing left to live for. They'll have a child, and I shall have no inheritance, no house, no wife – nothing!'

He flings himself at me, grabbing the lapels of my coat. I am really enjoying this.

'Kill me,' he begs, tears running from his beautiful, anguished eyes. 'Kill me instead.'

Oh, my pleasure.

Only I can't do it.

I hold Rupert close and we are the same height so he looks into my eyes for an instant before my head goes down to his throat. He is tense, desperate for oblivion. But then the inevitable happens. He softens in my arms and clasps my head. He sighs. He forgets what he was angry about.

We are locked together, his blood running sweetly into my open mouth, his groin pressed hard against mine. And it happens. I fall in love with him.

And I'm satiated so I stop drinking; I just want to hold him against me. But I haven't taken nearly enough to kill him and he knows it.

'You bastard,' he says weakly. 'You liar.'

He faints. I let him go. I leave him lying there, slumped on the roots of a tree, and I run.

I don't go far. There is an ancient rose arbour halfway across the grounds, with a dry fountain and some sad-looking, mossy statues. Here I hesitate, undecided, my mind full of Rupert and Meg and Daniel. I want them so badly. I am in anguish.

Karl startles me. I am not looking where I'm going and I don't see him there in the shadow of a rose trellis. I almost step on him. He's like a statue coming to life, with fire for eyes, and if I had been human I believe I should have died of fear. He's still following me, watching me, warning me – just for the hell of it, I swear.

'Are you simply going to leave him?' He grips my arms, forcing me to meet his gaze. 'You have a choice, Antoine. Go back and finish them all – or leave now, and never come back. Make a decision or this will destroy you!'

'Why don't you leave me the hell alone!' I growl, pulling free of him.

'I shall,' he says coldly. 'But I have seen so many of our kind sabotage their own existence through their obsession with mortals. I have even known them to kill themselves.'

'Kill themselves?' The idea is shocking to me. Abhorrent. What's the use of becoming immortal, only to waste it?

'As soon as I am sure that you understand – then I shall leave you to your folly.'

I laugh. 'Karl, do you really not see? How boring do you want our existence to be? Oh yes, I have tried all the things that new-made vampires think will thrill them. And it does thrill, just for a little while. I have climbed mountains where the cold and the lack of air would kill humans. I have swum deep in the ocean. I have thrown myself like a bird off the Eiffel Tower and walked away with a broken wrist.'

'And have you not found wonder in any of this?'

'The thing is that when such feats come so easily to us, there is no point in doing them. No challenge.' My voice is throaty and I hate myself for being sincere and fervent in front of Karl, but there it is. 'All that's left, the only challenge, the only chance of passion ...' I point across the garden at the grey-brown hulk of stone, 'lies in that house.'

'I disagree,' says Karl, but his eyes betray him.

'If you disagree, my friend, why are you pestering me? There is no reason under the moon for you to be haunting me, except that you get some frisson of excitement from it.'

Karl can find no reply to that. I dance away, quite pleased to have silenced him for once.

I am back at the house again. Moth to the flame. Of course.

I'm outside the parlour window and they are inside, sitting there by the light of an open fire and gas lamps. A brown scene, with little touches of green, red and gold. To my surprise, Rupert and his father are sitting in armchairs on opposite sides of the grate. They are not speaking but, my God! At least they are in the same room! They are sipping brandy from balloon glasses and the liquor shines like rubies in the fireglow.

Meg is perched on a couch, sewing. She wears a simple skirt and cardigan – not the maid's uniform I expected – and her hair is coiled on her head, beautifully dishevelled. They are listening to music on the wireless – such a big box to produce such small, tinny, jaunty sounds! But this is not a scene of happy domesticity.

There is a dreadful tension between them. Even through the glass I feel it.

They're waiting for me, thinking of me. I can feel the heat of their dreams and desires. For me they would forget their quarrels, even forget their relationships to each other, just to feel my lips on them again and my fangs driving into them … to lose themselves in bliss. I long to go to them. I want to feel their arms around me, and their bodies pliant under mine, and their genitals stiffening and opening like exotic flowers and their blood leaping into me, God, yes, their blood …

The woman pricks herself with the needle. I watch the blood-bead swell on her finger. Then her lips close on the wound, and my desires throb like pain.

My hand is on the window …

Meg looks up with her finger still pressed to the moist bud of her mouth, and sees me. I grip the frame of the sash window and push it upwards. The warmth of the room rushes to meet me and I hear her gasp, 'He's here!'

The men jump to their feet. Their faces are rapt, eyes feverish, lips parted. All three of them are coming towards me and I long to stroke their hair, to feel the heat of their bodies through their clothes and taste their skin. Brooding Rupert and leonine Daniel and sensual Meg. Three golden figures in a cave of fire.

'There you are,' they whisper. 'Come in, Antoine, come in to us.'

I reach out to them, as they are reaching out to me. Our fingertips touch–

Someone slams down the window between us. A hand grips my arm.

'They will suck you in,' says Charlotte into my ear. 'They will be your slaves and you will be theirs.'

Now if it had been Karl who shut the window I should have been furious. But I can never be angry with Charlotte; not for long, anyway. In a flash I am detached and ironic. 'That sounds quite appealing.'

Their faces are pressed against the cold pane, staring into the twilight. Charlotte pulls me aside so they can't see us. I yield, and we walk slowly along the back of the house, with grit and soil and the debris of autumn accumulating on our shoes. A graveyard scent. I'm looking for another way in. I feel like a revenant, scratching at windows, rattling door handles.

This path leads us into the kitchen garden again. In the gloom there are rooks on the furrows, pecking at the delicious morsels that Meg's father has turned up with his digging. Will he know what his daughter does with Daniel, and with Rupert, and with me? Will he join us? An old man, smelling of sweat and earth, creating green life from the ground ... I should like to taste his essence.

'If you go in, they won't let you go again,' says Charlotte. 'You won't be able to leave.'

I pull her to me and kiss her neck. 'I shouldn't want to leave. I love them. And you sound thrilled at the idea yourself.'

She laughs. 'Wasn't I right, Antoine? Yes ... this is excitement. This is ecstasy. Shall I tell you why Karl is so cold? Not because he's different from us. No, it's because he's the same, he can't leave humans alone. Only he hates the consequences. Oh, I always plunge in head first, I can't help myself, I always think it will be different this time. But Karl ... he's the realist.'

And Karl is there, as if he stepped out of thin air in the shadows. He has been waiting for us. Now he's strolling on the other side of me, his hand so affectionate upon my arm. They're trying to save me from myself! They are guiding me away from the house, along the grassy path towards the hedge at the top of the garden and the bare trees beyond, away, towards redemption. Every step is agony.

'The trouble is, there's a price to pay,' Karl tells me. 'You can say "yes" to them and you can let yourself fall – but you can't have them and keep them. They're dying, Antoine. The more you love them, the more you kill them.'

'Don't think it won't hurt you, when they die,' says Charlotte. 'Don't imagine the pain of it won't claw your heart to pieces!'

'But if I ...' My voice is weak.

Charlotte knows what I'm thinking. 'Yes, you could make them into vampires,' she says crisply. 'With a great amount of energy and will and strength, you could do that. But it won't be the same. Then you will have three cold-eyed predators, vying with you, resenting you, perhaps hating you. But your warm, moist, blood filled lovers will be gone.'

'So leave,' says Karl. 'Leave them now!'

We have reached the gap in the hedge. I stand there, despairing. I raise my arms in anguish and the flapping of my overcoat makes a dozen rooks rise in alarm. But one remains. It hops in circles on the grass, trailing a damaged wing. It cannot escape the earth.

I break away from Karl and Charlotte. I run back to the house and stand outside, breathing hard.

My lovers are inside, waiting for me. I can hear the blood thundering through their hearts, their red tongues moistening their lips in anticipation. I only have to turn away and they will remain like that for ever … aching for me, waiting, their lust turning to fevered agony … but alive.

Grief will, I think, be interesting.

I press my fingers to the cold glass of the kitchen door, and I go in.

The Ghost Who Looks Like You

Note: The vampire Stefan's untold story begins long before A Taste of Blood Wine and finds him a year after the tragic events of The Dark Arts of Blood.

I: Sweden, 1930

In the beginning, there was only Stefan. A golden boy, with a smile to charm the stars from the sky.

Not many know his secret, but those who do are surprised to learn that he was born a single child. His twin came later.

'Karl never knew you without Niklas, did he?' Charlotte asked. They walked arm-in-arm through Swedish pastures at dusk, where farmland swept up towards the edge of the fathomless forest. In pensive mood, he had wanted to show her his birthplace. The only sounds they heard were of the spring breeze, birdsong and the low music of cowbells.

'No. It was quite some time later, at least thirty years, that our lord and master Kristian fixed his attention upon Karl. Niklas was already with me by then. I never even told Karl the truth until … let me see … hardly five years ago.'

'Of course. I remember.'

'Look.' He pointed down the folded valley at a traditional red farmhouse, long and low under an angled roof. 'It's still there. There are more buildings around it than I remember. Barns, a new smithy perhaps. I'm sure they have replaced the roof, replaced and repainted everything over the decades, in fact … but the house itself still looks the same. Time has stopped here.'

He went quiet with his memories until Charlotte spoke. 'I cannot imagine that you were ever a farmer.'

'I wasn't. A farmer's son. But yes, a true peasant. I grew up here.'

'It is beautiful.'

'Not so beautiful, tending cattle in the freezing winter nights. And we always believed the land to be soaked with other races: elves and trolls, witches, hags that transformed into wolves, forest wives and wights … Those races went into hiding when Christianity came, but we still felt them.'

'And saw them?' Charlotte's eyes gleamed like lamps in the dusk. She was always full of curiosity. He considered her his best friend, as simple as that.

'Well, actually …' Stefan turned and set foot on the old familiar path that led uphill towards the wildwoods. 'Come. Don't be afraid.'

She smiled. 'We're vampires, dear.'

'And we both know that there are worse things than vampires in this world. Let me show you the place where I first saw *her*.'

II: 1765 – 1787

Stefan's family home, the red farmhouse near the coast, stood some two hundred miles north of Stockholm in the ribbon of hills and lakes and dairy meadows that lay between the Baltic Sea and the great forests. These pasturelands were delightful in the summer when the sky barely darkened, but in the winter they glittered with picturesque, inconvenient, merciless snow. Sometimes the sea itself iced over. You could have walked across to Finland, though Stefan was never of a mind to try it.

To the west and north, dark lines of woodland frowned over the green pastures. Trees rolled away for hundreds of miles until they met the northern tundra of Norway. As a boy he could barely imagine such a barren place. Surely only giants and the dreaded *Lindworm* lived there.

He had older brothers, but they grew up to be proper farmers, tough and God-fearing. Stefan was different. He had the face of an angel, soft pale-gold locks, eyes too blue and enchanting to be quite human. He was slender, almost feminine. Charming qualities in a small child, but as he grew towards manhood he failed to put on bulk or muscle, grew no beard, endured the tough work of farming with a distaste he could not disguise. Even his voice stayed soft. A male voice, but lacking the gruffness that might have averted the mockery of his peers.

His mother adored him. His father despaired.

His family were devout church-goers, naturally, but in private they still paid their respects to *den Gamle Tro*, the old beliefs. His father became convinced that Stefan was a changeling, left by the *Vaettir* or *Alfar*, the elves who'd stolen his real son.

Fortunately he was not a violent man, or Stefan might not have survived to adulthood.

Rather, Stefan's father was secretly, deeply superstitious. He would call out a warning to the invisible wights called *Vittror* before throwing out slops, or worse, since it was unwise to upset them. The *Vittror* were known to borrow cattle for their milk, but they always sent the animals back – as long as you did not anger them. Likewise, Stefan's mother unquestioningly left out food for the *Tomten*, sprites that must be kept happy or else your house and farm would fall into ruin.

They took the hidden world for granted. These rituals were part of everyday life.

And if such beings had left them an elf child, then the child must be nurtured.

Beware of the mist, his father told him, because the *Alfar* lurk in the mist. But whenever the sky turned to iron and shook with thunder and lightning, his father would say to him and his brothers, 'Look! That is Freyja making fire with steel and flint. She does so to watch over our fields and our cattle.' Then they would have to say a little prayer of thanks to the goddess of protection and fertility, their mother goddess, Freyja.

Stefan enjoyed bringing the cattle down from their summer pastures – for all he lacked the concentration to be efficient at the task – since that gave him a chance to wander the flower meadows and woods and high paths. He always felt nervous of something, though he knew not what. Trolls, dark elves, creatures unknown. He was always day-dreaming. Looking for something that he sensed just behind him, or just beyond the next hill.

Perhaps he was, as some claimed, simple. He knew he was not like others, but what was he? A frustrated poet? Or actually a changeling, one of the elven race?

'There was a tradition called the Year Walk,' he told Charlotte, decades later, in the modern world that had hardly touched his family farm. 'The walk was a divination rite, to see what the year had in store. To do so, you had to enter the supernatural world and ask the *Vaettir*, the otherworld folk. It was one practice my father rejected, because he thought it was too dangerous, or too blatantly insulting to the Christian religion. The only thing he feared more than the *Vaettir* was God himself. But this particular year – I was nineteen – I was determined to go. Somehow my father guessed, and he grew angry and we had a terrible fight that made me decide, once and for all, that I must leave. The thought of living my entire life on the farm made me desperate. I needed to ask the hidden folk, will I ever escape? Will I meet my true love? Find wealth and happiness? All of that.

'So, according to the rules, I sat alone in the dark until midnight came, then I made my way to the church. The first thing was to blow through the church's keyhole – that was to blow out my Christian faith and let in the supernatural. Then I walked around the church, anti-clockwise, to call the elves and enter the otherworld.

'I should confess I was quite drunk, and it was the kind of ritual that drunken youths undertake, like scaring yourself in a graveyard. I remember how very cold and dark it was. Cold, dark, and with something … watching me. You must remember that, even as Christians, we believed completely in the otherworld, but it was separate to God and therefore the realm of the Devil. We believed that unearthly women called *Huldra* waited in the woods, like sirens, to seduce young men who might never be seen again. People had even been put to death for consorting with such beings. So I was very afraid. In fact I terrified myself so thoroughly that night that my father's fury was only a gnat-bite in comparison. He had always complained to everyone that I was not right in the head. I hated him for it. But I feel sorry now, because I did not realise at the time just how deep his fear of the old beliefs ran.

'I don't remember much of the night. I was drunk, scared and lost. I may have passed out for a time – it's a miracle I didn't freeze to death, I suppose. Perhaps the *Vaettir* were watching over me. But when the dawn came, it seemed to me – still not sober – that it was a fine idea to go up into the forest.'

Stefan had climbed, his boots slipping on the fresh snow, his head full of the scent of pine resin. The snow appeared to be evaporating, filling the forest with cold mist, a milk-white vapour illuminated by shafts of weak sunlight. Rounding a curve in the path, he saw a woman standing in the clearing before him. She was tall, stately, dressed all in gleaming white garments – and she was almost entirely transparent. The tree trunks soared upwards all around her like the pillars of a cathedral. She stood in a sea of mist, like a ghost, floating. Pale blonde hair flowed in two waves away from her high forehead; her eyes were icy green.

She smiled at him.

She must be one of the *Huldra*, a forest wife: a demonic seductress who appeared out of the mist to tempt and destroy foolish men. But even as he thought this, he realised she was far more than that. She was Freyja – the great goddess, guardian of farmers, protector of the land, bestower of fertility. She who caused storms to rage in the heavens.

Stefan felt his meeting with her was inevitable. Since he was not right in the head, he was bound to start seeing things.

He wanted to fall down in worship, but he was rooted in place. The most appalling sense of terror and yearning washed over him. He had never felt anything so intense. The goddess standing there in the falling light … now raising a hand to point at him.

Or pointing at something just behind his shoulder. He shivered. He dared not look round.

'No,' he said in answer to Charlotte's question, as they stood together gazing up at the cathedral pillars of the forest. The clearing, now, was empty and silent. 'Sadly, there was no seduction. We stood and looked at each other until she faded and I ran for my life, falling over icy tree roots. At first I thought, if I were a Catholic, perhaps this would be a sign I should join the priesthood, but she was no vision of the Virgin Mary. She was Freyja. I saw her here, in this exact spot. I came back with wild flowers as an offering to her, a gift of thanks. And no – I have never seen her again.'

III: 1787: The Age of Enlightenment

His angelic looks, that had earned him mockery and bullying among the rural farmers, saved him in Stockholm. Stefan took menial jobs until he'd saved enough for a decent suit of clothes, and then he found clerical work, and learned to mimic the manners of the gentry to perfection. He charmed everyone with smiles and his beguiling nature. Women would turn to stare after him in the street. Men, too. Soon he was deluged with offers of employment from Stockholm's nobility.

The message he took from his vision of Freyja was this: *You do not belong here, Stefan. You are a changeling, born in the wrong place. You were not meant to be born the laughing stock of an ignorant family. You are a poet, a lover, an actor. Go to your proper place.*

So he went to Stockholm, city of handsome pastel buildings and blue waters.

Soon he found a position at the court of King Gustav III as secretary to an easy-going, pleasure-loving duke. He learned French, Russian, and English; he learned to play the piano and the harpsichord to delight guests of the royal family. He ran all over the palace and the town, delivering messages for his employer. Sometimes he performed in King Gustav's plays.

'What was it like?' Charlotte asked. 'The court, I mean.'

'Oh.' Stefan's mind was flooded with colours ... ivory and sky-blue, lavender, liquorice stripes, dark blues and blood reds. Old-fashioned traditional costumes for court, outlandish outfits for masked balls and operas. Paintings only slightly exaggerated the opulence of those vast royal salons and the physical beauty of the King and his brothers. Gorgeously tailored coats and breeches of the finest silks, braids and medals, and divinely-shaped male calves sheathed in white satin ...

Thoughtfully Stefan went on, 'Kristian used to say that when we joined him, we should forget our human lives. We had no life until we became part of the Crystal Ring, he said. We had no ties to Earth, no family, and no God, until we were reborn by Kristian's will. However ... I never forgot my human life. How could I? I can take you to the palaces. I'll show you the paintings and statues.'

'I would like that,' said Charlotte.

'My time at the court of King Gustav was ... unsurpassed. They called him an "enlightened autocrat". Before him, the monarch had been more or less the puppet of the *Rjksdag*, the parliament, for many years, but Gustav seized back his sovereign power, which meant he angered the nobility and all the other estates who objected to having their influence removed. All the same, court life was lively. Spontaneous. Music and parties, affairs, never-ending conspiracies and scandals. Oh, it was a fascinating time to be alive, Charlotte. Gustav loved the arts. He loved drawing and writing plays. He built palaces, opera houses and theatres. And he was a gentle, charming man, at least in public. He loved beauty. That made him popular, in spite of everything else. Imagine living at the Court of Versailles. It was like that, only more so.'

'It sounds … wonderful. Romantic.'

'Oh, it was. Especially with all the whispering in the corridors.' Stefan smiled to himself. 'Was Gustav actually the father of his son? Was the queen secretly married to someone else? What guilty secrets was his *sister* hiding? And so on. Even then, I had a taste for scandal. However, I built for myself a reputation for trustworthiness. I was the embodiment of the three wise monkeys: if you don't hear or see evil, you can't speak it. That's why the nobles trusted me with their messages. That's how I learned all their secrets.'

'Not to blackmail them?'

'No, of course not, although I could have done. Just so that I knew what was what. But I was well-paid for my discretion, that is true. At court, there was a girl …'

'Of course there was,' Charlotte said, smiling.

'Cornelia. The daughter of a minor Baron. She lived in the twilight, like me; I mean that her rank wasn't high enough for anyone to pay much political attention to her, but she had a merry disposition that made her popular. She was a beauty, small and slender with dark hair and blue eyes. She loved dancing, loved jokes and silliness. Loved me in her bed, too; such enthusiasm that night after night she almost wore me out. In truth, I would have waited until we were married, but she … couldn't wait to have her way with me, and who was I to argue?'

'You were going to marry her?'

'Of course. Don't look so shocked! She was a few years older than me, but that didn't matter. We were in love. Even now, when I remember her, I still feel the warmth of her body and all the delicious pleasures we shared. Despite all that happened afterwards, the thought of Cornelia still makes me smile.'

'It sounds as if you were happy, at least for a time.'

'Blissfully so, for three months. In that time, I didn't even notice the dark presence that had entered the court. I thought he was a visiting nobleman from Prussia or somewhere. Nothing to me. I was lost in the pleasures of the court, the operas and balls and plays. Lost in Cornelia. Her thighs …'

'Stefan, please,' said Charlotte. 'I don't need every detail.'

He went quiet for a time. He and Charlotte travelled south through the warped otherworld they called the Crystal Ring until they reached Stockholm, passing through walls as if they were no more substantial than drizzling rain. In the dark deserted gallery of a palace he showed her a portrait of King Gustav III: a handsome young man with languid eyes. For a long time Stefan gazed at the portrait as if he would never move again.

'Do you know what it is we call *Fanden*?' he asked eventually. She shook her head. 'The Devil. They say he has the usual horns and a cloven hoof, but they also say that he appears as a tall, lean man in a top hat. Well, Kristian had no hat, and nor was he particularly lean, but he was tall and dark, very imposing. I began seeing him in the palace and at the opera. I didn't learn his name for a long time. No one could tell me who he was. Just some foreign noble. I don't think people even saw him. However, he seemed fixated on me. Always staring. Not at anyone else, not even at King Gustav himself. Only at me. I truly thought I was imagining him, as I probably imagined Freyja that time, and I became worried for my own sanity. But somehow I felt he was the embodiment of the unknown, sinister presence I'd always sensed when I walked in the forests. Now, for the first time, I saw him clearly. And a voice inside me whispered, *Fanden.*'

'And he killed Cornelia?' Charlotte asked softly.

'Actually, no. This was around the time that she killed me.'

Take this message to the Marquis of Alfenborg, his duke commanded him. *Await his response and bring it to me without delay.* Obediently, Stefan took the sealed paper.

There was no servant at the door to the Marquis's quarters, so he went in. No one was there in the antechamber, either, but he heard explicit noises from the bedroom. *Bring his response without delay*, the duke had said. Having too much curiosity, and too little of the common sense that would have made him announce his presence and then wait outside until the Marquis emerged – disgruntled, but decent in a robe – Stefan instead crept towards the half-open bedroom door.

Thus, tragically, he found his dear true love Cornelia in bed with the Marquis.

'Oh,' said Stefan, hovering in the doorway. Alfenborg was forty-ish and silver-haired, known for his good looks and his quick temper. Cornelia was flushed, her eyes bright. Naked, they both stared furiously at him from the rumpled sheets and said nothing. 'I brought a letter from … Ah. My apologies. I see how it is.'

But he didn't.

Stefan dropped the letter on a table and walked away, soft and quick, too stunned to feel any deep emotion. Perhaps later he would go blind with tears, stab his own pillow with a dagger until the feathers flew, pretending the pillow was the Marquis, then get horribly drunk for three days … but now there was only shock. A huge cloud of disillusion wavered around him, weightless.

Outside in the corridor, he walked straight into her.

Cornelia.

Again.

She was fully dressed in a gown of lavender silk. They both stopped, and because he was staring, she stared too. 'Stefan, what's wrong?'

'How did you–?' He waved helplessly back at Alfenborg's quarters.

'Oh.' Her face went still. She took some moments to reply. 'My sister.'

After a pause of equal length, he said, 'You never made mention of a sister.'

As they stood, each trying privately to formulate what to say, the woman who looked exactly like Cornelia came out into the corridor, wrapped in a floor-length white robe. She pushed a folded paper into Stefan's hand and said, 'The Marquis's reply.'

Then all three of them stood in the lamplight, silent. Except for their attire, the two women were identical. Even the dark coils of their hair were the same. Both had the exact same expression of suppressed glee, eyes shining with amusement.

'Which one of you is … Cornelia?'

'I am,' both said at the same time. Then they pointed at each other and chorused, 'She is. I'm Matilda.'

The one in the white robe put her hand over her mouth. Their shoulders shook with mirth. When they'd managed to contain themselves, the one he'd met in the corridor – Cornelia? – looked down at the floor. Her eyelids fell beguilingly but there was no shame in her posture, no surprise, only amusement.

'And which one of you has a mole on her left inner thigh?' Stefan said sharply, loud enough to make a passing servant raise eyebrows at him. This gossip would be all over the palace by the day's end.

'That would be me,' said the girl from the bedchamber. 'I am Matilda. She is Cornelia. That is the truth.'

Stefan had no idea what to say. He was mortified.

'So you have both been in my bed? Cornelia … I had no idea. I don't – I don't understand. Forgive me – I would not have been faithless for the world. I've betrayed you, unknowing.'

'Yet suspecting,' said Matilda. 'You noticed the mole, after all.'

'I thought – I don't know. A tiny skin blemish or its absence was not enough to make me suspicious.' He put his fingers beneath Cornelia's chin, trying to make her look him straight in the eye. 'I did not mean to betray you, but your *sister* has betrayed you!'

He had expected shock from his betrothed, tears, rage. Perhaps she would slap him or strike her twin, if not both of them. But she did not. Neither woman moved.

'What is this?' said Stefan. 'I meant to marry you, Cornelia! How can I, now? I'm sorry. I don't know how this hellish thing has happened!'

'Oh, Stefan, my darling.' Cornelia stepped forward in her rustling lavender dress, her body brushing his, her hand rising to stroke his cheek. 'You are so sweet, so young. I was never going to marry you.'

'But ... What?'

'I'm so sorry,' she said, but couldn't stifle her giggles any longer. Both sisters collapsed in laughter, holding onto each other. He was humiliated; impotently outraged.

'All along, you knew? You both knew?'

They couldn't speak for laughter.

'But I loved you!' he cried. Pathetic.

'And I loved you too, Stefan,' Cornelia gasped. 'Who would not?'

'Then – why? Did you do this on purpose?' Still no answer. 'Apparently you planned this whole comedy. Took turns with me. Lied to me. Why?'

A few moments passed, heavy with tension and stifled gasps as they got their amusement under control. Eventually Matilda said, 'Because it's fun.'

'*Fun*?'

'Of course,' said Cornelia. 'Too delightful to resist.'

'Fun to deceive me. To make a fool of me.'

'Also a great deal of fun bedding you,' said Matilda, smirking.

'I am so sorry, dear Stefan,' said Cornelia. 'If I had known you would be so hurt ... We never intended ...'

'And what about your friend the Marquis in there? Does he know there are two of you?'

'Oh, he knows,' said Matilda. 'He doesn't mind. It's rather exciting for him, not to know if it's Cornelia or me he is embracing.'

'So he has you both. Of course. How excited would he be to know about *me*?'

Cornelia sighed. 'You're such a puritan, Stefan. He wouldn't care. He might shoot you for making an issue of it, but he wouldn't actually mind. Most men are rather thrilled when they find out. Then they want us both at once. Don't you want ...?'

'You've done this before.' As he spoke, Stefan felt like the greatest idiot in the entire world. 'You do this all the time. All I am is a toy for you to share. People must know! Why did no one warn me? What, was the whole palace laughing at me behind my back?'

'People are cruel,' said Matilda.

'That is why I began to speak of thighs,' he told Charlotte. 'A couple of times, I noticed a small brown mole that I had not seen before. Other times, it was no longer there. Mostly, I entirely forgot to look. I was mildly puzzled, but gave it no more thought. You know I'm a trusting soul, and I never dreamed ...'

'Oh, Stefan. To think you thought you'd found your soul mate. I'm sorry.'

'I bear no grudge. But at the time, I was cut to the heart. Blind with tears and humiliation, I walked away with their laughter echoing after me. Ah, my wounded pride! So I marched out of the palace and did the worst thing possible. I joined the army.'

Within months, Gustav had declared war on Russia. Stefan found himself in Finland, on some godforsaken cold wasteland, marching towards the battlefield.

No role could have suited him less. From the start, his superiors had marked him as weak and picked on him relentlessly. A particular officer, a sharp-faced, precise man who looked more like a priest than a soldier, dragged Stefan into his own quarters and told him, there in the near-darkness, to strip naked.

'There was no need for him to hold a sword to my throat,' he told Charlotte. 'I would have done what he wanted in any case.' He shrugged. 'I didn't care what happened to me. It was all the same. I'm not proud to admit it, but I found I had rather a taste for other men. Oh, not the brutish ones ... but the ones who were gentle, and grateful. I became ... I cannot put this delicately ... I became the barracks whore.'

His fellow soldiers bullied him. He hated the uniforms, the training, the food, the priests, the ghastly sea voyage to meet their enemy on Finnish soil, the stink of bonfires, the swamps of mud and manure in which their tents were pitched. Marching through the muddied snow. Hated everything.

And now, the culmination of the nightmare. Advancing on the Russian troops.

'They should have left me behind with the camp followers, but no, I was still a supposed soldier, after all. My first battle was my last. I don't even remember much about it. Deafening noise – men yelling, galloping hooves, pounding boots and cannon fire. I was too busy trying to see and hear, and to comprehend which way was up, even to be afraid. A Russian musket ball went into my chest. I didn't even know why I was suddenly on the ground, but I knew my life was over. I was dying and, oh well – it all happened so abruptly there wasn't time to be upset about it.

'But then, the *Fanden* came. Kristian appeared out of nowhere, like a great dark shadow over the battlefield. He scooped me up and saved my wretched life.'

IV: We Fold the Night

Kristian, a vampire of singular habits, not entirely sane, had the nature of a hermit and the instincts of a hoarder. But this was contradictory: in order to hoard, he must leave his lair and go out into the world in search of prey.

'He didn't have a type, as such. Certainly he was drawn to beauty – he took Karl, Andreas, Maria, Katerina and Antoine, to name only a few, as evidence of that – but he would also take in the strange, the mediocre and the sinister: creatures such as John, Matthew and Cesare. Kristian saw something in humans that no one else could see, something that he needed in his vampire flock.

'Kristian would leave his Rhineland castle and travel through Europe, haunting palaces and monasteries, great houses and hovels, churches, taverns, anywhere and everywhere in search of his Chosen Ones. And in the 1780s, following whatever strange holy muse guided him, he was in Sweden. And he chose me.'

'For your lovely face,' said Charlotte.

'And my rampant stupidity.' Stefan grinned morbidly. 'He transformed me into a vampire in the usual manner, the alchemy of three. You know how that goes.'

'The clarity,' she said. 'You see the world differently, as if you'd always seen it through a dusty window before.'

'Yes. And the gorgeous blood, the fountain of life. The gorgeous *victims*.'

The first thing Stefan did, once Kristian's followers had finished with him and he knew, with a kind of stunned delight, that he was changed forever, was to take himself north.

'We fold the night and travel through the folds,' Stefan said. He meant the Crystal Ring, also called Raqia: the strange hidden ether that only vampires (usually) could enter. 'That ability was so strange and magical to me – almost more enchanting than the divine liquor of blood itself. Nothing could stop me travelling. Folding space itself and piercing straight through like an arrow! How wondrous.'

So he went up to the very north, across the tundra to the brink of the Arctic Ocean, where the air stung bitterly and the stars flowed like a river of light and shadows above, as if a snow blizzard whirled across Valhalla. Thick bulky clothes of reindeer leather, boots, scarves, fur hats, gloves – he needed none of that. He travelled in courtly clothes, silken brocade coat and breeches.

Although Stefan felt the cold, he knew it could no longer harm him. He sat on the edge of the world, hands wrapped around his knees, and watched the aurora. The wedding veils of the gods swirled down from heaven, ever-changing. Such colours he'd never seen as a human. Emerald and violet, fiery pink and ethereal shades of blue never imagined on Earth. For hours he remained there, captivated by the aurora and the stars and the planets … God, the *planets*. Strange worlds of swirling storms and rings, dozens of eccentric moons. Who needed a telescope?

He stayed there, falling in love with the entire universe, for countless hours. Only the thirst for blood moved him. Then, like a wild predator, he shadowed a group of *Sami* as they herded their reindeer, stalked them until they made camp and all but one of them slept.

Soft as a shadow, he crept up on the one who kept watch and took him so gently the man did not even cry out.

The blood was almost too rich: thick and nutritious from a diet of reindeer meat, oily fish and game. Stefan came as he drank, a violent rapturous spasm that shook his whole body, as if he were in love with his victim. He was in love with all of creation at that moment. He didn't drink enough to kill the man. The blood was too much, too luscious. He fell away gasping, in a stupor of bliss beneath the Northern Lights.

Clearly he was going to enjoy this new life.

V: Schloss Holdenstein

Kristian's castle, Schloss Holdenstein, was always a place of horror for him: a dank, crumbling maze containing too many rooms without windows, more a prison than a seat of power for the self-made Lord of Vampires. Kristian's lair was the antithesis of the grand salons that were Stefan's natural habitat. At the same time, Stefan did not mind being there.

'A strange dual layer of perception exists in vampires – multiple layers, often – that allows us to see a thing as our human selves would have seen it: horrifying, filthy, frightening, undesirable, and yet to find those things interesting rather than repellent,' he said. 'We see through multiple layers that a thing may be subjectively ghastly, yet objectively neutral, even fascinating. Just an arrangement of elements like everything else in the universe.'

So although Stefan hated the castle, when Kristian insisted on his presence there, he did as he was told with calm acceptance.

'Did you love Kristian?' Charlotte asked. 'Karl said you were devoted to him, not so long ago. You would sit at his feet, like a pageboy.'

Stefan shrugged. 'I've never denied that I'm shallow, and prefer an easy life. I was Kristian's lapdog for a long time. I am not proud of that. It was Karl who persuaded me to turn away from him. Karl and you. But did I love him?'

Charlotte knew only too well, so Stefan did not need to explain, that Kristian was a great dark brute of an immortal, jealous, violent and possessive. He held terrible power over his flock. Those who opposed him tended to perish in states of extreme shock. Those who displeased him … on a whim he would take them up to the highest layers of Raqia, to a frozen, floating ice realm called the *Weisskalt*, and leave them there to sleep for ever. True hibernation. Few returned. Those who were able to recall the experience described it as worse than death. Not oblivion, but eternity under a blinding, burning-cold light.

So Kristian was hardly lovable, and yet he inspired a strangely overwhelming devotion in his followers. He talked a great deal about God, rationalising the existence of vampires as punishing angels sent by the Almighty.

In private, Stefan never took his theology too seriously.

'Yes, my own way, I did love Kristian. He didn't give me much choice, so I surrendered. That's how he kept me in thrall for so long, serving him even when my instincts told me to flee. He was a brute, yet not unattractive. Handsome in his dark, granite way. I tried to seduce him, naturally. Oh, how I tried! But his interest in his flock was never sexual. Or if it was, he kept the urge severely in check, and released it in rage and violence instead. Once or twice, I tried to touch him - just the cheek, or the thigh - and he threw me across the chamber so hard that my bones broke against the stone walls. I learned my lesson. He only wanted me sitting at his feet, lapping up his wisdom and doing his will.'

'He was vile,' Charlotte said softly.

'We are all vile, in our different ways. At least he let us go out, as long as we came back. In my first few months as a vampire - especially after I sat there under the aurora feeling god-like, certain that nothing could harm me, ever again - I grew overconfident. Truly I thought I was untouchable. And after a time I conceived a plan to revisit that army officer who'd first abused me, and have my revenge. First upon him, then on all the others who'd made my life in the army a misery.'

'And did you?'

'Well, I found him. I terrified him and I fed upon him. That part was a delight. Unfortunately, so lost was I in the pleasure of draining his blood that I did not notice his adjutant stepping into the candlelight behind me, drawing his sword and sweeping it towards my neck.'

VI: Niklas

'When a human is beheaded, does their consciousness persist for any time at all? Even for the micro-second it takes all the blood to leave the brain? Is there a moment of shock - or ecstasy - in which you realise your head has been severed from your body and here is that all-important moment: the end of you? No one comes back to tell us. However, with vampires, it's said that consciousness does persist. Not for long. Just a few seconds that seem like eternity. Staring, perhaps trying to speak - and then the curtain falls. Some say the curtain is a dazzling white veil, others speak of utter blackness. For me, there was blackness.'

Stefan felt he was travelling down a long smooth tunnel that went on forever. As in a dream, he felt no emotion at this, and no curiosity. It simply was.

When he opened his eyes again, he felt as if he'd woken from a long sleep. He had no idea where he was or why, or even who he was, yet it didn't matter. He was still half-dreaming. Over him was a low, vaulted stone ceiling, lit by a dim red glow. Everything else was dark. He lay on his back, confined by … he couldn't tell at first. He seemed to be in a stone horse-trough. Or a very old coffin. Its sides squeezed his shoulders. He was lying in some kind of dark, gelatinous, iron-scented liquid.

Blood, old blood. He was lying in a coffin submerged to his ears in blood.

He sat up. This was not easy, since he had no strength. The thick congealed mass held him down like glue, and he couldn't wriggle his arms free to lever himself up. Eventually he got one hand onto the coffin rim, then the other, and pulled himself into a sitting position.

He found himself next to a huge mirror that covered the entire wall. There was his reflection: sitting up in a coffin on a plinth, covered in gore, his hands white on the stone sides, his face a picture of staring horror with wide-open eyes.

His eyes had changed colour from blue to pale saffron. He put one hand up to his neck … his head was attached to his body again and he felt no scar. His reflection mimicked the action. White skin showed as the blood oozed away and he saw, beneath the gore, that his mirror image was beautiful.

He began to climb out of the trough, but his reflection stayed where it was, staring at him. Stefan's mouth opened in shock while the reflection only smiled.

He put out his hand towards the glass but found thin air. There was no mirror. In reality, there was a second stone sarcophagus, and a second pale being that was an exact copy of him

Except for the colour of its eyes.

Stefan fell to his knees. It was not terror that struck him down, but a sense of overwhelming relief. Then he crawled towards the second coffin and reached up to hold his duplicate's cold hand between both of his own.

'I can't explain. Anyone normal would have fled screaming, but not me. All I thought was, "I never have to be alone again," and, "Here is someone to love. A companion who needs me. My brother."

'Kristian rose out of the shadows and called for his acolytes. They washed us, as midwives might wash the blood from newborn babies, and dried and dressed us. I was in shock, my memory blank. Days passed before I understood what he had done. Kristian had taken my severed head and body from the officer's quarters and carried them back to his Schloss. There he drenched the two in fresh human blood, separately, day after day for months. Eventually my head grew a new body, like a lizard regrowing its tail, and the body produced a new head. This regrown head – Niklas's head – had no intellect. That's what everyone concluded, that the brain and the mind could not regrow and he was just a blank copy of me, like a life-sized mannequin. But I felt him. I know he knew *something*, even if he never spoke. I know he had awareness, if only an echo of my own.' Stefan put a hand to his chest. 'I felt him, *here*, all the time.'

'I still don't understand why Kristian would do such a thing,' said Charlotte.

'Some kind of alchemical experiment. To prove it could be done. Who knows? Twice, Kristian saved my life, yet his curiosity seemed to go no deeper. He was desperate for vampires around him, but only so that they could worship him. Niklas was just one more.'

'Who named him?'

'I did. Kristian allowed me that. And my sudden twin was not aggressive or dangerous – if that had been the case, they would have destroyed him. He was gentle. He was watchful, with his mysterious golden eyes. I had to lead him to our prey. He could do things if I showed him, and he could follow simple instructions. Without going into detail, everything about him worked … but he did nothing unless I guided him. Yet, I felt his feelings, which were only echoes of my own, but still … He was real to me. I loved him as I have never loved any creature before or since. When we sat before a mirror, the two of us became four. So strange and wonderful.'

'I remember how you cared for him,' Charlotte said. 'You always put him first.'

'After I told Karl how Niklas came to exist – that he was not my natural twin – I also made him promise that, if anything happened to me, he would look after Niklas. Karl said he did not think that Niklas could survive without me, any more than our reflection stays in a mirror after we've moved on. But I answered, suppose you're wrong. Suppose I'm dead and Niklas lives on, helpless and alone. Promise me. Karl asked why, and I said – because my beating heart lives in his chest.'

VII: 1792: A Masked Ball

'Kristian made Niklas, and yet did not know *what* he had made. He thought that everyone and everything revolved around him, the centre of his own universe. He barely seemed to realise that others had lives and feelings and realities of their own – or if he did, he would try to snuff out such subversion. Thus Kristian failed to notice that centre of my life was no longer him, but Niklas.'

A very few years had passed since Stefan had become a vampire, and then become two vampires. And Niklas was so beautiful, the pair of them so striking together … Stefan was beset by the desire to return to Stockholm. He missed the royal court.

He wanted to be part of it again. The lavish clothes, the etiquette, the intrigue, the parties and operas, all of that.

'The colours,' he told Charlotte. 'The costumes. In those days the women had these great dresses of the most ridiculous proportions, so voluminous you could barely get near them, except that they were somewhat flattened in front and flaring out to the sides like lavish upholstery. Utterly ridiculous, yet delightful. And the wigs, the monumental silver wigs they wore! Part of me likes the plainer clothes that we wear since the Great War ... but I never saw such fashions as I saw in the latter days of King Gustav.'

So Stefan returned to Gustav's court. Since he could pass easily through walls, invisible in the Crystal Ring, he had no trouble gaining entry to the palace. No trouble stealing two fabulously-tailored suits from the rooms of some duke who had a similar slender build, and also swiping a decanter of cognac. No one challenged Stefan as he wandered the grand corridors until he caught a warm familiar signature. He found a niche for Niklas to hide, told him to wait there.

Alone, he entered a small pleasant parlour where Cornelia and Matilda sat embroidering. By happy fortune, there were no maids or relatives present to derail his intent. The twins wore identical white dresses sprigged with blue and pink. They were as beautiful as ever.

He entered without Niklas and without sound, standing there until Cornelia finally noticed him and started up in shock. 'Stefan!'

Her embroidery frame fell to the floor. Both women rose and he bowed and kissed their hands. Then he embraced them – Cornelia first, then Matilda – and they kissed. Light kisses on the cheeks, then a brush of the lips. And they were all three smiling.

'We thought you were dead in the war!' Cornelia exclaimed. 'Where have you been? Oh, how wonderful to see you. Stefan, darling Stefan. You look magnificent.'

'As do you, ladies. You are keeping in good health, I hope. Are you married?'

They glanced at each other and laughed. 'No. We're quite the pair of old maids. Ladies-in-waiting, to earn our keep.'

'But you are both still so beautiful, and not a day older. Don't speak nonsense of old maids.'

Matilda said, rolling her eyes, 'Father wants to move us to some other palace, perhaps to another country, where our reputations are unsullied and he can find a pair of ghastly old noblemen who will have us. But we prefer to stay here. We still like our ... furtive pleasures.'

'I am quite sure you do.' He held up the decanter. 'See, I have brought a peace offering.'

'Ah, you've become a man of the world?' Matilda's eyes sparkled.

'Of several worlds,' he said.

Half an hour later, Stefan lay between them in a vast bed – or rather they all lay in a heap of warm satiny skin, enmeshed limbs, erotically musky fluids. Occasionally the sisters embraced each other, forgetting he was there for a few minutes. So he would remind them, and they would gasp at his stamina, and be all over him again, gently struggling for possession of him – for his mouth and hands, if one sister was first to claim his loins.

Then he sent out a wordless signal, and Niklas moved invisibly through Raqia and stepped into the bed chamber. Niklas was nothing if not obliging. The sisters did not even notice him as he stood there – saffron eyes blank, silently removing his clothing until he was naked, as lean and perfectly formed as Stefan – in fact, they did not notice Niklas at all until he moved towards the bed and leaned down over the three of them.

Cornelia screamed. Matilda uttered a series of grunting breaths as if she were trying to scream too but couldn't force any sound out. Stefan had never seen anything as thrillingly, delightfully hilarious as their shock in that moment.

They both scrabbled, but were too tangled up in the bedclothes and in his arms to escape the bed. With effortless strength, Stefan held them both.

'What the hell – what in God's name – Stefan, what …?'

'Oh,' he said, grinning. 'Did I forget to mention my twin brother, Niklas?'

'As revenge goes, it was the best ever,' Stefan murmured, smiling at the memory. 'Their terror turned into furious indignation, and we had quite a lively exchange of words. But no one fled the room. I apologised. They began, how can I put it, to see the funny side … The possibilities. And soon Niklas was in the bed with us.'

'Did he … know what to do?' Charlotte's eyebrows were raised, her lips parted with surprised curiosity.

'Evidently. As I said, he would do whatever I showed him, or asked him to do. And he felt pleasure. Gave pleasure, too. That much was obvious.'

'It must have been quite an evening.'

'Oh, it was. Niklas and I dined very lightly upon our lovers' veins, so no harm was done. Perhaps a touch of delirium in the morning, and wondering if they'd dreamed the whole thing … But it was not the only time. We four were a tangle of molten indulgence for many nights … I would even say addicted to the situation … but it couldn't last forever.' He sighed. 'I always knew it couldn't last.'

'King Gustav, the lover of beauty and music, threw a masked ball at the Opera House he had built so lovingly. Niklas and I were there with our paramours, Cornelia and Matilda, in our costumes and our masks: two identical pairs. They were flower-sellers, we were harlequins. What a splendid sight we made. I remember telling the women, 'You were right. This is fun.'

'Oh, and how we laughed together, and how strange it all was. Artificial. For they knew we drank from their throats, but they never said the word *vampire*. Perhaps they thought saying it out loud would break the spell.'

And the four of them had whirled for hours – Stefan now dancing with Cornelia, now with Matilda, swapping partners with Niklas between each dance – and he was drunk on the glittering reflected lights, the jewel-colours of the dresses, the human heat and excitement, so many eyes gleaming in the shadowed eye-slits of masks ... and he drank in the bright laughter of Cornelia and Matilda as the guests all waltzed and conspired together, drank in all their carefree, heartless jollity ...

At some point, King Gustav himself joined the party: a man in a dark cloak, with a three-cornered hat and domino mask, looking somewhat like a highwayman. Stefan barely noticed him. Barely noticed a small group of men in black cloaks moving to surround the king.

Someone struck a drum. It was that kind of muffled noise, a thud in the wrong place. Then a wave of shock spilled out around the King – people ceased dancing, the music stopped, guards were suddenly everywhere. There were shouts and screams. Someone began shouting '*Fire!*' as if to clear the house, but the guests only kept milling around. Chaos.

Some minutes later it became apparent what had happened. A would-be assassin had shot King Gustav in the back.

'He lived for another two weeks,' Stefan told Charlotte. 'As I mentioned, he had enemies. He'd infuriated the nobility by curtailing their powers, so a group of conspirators decided the only answer was assassination. And, imagine this: one of them had lost his nerve and sent the king an anonymous message. Gustav chose to ignore the warning, and came down to the ball regardless.'

'Kings think they are invincible,' said Charlotte.

'I don't know what he was thinking. It wasn't the first threat he'd had, so I imagine he didn't take it seriously.'

'Did you know Gustav? Was he another of your lovers?'

Stefan paused. He and Charlotte now stood in a different gallery before another portrait of King Gustav. Stefan felt a shiver of regret, something long blunted by time but still there.

'To both questions, no,' Stefan said softly. 'He'd only ever spoken to me while directing me in his plays. I might as well have been a piece of scenery. It's true I had a kind of infatuation with King Gustav ... Look, you can see he was a handsome man, so magnificent in his white wigs, his silver brocades and white ermine furs, his gold chains dripping with blue sapphires. He was known for his charm, but I had never dared approach him. Why should I? I had been just a commoner, an occasional actor, a servant. But now ... You see, everyone thought he would recover at first. Despite the wound, he was soon back in action. He took command and dealt with his enemies, had his attackers arrested and received apologies from the nobles who'd quarrelled with him. But a few days later, the wound turned septic. Fever overcame him and he took to his bed.

'I don't know what came over me. Yes, I'd been a common servant, but now I was a vampire – outside human hierarchies – and Gustav was laid low by the shrapnel in his back. The idea of him lying helpless in the royal apartments obsessed me.'

'Oh, Stefan,' Charlotte sighed. 'Can I guess where this is leading?'

'To have power over a king, even just for a little time ... I couldn't resist. Deep in the night I went to the grand state bedchamber where he lay, passing in easily through the Crystal Ring with Niklas beside me. His guards and physicians did not see us. There was no need for anyone to know we were ever there. I wanted to know how the blood of a king tasted.'

'And how did it taste?' Charlotte whispered. She put her hand through his arm. He felt her trembling a little with excitement.

'The same as anyone else's blood. Very good. Delicious. There was just that little taint of illness on him – you know, when they have a fever, or have taken opium, or are simply exhausted, and it adds a curious flavour, like a rare spice? I tasted that. But otherwise, his blood was like any human's: the very ichor of heaven.'

'Mmm.' She made the soft noise in her throat.

'I took only a few sips. Five, to be exact. It was hard to stop, but I stopped. Then I let Niklas have his turn, so that he too could say he had drunk the blood of a king – had he been able to speak. Then Gustav opened his eyes and looked at me. I wonder what was in his mind? He didn't seem afraid. His eyes were calm and hazy; perhaps he thought I was a fever-dream. The angel of death, ready to carry him to heaven. We looked into each other's eyes – he had the most lovely, large and languid eyes, and for those few seconds only Gustav and I existed in the whole cosmos – and then I drew Niklas back into the folds of Raqia, and we left.

'King Gustav died the next day. We fled the palace and never went back. Not because I feared being found out, but because nothing was the same without him. They said he died of blood poisoning and pneumonia. Perhaps that is what happened, but I can't help thinking ... that it was my fault he died. If I hadn't taken the last few drops of his strength ... I didn't mean to.'

'We never do,' said Charlotte.

'He was a beautiful man. There were rumours he had a fondness for men, and he had his close male confidantes, but he never glanced at me. Perhaps I was too feminine for him. Who knows? But I had him that night. It's a nice secret to hold, Charlotte, when I am feeling lonely and a little sorry for myself. I tasted the blood of a king. I know how it feels … to have killed a king.'

VIII: 1930, Svalbard

'You know the rest,' he said.

'I doubt that, but I know everything you are willing to tell me for now.'

'Well, you were with me for the worst of it. The end of Niklas. My punishment for overreaching myself, causing Gustav's death? It does me no good to think too much. I was made for pleasure, not for philosophy.'

She put her arm around his waist, a light touch of love and friendship.

Stefan and Charlotte were very far to the north, on an island deep within the Arctic Circle. Not minding the cold, they sat on deep snow, drenched by falling chiffon waves of light. Electric green, fuchsia pink, bursts of icy blue rays. The aurora borealis dwarfed them with its sheer vast scale – rippling streamers vaunting towards the stars, sheets of light undulating in translucent folded layers. And in a flash, their structure changed again.

Now aqua streamers spread out from a point on the horizon into curved waves, like the whorls of a conch shell. The sky to the left of this spectacle turned fiery pink, while on the right it glowed violet.

No doubt Charlotte could have explained the science, lectured him on electrons and magnetic fields, but he had no desire to hear it. All he wanted was to bathe in this unique enchantment. There would be other nights, other wonders, but never this particular night again.

'Freyja's wedding veil,' said Stefan. 'Or light flickering from the armour of the Valkyries, as my father used to say. Has it struck you that, although we see great beauty in the Crystal Ring, we never see this wonder? This belongs to Earth.'

'And that's awe-inspiring in itself. Stefan, you said you believed in the hidden worlds of the *Alfar*, the elves. I wonder if that world and the Crystal Ring are the same, or if they overlap? Have you ever seen your sprites, forest wives and trolls there?'

He considered. 'I've seen strange things, but not the folk creatures of my homeland. Never.'

'Yet you saw Freyja.'

'But I was still human then. She was not part of the vampire realm, and nor was I.'

'All the same … if the human subconscious creates the Crystal Ring …'

'Then what?'

'If other realities intersect in layers, just like this …' She tipped back her head and watched the folded light-fall flashing across the dome of stars and shadow-clouds. Pure green, red flushing into apricot. 'You saw Freyja, and she gave you a vision that changed your life. You speak of seeing Niklas in veils of mist. You know I had a strange time when I thought I'd split in half, and saw myself outside myself, and others mistook that apparition for one of the *Weisse Frauen* who haunt the Swiss Alps, who are really just the same as your *Huldra*, the forest wives ... I don't know what I'm saying.'

'She looked a bit like you,' Stefan said. 'Freyja. She was taller, paler, more statuesque ... but when I look at you, Charlotte, I recall her. My beautiful white muse standing in the mist and snow.'

'I think what I am saying is that there are deep mystical currents interconnected in a way that we can't understand. Not yet, at least.'

'This means something, though,' said Stefan. 'I can't grasp it. Not yet, not tonight. I don't wish to be maudlin and dwell on the past, or wallow in grief forever, but sometimes ...'

'Sometimes you need to talk about Niklas.'

'And you're the only one who really listens to me.'

'Always,' she said tenderly. 'And now? It's only been a year. How are you?'

'What would you like me to say?'

'Whatever is true. You seem like your old self: carefree, full of mischief. And that's a delight to see, but ... I know the pain never entirely goes. And there's no shame in talking of loss. Darkness. I have seen so much. I was there.'

'Yes. You held me while I wept and raged. Now I know I was right always to protect him, but it still wasn't enough. Humans on a murderous mission came for us both, but only Niklas died – apparently because I was a true vampire, as hard as diamond, and he was only a facsimile, just a china doll that would shatter at the first blow. But don't try to tell me that Niklas did not matter, that he was only a shell who looked like me, and not real.'

'I would never tell you that,' said Charlotte.

'I know. I need to tell the universe, though. He was beside me for so many years, longer than any humans are together. Now he is there no longer, and yet he is. I see him from the corner of my eye. I feel him. I look in the mirror, and there he is. Two of us again. I can even touch him, and not care that he feels like cold glass. I look out of a darkened window and he's outside, looking back in at me. Sometimes he comes towards me through the fog, but the fog is a veil that neither of us can penetrate.'

'Yes,' she said. 'I understand.'

'It's strange, Charlotte. I'm always looking around, expecting to see him at my shoulder, but at least it's no longer a shock when he's not there. I always want to talk about him, but who am I talking about?'

She waited for him to go on. Above them the winter sky was crowded with stars, the river of the Milky Way flooding across the black obsidian dome, the ethereal lights swaying and dancing. Freyja's wedding veil, Stefan had said.

'I am Niklas. He is me. Perhaps it was Stefan who died, and Niklas who sits beside you now with all Stefan's memories. Charlotte, it's what you were saying about layers. I think I understand. We split in two for a while – we split into four, when we both stood before a mirror, and into eight with Cornelia and Matilda. And if I stand between two mirrors, I split into an infinite number … but the thing is, Niklas and I split in two for a while, and now we are one again. So what is there to mourn? If my heart beat in his chest, his soul lives in mine.

'When I spoke about drinking the blood of King Gustav, I bent the truth a little. It's true I expected Niklas to drink from the wound I'd made, but he refused. I almost never knew him to defy me in anything – but that one time, he stood back and only stared at me, as if I had done something appalling. Why? Was Niklas actually my conscience? Because of him, I am not the brutal vampire I might have become otherwise. In saying nothing, he said everything.

'I see now that it wasn't Kristian I sensed behind my shoulder, all those years ago. It was Niklas. Always Niklas. Deep inside all the layers and reflections, elusive … until Freyja pointed the way. All my life, I was waiting for him. Now he waits for me.'

My Name Is Not Juliette

Philip knew there was something wrong with Jennifer. All the way to the theatre she'd seemed on edge for no reason. Now as the house lights dimmed her smile was fixed, her eyes scared. He felt irritated. If something was up, why couldn't she just come out with it?

He leaned across their small daughter, Sarah, who was sitting between them, clutching the programme. *The Ballet Lenoir presents Swan Lake*, said the curling letters.

'I'm told this is going to be something pretty special,' he said. 'It had better be; tickets cost a bloody fortune. Glad the *Mercury* is paying for us.'

Sarah – seven years old, her feet dangling over the edge of the seat – was wide-eyed. Philip envied her innocence. This was an event that would cast its magic through the rest of her life. For him, a theatre critic, it was merely a job.

In the moments before the overture began, the auditorium was filled with rustling darkness, a palpable anticipation. But Jen was smiling too hard, as if she was here under sufferance and trying to be nice about it, as always.

'Just relax and enjoy it, okay?' Philip said brusquely. She winced at his tone, which only annoyed him more.

Blonde, compliant Jen, always putting everyone else before herself. No man could wish for a better wife. But God, her ridiculous moods made him angry sometimes. He'd have it out with her later, but now the curtains were gliding apart, the green and silver world of *Swan Lake* opening up to absorb him.

Jennifer could hide nothing from Philip. She knew she was irritating him and that there'd be a row when they got home. Anxiety formed a hard ball in her chest. She had these few hours, while the swan maidens spun their magic on the stage, before the showdown – but suspending real life was a trick that eluded her.

She envied Philip's ability to detach himself. She envied Sarah, who was oblivious to everything but the unfolding story. The ballet was a classical production with no modern grotesquerie. The dancing had an underwater quality, an ivory-tinged slow-motion dream seen through rippling light. The effect was mesmeric. Yet, like a nervous swimmer clinging to the side, Jen could not completely lose herself.

She knew her worries were trivial, even pathetic. Only that her mother had wanted Jen to stay with her over the weekend, and Jen, as usual, couldn't say no and dared not tell Philip. He would be furious.

'Not again!' he'd shouted the last time. 'You're my wife, you can't be at the beck and call of your mother all the time. She'll never get her claws out of you if you keep giving in.'

Easy for him, when he wasn't prey to her parents' subtle emotional blackmail. Jen tried to please them all, ended up being slammed between them like a squash ball. It was her own fault, of course. She could be bright and breezy and cope with anything – until there was a row with Philip. Then his voice raised in anger and his piercing stare were all it took to wake the demons of her childhood. His hostility made her a little girl again, frightened and confused. She couldn't bear it, would do anything to be loved again.

Anything to protect herself from the demoness of her nightmares, the slayer and punisher of bad children: Lilith.

It wasn't rational for a grown woman still to be afraid of a myth, Jen told herself. But she couldn't rake out the poisonous weeds sown in childhood.

Not her parents' fault, even though her father was something of a tyrant, her mother an emotional manipulator. Her Nan – her father's mother – was the one who'd told her stories of Lilith.

Jen tried to concentrate on the ballet but the stage seemed as distant as a television. Memories fell like a veil between her and the real world. A dark, high-ceilinged room. Nan bending towards her, streetlight outlining her thin, beaky nose. Nan smelled of mothballs, lavender and the damp that pervaded her house; and although she wore bright, cheap crimplene, Jen seemed to picture her in black satin and lace.

Six-year-old Jen had been disobedient. Her father had told her to stop playing with a china figure she'd picked up. She had defied him, and a moment later the figure had slipped out of her hand and shattered. An accident, but her father, incensed, had dragged her along two streets to her grandmother's house.

'I'm not having this child back in the house until she learns to behave like a civilised human being,' he said, and dumped her there.

He never explicitly asked his mother to punish Jen. He didn't have to. Nan had her own ways of dealing with disobedient children.

'D'you know who Lilith was?' Nan had Jewish European ancestry but her accent was from Sunderland, where she'd been brought up. Jen didn't even know where Sunderland was, but she thought of it as some strange dark netherworld where witches came from. *Sundered Land. Underland.* 'Adam had a wife before Eve. The first wife's name was Lilith, but she was wicked and disobedient, just like you, pet. She wouldn't do what Adam told her. Instead she ran away into the wilderness and turned into a horrible demon who flies around at night looking for bad children. Lilith married the Devil, see, 'cause she's as wicked as him and can't ever have real babies, only demon babies. That's why she takes revenge on women who can. She hates them.'

The story was always muddled, senseless, yet unspeakably frightening. Jen felt Lilith's presence in the room, snake-like and shadow-black. 'Hates them. She'd like to take all their children away and suck their blood. But God won't let her because it wouldn't be fair, would it? So he did a deal with her. He said, 'I'll protect the good children and you can have the bad ones, because they need to be punished. So when a child is wicked, along comes Lilith and takes them away. Do you understand me, pet?'

Little Jennifer nodded, chewing the hair of her doll in fright.

'If you're bad, she'll take you away in the night, bite your throat and suck out all your blood,' Nan said confidently. 'Have you been naughty enough for Lilith to come? Wait and see! If you're still here in the morning, it means God's forgiven you. Then you'd better not be disobedient, ever again.'

Then Nan had locked her in the bare, damp bedroom and left her there until morning. Left her to watch for movement in the shadows, to transform the bulk of clothes or furniture into threatening figures. Jen had a clear picture of Lilith. A grotesque woman with long black hair, who wound across the floor like a snake, her body clothed in coal-black wings. All night she waited for Lilith to slither from under the bed.

She cried herself to sleep, clutching her doll. When she woke in the morning, the doll was gone. She went half-mad trying to find it, until her Nan led her up to the attic, saying, 'Perhaps Lilith came after all.'

There was the doll on the dusty floorboards, its dress torn off, its plastic limbs mutilated, red stuff smeared all around its neck and trickling down the pink torso.

'Ah,' Nan said wisely. 'Lilith didn't take you, but she took your baby. It's a warning, see? You've got to be good all your life, or she'll take your real babies away. Be an obedient girl and you'll be safe.'

Such a warning, Jen could never forget.

The grown-up Jen felt white-hot anger at her grandmother for terrorising a small child, but the fear had come first and was stronger, more primeval. Nan had been obsessed with the mythology of sin and punishment; perhaps she thought she was doing Jen good, or perhaps she was plain evil. Whatever the truth, Nan's death, when Jen was fourteen, did not make Lilith go away. On the contrary, it only seemed to unleash Lilith from all restraint to fly free in the darkness. Only now, Jen did not fear for herself, but for her own daughter.

When Sarah was born, Philip had mocked his wife for putting a Hebrew amulet in the cot to protect the baby against Lilith. 'Since when have you been Jewish?' he said, incredulous.

'You don't understand. My grandmother–'. She tried to explain, but Philip wouldn't listen.

'I'm not having this superstitious nonsense! I don't know what's got into you. You don't even believe in God!'

No, nor in angels or devils or Adam and Eve. Only in Lilith. And she'd had to stand and watch Philip tear up the paper charm and throw it away. Since then she'd learned to hide her true feelings from him with lies.

That was Jen's fault too, for marrying a man just like her father: a big, dark, self-obsessed man who took her completely for granted. Both loved her conditionally according to how 'good' she was. But being perfect for her husband and perfect for her parents were two different things, and the difficulty of balancing them was wearing her thin.

Suddenly, in Act III, the ballet's enchantment hooked her at last. The ballroom scene, where the sorcerer sends his daughter Odile to seduce Siegfried away from his true love, Odette. The ballerina spinning across the stage in glittering black was a striking contrast to the dazzling white of the swans. Odile was breathtaking, and she caught Jen's attention as the other dancers had not. Such expression in her long white limbs, her gracefulness, the way her dark costume moulded to her body. She radiated arrogance, yet mimicked Odette's vulnerability to perfection. She seduced Siegfried and audience with equal ease.

Odile pirouetted, eyes fixed on one spot to keep her balance as she turned – and that spot was Jennifer's face. In lakes of kohl, Odile's eyes were jewel-cold, and they hung on Jen's gaze, scorching her with their coldness.

And they recognised each other.

I know who you are, said the dancer's stare. *I know your disobedient thoughts and all the little lies you tell to keep people quiet, so they won't see you as you really are. But your sins will find you out and you'll be mine.*

And Jennifer thought, *Lilith*.

This was idiocy, of course. This was paranoia. She realised it but she couldn't stop it. Knowledge impaled itself in her like a thrown knife and quivered there. *This woman is Lilith. This woman wants to hurt me. She is going to steal my husband and kill my daughter.*

Jen glanced at Sarah. Her daughter was spellbound. So was Philip, in a different way. She'd seen that look before, when he saw a stunning woman and thought Jen wasn't watching. He ran his tongue over his lips, twice.

Jen began to feel sick and shaky. There was a sack of sand in her chest. Beginning of a panic attack, no reason for it – but that was the essence of phobia. Irrationality. She clutched the scratchy velvet arms of her seat. Breathe, damn it. Just remember to breathe.

'Bloody superb,' Philip muttered. 'There was pure evil radiating from her.'

When *Swan Lake* came to its poignant end, and the company took their rapturous curtain calls, Odile was absent. The audience shouted ecstatically for her; still she did not appear. As the house lights came up, Philip rifled through the programme. 'Strange. Odette and Odile are traditionally danced by the same ballerina. But that Odile wasn't Odette.'

Jen was exhausted with tension. All she wanted was to go home, take a valium, and sleep. Leaning over, she said, 'Look, it says there: Odette/Odile, Marie Darby.'

'I know, but it wasn't the same girl,' Philip said excitedly. 'Was it, Sarah? They looked quite similar, but it was just clever make-up.'

Jen didn't know why he was so worked up about it. She found his excitement distasteful, like inappropriate lust. 'Who is it, then?'

'The owner of this company is a woman called Juliette Lenoir. But no one knows anything about her, no one ever sees her. I think that was her dancing Odile! Why does she make a mystery of herself? Why dance anonymously? There could be a real story in this, not just a one-column review. Come on.'

'Where?'

'We're going backstage.'

Jennifer's heart sank. 'We should go home. Sarah's tired.'

'No, I'm not, Mum,' Sarah said vehemently, bright-eyed.

'They won't let you in,' said Jen in desperation.

He tutted, exasperated. 'Come off it, Jen. I'm known by the theatre staff. It's part of my bloody job, for Chrissakes.'

'Don't swear in front of-'

'Oh, go on, Mum, please,' said Sarah, looking up with dark excited eyes. Jen gave in, covering her anxiety with a smile. What the hell did it matter who danced Lilith? Slip of the tongue. Odile.

The painted brick corridor behind the stage stank of dust and damp and musty material, years of sweat and greasepaint. Ropes hung from the shadows and the walls were lined with hampers. A murmur of voices came from the dressing rooms.

'God, I hope she's still here,' said Philip.

Jen, feeling awkward and out of place, prayed she was not.

A swan maiden in costume went past, delicate in snowy tulle. Sarah stared at her in awe. 'Excuse me, mademoiselle,' said Philip, all business-like charm. 'Could you tell me where I might find Juliette Lenoir?'

The dancer looked startled. 'I'm sorry, sir, she's not available.'

Jen was relieved, but Philip persisted. 'That was her dancing Odile, wasn't it?'

From the girl's guarded reaction, he'd obviously guessed right. 'When Madame dances, she doesn't advertise the fact. You'd be wasting your time trying.'

'That's a shame. It would mean so much to my little girl.'

The swan maiden smiled and bent down to Sarah. 'Well, she can meet the rest of us. Would you like that? What's your name?'

As they were talking, a woman slipped past in the background, wrapped in a lavender cotton robe. Jen's heart gave a heavy thud of recognition. She said nothing, but Philip had spotted her too. Rudely he rushed in pursuit, calling, 'Madame Lenoir! Could you spare a moment, please?'

The woman stopped and turned. Her face, scrubbed of make-up, was unexpectedly fresh and young, but her eyes again turned Jen to ice. Clear polished agate swirling with shades of silver, violet, blue, captivating and glacial. Her hair was loose over her shoulders, a crinkled mass of black all dishevelled from being compressed under the feather head-dress.

She seemed smaller than she had appeared in costume, but no less stunning. Hers was an unapproachable, transcendent beauty. Watching Philip with icy appraisal, she stood half-turned away from him as he spoke to her, denying him, shutting him out.

'You danced tonight, but your name wasn't in the programme.' Philip had – on the surface, at least – an easy manner that usually disarmed stubborn interviewees. 'You're extraordinarily young to be the director of a ballet company. I imagined Juliette Lenoir to be much older. I'm Philip Linley.'

'A journalist?' she interrupted. Despite her name, her accent was English. Her voice, cool and gentle, gave nothing away.

'I'm the theatre critic for the *Evening Mercury* and I'm about to write an ecstatic review of tonight's performance. The problem is, there is very little information available about the Ballet Lenoir. I'd be so grateful if you could spare a few minutes to tell me something about the company.' He smiled. 'I assume you'd prefer it if we got our facts straight?'

Juliette Lenoir almost returned the smile. Not quite. 'Journalists are vampires, are they not? They suck out their victims' lives and smear them in black and white over something that's not fit to be used for cat litter.'

It struck Jen that Madame Lenoir was teasing Philip.

'No, it's not that sort of newspaper. We're perfectly respectable.'

'I'm sure you are, but I don't give interviews.' She sounded final, but then she turned, looked straight at Jennifer, and seemed to change her mind.

Again Odile's searchlight stare went into Jen. A beam of hostility. A look that actually could kill. Jen felt a fist clench in her stomach. She glanced around anxiously for Sarah, relieved to see her still with the swan maiden.

'That is, I don't give interviews as a rule. But this time ...' Lenoir spoke slowly, still gazing at Jen. Then her gaze flicked to Philip and she smiled. *Serpent!* Jen thought. *God, why do I hate her so? I've never hated anyone on sight like this.* 'We'll see. But not now.'

'Over dinner?' Philip said eagerly, subtlety deserting him.

'No. Meet me here ... on Sunday evening. There's no performance then. I'll talk to you only on one condition: that you bring your wife and child with you.'

He looked dismayed, but hid it with a laugh. 'I don't normally take them to work.'

'I don't care what you normally do, Mr Linley,' Juliette Lenoir said sweetly. 'If you want the interview, bring them. I would like to know you all.'

Looking at Sarah, she touched her tongue to her upper lip.

Philip was about to leave for their assignment – for once not feeling seen-it-all-before jaded, but giddily excited – when Jen started again.

'Don't go, Philip.' She was standing in the hallway, having made no attempt to get ready. He felt like slapping her. All weekend she had tied herself in neurotic knots over a simple interview that was actually nothing to do with her.

'Why the hell not?'

'I don't know,' she said helplessly. 'It's late. I don't like her. Just – don't.'

'For God's sake, Jen, how can you not like her? You don't even know her. Anyone else would give their right arm to meet an artist like her. What is your problem?'

Jen didn't answer. He felt too preoccupied to get really angry with her. He held her shoulders. 'Look, she insisted I take you and Sarah with me. If you don't come, I might not get the damned interview and it'll be your fault. Now get Sarah ready and get your coat.'

Jen wasn't usually this stubborn, but she pulled away. 'It's much too late for Sarah to go out. We're not going. Why is it so important anyway?'

'Shit!' said Philip, losing patience. 'I've had enough. Stuff it, I'm off.'

As he made for the door she followed him, pleading. He grabbed his coat and slammed the front door in her face. *I can't handle this cryptic hysteria*, he thought savagely. *Why the hell does she have to get into such a state about nothing? Anyone would think I was hoping to have an affair with Juliette Lenoir.*

As his car slipped through the orange glow of streetlights, Philip worked out how he'd explain his wife's absence to the dancer. Sarah not well. Yes. Why the hell did she want them there anyway? If it was a chaperone she needed, she could provide her own. He must see her again at all costs, and he didn't care whether he got a story out of it or not. Lovely Juliette. Love, lust, whatever it was, he couldn't get her out of his mind.

When he arrived, he found the theatre in complete darkness. Sunday, no performance, everything locked up. His heart dropped with the certainty that there was no one here, that she'd forgotten or never meant to come in the first place. 'Bloody prima donna,' he muttered.

But he found the stage door unlocked so he went in, feeling for a light switch in the darkness. He found one, but the dull click brought no burst of light; power must be off at the master switch. Looked like she hadn't turned up; still, he must make sure. Holding a copy of Saturday's *Mercury* under his arm, he felt his way along the wall towards the dressing rooms. The stillness had a strange intensity, as if the ropes and curtains and played-out emotions exuded weight into the darkness. The building creaked, ancient pipes gurgled. Suddenly his foot hit something solid and he stumbled, barking his shin on a hard edge.

Swearing, Philip remembered the box of matches in his pocket and lit one. The glow flared white on a 'No Smoking' sign and slanted across the short flight of steps into which he'd blundered. They led up to the stage. Might as well check, nothing to lose.

The flame burned his fingers and died just as he reached the wings. In blackness, the stage sets were a maze around him. As he fumbled for another match, he heard a disembodied voice.

'You shouldn't play with matches backstage, Mr Linley. Fire regulations. Didn't you see the sign?'

Philip drew a sharp breath. Her voice seemed to come from the centre of the stage. Carefully he eased his way around the painted panels and felt the cool space of the auditorium opening in front of him. She said, 'But could you lend me a match anyway?'

He managed to light another one. Her hand touched his and he jumped, not realising she was standing so close. He caught a glimpse of her opalescent face as she took the match from him and turned away. She was a fragment of a silhouette: a cobweb of hair and a curved shoulder. She bent down and other small lights began to appear. Juliette Lenoir was lighting a circle of candles around herself. When she had finished she straightened up, and he saw her at last.

He gasped out loud. She was wearing a black T-shirt, skin-tight black leather trousers, a lace shawl looped casually around her neck, and heavy, buckled boots. He simply hadn't expected her to be dressed like that; he'd imagined her in a classic dancer's style, maybe a pale leotard and wrap-around skirt. But it was very nice. She was unbelievably enticing, with the candles throwing light and shadow from below.

'Is something wrong, Mr Linley?' she asked, sitting down cross-legged on the boards in the circle of light. The way she looked at him seemed hostile, mocking. He couldn't work her out at all.

'Good evening, Madame Lenoir,' he said. 'No, I'd just made up my mind there was no one here. Thank you for meeting me. I brought last night's *Mercury* so you can read my review.'

He held out the paper to her, but she made no move to take it. He dropped his arm, feeling awkward. He said, 'Rather than scramble around trying to find the master switch for the lights, shall we go somewhere more comfortable? There's a very nice wine bar ...'

'I'm quite comfortable here,' she said. Then she smiled. 'You think I'm peculiar, don't you?'

He grinned back. 'Well, I have to admit I've never met a director of ballet quite like you.'

Her sweet tone turned to steel. 'I asked you to bring your wife and child. Where are they?'

'I'm sorry, but Sarah was running a temperature. Jen couldn't leave her.'

He saw from the coldness of her eyes that she knew he was lying. 'I asked you to bring them,' she repeated patiently. 'It was important.'

'I'm afraid I don't understand.' He lifted his hands in a *Give me some help here* gesture. 'Madame, I only want to write a feature for my paper, I don't see–'

Fluidly she stood up and took a step towards him, hands on hips. Candlelight slid over the satiny contours of her legs. 'Why would I think you wanted to do anything else?'

How the hell did you break the ice with this woman? 'Peculiar' was an understatement.

'No one could deny you're an extremely attractive woman. The truth is, I think Jen is jealous. She seems threatened by you. I just couldn't persuade her to come. However, I can assure you, Madame, that I intend to keep this on a purely professional level.'

'Unless,' said Juliette. She moved towards him and put her hands on his shoulders. 'Unless, you thought, something like this would happen.' And to his absolute astonishment, she put her arms around him and kissed his neck. Philip was so startled he froze. Juliette didn't know he'd fantasised all day and night about just such a scene – but the reality of it was nothing like the fantasy. It was weird, unsettling, passionless.

'Perhaps I'd better go,' he said.

'Doesn't Jen do this to you?' She nipped the angle of his jaw between her front teeth. It hurt. He began to feel both frightened and aroused, his groin stirring, aching. 'I asked you to bring her! I don't care about your newspaper or your ego. It's your wife and little girl I want.'

Her words chilled him. He held her arms, torn between pushing her away and kissing her. She was shaking a little. She seemed ... angry.

'What the hell do you mean, you want ...?'

'I bet Jen doesn't do this,' Juliette said tightly. Her teeth closed on his throat. Jesus, she'd leave him with a love bite. Philip began to panic but he couldn't push her off. She bit harder ... and harder ... until all the tendons down his neck screamed and then what felt like two little scalpels stabbed through his flesh and he began to fall down into the darkness.

In the darkness, Jen was talking to herself.

'You say, "Do you love me?" and they say, "Forever," but what they really mean is, I love you today because I'm in a good mood. The next day you ask again and it's, "Not today, you've been a bad girl." That's how they control me, my father and mother, withholding their love then dispensing it in little parcels as a reward. I'm like a dog begging for the crumbs they drop. Now I do the same with Philip because I don't know any other way. I don't know any other way, Lilith, so please, for God's sake, leave me alone.'

She lay in bed staring at the ceiling, listening to the slow thick beating of her heart. Their house was a Victorian terrace, like a smaller version of her Nan's house and just as eerie at night. She lay waiting for Philip to come home. She pictured him conducting the interview in the ballerina's hotel bed, both of them sipping champagne in a post-coital haze. Once she fell asleep and dreamed that she got up and went into Sarah's room and there was a serpent rearing up over Sarah's bed, its thick black neck glittering like sequins. It had a beak like a swan, and in the beak was the paper charm that was meant to protect Sarah. And on the bed Sarah lay cut and mutilated, only she was a doll with pink plastic flesh and glass eyes ...

Jennifer twisted violently out of sleep, sweating. Something other than the nightmare had woken her, some sound intruding on her doze. She lay rigid, straining to hear something. She sensed the house lying dark and still around her. Nothing to fear, Sarah safe in bed.

She thought she heard the front door open. She sat up and put on the bedside light. Utter silence. Must have been the neighbours. Trembling, she took her valium bottle from the bedside drawer and was fumbling with the cap when the bedroom door burst open.

The handle hit the wall with a bang that made the door shudder in its frame. Philip stood in the doorway, his face the colour of damp newspaper, streaked with sweat. His eyes were terrible.

'Jen,' he said hoarsely.

He surged into the room like a drunk, kneeling on the edge of the bed and crawling towards her on hands and knees. She struggled to evade him but the bedclothes pinned her in and she couldn't move.

'Stop it!' she said, high-pitched. 'For God's sake, what's wrong with you?'

He thrust his face towards hers. 'She's here, Jen. Don't know how. I was in the car and she was on foot, but she still got here first. Got to get you out, she ...' His eyes went blank and he passed out across her, a dead weight.

Then she saw two purple wounds in his neck, streaks of blood running along his collarbone.

Weak with panic, it was all Jen could do to pull herself free of him. 'Philip!' She shook him, bent her head to his heart. Still beating, slow and heavy. He was breathing steadily but she couldn't bring him round.

While she had lain listening for her husband, had Lilith already entered the house, silently, without breaking windows or locks? How long had she been here?

Jennifer felt overpowering terror, but no surprise at all. After all, she had been waiting for this all her life. She looked at the telephone. What could the police do about Lilith? Could a doctor heal her bite?

No one could help her. She had to face Lilith alone. Sarah ...

Suddenly she was no longer timid Jennifer but the feral mother who would fight and claw to protect her child. She was up and running across the landing to Sarah's room. There was no serpent, no dismembered doll's corpse. There was nothing.

The bed was empty. Jen flicked on the light, as if that could make her daughter appear. 'Sarah!'

Gently now. Don't panic. Lilith is coming.

Jen crept downstairs, making as little sound as possible. Through the crackled panel of glass in a hall door she could see lights in the sitting room, strange faint glimmers that came from no lamps she and Philip possessed. Fear strangled her. She dare not, could not go in ...

Think. She slid softly into the kitchen and took the biggest, sharpest knife from the block. She gripped it hard. They were vegetarians so she'd rarely used it: sliced through a tough head of cabbage, but never slipped it into flesh ...

The lights gleamed red through the glass. She paused, staring at two distorted shapes moving behind the dappled panes. One belonged to a slim woman and one to a child ...

Jen flung open the door and cried, 'Sarah!'

Her daughter, in pyjamas, turned to the door, looking startled. Behind her, hands on the child's shoulders, was that woman. Juliette, Odile, Lilith, with her huge cold eyes and fountain of serpent-black hair. They both gazed at Jennifer as if caught in some shameful, intimate act.

For a moment, all Jennifer's anger was directed at her daughter. 'What are you doing, you naughty little–'

Sarah's face fell. 'Juliette was teaching me how to dance. Look, Mum.' And she arranged her feet in first position and curved an arm to the front, side, above.

'We were waiting for you,' Juliette said softly. Her gaze spilled ice-water over Jen's rage. 'Sarah wants to be a dancer. I think she would be very good. Don't you think ...' Her gaze swept down to the knife in Jen's hand, 'that you had better put that down before you frighten Sarah? *You* are upsetting her – not I.'

Lowering the knife, Jen tried to sound calm and in control. 'Darling, go to your room.'

'But Mum, I like Juliette, she was ...'

'Don't argue.' Jen stared at the demon, willing her to let Sarah go. 'Go to your room and stay there.'

Juliette lifted her hands from the child's shoulders and Sarah ran out of the room, shutting the door behind her. Jen's relief was momentary. Now she was alone with the creature who'd sucked Philip's blood. And the creature was sitting down on the sofa, composed and malevolent in the light of five black candles she had lit on the coffee table. Heavy scents drifted from them: sandalwood, jasmine, myrrh, making Jen dizzy.

'Why did you attack my husband?'

Juliette shrugged a little. 'He made me angry. He offered me a drink. Take your pick. But what makes you so sure it was me?'

'Because I know you!'

'Really? And who do you think I am?'

Jen was holding the knife handle so hard that her hand went numb. She said, 'Lilith.'

Juliette looked genuinely startled. 'How did you know?'

The admission was a kick in Jennifer's breastbone. Until then she had subconsciously hoped Juliette would deny it; as if it would have been easier to deal with a simple vampire or homicidal maniac. Anyone but *Her*. 'You're not in the shape of a serpent, you haven't got wings, but I always knew you'd come for me. I could never be good enough to keep you away. But it's not fair. I've tried so bloody hard!'

Juliette looked hard and quizzically at her. 'I knew I must come to you when I noticed you in the audience. When I see someone like you, I can't leave them alone until it's finished. I have to kill the child.'

'No.' Metallic shivers slid down her shoulders, her spine. 'Take me, not Sarah. I'm the one who's been bad. Please, I'll do anything ...'

'That's it. You'll do *anything*.' Juliette stood up and began to walk around the room. Her volatile restlessness filled Jen with dread. 'By pleading with me, you give me this power over you!'

'Give you–?'

'God, I hate this,' Juliette murmured. Her face gleamed like nacre and her lips lifted to reveal neat teeth. She looked insane. 'I don't want to do this, I hate it, but you give me no choice! The child is bad. The child makes you unhappy.' She came towards Jen with all the electric energy of Odile, her hair like a cloud of black silk. 'Who is Lilith? Who do you think she is?'

'A demoness,' said Jennifer, breathing fast. 'The mother of vampires and the enemy of mothers. She comes in the form of a great serpent with rustling black wings. Seducer of husbands, child-killer.'

'I thought so. You listen to their voices, but you ignore your own voice.' The vampire stepped closer, smiling bitterly. Jen raised the knife, determined to keep her away from Sarah. Juliette gave the weapon a contemptuous glance. 'You can't stop me. The child is here.'

'No.'

'Here in this room, Jennifer. *Inside*.'

Then Juliette came forward in a rush and she was Lilith: dark, corrupted beauty, rage and pain. Her mouth was open, her neat canine teeth lengthening as Jen stared, sliding down in their sockets and locking into place with a faint crunch. Sharp white fangs. The weird familiarity, the near-ludicrous image from so many films, only heightened Jen's horror. The reality was ... hideous.

She made a lunge with the knife, missed. It fell from her fingers as Lilith caught her arms and pinned her against the door. Her fangs drove into Jen's neck like nails. Pain throbbed through her from head to foot.

She felt the blood leaving her veins. Vile sensation, a diffuse tingling all through her body, a swimming sickness. The whole room was falling on her like a billowing brown tent ...

She was lying back in an armchair. She must have blacked out for a moment because now Lilith was a few feet away in the middle of the room with light from the black candles flickering over her. She did not look sated or content. Instead her lungs filled and emptied as if they would burst her slender ribcage apart. The look on her face was one of such terror that Jennifer forgot herself in an instinctive rush of concern.

'Juliette? Oh God ...'

The vampire lurched back and caught herself on the arm of the sofa, seeming to brace herself against some internal pressure. Then her mouth opened and she began to breathe out what looked like a wobbling bubble of blood. The blood did not fall but hung in the air above the carpet, like a mass of liquid in space, undulating.

It began to drift towards Jennifer. It took on a shape. A little girl.

Jen let out a cry. The child was rippling, dark, featureless. And it was still attached by a maroon strand, like a hideous umbilical cord, to Lilith's mouth. Her lips were a stretched O around the viscid string and her eyes bulged as if they would fall from her skull.

Jen put up her hands to keep the blood-child away, but it kept coming, impaled itself on her fingers and broke, like a soft-walled sac of fluid. Blood gushed and formed a gleaming pool on the carpet. No child. Just the dark lake on the floor. Lilith spat out the end of the cord and slumped back, gasping, like a woman delivering herself of an afterbirth.

The silence roared like machinery in Jen's ears. She hung over the side of her chair, dry-retching.

Hands stroked her head, gentle. A glass of water touched her lips, the cold liquid as compelling as wine. She looked up into Lilith's face and saw that the vampire was calm again: cloud-white unhuman beauty, eyes of amethyst and lapis, her hair the long black wings of a fallen angel.

Jennifer found she wasn't frightened any more.

'I am sorry, Jennifer,' Lilith said quietly. 'It almost kills me to do that. Sometimes I wish it would. When I see a child, I have to kill it.'

'I don't understand.'

'Let me tell you who Lilith really is, though you will soon come to know for yourself. You said she was evil; but men have only called her evil because they fear her. They split women in half: good and bad, virgin and whore, submissive and disobedient, Eve and Lilith, Odette and Odile. But we are all one. Lilith's crime was her refusal to be dominated. She is rage and freedom and sexuality, all the things that women are not meant to be, even today, because men fear those things so greatly. Yes, she is dark, but darkness is only the essential complement of light. It is mystery, not evil. How people fear mystery!'

'And love it,' said Jen.

'Yes.' Tenderly the vampire stroked her arm. 'To deny Lilith brings disaster, but that's what men and women have done for centuries. The child I kill is the child inside the adult, Jen. The infant that craves love and approval, keeps you helpless and dependent on others for your sense of worth. Lilith despises that need. She strangles it so that you can grow up and be your true self.'

'Did you do this to Philip as well?'

A sour half-smile. 'It is not so easy with men. Sometimes they do not … survive. But sometimes …'

Jennifer wasn't concerned about Philip. She realised that her anxiety had gone. This was the first time she'd been free of it for years. In sheer relief, she put her arms around the vampire's neck. 'Juliette,' she said.

But the vampire took Jen's wrists in her cool hands and disengaged herself. 'My name is not Juliette. Juliette Lenoir does not exist. Stop this. You never need to cling to anyone again.'

And Jen knew this was true. The inner child was dead, her true self rising from the ruins. 'But how did this happen to you? Were you ever human?'

The dancer moved away, avoiding her eyes. 'I don't speak of it, my dear. Let us just say that this is the price I pay to go on dancing.'

The air was narcotic with incense. Jennifer looked at the dancer's slim form moving against the smoky light and thought how beautiful she was. *I would like to stay here and look at her forever …*

She heard the cry coming from far away but rushing in fast: a throaty yell of despair, a battle cry. Philip burst into the room, his face wild. He saw the knife lying where Jen had dropped it, seized it and lunged towards Juliette.

'No!' Jen screamed. She flung herself between them, thrusting out her hands. She did not feel the blade enter her flesh. She fell back onto the carpet, found herself staring at the black handle of the knife sticking up from her left palm, her fingers curling up around it like red petals from a swamp of blood. But Juliette – Lilith – had vanished.

They sat together in the firelight, Philip gently holding Jen's bandaged hand. She looked at him affectionately but remotely, seeing now that he wasn't like her father, not some monstrous patriarch whose word was law. He was just like her. Too stupid not to play the roles they thought were expected of them. The same went for her parents, for that matter.

They sat without speaking of what had happened. Jennifer was not sure Philip understood or even remembered too clearly. But he had changed. And she would never forget.

Sarah was sitting on the floor, reading a book about the history of ballet. One of Philip's reference books that he'd owned for years. She loved the pictures. Watching her, Jen thought, *Am I repeating the same mistakes my parents made with me, brain-washing her in a thousand tiny ways to believe that only a smiling doormat is worthy of love – while the Lilith part of her is feared and shunned until it rises up in rage and bites back?*

Over Sarah's shoulder, Jen saw a photograph of Margot Fonteyn in mouthwatering red net, languishing in the arms of Rudolf Nureyev. *Marguerite and Armand.* But the child pressed her finger to the portrait below it. 'Look, Mummy.'

Jennifer leaned down and recognised a scene from *Swan Lake*: poised in grainy monochrome, the sorceress in black, Odile. The photograph had the ashen charm of an older time, and the caption read, 'Violette Lenoir, world-renowned ballerina of the 1920s and 1930s, still considered one of the greatest dancers of all time.'

The dancer was unmistakably Juliette. Her elegance, her cold compelling eyes, everything about her shone through the veil of distance and time. Unchanged in seventy years. Unchanged in eternity.

While Sarah, too serious and reflective for her seven years, with her long dark hair and grey eyes, seemed to take on an eerie resemblance to Juliette – Violette, Odile, Lilith. Jen shivered, seeing that her daughter was not an extension of her but something apart.

Someone who would never need a visit from Lilith.

Little Goose

Spring was swelling the land, the night I met her. Sap was jumping like clear blood through the veins of leaves, flowers slithering yolk-yellow from fat white bulbs, lambs somersaulting in the moist red wombs of their mothers. In the city, tourists revealed plump limbs to the sun. So much fecundity, so much insolent life, and I picked my way through it like a journalist stalking a battlefield. I, vampire, outcast, voyeur. Like a skeleton I tiptoed, bone-white, bone-dry, infertile, looking upon this rich green egg of a season with a mixture of revulsion and tongue-lolling appetite.

The nights were frost-bound still and left the blossom burned brown at the edges and curling. All along the walkway to the museum, petals were falling like wistful confetti on a bridal bower. I love museums and galleries by night, when the visitors have gone, when birds have pecked every last crumb from beneath the green trees and gone to roost in the branches. (Above my head I imagined their tender nests full of eggs.) I love the stillness inside; the exhibits, frozen effigies in a great, taut silence through which a footfall snaps like gunshot. The tremble of a questing torchbeam, the terrified face of the security guard as his eyes meet mine …

I have learned not to set off alarms, nor to appear on security cameras. Such diversions have afforded me amusement in the past but the excitement palls. What I seek is that exquisite vast stillness, and all that treasure spread out for my eyes alone.

This night, though, the museum was not quite deserted. They had been setting up a new exhibition – jewellery design of some kind, the poster said, though I had only half-glanced at it – and, accompanied by the fading sounds of people calling goodnight, locking up, leaving, one woman still remained.

The display cases looked tiny in the grand vaulted hall. It was a corridor for the gods, going on forever. And in this half-lit sepulchre a small figure remained, her dark head poised over the sloped glass of the cases; perusing, moving on in a slow, slow reverie; pausing again. Her knuckles were taut, her breath unsteady. Her scent and body heat came enticingly to me, and all her coiled emotion.

I was loath to interrupt, so for a while I only watched. There was something compulsive in this secret intercourse. Her, I mean, with the exhibits … and me with her.

Points of light winked in the cases, tiny enamel gleams. Drawing closer, I saw that the exhibition was on a theme, and one appropriate to the time of year. In each case, nested upon crushed velvet of darkest purple-blue, sat eggs of every scale; quail-eggs, duck-eggs, goose-eggs. But fashioned for emperors were these, of nacre and diamond, of ivory, jet and heavy silver, eggs hinged and lined with sapphires, eggs crowned with gold flame and circled with rubies.

I moved from one case to the next, shadowing the woman. Here were eggs of green jade and of crystal, so exquisite you would wish to touch your tongue to them, to feel the cool ice of them sliding and melting. Quartz, clear as glass, and the polished greens of turquoise and chrysocolla, clasped in webs of silver, set with amethyst and pearl. How deliciously the fruits of the sea and the earth blended, clinging like lovers.

I opened my lips, wanting to taste their coldness, wanting it as badly as the soft heat of a victim's throat under my lips. I smiled. Their solid perfection made me want to laugh with simple joy

'Fabergé,' I whispered, because they called to mind the famed maker of jewelled eggs, the only one whose name I knew. I did not mean that I thought these were his; they were too modern, too different in style. But the woman heard me.

In the background was the throb of machinery; heating, plumbing, or some such in the museum's underworld. Against this metallic heartbeat she turned to me, her face waxen, her eyes huge shadows.

'Not Fabergé, of course not,' she said, startled to see me, and angry. Her expression read, *who is this ignoramus?*

From the tail of my eye, with my marvellous vampire eyesight, I took in the gist of a poster that was curled around a pillar yards away. *Rebirth. A journey in jewels by Bartholomew de Grise.*

'I meant,' I said, lifting one eyebrow, 'that de Grise is surely the only natural heir of Fabergé.'

Really, I sicken myself sometimes. But it worked; my words threw her on the back foot, yet pacified her.

'You're not the first to make that observation,' she retorted. She had a strong look; big nose, intense Cleopatra eyes, masses of earth-coloured hair. She wore a white pashmina and ropes of garnets around her neck. Jeans underneath. Too much driving lifeforce for such a small frame. Her energy washed me in red waves, drew me in.

'You must like his work,' I said. 'The exhibition is not even open yet.'

'He is my father,' she snapped back. 'And no, the exhibition is not open.'

'I'm over from a Dublin museum,' I lied glibly. 'Forgive the intrusion, Miss de Grise. But it was too much of a temptation to see all this before the crowds come. And a great honour to meet you.'

I told her my name; she extended a wary hand, bent like a ballerina's, to clasp mine. Ah, how I love the slow dance of seduction! I added, for I was already in love with these wondrous objects, 'Your father seems to have had a great change of style … from the use of classic materials, gold and silver, enamel and gems, to these …' I indicated the semi-precious ones, those of sea-green and pearl, held in nests of jet, stabbed with great chunks of amethyst. 'These, which have a more contemporary feel.'

Tiny muscles tensed in her cheeks. 'My father's style has developed over the years. But the ones you are pointing to, those are mine.'

'Of course,' I breathed, and caught the small print just in time. 'Rebecca de Grise. Forgive me, I've had a long day.'

She arched the firm black bows of her eyebrows. 'You've heard of me?'

I hadn't, but I could dissemble for Ireland. 'You mind, that your name is in much smaller type than your father's?'

She smiled. Her eyes flashed rusty fire. 'Naturally I don't. He is the world-famous jeweller; I am, as yet, only his apprentice.'

Her modesty seemed genuine, not bitter. 'He must be very proud of you.'

'He is the finest of teachers.'

'He had better look to his crown,' I said softly. 'The king is dead. Long live the queen.'

She gave the tiniest gasp of shock. 'Sacrilege,' she said. But she was pleased, and embarrassed by the fact. Relaxing, she took my arm, and took me on a tour of her father's work, pointing out the skill, the attention to detail, his artistry, his mastery. 'See this one, all gold leaf, garnets and rubies, an egg within an egg; the inner one rising on a tiny mechanism when the outer one is opened, like a smooth little womb. Marvellous.'

Her father had made the outer shell, Rebecca said, and she the inner.

'Are these Christian eggs or Pagan eggs?' I said, halting her flow.

'What?'

'Rebirth. Do they symbolise the resurrection of Our Lord, or the rebirth of the land in spring? Or something else … more personal?'

She paused, staring aggressively at me with her head cocked on one side. Then a spiky whisper. 'Whichever you want. They are just eggs.'

She was an egg herself. A shell of sophistication, ivory and black diamond and blood-red garnet, sealed around an anxious, striving child. Our love-making was frantic, noisy, wolf-wild; but when I drank the divine raw yolk of her blood, she made not a sound; said not a word, only sighed afterwards, as if what I had done were perfectly normal; or part of some weirdness she had come to expect.

I contented myself with just a little; I never intended her to die, that's not why I wanted her. In the days that followed she became feverish and obsessive, as the lovers of vampires often do. She said I inspired her …

But I am running ahead of my story. She invited me to the private viewing and I went, eager as a child given free run of a toyshop. Such a press of art critics and journalists, buyers and hangers-on. A casserole of human bodies trussed in tight silks, sparkling gems, feather-soft shawls – ha, and the women equally magnificent. Oh, their gasps of admiration and sycophancy, mostly unfeigned. I smile to remember the feast ... although, for once, I took little interest in their blood. Too entranced was I by the artists, father and daughter.

'Too much nonsense is talked of art,' I heard him telling the rapt journalists. 'What's happened to craftsmanship? This is a craft, a *craft*. It's high time we celebrated skill again! Yes, this is a celebration of skill.'

Yet he had the temperament of an artist; intense, flamboyant, obsessive. A face beautiful with age and wisdom, a shock of grey hair, no tolerance for fools. He and Rebecca worked the room together, doting upon each other, feted like stars at a film premiere.

I watched from a distance. This I was compelled to do, since Rebecca refused to introduce me to her father. I must not approach her, she insisted. If she approached *me*, I must not reveal that I had met her before. Strange, yet I obeyed. From behind the rim of a glass of champagne that I never tasted, I watched them.

De Grise tidied her hair, patted her hands, clasped her against him as he sang the praises of his talented daughter, his apprentice, his protégé. His eyes crinkled with love as she protested no, no, my father is the master, my own work a poor shadow.

I heard the searing whisper of prices. Dealers muttered in strange jargon, not saying exactly what they meant, but with a breathy excitement that signalled hundreds of thousands ... perhaps millions ...

'Six months it took him, to make this one. This, a year! So painstaking his work, he can never keep up with demand, never in a thousand lifetimes can he meet the demand. And his daughter almost as sought-after now, and her prices catching up with his ...'

Passionate was the talk of money, lascivious their eyes sliding over the gleaming shells of the eggs. Collectors would pay this or pay that, collectors would do anything, there is a woman in Canada who would pay *whisper*, a Japanese man who paid ... *gasp*!

Father and daughter floated above the coarse talk of value. I looked for a flaw in their devotion, could see none. If she felt he controlled her, there was no sign that she minded. She needed the security, perhaps.

'Since her mother died she has been my life,' I heard him say, and his gaze was tender upon her. They were golden, bound together, an entity greater than the sum of its parts. Hard, glittering, magical. A glowing duo, mysterious and perfect as their tiny offspring, their bejewelled eggs.

I wanted ... oh, more than their blood. I wanted to climb inside them, to know how their minds worked, to see through their eyes and feel the sensation of nerves and sinews as they worked. Impossible. I had a nickname for her in the dark, Little Goose; for I did love her, in my way, which I suppose for vampires is a kind of envy; trying to recall how it was to be mortal, to reach into them, but forever separated by that thin cold sheet of glass, as if I were pressed flat against a museum display case, panting for treasures beyond my reach.

For weeks Rebecca played a nervous game, keeping me away from her father. I must never be seen with her in public. He came rarely to her flat – correction, her loft apartment, for that is the fashionable thing, to make homes in old factories – but when he came, I must not be there.

'Why? You are not sixteen.'

'He thinks boyfriends will stop me working. He scares them away! It's less trouble if he doesn't know, believe me.'

As I have said, I didn't stop her working; far from it. The vampire's kiss wreaks strange wonders on the mind. Zombie-eyed she would stagger from our bed to her studio – set on a gallery against the apartment's wall of windows – and work, work, work like some mad Rumpelstiltskin character in a fairy tale. The more often I pleasured her, pleasured myself on her body and blood, the more feverishly inspired she became. From the prosaic equipment of cutters and polishers, blowtorches and pliers, drops of shining perfection emerged.

Her designs grew wilder. Eggs of dark pink tourmaline cupped in storms of jet. Snow-white jade, cracked with veins of blood ruby.

One day her father came unannounced, and I must be stuffed like a corpse into a cupboard. Yet I have ways of watching unseen, and I saw.

He stalked the gallery, a forensic examiner. He frowned. His nostrils flared as if he could smell me. Rebecca watched in silent annoyance as he perused her workbench; the designs scattered everywhere, the new pieces taking shape in chaos. He picked up drawings, judged and set them down again, lips pursed.

'You have done all this in so short a time?' he said.

'Why?' Her voice was high and taut. 'Is the work substandard?'

'No. No.' Then, harshly, 'How long have you been taking drugs?'

She was indignant, outraged. 'I'm not taking anything!'

'Have you looked at yourself in the mirror?'

She clutched her dressing gown to hide her throat. For she had indeed the look of one who makes love to a vampire, then rises from bed to work the night through. Drained, pale skin. Eyes like feverish rubies deep in purple-brown pits. 'I've been working hard, that's all.'

'You will burn yourself out! What is it that keeps you awake, speed, cocaine? For God's sake, Rebecca, what's happening to you?'

I chose my moment. Stepped out of the shadows, strolled up the gallery stairs in my robe, dishevelled, cool and ironic, as if in a movie. I said, 'Rebecca, are you not going to introduce us?'

She looked mortified. There was a terrible silence. At last, in a small voice she said, 'Father, I'd like you to meet Sebastian.'

It was worse than I had expected. When he looked at me – I say looked; really it was like being X-rayed – he saw what I was. Not literally, perhaps, but so keenly that he was half a whisker from the truth. His eyes burned me black.

'I knew it would be something like this. Knew. I see it all. He's the one forcing you to work too hard. He's the one who procures the drugs, yes?'

'No! He is my inspiration!'

A hissing sneer of contempt. 'I know him, and dozens like him. They're all the same. They want to feed off your glory, your money! "One more *objet*, dearest, for us. A few extra works, and we'll be rich." He'll bleed you dry!'

'Get out!' she screamed. 'You've never let me live my own life! You have to let me go!'

'Make a choice,' he said, droplets spitting from his lips. 'Go on seeing him and you will never see me again.'

In answer, she drew close to me and slid her hand through my arm. '*You* make a choice, Daddy,' she answered. 'Let me grow up, or get out. They're not all the same. Everyone I've ever loved, you've driven away! Well, not this time. Not this time.'

White-faced and vibrating with emotion, her father left.

And I would have been proud of her if only, sadly, he had not been so right.

Apart, they were paralysed.

For weeks they sulked and grew gaunt, while their workbenches lay idle, and their phones rang unanswered. I know, for I watched them both, even when they had no idea I was there. They wasted in every sense. Yet neither, straight-backed and stubborn, would give in.

I haunted the old man's house. He was there at his workbench, playing a file, not on gold but on his own callused fingertips. Staring at the dark.

'Go to her, Bartholomew,' I whispered. 'Take her in your arms and tell her you're sorry.'

He started, but looked at me without surprise, didn't even ask how the hell I got in. Hoarsely he said, 'She sends you as a go-between?'

'No. I came because I can't bear to see her pining.'

'She has her lover, what use has she for a father? I have only loved her all her life. I only taught her everything she knows.'

'And this is how she thanks you,' I added. 'Have pity on her. She can't work.'

'Can't she.' A sneer of grim pleasure.

'Nor can you.'

'You only care for her work, for the wealth and glory you leech from it! I know you were forcing drugs on her. Nothing else could make her look so ill. I know your sort, predators on my daughter. Happy now, are you? You cut the goose open in your greed and look! No more golden eggs!'

'I am irrelevant,' I said softly. 'It's that your daughter dares to defy you, that's what you can't accept. It's that she dares to step from under your wing and be an artist in her own right, to be better than you. And you know you're in the wrong but you can't admit it. You'd rather torture her for the rest of time with your hubris than admit you're wrong.'

'You devil!'

With a roar he leapt at me and I, taken by surprise, defended myself. The file jabbed into my eye. Searing pain jolted through my skull. My hand sprang out to grip his throat. What must he have seen? My white face, my eye socket a gelid mess with the file sticking grotesquely from it. And I, not screaming but enflamed, monstrous. For then he was unmanned. He turned purple, he screamed, he twitched and I – I swear I did not mean to harm him but the pain, turning from fire to ice as my unnatural body pushed out the foreign object – the pain took over and I had him to my lips, my mouth full of his neck, his neck a spouting hose of blood, delicious, hot …

She saw, when I went back to her, that something dreadful had happened. My eye was healing but still clotted, hideous. I sat in shadow to hide it but my hands were flushed and trembling. She saw, and suspected, but made no comment. I can't blame her for preferring not to know.

All she asked was, 'What did he say?'

'He won't give in.'

'Well, neither will I,' she said. 'Not this time. All my life he has controlled me. Not any more.'

'Even if you never speak to each other again?'

'Even then.'

'Even if you never work again?'

'I shall work,' she said. 'I shall. I'll show him!'

For he lived, against the odds. I'd left him groaning, barely conscious; but not dead. He would live, but – I already knew, and was proved right – he would never be the same again. And I despaired that he had created his last, his last exquisite piece, and would create no more. Was it my bite that destroyed him, the world-renowned master jeweller, or Rebecca's defiance, or had he been teetering on the brink of secret self-destruction for years? Who can say, but oh the tragedy, and now the rarity of his work …

At that moment, though, I didn't want Rebecca to know, or mind, or be hurt. I was desperate for the beauty to continue; if not through him, then through her.

'Yes, you will work.' Clasping her shoulders, I swayed her with the power of my design. 'Imagine if you could live forever, without fear of age, illness or death. No pressure, no terror that time is running out. Never any end to the beauty you will create ...'

She turned huge eyes to me, mad, trusting. Altogether my creature, knowing what I was, accepting it, loving me in spite of it. 'You can do that?'

I can. I did. And now, oh God, she is a tiptoeing skeleton like me.

She says that she stares into the void of infinite time and it is too much; without a limit in sight, without an end, she cannot begin. And all that fills the void is human blood, not cold jewels. I forgot, I forgot that when we go through the veil we always change, and the things that were so desperately important in life cease to matter. There is no eternal frenzy of creation from Rebecca. Only silence.

Absorbed only in her own new, wondrous, terrifying vampire existence, still she will not speak to her dying father, nor he to her. She knows he is dying; he knows something appalling has happened to her; yet neither will acknowledge it, nor speak, nor heal.

Disgust forces me to walk away. My remorse is savage.

A few souvenirs I took, for even vampires need money; more than most, in fact, since we must plan for an elastic future. My pockets are filled with baubles enough to make the jaws of dealers fall through the floorboards. One alone I will keep, the Rebecca Egg I call it, in memory of my little goose. All gold leaf, lacquer and bloody garnets is this delightful object. The top flips back and up slides a daughter egg on a delicate mechanism; and down again, swallowed back into the parent shell. So perfect.

Summer offends me. Its greens dazzle like migraine, the opposite of sweet red. Soon I shall taste smoky autumn in the air and walk through cemeteries with my hands in my coat pockets – my bulging pockets – mourning the world's loss. Ah, the sorrow, the speculation in the broadsheets, an end to the production of de Grise eggs, and the value of them rocketing as they pass like fever from hand to hand ...

For I, a vampire, am bound to destroy what I love, and suffer for it. That is our condition and our punishment. It's what we do. So if we must do it, then I am dedicated to doing it well. And, believe me, I am the best. I am the master.

The House of de Grise was crumbling. I merely touched it with a fingertip, and down it came, all its forbidding towers revealed as thin hollow shells, fragile as calcium, falling in dusty glory. I did that. Glorious destruction. Stand, then, as I do, and marvel at my latest creation.

A work of art.

Las Muertas Invidas
(or, The Living Dead)

Luxury was a mattress, thin and grey and heavily stained, alive with bugs. Most newcomers had to make do with the hard dirt floor, but a girl with wide, dark, expressionless eyes had beckoned Claudia to share the mattress with her.

'You seemed the one least likely to knife me in my sleep,' the girl told her later. Her name was Irene. Like Claudia she was skinny, bronze-skinned, dressed in cast-off jeans and T-shirt. Tough, like wire. Even in the steambath heat of the prison, Irene barely perspired. Claudia felt sweat oozing constantly from her pores. She knew she smelled bad, but then so did everything and everyone. Her hair had matted into twisted black rats' tails.

The sun was a white inferno. It turned the exercise yard into a furnace, but its rays barely reached inside. Their 'window' was a misshapen gap in the adobe wall, with rusty barbed wire woven between the bars. Someone had hung a tiny fabric doll with a skull for a face on the wire, like a mascot.

To reach this rough aperture, Claudia had to step across the latrine and poise herself on a thin brick ledge in order to see outside at all.

They possessed the mattress, and kept it, simply because it lay on the last three feet of floor space beside the grim hole in the earth. All night long, women would be stepping over their feet to squat over the pit.

The first few nights, Claudia had barely slept. People kept treading on her, even kicking her, swearing as they passed. Foul smells wafted around. At first she lay awake, crying silently with her face in the mattress to stop herself retching. Eventually, she grew accustomed to the stink. She pretended she was in her grandparents' farmyard and that the smells were no worse than animal dung. When the sound of inmates yelling and chattering and fighting crept into her nightmares, she made herself imagine it was just the bleating of goats she could hear, or wild dogs howling in the night.

'I like you because you're quiet,' said Irene. 'The others, they never shut up. I understand. They're angry. They have nothing to do but complain. But, *Santa Sebastiana*, how I wish they would be quiet.'

'How long have you been here?' Claudia's voice was hardly a mouse-squeak.

'Months.' Irene sat with her arms around her knees, staring up at the barred window. A single bright patch of sky.

'What ... what did you do?'

'They say that I pushed a knitting needle up myself and aborted my baby.'

'And did you?'

'No. I had a miscarriage. I bled and bled – I tried to stop the bleeding, but ...' Irene shrugged. It was the first and almost the only time Claudia saw her blank expression waver. Her mouth cramped, turning down at the corners. A few tears leaked from her eyes. 'It was God's will, not mine.'

'Didn't you tell them that?'

'Naïve soul,' said Irene. 'Of course I did, but the authorities don't care. To them, I committed murder. What about you?'

'They said I stole a ring.'

'That's different. It's usually drugs. And did you? Steal a ring?'

'No. A fine lady gave it to me, but a policeman saw us ...'

'Sure she did.'

'No, it's true. She ... I don't know what she was doing in the worst part of town. Perhaps she got lost, a stupid tourist. Perhaps she took pity on me, but it's true, she gave me the ring, a beautiful big ruby like I'd never seen before, but the policeman saw me take it from her and he arrested me for robbery, so ...'

'That's bad luck.'

'I was stupid to accept it. How could I have worn it, or sold it for more than a few dollars? The woman ... she took her ring back, and she vanished, never even came to the police station, but here I am anyway.'

'How old are you? You look like a kid.'

'Sixteen, I think,' said Claudia. 'Not a kid.'

'Me, I'm twenty. Ancient. This place makes you feel very old, very quickly.' Irene closed her eyes, leaning back against the wall. 'Describe the woman for me.'

'Why?'

'Because I'm bored.'

'Just a tourist. Pale, with a big sunhat, sunglasses. I could only see a bit of her hair but it was blonde, nearly white, so she might have been young or old. She spoke Spanish, but her accent wasn't American. I don't know where she was from. Europe, maybe. I don't know.'

'Well, she was the stupid one, flashing her giant ruby around. Shame you didn't keep it. Me, I would have swallowed it and ... waited. Things like that can buy you special favours in here.'

'If I'd kept it, I wouldn't be here, would I?' said Claudia. 'I mean that if no one had seen us, I wouldn't have been arrested.' They sat in silence for a few breaths. The air was thick with heat, smells and bugs. Eventually she asked, 'What about your husband … boyfriend …?'

'Him.' Irene spat. 'We're not allowed male visitors anyway, but he's long gone with some other woman. He's nothing to me.'

'How long … how long is your sentence?'

'Life, I expect,' said Irene, gazing listlessly at the mottled walls. Flaking paint, desperate defiant graffiti. 'I'm still waiting for my trial. You?'

'Same. Waiting.'

'So you realise they can hold us here on remand, waiting, for months, years. Forever.'

Later that night, Claudia stood on the latrine edge and looked up at the patch of sky. The full white moon beamed down at her. It looked huge. She could see every detail, every crater etched like lace shadows on its round shining surface. So beautiful.

She hadn't told Irene the full truth about the 'tourist'. She couldn't. It wasn't something to be said aloud. She couldn't find words to make the encounter sound real.

She remembered being brought to the women's prison. There was a bleak corridor, lined with doors, and in each cell door a slot from which human arms poked, hands waving in the air – pleading for help, attention, food, mercy. Voices clamouring their innocence.

Then being pushed into this communal cell, a grimy oblong room with bars all along one side so the guards could keep constant watch on their prisoners. The cell was crowded with women of all ages. Some had children with them. Some were better dressed than others. Many had hard eyes and a casual attitude as if to tell the world they didn't mind being here one bit. This was their kingdom.

Claudia learned quickly to keep out of their way.

Or if they told you to do something, you did it. Special favours came if one of the boss ladies took a liking to you, but none of them had fixed her eye upon Claudia yet.

Then there was this secondary space, leading off the main cell like a corridor. Just a short passage to the latrine, yet also a dormitory. Every bit of floor was somewhere to sleep, territory to be fought over.

In the mornings they would be let out to wash in cold water and eat some unappetising food, usually sardines and rice. Then the prisoners came and went all day, trading and arguing, playing games and dealing drugs. During the day, Claudia would look out of the little window and see them dancing in the exercise yard. Practising the tango with each other. There was even a market stall where goods and tobacco could be had. There were ways to earn little bits of money, and purchase small luxuries such as toothpaste.

A fist-fight always drew an enthusiastic audience, keen to place bets.

From inside, she watched. She dared not go out there.

In a way, the prison was like a claustrophobic village. The prisoners carved out life as best they could. But you could not leave. Many here would never leave.

Sometimes tourists came – let in by the guards for a heavy bribe – and wandered around staring and looking concerned, as if visiting animals in the zoo. Claudia stared back, wishing with all her soul she might fold herself into a backpack and be carried to freedom. In the outside world, she had had nothing – her mother was dead, her father long gone, and every night she must find a new hiding place to sleep beyond the town's edge – but she had been as free as a wild animal under that splendid pearly moon.

A woman walked across the scrubby desert under the same full moon. She wore black: a tight jacket, split skirts flaring nearly to her ankles, rugged boots, a wide-brimmed hat. She looked like a gaucho, but with the elegance and bearing of an empress. Anyone who saw her pass would note that she seemed to glide, as if the gravity of this world hardly touched her.

She was thinking of everything and nothing. She was as old as time, or felt so: when you had contemplated every possible aspect of life, eventually all the thoughts went still inside you and simply floated there, as if your mind had become a great ethereal library. But she still found the nights glorious. She could still, always, meditate on beauty.

Through Mexico and down through Central and South America she had walked endlessly across prairies and deserts, through jungles and humid rainforests, over the peaks of mountains and through the caves beneath. She had followed the course of rivers and she had stood in streams, bending down to sift the gravel in hopes of finding gemstones washed out of the host rock. Her life was a constant search.

She slid through towns like an assassin. Humans – they were sacs of blood and heat and suffering. Here and gone. But once in a lifetime, there would be a human that stuck in her memory, an irritation like a tick piercing the skin. Then she was tempted to go in a circle, to find the source of irritation and crush it.

Yet she never did. She knew that as long as she did not look back, the sting would eventually fade.

Night in the desert was cold, but now the sun was rising swiftly, blinding-hot and brutal. She would find shade beneath a rock before the whole plain turned to white fire and the ground itself turned to molten – that was how the sun seemed to her here, a merciless blaze like a blacksmith's furnace in hell. She could endure it – her hat and dark glasses helped – but she preferred to avoid the worst of high noon.

On her right hand, a clear stone flared and glittered like the moon trapped inside a giant diamond.

One morning Claudia looked out at the exercise yard and there were three heads growing out of the ground. Their hair was tangled and dusty. Big criss-cross stitches held their lips shut. A sign roughly painted on cardboard stood behind them. She couldn't read the words but the letters were jagged and angry. '*Something something … help us.*'

Only their eyes moved. Glaring, blinking.

'What are they?' Claudia jumped back across the pit and landed on the mattress, shaking Irene awake. 'Out there. What the hell is happening?'

Irene got up, cursing under her breath. She hopped across the stinking latrine and clutched the window's edge to steady herself. After a few moments, she came back and sat down.

'The living dead,' she said.

'What does that mean?' Claudia crouched down, balancing on her toes. Irene sat back against the wall, her eyes distant, but Claudia was all nervous energy, horrified and scared. 'Why have they been buried? Are they being tortured?'

A clanging sound arose. All around the prison compound, women were beating on the bars with spoons, saucepans, anything they could find. Louder and louder the noise grew.

'No. They do this to themselves. Sew up their own mouths so they can't eat, bury themselves in the ground.'

'Why?'

'As a protest, you idiot. They are protesting about the conditions we live in. Look, the one in the middle is Lucia. She's a good guy. She's so brave!'

Claudia went to look again. Scorching hot rays burned down into the suntrap of the yard. The three buried women endured. Sweat made tracks on their dusty faces. Claudia watched them for an hour, until she couldn't watch any more.

The little skull-faced mascot hung on its barbed-wire hook on the bars – was it there to curse their enterprise, or to protect them? Claudia detached the doll and stuffed it into her jeans pocket.

'What will happen to them?'

'Oh, don't start crying. They do this every now and then. They hope a tourist will photograph them and show the world this scandal and embarrass the authorities into making things better. But nothing ever changes.'

'Can't we do something to help them?'

'That would spoil the protest, wouldn't it? I expect the guards will dig them out later and carry them away to cool off somewhere. There's nothing you can do, darling Claudia. They're trying to tell the world that living here is no better than death. But this is our life now. Get used to it or die.'

That night Claudia was sick with a fever. She lay shivering, plagued by nightmares – or by reality, expanding into grotesque horrors. Cockroaches ran over her feet. The women tripping over her as they went to the latrine and back, cursing her – they had the form of skeletons. An endless parade of skeletons, squatting over an abyss. All the noises of the prison filled her head, magnified as if they echoed inside a giant cauldron. Children crying. A woman screaming in childbirth. The sexual grunts of inmates copulating with prison guards, some willing and others plainly not. A woman's voice raised in prayer, chanting in a desperate, horrible-sounding appeal to some saint. *Senora Blanca. Santa Sebastiana. Santa Muerte, please aid us.*

The white lady, *Senora Blanca*, drifted into Claudia's dream. She was all in black, with a wide-brimmed hat and flaring skirts, but her skin was like milk, her hair honey-tinted cream. Claudia had met her at the edge of town, where the slums petered out into baked scrubland – Claudia sitting on a formation of orange rock because she had nowhere else to be, no home. She would rather snare and roast wild animals than turn to prostitution.

In the dream she was embroidering the robes of a tiny doll: the image of a female saint with a skull for a face.

As she saw the female tourist approaching, she held out the doll, hoping to sell it so she could eat that day. Dusk was falling, the hot day chilling suddenly, yet the woman wore sunglasses. Seeing Claudia she stopped, threw off the sunglasses and the hat, unleashing a long wavy flow of pale hair. Her skin glowed. Her eyes were like those of a cat, emotionless, icy green, utterly compelling. She seized Claudia's wrists and pulled her upright.

The saint doll fell into the dust. That was not what the traveller wanted. Claudia saw on the woman's finger a huge white gemstone, a diamond surely, that shone and flashed with rainbow colours. She saw the ring, a second before she felt crushing pain in her wrist.

The woman had her teeth in Claudia's veins, biting, pulling on the blood. Claudia felt the subtle wrist pulse increase until it thudded through her whole body. Because she was paralysed and in thrall, she felt no fear. What she felt was a kind of shock, as if she'd suddenly been thrown into an ice-cold lake …

But someone held onto her, pulled her to safety …

Then it was over. The woman was standing two feet from her, and she seemed different. Softer. Less menacing. Red was added to the ink-black of her clothes and whiteness of her skin. Her mouth was red with blood. Her tongue, emerging to lick the blood away, was scarlet. And the big white gem on her right hand had turned the crimson of fine ruby.

'Take this,' the woman said gently, removing the ring from her hand and pressing it into Claudia's palm. 'This jewel in exchange for your precious blood. Forgive me.'

Then she was gone. Claudia, dizzy, called after her retreating figure, but it was too late. The police were coming for her. A dozen policemen, skeletons in uniforms, were dragging her to prison with their bone hands …

'Get away from her, you devil!'

The shout woke her. Irene was lying next to her, half-sitting up and throwing a shoe at something. In the grey daylight, Claudia saw a rat scampering away. A rat the size of a rabbit. All the prisoners sleeping along the row thrashed awake in turn as the creature went scampering over them.

It was comical, almost.

'It bit your wrist,' said Irene. 'I'm sorry, I couldn't stop it in time. Dear, let me fetch you a drink. You have had a terrible night.'

'Everyone has had terrible night, I think.'

'You've stopped shivering, at least. What were you dreaming about?'

'How do you know I was dreaming?'

'You were writhing and crying out so much. I have lain here all night holding onto you, trying to keep you warm.'

Irene tended her all day, too, even bringing a health worker to see her: a kindly but harassed French volunteer who had bribed her way inside the prison in order to help the inmates as best she could. Irene said she brought medicines and condoms and health leaflets. Now she brought fruit juice, and painkillers to reduce fever, antiseptic and bandages for the rat bite.

'You cannot sleep next to this hole,' said the volunteer. Her eyes were watery with tiredness and plain disgust. 'No wonder you are ill.'

'Don't you understand, we have nowhere else?' Irene said sharply.

'Of course, I know that. This overcrowding is impossible. Believe me, I'd shut this place down tomorrow if I could. I'll come again, if the guards will let me in. It depends who is on duty, you see. Some wave me through for a bottle of whisky, others want more than whisky or even money, so …'

'Don't come again,' said Claudia. 'It's not safe here.'

'Oh, don't worry. I've had knives held to my throat, but the others protect me because they know I'm trying to help them.'

'No, you don't understand. It's too dangerous. Please stay away.'

'Take no notice, *senorita*. She's feverish,' said Irene. 'Thank you so much for helping her. Oh – would you do something else for us? Take a photograph of the protestors?'

'They're not there anymore,' the aid worker said in a low, sad voice. 'I do my best for them … they all have heatstroke, and their mouths are torn and infected …' She shook her head.

After she had gone, Claudia sank into a depression she'd never felt before. She felt as if light and sanity had left the world. The volunteer, for all her compassion, could just walk away whenever she liked … Irene sat beside her and held her hand.

'Tell me about the dreams you had.'

'Why?'

'Because I want to hear. We have to cheer each other up somehow.'

'I dreamed about the tourist lady. She was different in the dream, yet she was the same. The difference was that I was seeing her more clearly.'

She described the dream. The events were almost exactly as they had played out in real life – except that, in reality, she had not been embroidering a figure of *La Santa Muerte*, the Blessed Lady of Death. Nor had the woman let down her glorious hair. And only one, solid policeman had arrested her, not a dozen living skeletons.

Claudia fingered the skull doll in her pocket as she spoke.

'But the rest really happened. The gem I saw on her hand was *ridiculous*. A diamond like the moon, a big round diamond as wide as her finger. All the colours of the rainbow came out of it. The setting was silver-coloured. Platinum, maybe.'

'But when she gave it to you, it had turned red?'

'Like a ruby.'

'Are you sure it was the same ring?'

'Yes! She only wore the one. When she drank my blood, the blood soaked into the stone. Even into the stone.'

'And that happened in real life?'

'I swear.'

'But in the dream you were also embroidering an image of *Santa Muerte* …'

'Exactly. I heard someone praying to her last night, addressing her as *Senora Blanca*, and that's how she got into my dreams, obviously, the white lady, but the part about her drinking my blood – that actually, truly happened. She gave me the jewel in exchange for my blood. It must have happened, or what did they arrest me for? I don't blame you for not believing me, but I swear it's true!'

'Shush. Calm. I do believe you. Do you pray to her? Our Lady of the Holy Death?'

La Santa Muerte. She who presided over life and death, with her skull face and her saint's robes. The patron saint of the poor, the dispossessed, the criminal and the desperate. Because she was the Holy Mother of Death, she could grant respite, health, better fortune, or a few more grains of life at least. *Santa Muerte* would listen when every other saint and even God himself had turned away.

'No,' whispered Claudia. Guiltily she pushed the doll to the bottom of her pocket and let it alone. 'When I was a child, before my father ran off and my mother died, we used to go to church. The priests always warned us against worshipping *Santa Muerte*. Now I pray to no one.'

'I think we'd better start.'

'Why?' Claudia felt a trickle of fear. *Senora Blanca* was a demon, the priests had said. Call on her and you call on the Devil.

'Who else will listen to us?'

'But half the women here pray to *Santa Muerte* anyway. I've heard them. I've seen their little shrines. Even a tiny figure stuck on the window bars … I took it down, because … I don't know why. I'm tempted to ask her for help but … I daren't. What good can it do?'

'Because you're different,' Irene whispered. 'I think you have actually *met* her.'

Claudia shuddered from head to foot. 'The woman I met did not have a skull for a face.'

'So? She is a goddess. She can change her form as she pleases. You have met her, so you're the one she will listen to. Start praying to her. Start calling to *La Santa Muerte*, with all your heart and soul.'

She rarely retraced her steps, the milk-white woman who delved in streams for treasure, but this time was different. She'd taken the peasant girl's blood, and tried to give her the beautiful, accursed Elfstone ring in return, only for the girl to be hauled away and punished. Punished, for an act that was not her fault, certainly no crime.

Sometimes it was very hard indeed to understand humans.

Still, she knew for certain now that the jewel was her burden to carry. She should never have tried to pass it on to someone else, least of all someone so vulnerable. That had been an unforgivable mistake. So she still owed the girl *something*. Not the jewel, but something more vital.

She looked up at the enormous moon and at the river of stars that bore the celestial body across the sky. She thought about heat and clouds and thunder. Her booted feet began to take her along a curve … around a spiral that would draw her back inwards to where this had begun.

'*Santa Sebastiana, Dobeiba, Chia, Aphrodite, Madre Vieja, Mama Quilla, Ningui, Lasya, Aine, Anahita, Artemis, Cerridwen, Hekate, Freyja* …'

Voices called to her, but she had been called by many different names in her time.

Irene left, but came back an hour later with a piece of thin, worn wool.

'Look, I got us a blanket. Ignore the fleas. Some people here are kind.

Have you been praying?'

'Not much. I'm so tired.'

'Oh, you're too tired to pray? Go to sleep, then. Sleep forever, like Lucia.'

Claudia heard the edge in her voice, something deep and dark.

She rose onto one elbow as Irene sank back in her customary position against the wall. Irene's mood had entirely changed. She seemed to be in shock, distracted, her eyes shadowed. Anger gathered between her eyebrows. She slumped down with her hair over her face and her hands curled loosely at her sides.

'What's wrong, what has happened?' Claudia asked three times before Irene responded.

'When they pulled *Las Muertas Invidas* out of the ground ... Two of them are okay, but one of them ... She's dead. Lucia. She was my friend.'

I'm so sorry, Claudia tried to say. The words didn't come out, so she gripped Irene's hand instead.

'Go to sleep, then.' Irene freed her hand and tucked the blanket over her, kissed her on the forehead. 'Dream of *Senora Blanca*, and she'll come. Saints bless you, beloved sister.'

Claudia slept the night through and most of the next day. She had no idea how long she'd slept but there had been no dreams. Her body needed to recover from her illness; sleep would not be denied. Even the daily prison racket and the stream of people kicking her ankles had not roused her.

Now scarlet light oozed through the rough window, revealing that the sun was setting and that Irene was not there. Claudia swayed to her feet, pulled down her jeans and crouched over the disgusting latrine to relieve herself. Then she stood on tiptoe on the ledge, and looked outside.

Down in the exercise yard there was a single head growing out of the ground. The face, tipped upwards, was bathed crimson in the dying light. Claudia saw the thick black criss-cross lines of thread sealing shut the lips.

Irene.

For a while she couldn't breathe. She tried to grab onto the window bars but gashed her palms on the rusty barbed wire. Irene. *Oh God, why? Dear God, please help her. Saints in heaven, help her. What can I do?*

'Hey,' said a woman's voice behind her. Claudia didn't know her name. She was one of the boss ladies, squat and tough-looking, with a hard voice like metal. 'What you looking at? Is she still out there?'

Claudia crossed herself. The action upset her balance and she fell towards the latrine, one leg going down into the pit. She caught herself by grabbing the sides with both hands, hanging there awkwardly with the sewage fumes from hell clouding up around her. Then the other woman caught her under the shoulders and dragged her to safety.

'Ugh, what the hell are you trying to do? Jesus.'

'Irene out there, she's my friend.'

'Yeah, I know. Bed fellows. She's been out there all day, honey.'

'*All day*?'

'One of the guards pissed on her head. Said it was to cool her down.'

'Fucking *pigs*. We have to help her.'

'You know we don't do that. She's making the protest for her friend Lucia, isn't she? So we don't take away her pride and dignity.'

'I know that, but ...'

A few more inmates were gathering where the main cell met the toilet corridor, drawn by their exchange. Their dead eyes gleamed with a faint flickering of curiosity. Something flared up in Claudia, bigger than rage or anger. She no longer feared them or what they might do.

'This is my fault,' she said.

'How is it your fault, little idiot?' the boss lady said.

'Because she asked me to pray to *La Santa Muerte*, and I didn't!' She began to try, murmuring under her breath, '*Senora Blanca. Santa Muerte.* Please help us. Please ...'

She fingered the skull-headed doll in her pocket. She brought out the figure and held her up in the air. A crudely-embroidered little thing, dressed in a scrap of cloth like a veiled Madonna. The death-headed saint.

With a weird rising sound, like mourners wailing at a funeral, all the women around her joined in. 'Our Beloved Lady of the Holy Death ... *Santa Sebastiana ... Santa Muerte ...*'

Louder and louder their voices swelled. The whole cell swayed with bodies, hands raised towards heaven. Such a racket they made that a guard came and started banging on the bars in the outer corridor, yelling at them to shut up. Claudia raised both her hands too and roared the name of the merciful goddess, Saint Death.

She had no idea, though perhaps one day she would learn, that it was not the passionate, deafening pleas of the inmates that caught the attention of a goddess, but the scent of her own blood. Blood leaking from barbed wire gashes on her hands. Somewhere out in the scrubland, the pale immortal came spiralling inwards in search of a girl to whom she still owed a debt. If not the Elfstone ring, then something far greater.

A dense bank of cloud rolled in, consuming the sunset. Gigantic thunderheads thickened the sky, a terrible fleet merging into a single mass of purple, iron grey and green.

An eldritch light filled the exercise yard. Irene tipped back her head, as if longing for raindrops to fall onto her face and wash away the dust and the ammonia stink of the guard's crusted urine – but no rain came. The storm was as dry as bone, the air baking hot, bristling with electricity.

Lightning strobed behind green clouds. The rumbling *basso profundo* of thunder shook the atmosphere. The bombardment came closer, louder, ripping the sky apart. Lightning and thunder moved into synchronisation as the storm poised itself overhead. Ear-splitting noise and searing light detonated together, like a sudden outbreak of war.

All around the prison, inmates began shouting.

An immense bolt of lightning cracked out of the clouds. Throwing out jagged branches, it lit up the clouds from iron-grey to blazing white, bleaching the world like a nuclear explosion. That lightning bolt struck the barred window of Claudia's cell.

The whole wall exploded and collapsed, leaving a massive hole and a heap of debris.

Her mattress caught fire – she'd been standing by it, minutes earlier – and the fire began to smoulder from one makeshift bed to the next. Towels caught, clothing caught.

'Fire,' Claudia said under her breath, as if whispering the word to a lover. Then she found a piercing voice. 'Fire!' she yelled.

Fifty pairs of shocked eyes stared from the darkness. She saw ball lightning racing along the main corridor beyond the inner wall of bars. She heard stampeding boots as the guards fled.

'This way! Run!' she cried.

She started to haul the burning mattresses sideways-on. Their ends overlapped, spreading flame from one to the next like fever. This would increase the fire, she knew, but the most pressing need was to clear space in the passageway. After that – let the place burn.

Fire scorched her legs as she waved everyone along the narrow toilet passage towards the breach in the wall. Rubble had filled the latrine pit. She stationed herself there, to help those unsteady on their feet across the broken treacherous surface. With rats running among their ankles, all the prisoners ran and scrambled across the rubble towards the great gap. In twos and threes they ran through and outside, into the storm.

Throughout the prison there were explosions, one after another: lightning igniting gas canisters or illicit weapons. In every barred window, yellow flames were flickering. Claudia's eyes ran with fumes. Smoke and flame roared up from the roofs.

All through the prison, fire whooshed along corridors. The very walls were catching alight. Mattresses, towels, garbage, anything combustible began to burn. Claudia, choking on smoke as the last woman and child rushed past her, finally staggered out into the yard.

From every part of the prison, inmates were spilling through gaps and broken gates.

Streams of prisoners fled past her, a dark flock against scarlet fire, bleached every few seconds by lightning. Claudia fell to her knees on the dirt and crawled towards Irene's head poking from the ground. Hot feathery ash coated them both. With her bare, wounded hands she began to dig.

'*Mmm.*' Irene made a pained noise of protest. Whether it meant, *No, leave me here*, or *Help me*, Claudia could not tell. Maybe both.

'Irene, it's okay,' she said. 'You might be older and braver and wiser than me, but I know all the places to hide.'

The stony soil was loose. She dug and dug, ignoring her ripped fingernails, ignoring the crowd that surged past her: black silhouettes against the leaping flames.

Lightning had blasted the perimeter wall to ruins and torn down two sets of wire fencing. She glimpsed the gap towards which the inmates were fleeing. All that lay beyond were dirt tracks and the dark wild plains where the escapees would spread out and vanish.

She hauled Irene from her rough burial pit, held her upright, and followed.

Every building that surrounded the prison yard was on fire.

Later, later she would find a place to hide, cut the stitches out of Irene's lips, trickle water into her mouth, scrounge food and medicine, and spend days or weeks at her friend's side until she healed. Eventually there would be freedom, and a future of some kind. Eventually they would give thanks to *La Santa Muerte*, also called *Senora Blanca*, or whatever strange deity had taken the shape of the moon-haired traveller in black.

Perhaps, one day, they would even see her again. But for now–

Claudia and Irene went stumbling together towards that fire-blackened opening. No sign of guards. What would the guards do, but flee? They wouldn't stay inside a burning compound. They wouldn't try to stop the mass of prisoners who were boiling out onto the dirt roads. More likely, they'd run for their own lives and leave the gates unlocked behind them as they went.

The prison roared red and yellow towards the sky, unleashing a stench of smoke and burning metal and infernal fumes. Sirens sounded, vehicles roared, crowds of locals gathered to yell and marvel at the flames consuming the night. The conflagration filled the world as if a great bomb had exploded.

But, with each limping step they took, the spectacle began to dwindle as Claudia and Irene left it behind. Eventually the blaze was no more than a plume on the horizon, swallowed by the great dark welcoming arms of the wilderness.

Above, the storm clouds rolled away. Stars reappeared, pure and bright, enthroning the moon.

And Their Blood Will Be Prescient to Fire

Violette: she is the Death Lily. Her eyes blaze violet, drawing you in with the light of forbidden wisdom. Her midnight hair and glacial skin leave you wrecked upon the rocks. I love her. I would give my life to meet her. Off-stage she wears silver and lilac and black diamonds and that is her: soft as silk, hard as gemstones.

She is the mysterious celebrity in the shadows. Fêted, celebrated, unknown. The latest in a family tree of prima ballerinas called Violette, Juliette or Mistanguette Lenoir; when one fades, another young protégée steps into the white satin shoes. For seventy years this has continued. A niece, then a grand-niece: sure. No one realises, since it's impossible, that they're all the same woman. But I worked it out. I know her secret.

I've loved her all my life. I have collected every old book, every press cutting, taped all the arts programmes. I've travelled to every performance I could afford – and those I couldn't. Violette is an expensive obsession. From the audience I watch her create her bright world of enchantment and I fantasise that she is dancing just for me.

In reality she would never notice me: a small, skinny nobody. In our family, the looks, height and charisma passed me by. Not in her immortal life would she ever look at someone like me.

And yet, I heard she fell. It burns me even to say this. She fell for my sister.

'It's a dessert wine,' said Charlotte. 'Try it.'

She slid a dewed glass across the darkly varnished table. Within, liquid shimmered straw-gold. Violette stared suspiciously.

'What the hell is this?' She looked ragged tonight, Charlotte thought; black hair a bird's nest, toned body airbrushed into black jeans and purple tie-dyed cotton. Around them stretched the anonymous semi-darkness of a bar in the basement of a large hotel. Low music, murmuring voices, Tiffany shades glowing in the dark.

'Muscat with a twist,' said Charlotte.

'We don't drink wine.' Her smile was sardonic, dangerous.

'A little something created by our good friend Stefan. He thinks it's a bore to sit in a bar and not drink along with humans. Think of it as protective colouration.'

'Blood tastes like the finest wine,' said Violette. 'Actual liquor, however, tastes like bleach with a dash of battery acid. If you think I'm putting that to my lips, you're out of your mind.'

'That's what I said, but …' Charlotte took a mouthful, to show it was safe. A burst of familiar nectar, laced with spice and a fiery afterglow. Violette took the smallest, hesitant taste, held it in her mouth, swallowed with the shudder of a human sampling his first raw oyster. Her compelling eyes opened wide.

'It's wonderful. What is it?'

'Plasma, fermented with herbs and other ingredients according to Stefan's secret recipe. He's been working on it for a while.'

'Why?'

Charlotte shrugged. 'For the pleasure of immortals.' She felt heat swimming in her head. A pleasant feeling, but strange; alcohol from human veins only induced a flat headache.

'It tastes …' Violette frowned, turning the glass between elegant fingertips. 'Intoxicating.'

'I believe that is the idea.' Charlotte smiled.

'Stefan is the devil.'

'He really is,' said Charlotte, amused. 'He loves to put humans in thrall, often using more than his own charm. Opium was a favourite, in the old days. Perhaps he's found an addiction for us, too. I wouldn't put anything past him.'

'So, are you trying to get me drunk?' Violette was sweet and sharp at the same time. In these unpredictable moods she could tip into playfulness or fury.

'No. To relax.'

'Only, the last time you got me drunk, I passed out human and woke up crazed vampire goddess. What was it you used?' Violette tipped her face sweetly towards Charlotte. 'Laudanum?'

'That was decades ago.' Shocked, Charlotte drew back. She ran her fingers up and down the stem of her glass. 'Surely you've forgiven me by now.'

'Forgiven, yes, but not forgotten.' The teasing edge to Violette's voice sounded dangerous. 'I never forget anything.'

'All right, what's wrong? Whenever you're upset, you play games.'

'Nothing, sweetheart.' Violette reached out and stroked the tender skin of Charlotte's forearm, where it lay relaxed on the table. Her hand strayed upwards, over the silk and lace of Charlotte's old-fashioned dress, caressing the bronze and gold fabrics. These days, if Charlotte wanted to be pre-Raphaelite and Violette a Goth chick, no one noticed any more. 'Boston gets to me.'

'Yes. Sorry. I know.'

'I'm restless,' the dancer went on. 'Danced my feet off for weeks, one city after another. Endless receptions, after-show parties, press calls. Always on my best behaviour.' She smiled, suddenly looking endearingly tired and human. 'I can't be the great Lenoir all the time. The demon-goddess part really ticks me off as well. I needed to be in a different world, where no one knows or cares who I am.'

Charlotte flicked a glance at the ceiling. 'Hence we leave a perfectly good hotel and end up in another with a huge business conference upstairs?'

'Different world.' Violette sipped her wine. 'They wouldn't know the ballet from their arses. I want to be among strangers who are not fascinated by my every move. It makes for better hunting.'

Charlotte glanced around at other tables and became aware of guarded but intense male attention.

'You can't escape. There are drink-sodden businessmen ogling us.'

'Eugh,' said Violette. 'I've lost my appetite.'

'Perhaps they think we're lovers,' said Charlotte.

Violette leaned in and kissed her on the mouth. Charlotte tasted Stefan's wicked nectar on her lips. 'Are we?' Violette whispered.

The unanswerable question. 'I worship you. You know that.'

'I know the love that made you turn me, Charlotte. I raged and hated you for it, until I understood that you only made me become myself. Don't keep fishing for absolution. You love someone else, and my nature is solitary.' The dancer sat back, her dark tone lightening. 'They're looking at you, not me, dear. The voluptuous one, hair shining all shades of gold. Sometimes it's fun to have sex with your supper. Is there nothing to tempt you?'

Charlotte surveyed the bar. Amid an ocean of trolls, she saw one tempting blonde young man in a fall of light. He caught her eye in startled fascination. She looked away.

'Nothing.'

'Liar, liar.'

Then the woman walked past. A conference delegate, neat in a grey tight-waisted suit, name badge on the lapel, leather folder under her arm. Passing their table, she bumped into an empty chair and dropped the folder. The table shook, spilling wine. Papers fanned out on the carpet. Swearing, she bent down to collect them up. As she did so, the mass of her long chestnut-brown hair fell forward across her face.

Quick as a snake, Violette was down there helping her. And as the woman rose, pushing back the glorious hair, Charlotte saw her face, heard the precise upper-class-Boston accent.

'I'm sorry ... thanks so much ... that was really clumsy of me ... oh no, did I spill your drinks? I'm so sorry.'

'That's all right,' Violette said softly. 'Only a drop, it's fine.'

Her hands, giving back stray papers, brushed the woman's.

'Oh, you're British, right?' said the stranger. Violette inclined her head. 'Well, have a nice evening.'

She went on her way, her step quick and business-like in high heels, luscious hair swinging against her back. Violette's face was frozen, her lips parted. All her languid teasing sarcasm had vanished. She looked nakedly shocked.

'That was Robyn,' she said.

'No, it wasn't,' Charlotte gasped. She'd seen the resemblance, but Violette's reaction alarmed her. 'I know it looked like her, but ... Violette, it wasn't.'

'Yes,' the dancer whispered. 'It's her, it's Robyn.'

Robyn. Eighty years dead. Violette, who thought she couldn't love, had loved her. Perhaps she'd come close with others since, but Robyn was the ruby set in her heart. A glorious courtesan defying Boston's high society; a wounded soul, beautiful, warm and funny. The miracle was that Robyn had wanted her too. But Violette had turned her away. *Robyn, if I let you come with me ... I will destroy you.*

It had seemed the right decision at the time. Even with the prescience of a goddess, how could she have known that Robyn would die at the hands of another vampire? The joke was that he'd loved her too. He'd been trying to transform her. But Robyn hadn't wanted to become a cold crystalline shell feeding on the living. The transformation failed because Robyn chose to stay human. She chose death.

Violette was hardly aware of her surroundings. She could only see Robyn's face, smell her hair. Charlotte's voice startled her.

'Where are you going?'

'To speak to her.'

Charlotte's hand shot out and circled her upper arm. 'Don't.'

'Do you think a day goes by that I haven't longed to find her again?' Violette hissed. 'Let me go.'

Too much liquid swam in Charlotte's eyes. Fear, jealousy. 'Violette, it isn't Robyn.'

The dancer plucked Charlotte's hand off her arm and pushed it away. 'Let me go. Whoever she is, at least let me look at her face again for a few minutes.'

The main lobby of the hotel was bright, sparkling with huge chandeliers. From the marshmallow comfort of a sofa, Violette watched the woman pacing, talking into a mobile phone, high heels clicking on the marble floor. At last she ended the conversation, turned and saw Violette.

'Hi again,' she said, about to walk straight past. Violette sat forward and made brazen eye contact, her posture demanding conversation. With those brilliant kohl-ringed eyes she could convey emotion to the back of the stalls. The effect on the woman was virtually physical. She halted, bemused as if Violette had tripped her.

'Hi,' said Violette. 'Is your evening going as well as mine?'

'Oh, my dinner date stood me up. Migraine, sure; too many brandies at lunch is more like it.'

'Same here,' said Violette. 'That is, my friend was called away. Ordered this bottle, and now no one to drink it with.' She indicated Stefan's demon-brew, which she'd seized and brought with her. The thick green glass of the bottle glistened. There were two fresh glasses beside it. 'I'd love it if you'd help me out.'

Despite the cool poise of her exterior, Violette was trembling inwardly like a teenager. Her approach felt inane and desperate. The desire to keep this gorgeous, distracted stranger beside her was turning her into a fool.

'Oh, sure, why not.' The woman flopped down, stretching stockinged calves. She took out a tablet computer and began tapping at it, at the same time trying to keep the folder from sliding off her knee. Violette, hypnotised, watched Robyn's warm face with its mischievous dark eyes, Robyn's unruly thick hair falling forward and being pushed back. 'It's such a damn nuisance … hope the guy's okay for a working breakfast … Oh, and my sister's picking me up at nine … Damn, I need to email Mark; that's my husband …'

Violette had a vision of breaking into a strange house and sucking the life from a faceless man. No more husband. She poured syrupy straw-gold plasma into the woman's glass.

'What do you do?' she asked softly.

'What? Oh, pharmaceutical company. Really dull.' The woman flipped the tablet case shut and into her purse. 'Sorry, I'm not normally this rude. You so don't look part of the convention, and you'll turn out to be head of some huge corporation and I'll have blown a billion-dollar deal.'

'Relax. I'm not.'

'I'm Ruth Sarandon.' She reached out and shook hands, her fingers warm in Violette's cold ones.

'I read the name tag.'

'You're not wearing one,' said Ruth. She took the glass. There was no sign of Robyn's calm, sensual personality beneath the brittle energy.

'I'm Violette.' She didn't think to offer a false name.

'Well, cheers, Violette.' The dancer watched as Ruth-Robyn took a mouthful of blood plasma. She swallowed hard, eyes watering. 'Wow, that's different. Kind of bitter, like an aperitif. Not bad.' She turned the bottle, holding it by the neck. 'No label. That's scary.'

'It peeled off. Condensation.' Usually Violette dealt in the truth. Tonight it felt all too easy to spill one lie after another. The spiked blood made her unguarded and she was floating in a dream where all that mattered was what she wanted.

'So, what brings you to Boston?' Ruth asked. She took large mouthfuls of her drink, shuddering a little with each one. Violette looked at the chestnut hair lying against her throat.

'Oh … working trip,' she began, but Ruth sat forward, speaking over her.

'You know, you look incredibly familiar. Did you say your name was Violette? Are you a ballet dancer?'

Violette bit her lip, cursing inwardly. She felt the magic bleeding away. The chatter of people in the lobby became deafening. She shrugged, gave a self-effacing smile. 'I'm off-duty.'

'You're *the* Violette Lenoir, right?' Ruth put down her drink and clapped her hands. 'Oh, my God, my little sister worships you. She will *die* if she knows I met you.'

Violette's eyes widened. She had an image of a small girl, like a child in an Edward Gorey cartoon, literally expiring in the face of her big sister's news. Meanwhile Ruth's chatter went on: 'I say little; Sara's twenty-three. Oh, her room's a shrine, she has every one of your ballets on DVD, she truly spends every cent of her wages on you …' and Violette sat transfixed by dismay. This was the last thing she wanted. She wanted Robyn, the wordless bliss of finding each other again. Not the inane flutter of a stranger. She wanted Robyn so badly the feeling pushed tears into her eyes.

She drank down the herb-fragrant blood. It gelled inside her like disappointment. She let the words wash over her until she couldn't hear them anymore. The world was buzzing madly around her, speeded up in time while she sat utterly still. No longer seeing the babbling woman there, only seeing Robyn.

She became aware that Ruth had stopped and was staring uneasily at her. 'So – I guess an autograph's out of the question? For Sara, not me.'

'Forgive me.' Violette's attempt at graciousness sounded wooden. 'It's wonderful that your sister … To know my work's not in vain.'

'I'm sorry,' said Ruth. 'You must get this all the time. Another gushing idiot, and here you are trying to relax. I'll stop.'

Her voice had an edge suggesting disapproval of stars who weren't meltingly grateful to their fans. Violette didn't care. She leaned into the sofa, her body turned towards Ruth's, one hand supporting her head and the other resting lightly on her hip.

'Actually, I'm trying to pick you up,' Violette said coolly, not blinking. 'Can we please go to your room before everyone in this bloody hotel recognises me?'

The narcotic wine dissolved boundaries. It blurred the room into a cocoon of gold, softened edges, intensified feelings, elongated time. They were falling in through the door, kissing. Violette twirled away, peeling the t-shirt over her head; her small breasts were bare beneath. How wonderfully strong and arched her feet were, stepping out of jeans and a tiny violet thong. Ruth followed, mesmerised by the slender body, lily-white as if the sun had never touched it. The sable triangle, black as her hair. Now Violette was kneeling in the centre of the bed with Ruth perched on the edge, languorous but uncertain; the dancer leaning forward, turning her so their mouths met.

Ivory fingertips worked at Ruth's buttons. Her skirt and jacket with their satin linings slid easily to the floor. Cool hands moved onto her naked flesh, sliding beneath her underwear, impatient to remove it. Dancer's hands, smooth yet unbelievably strong. Their lips folded together, moist and hot. Violette's tongue, parting her teeth, sent a snake of heat all through Ruth's body, a hot stiff column of aching fire. Pulling each other down, they lay alongside each other; nipples touching, Violette's thigh loosely bent and raised to cover Ruth's darker limb. Ivory on amber.

When Violette rose above her, she was everywhere, a soft bell tolling. Her hair was a black waterfall. Eyes two violet moons, arousing werewolf madness. She filled the world. Her face almost touched Ruth's, so close the eyelashes brushed her cheek. Her scent ... hardly there at all. Lily of the valley, faint and pure. It was Ruth's own musk that perfumed Violette's body.

Her tongue tasted Ruth's breasts, trailed all the way into the centre of fire, explored exquisitely until Ruth cried out. The goddess rose again. They devoured each other's mouths.

In this fever no inhibition remained and Ruth caressed the dancer everywhere; felt strong sweet notes of pleasure where Violette's thigh pressed hard between her own ... felt the muscular contractions of the dancer's climax against the hot wet palm of her hand ...

Ruth's head fell back, eyes closed. The piercing convulsion of orgasm lit another sensation, a burning pin-prick in her throat. Violette's head was heavy in her shoulder, silken hair spilling over them both. Strangest pain, like something pulling, pinioning her. She was drowning in hair. Spinning in the darkening honey light, Ruth looked down at her own body and saw that it was covered in bruises; each a black flower with a red centre.

I have never tried to meet her.

This may seem unbelievable, but I never dared. 'Giving my life to meet her' is a dream; dull prosaic reality is that I'm afraid. If I met her, everything would change. Perhaps she'd be enchanted and take me under her wing as some kind of fledgling assistant; yeah, right. She might turn viciously on me, one adoring fan too many. But her indifference would kill me.

Hell, I saw her dance on stage only three nights ago! But I sneered at the fans clustering pathetically around the stage door. Sneered, and walked away.

So I am listening as Ruth spills out this incredible story.

She is pale but too animated; hardly able to talk at first, then stumbling on the words. 'You'll never guess who I met ... oh my God ...I know she's your idol but ...'

almost in pieces. I'm not even clear what she's trying to tell me – until I take her hand. Then I see everything.

Images of black and bronze hair tangling, small rounded buttocks rising and falling. Violette must have made comparisons with her hands ... the texture of the breasts softer perhaps, the hips narrower, scent and taste subtly different from that of the long-dead lover. Did she like the differences or hate them? How could the two women be the same? I know nothing about Robyn, but I know there is only one Ruth.

Who now veers from shock to amazed laughter to sudden gentle horrified apology. 'God, Sara, I know she's your hero and I'm so sorry to destroy your illusions, but you had to know. She's not what you think.'

But how the hell does Ruth know what I think?

I grip her hand so hard that she jumps and says, 'Ow, what was that for?'

'You touched Violette,' I explain.

Ruth woke from a heavy sleep, her mouth dry, pain hammering delicately behind her eyes. She pushed her hair out of her face and remembered ...

Not shame or guilt, but disbelief. Before Mark she'd had affairs she'd regretted, but never in her life had she succumbed to a stranger, a celebrity, a woman. Her skin felt burnished smooth like leather, beautiful. She remembered sensuality, heat, orgasm, all laced with a nightmare of being pinioned and drowning. Her neck throbbed. As she tried to move it began to hurt, really hurt, shooting pain deep into her shoulder. She reached across the crumpled landscape of sheets but the space beside her was empty.

The ballerina sat on the end corner of the bed, staring at her. Violette's knees were drawn up, arms wrapped around them, ankles crossed. Under the shower of raven hair, she was a white statue. She gazed at Ruth like some lavender-eyed cat, unblinking. There was blood on her mouth.

Pushing herself up on her elbows, Ruth asked, 'You okay?'

No answer. The ballerina appeared catatonic.

'Violette? What's wrong with you?'

Blood gleamed freshly on the parted lips. Ruth put her hand to the sore place above her collarbone and her fingers came away red. A recent nerve-memory of pain lanced her, of being pulled down into a red-black whirlpool where pleasure and horror congealed together.

'What did you do to me?' Fear made Ruth angry. 'You have to be some kind of ...' The word *maniac* didn't touch the slow, oppressive heartbeat of fear, the wrongness of an atmosphere tainted with the bitter honey of opiates. 'For God's sake, say something!'

Still no response from the thing on the bed. Ruth panicked. She was on her feet, struggling to dress, stuffing her belongings into her designer holdall, muttering, 'Oh God, oh Jesus.' She couldn't breathe properly.

Couldn't make her limbs move fast enough. As she floundered to escape, the only parts of the ice sculpture that moved were the eyes, watching her.

At daybreak, Charlotte wandered the hotel looking for Violette and in a corridor she found the woman who looked like Robyn. She was emerging from a room, struggling to heft a bag, fasten strappy shoes and talk into her mobile phone, all at once.

'No, I'm done with the conference … Something happened and I'm kinda freaked out … I sound weird? Babe, wait 'til I tell you … Yeah, come pick me up like now. Yeah, you can park in front of reception like we said … okay, 'bye.'

'Anything wrong?' Charlotte asked.

Ruth Sarandon jumped so hard she nearly dropped her phone. Pushing uncombed hair out of her face, she looked at Charlotte wild-eyed. 'Your friend is out of her mind. I don't give a rat's ass how famous she is.' She pointed at the half-open door. 'She's just sitting there. And who the hell is Robyn?'

Charlotte let her face betray nothing. She probably looked as strange to Ruth now as Violette did, all porcelain and glass. 'I'm sorry,' said Charlotte. 'I wanted to warn you …'

'Warn me – what?'

'You reminded her of someone else.'

'No kidding.' Ruth's face was beautifully flushed with anger. She rubbed at faint bruises on her throat. 'She used to bite them too? That's assault. She put something in my drink. I should call the police!'

'I'm sorry you were hurt.' Charlotte meant it; her low tone seemed to calm the woman. She pushed her hair back again, sighed shakily.

'It's okay. Consenting adults, and all that. But she is seriously disturbed. I have to go meet my sister.'

Ruth went striding away, shoulders back, as fast as she could without actually running. Charlotte watched her from a distance, stabbing at an elevator button. Then she entered the room.

The dancer sat folded on the end of the bed, a dark elf.

'Violette?' Charlotte said softly. 'What are you doing?'

'Wondering if I can love her or not.'

Charlotte gave a short sigh. 'It's academic, since she's bolted.'

'She wasn't Robyn.'

'I tried to tell you that.'

'But I had to touch her and taste her before I could believe it.' Violette relaxed, turning to drop her feet to the carpet. Her hands rested loosely on the bed cover and she sat forlorn. 'The question is, would I hate her for being so like Robyn but not actually her, never her? Or could I accept her as a different person and love her anyway?'

'The thing is,' Charlotte said, folding her arms, 'that while you were having this debate with yourself, you freaked the living daylights out of Ruth, and didn't even notice.'

Violette's eyes flashed up at Charlotte through a winter lattice of hair. 'Did you try to warn her away from me?'

'No. I wish I had!' Charlotte put up her hands but Violette came at her and seized her arms.

'Yes, you still think you have a right to interfere with my life. Still want to control me, all out of guilt for having unleashed me on the world.'

They stood face to face, glaring. Violette's words hurt, but they were true.

'I'm only pointing out the obvious, since you can't see it,' Charlotte snapped. 'You're only thinking about what *you* want. You don't even know her! You're in a dream, wondering can you or can't you? Meanwhile, she's too terrified out of her brain to know or care what's going on in yours. You drugged her, drank her blood and called her Robyn all night. From her point of view, this is not the start of a promising relationship.'

Violette released her. 'It was Stefan's wine. What a sad excuse.' Outlined by the glow through the curtains she was a creamy silhouette like Venus rising. 'It was a dream, a lovely, depraved dream.'

'Come on,' said Charlotte. 'It's time to leave.'

Violette's bloodied mouth twisted in a smile. 'I can't.'

'Why not?'

'I think Ruth, in her haste, took my top. I'm not asking for it back. Best we never meet again.'

Charlotte half-smiled. 'She's in no mood for an apology. Take this.' She took off her cardigan, a lacy thing crocheted of gold silk.

'Poor Ruth,' said Violette. 'That's it: I've forgotten how even to pretend to be human. I'm designed to be alone. I know that. I bring light to others, but I'm damned if I can find it for myself. I feel as if I'm made of bone.' She came forward again, slim hips swaying; so beautiful, Charlotte could only stare. 'That sounded wonderfully self-pitying, didn't it? I should be beyond all that. But it still hurts.'

'You've always got me,' said Charlotte.

Violette shook her head sadly. 'No, I haven't.'

Charlotte leaned in and kissed her on the mouth, tasting Ruth's blood, lapping the red sweetness from Violette's tongue and lips until the stain was gone. They stood looking at each other, hands soft on each other's arms, as they had a thousand times in the past.

'Ruth tasted nice,' said Charlotte.

She touched Violette.

Safe in my parked car, Ruth spills it all out. 'You have to know the truth, Sara,' so apologetic – as if she's doing me a favour, while plainly relishing every moment of the scandal. Calm at last, she even starts making little jokes about it. 'What a night! (Oh, Mark must never know, right?) Wow, what a kick.'

She doesn't notice my silence, my knuckles turning white on the steering wheel. Ruth of all people – with her perfect career, perfect marriage – Ruth has had what I've only dreamed of. Violette's attention, her desire, her yearning, her body, her pleasure and anguish. And it meant nothing to her. Just as she didn't truly see Violette, she doesn't see me either.

I feel like telling my sister the simple truth. When she bit you, it was me who felt it. When she realised she couldn't love you, those were my tears that fell.

But I can't speak and suddenly she's getting out of the car again. 'I'm acting crazy,' says Ruth, fishing in her bag. 'I can handle this. I'm going to go right back in there and give Violette her shirt back.'

Daylight couldn't burn Violette's skin any more than it could burn limestone. In morning splendour the lobby was palatial, so bright it hurt the eyes. Fresh white lilies on plinths filled the air with fragrance. Violette walked dazed through the brightness; paused by a sofa and watched a housekeeper clearing last night's wreckage; the unlabelled bottle of thick green glass and the empty glasses. For the pleasure of immortals, indeed.

Looking up, she started. Ruth was standing in front of her. Ruth, not Robyn.

'Oh, you started blinking again,' said Ruth. 'That's good, right? I realised I ...'

She held out a purple scrap. Violette took it and whispered, 'Thank you.'

Ruth ducked her head nervously. 'I'm sorry I ran out. I panicked.'

Violette tried to smile. She knew her smiles looked cold, however warmly she meant them. 'Your sister will have to tear down her shrine.'

'Oh, god.' Ruth lowered her eyes.

'This is all my fault. I should have warned you, I'm quite mad.'

'Just a little drunk, both of us.' The woman sighed. Their eyes met briefly, awkwardly. 'I wanted to say ... it was weird and wonderful, and no hard feelings?'

Violette nodded. Turning to go, Ruth added, 'I hope you find her. Whoever it is you're looking for.'

Light dawns. It didn't happen to make me jealous. No, Ruth was there to become my bridge. My only chance.

As I said, I've never tried to meet Violette. I know I could never be anything to her. Just another obsessed fan. I know that.

But in my own mind I'm something special. I'm her archivist. I'm the one who knows what she really is: Lilith, the immortal Death Lily. Perhaps this knowledge makes me dangerous.

I climb out of the car. Sunlight cascades down the tall glass doors of the hotel. There are two veils of glass between me and Violette and I can't see her, can only see my own small reflection, sliding off the door as it hisses open for me like stage curtains. Then the last veil parts and I'm breathing the same air as her. The foyer is a softly shining theatre centred around its star and she's there, in all her magnificence. Snowy skin, raven hair; a poised figure, exotic even in jeans; more petite than I expected. My fate.

My sister is stepping away from her. I hardly notice. I am thinking, Violette fell. She's not perfect after all. Her wings caught fire and she fell. Do I love her more for that, or is she tainted – no longer above me? I have to know.

The air is white with fire. I walk steadily towards her. Violette glances up and, with those brilliant uncompromising magisterial eyes, she watches me coming.

PART TWO: OTHER TALES

The Journal of Elena Kovacs

25th July

I mean to keep a journal in imitation of our gracious English visitor, Madam Harker. She gave me the book, pens and ink. I will write very small, so that paper and ink shall last a long time – I could get none from Father without explaining why I need it. And I shall practise my poor English, to improve – and so that my father may understand my words less readily, should he ever find this.

I wish I need not write in secret, but I must. Father must never see this precious book. I know it would make him angry. And what might I record that must be concealed from his eyes? Simply the thoughts in my head, since I am not supposed to have any. Secrecy is sinful, but I will not dwell on that or I will never set down a word.

I have a little downstairs room to myself, which overlooks the rear farmyard. I can see the well, the side of the great barn and the orchards, pigs and poultry running about. Beyond the fruit trees, the forested ridge rises up as a great misty wall. It makes me feel lonely; I imagine jumping over the window sill, running away and being lost on that ridge …

The farmer's daughters are as dear as sisters to me, but I am glad I do not have to share their room or I should never have a moment to myself. They are good girls but so simple, wanting nothing but to marry shepherds and breed more little shepherds. We have nothing in common. They could never understand me – why should they, when I do not understand myself?

I don't know what I shall write, in any case. I have spent so much time on this farm that nothing is new any more. Shall I write of turkeys and geese, the daily coming and goings of peasants, the long hours spent sitting at my father's feet while he paints on the slope of some pasture? Well, I may write about the visit of our English guests, at least.

I feel a strange yearning. Madam Harker did not create it, but she enflamed it. If she had not visited us, if she had not taken so kind an interest in me, surely this ache in my breast would not have stirred so fiercely! She brought the soul of England with her, with her beautiful sombre clothes and her lovely manners and fair complexion. She will never know what excitement she brought to my life … but now she is gone, how small my world seems. Not the physical world but the world with my father. I can see how vast and beautiful the world is, but he puts me in a little glass box.

Why do I feel this urge to defy him? Am I a changeling? If I were the dutiful daughter he wanted, I would not feel so afraid – so trapped!

God forgive me for such sentiments! There, that is why these words must be hidden from his eyes. I want so much from life and here there seems so little.

I wish I knew where they went on their mysterious carriage journey. It made a change in all our guests, but most of all I noticed it in Madam Harker. Before she went to the Borgo Pass she was troubled, as if they brought some dark secret on their 'holiday'. Perhaps I imagine too much. But when they came back they were different, all light of heart and laughing, as if they had found out something that pleased them. I don't mean they were (I must consult my dictionary …) frivolous. Madam Harker could never be frivolous or silly, as my father says women of foreign cities are. She was serene, glowing and happier than before she left. Perhaps it was only that she is returning to her son.

The change in her mood made me feel strange. It made me … frightened. Why? I did not realise until I wrote it. Oh, now I scare myself for no reason. How I hate the superstitions of this land! I hate them the more because I cannot dismiss them. They creep into the blood and become real. I wish I was like Madam Harker, brought up in a land free from beliefs that men change into wolves or that the dead can – no, no more. I wish that I lived in a land of reason!

When Madam Harker first arrived, there was a shadow of sadness inside her. But when she and her party returned from their unexplained journey, the shadow had changed. It was still there, but outside her, so she was no longer aware of it. And it fell on me instead. By 'shadow' I mean a feeling, a mood … some wisp of pain, fear and excitement mixed, but when I try to get hold of it, it vanishes between my hands. And then I forget, and it appears again. Like something watching. This makes me shiver, I need my shawl. I did not begin this journal to frighten myself … or was the fear inside all the time, and writing only brings it out? There, I have learned something, but not the knowledge I thought I was seeking.

Father is calling me. My precious book, I must hide you!

30th July

I have been wondering about my mother. I barely remember her. She died of fever when I was a baby, my father says. This morning I was looking at the farmer's wife, her hands red-raw from endless washing, cooking, sewing, goat-milking, her face red-brown from the weather, and her daughters the same, and I wondered if my mother was like that! Or was she elegant like

Madam Mina, intelligent and accomplished, with white hands and beautiful clothes? My father hates me to ask questions. I could ask Uncle André, when we meet again.

Father has been sketching the peasants at work in the fields. The pastures are lush but life is harsh here, especially in winter. The farmers see no beauty in the mountains, only that wolves may come down from the heights and kill sheep. My father is very taken up with this idea – the battle between man and nature – and pays me no attention, which gives me time to think. Shall I write poetry? I could become a great and famous Hungarian poetess!

I had a dream last night. It lingers with me, like a strange atmosphere that makes a silver mist over everything. Let me try to remember ... I am in a dark place where all I can see is a thick white mist flowing very close to the ground. All is chill, with a smell of damp stone. A light shines inside this mist, throwing upwards a kind of radiance, against which stands a tall, thin, dark figure. This figure is all in black but it has no face. It is covered in a black shroud. This figure does nothing, it simply *is*. And I am filled with terror.

I can't say what so alarms me. Just to know that such a thing exists.

I frighten myself again, thinking of it! I could not wake up, I struggled for breath. I thought to cry out and wake someone, but could not make a sound. At last I woke suddenly with a great effort, and found myself sitting up in bed. I felt an overwhelming urge to get up and look out of the window.

Moonlight flooded the farmyard, the orchard and the steep forested ridge beyond. But nothing stirred. I wonder why I feel so strange?

Now I know the value of this journal. Not to record the details of my life, which is dull, but to record my dreams and thoughts.

Oh, if I were a man, I could be a poet. I could go to Paris or London! If I married Miklos, would we travel? Would marrying make me more free, or less so? My father will never let me do anything alone!

2nd August

Something dreadful is happening.

Let me set it down. I must know if writing will make it worse, or better.

Last night I could not sleep. Rather, I went in and out of dreaming. Not pleasant dreams, these, but a distressing, heavy state in which I was too hot, and my head ached, and I could neither wake up nor fall fully asleep.

As I lay like this I heard a faint sound outside, the thin hard whine of some animal in distress. At first it seemed far away on the mountains, then as if it was right outside the window, then far away again. It was a horrible noise, which pained my nerves. I prayed for it to cease, yet I wanted to go out to whatever made the sound – to silence or comfort it, I do not know.

This keening went on and on, near and far away. When I tried to get up and look outside, I could not move. This alarmed me greatly. I saw unpleasant things in this half-dream. The heavy white mist again, with red wisps swirling into it, like blood in water. I am trying to climb a dark mountain wall but I am struggling and slipping back; it is too steep. I see some splintered timbers lying on a path, all rotten and glistening with rain. These images make no sense but each is terrifying and upsets me deeply. Even writing this down, I can make no more sense of it. And always that irritating bleat of pain!

I must have slept in the end, for I awoke at dawn and all was normal. But as we ate breakfast, a shepherd came to the kitchen door and told the farmer that a wolf had come down from the forests and taken a lamb.

Was that the sound I heard, that I thought was only in my nightmare? The lamb, bleating for help?

The men have gone out with guns to hunt the wolf. I hate to think of it being chased and shot, the poor wolf, which was only hunting to live. Must two animals die instead of one? My father would say this is sentiment. He would think me mad.

But the worst thing that happened was this. While he talked, the shepherd – a young, unappealing man with red cheeks and a long greasy moustache – kept staring at me. Perhaps he meant no harm, but I found his looks insolent, and they made me feel defenceless and somehow ashamed. If I could have left the room quickly, it would not have mattered. But my father saw the looks, and got in a rage, and would have attacked the shepherd had not the farmer and his sons held him back! It was an ugly scene. When the shepherd had gone, amid raised voices, Father pushed me into my room and shouted at me that it was all my fault, I must have encouraged him, and I was nothing but a hindrance to Father's artistic career, and the sooner I am married and out of harm's way the better, and so on. Then he embraced me so hard my ribs were bruised, and said he could not bear me to marry, no man would ever take his Elena from him, and all this so rough and fierce that I found no comfort in it, only more pain.

I was left weeping. I still tremble now. Suddenly everything seems very dark and wretched and I wish I could leave, but I cannot. Where would I go?

There is a commotion outside. The men are home.

3rd August

Father has been kinder today; or at least, he has kept me constantly busy, fetching and carrying, cleaning brushes. He commands me to sing folk-songs as he paints, then complains that my voice is weak and shaky. I wish I knew how to please him! Everything I do seems to disappoint him. If I had been a boy ... Sometimes I wish I had never been born! I think he wishes it too.

They shot the wolf that took the lamb. The poor creature dragged itself off to die and no one can find it. I hate to think of any creature dying slowly in pain.

5th August

Last night as I lay in my bed I heard a wolf howling, a lonely, high keening that pierced the silence and brought me awake. It sounded uncanny, high at first then falling and trailing mournfully away. The sound of it turned me cold. But I had to get out of bed and look.

Down in the yard, standing in the centre of a white splash of moonlight, there was a great silver wolf! He was beside the well, his ears almost on a level with its carved wooden roof. He was pale in the moonlight, but his eyes glowed red. He stared at me. I could hardly move for fear. This terror of wolves is very old and deep in the Transylvanian peasants – and in me, as if their fear has stirred and woken my own. Yet I opened the window wide, as if I were acting in my sleep.

The animal was there, looking up at me. We stared at each other. I felt a compulsion to climb out of the window and go to him. But he let out a faint keen, and suddenly the howling of dogs rose up from the village, from other farms. This was joined by the howling of wolves on the ridge, until the whole landscape was filled with their mournful keening. So disturbing was this sound that I drew back quickly and closed the window.

When I looked out again I saw the creature turning and slipping away into the shadows. But he went slowly, very lame, and I saw a dark splash like blood on his flank. My heart beat hard. This must be the wolf that was shot! He was wounded and in pain, I could not leave him! But he had gone, and I dared not go after him. All of this was dream-like. I lay down and slept until morning.

I tried to find the wolf in daylight but there was no sign of him. How far could he have gone, so sorely wounded? I have told no-one. I don't know why. I feel it is my secret. I am afraid of the wolf, yet I want him to come again.

7th August

He came. I am fearful, but I must write of it.

Last night I was woken suddenly – not by any sound, but by an urge to look out of the window. I crept out of bed and looked out, and the great pale wolf was there again.

He stood very still, his haunches all bent under him, his eyes as scarlet as sunset. I was very afraid, but felt I must go to him. I undid the window and climbed over the sill, nearly tearing my nightdress. I had saved him a little piece of meat. I crouched down and held out the meat to see if he would come, and he did. He came limping to me and ate out of my hand! Then he let me stroke him. I never dreamed I would dare to stroke so fierce a creature.

He put his big head on my knee and let me rub his soft ears. There is a big ragged hole in his haunch where the bullet went through. It looked as if it should have killed him. His eyes, which had seemed red before, were dark and filmy with weakness. He licked my hand as if to thank me, then he left.

I followed a little way through the orchard, hoping to find his lair, but I lost him. Suddenly the trees around me seemed full of menace, and I looked around as if I'd woken from a trance. Something was watching me from the darkness; I couldn't see it, but I knew. I turned and ran back to the house, and soon I was in bed with the window shut, feeling safe again but foolish.

I hope the creature will come again. I will keep food for him. If I don't feed him he may starve to death. Perhaps he cannot live anyway but I must try to help him.

No one must know, or they will kill him, and punish me.

9th August

All I can think of during the day is the wolf. While I am helping Father, I am only waiting for night to come. I am clumsy, I cannot pay attention. Father berates me but I don't hear.

The great wolf led me a little way into the trees tonight, and ate all the food I had saved. He was famished. I cleaned the edges of the wound as best I could with clean water, but it is very deep and not healing as it should. Something is wrong. He is too vigorous for an animal that must be dying. When he licked my hand, as if to say thank you, his tongue was cold. And before he left his eyes again glowed scarlet, so bright I could not mistake it. I was frightened when I looked into his eyes. I felt dizzy, as if I would fall.

When I went to bed afterwards, I had a nightmare. It was real and vivid, but the events so wild and squeezed together I could make no sense of them.

I am lying in a box of earth, a big mouldering box like a coffin. Everything is moving violently around me, as if there is a cart beneath me, and I am afraid. No, not quite afraid, but urgent, angry and full of hatred. I see and feel, but cannot move. Now I see the sun dipping above me, red as blood. I smile. I know I can move once the sun sets. Then I will do something very terrible. (I shudder even now to remember that gloating anticipation.) I am about to do something violent and evil, yet I long to do it! Now I see two faces above me – pale, shadowed and colourless with the cold crimson sky behind them, and snow blowing around them. I see two shining steel blades flashing towards me. I scream, my whole body jolts.

Then there is a deep, peaceful blackness.

This seems to go on forever. I have no thoughts, no feelings, only a dull awareness. I know I am dead, but there is no Heaven or Hell waiting, not even purgatory ... only this limbo. Nothingness.

(How horrible it seems, now I write it down! The faces, I recollect ... One I did not know, but one was that of Madam Mina's husband, Jonathan Harker. I feel violent hatred for him as I write. What does this mean?)

After an indefinable length of nothingness, I hear the fleeting murmur of a voice I know. A spirit brushes by me, like an angel! I stir. Something pulls at me and I open my eyes, but no one is there. Instead I see a stony road winding between the mountains, a thin bleak twilight lying on the cold stones. I see some greyish soil, like ash, lying in the cracks between the stones. The sight of this dust, for no reason I understand, fills me with despair and I want to roar with grief. But I have no throat with which to cry out.

Thank God, I woke then. I was hanging out of bed, shivering with the cold, and my chest aching from the position I had twisted into in my sleep. It's over. I said a prayer. I never, never want to have a dream like that again!

10th August

Prayers not answered. The nightmare again. The same, but it goes a little further this time.

As I stir from limbo, I see the angel who woke me. I hear her warm voice and see a fleeting form like a white ghost – and it is Madam Mina! Her presence is a hot, fragrant river. I am a ghost while she is alive, mortal, full of blood and life ... and I long for her, I must touch her at any cost; she is as vital to me as a mother to a child! But I can only watch. I watch, coldly, the figures of her and her hated companions, standing with their heads bowed. I don't know what they are doing. The tableau of their heated, mortal, ageing forms fills me with despair, as if I fall for ever into an abyss.

When I say 'I', I mean whoever I was in the dream – for I was not myself. These visions and nightmares distress me more than I can say.

13th August

Each night I stay as long as I dare with my friend the wolf, because I do not want to go to bed and endure the dreams again. But they always come eventually. I fight sleep as long as I can, and my father says I look pale and tired, and berates me for my lethargy. I think he has made up his mind I shall marry Miklos now. He says my illness is because I am spoiled and lazy, and I need a husband to keep me under control. Unwell, I am a burden to him, so he wants me to become the responsibility of someone else. And again I disappoint him!

I tell my friend about the dreams. That comforts me, though I know he cannot understand. He lies with his heavy body over my legs and I stroke his fur as I tell him every detail. His ears flicker as if he listens. When I look into his glowing eyes he seems almost to speak to me. He seems more real than my father, the farmer's family and the insolent shepherd all put together!

I cannot wait for night to fall, and the shaggy white wolf to stand under my window and call to me. I worry about him. Although he eats the food I give him, he remains very thin under his coat. He drags his hind leg and his wound does not heal. He neither regains health nor loses it; he is always the same, as if … as if he were dead, yet still walking.

I wish I hadn't had that thought! This room seems so tiny and ill-lit, while the world outside oppresses me with its wild, cruel darkness.

15th August

I think I have lost him. I am very afraid.

Last night he looked into my eyes and I felt him trying to tell me something. His eyes were like two great lamps, burning into my head. I had to look away, to push his head away, because I could not bear it. I couldn't understand. Then he began to snap and snarl at me. I cried out and ran away from him, through the trees and back to my room. He came after me! Surely he could have caught me easily. Just as I shut the window he jumped at the glass, making the whole frame shake. I yelped in fear. He stared at me through the glass, his lips drawn back and trembling. His long fangs shone and they looked so cruel and hard.

I was terrified he would burst through the glass. We stood eye to eye for a moment. Then he took his big paws off the sill and ran three-legged into the shadows of the trees.

I cannot believe he has changed and turned on me. What have I done wrong?

I did not sleep until the cold hour before dawn. But then I had another dream, the worst yet.

I see cold mountain slopes, a castle rearing above a precipice and folds of thick dark forest, as if I am a spectre wandering over a land I once loved, but which is now bleak and lifeless. I would weep if I had throat, mouth and eyes to weep with. All I ever loved has passed away to dust. All my loved ones are long gone. There is nothing but darkness to the end of the universe. Nowhere I can find rest.

As I describe the dream I cannot express the feeling of desolation that filled me. It is the most terrifying feeling I have ever known. This God-forsaken landscape is my own soul. I haunt the walls of the castle but I am exiled.

Someone woke me from oblivion, but she is gone and I cannot find her. Have no body in which to find her. I drift a long way over mountains ...

I see a hairy wolf, dying at the foot of an oak tree with the glistening wound of a bullet in its haunch. I enter its body as its own spirit departs. Its corpse is mine and now I have a form in which to move. Now I can find someone to help me ... One who has been touched by the same gentle spirit.

I can write no more. This is all I remember. The dream faded and as I try to recapture it I can only think how ridiculous it sounds.

I will steal a good piece of meat from the kitchen, in hopes of sweetening my friend. He eats most of my dinner and supper these days, while the farmer's wife frets that I grow thin. He thrives at my expense, then dares to snap at me!

16th August

He came back. He ate the meat, very slowly and lovingly, licking and tearing it into thin slivers. As if he knew the risk I had taken to steal it for him.

Then he came and licked my hands. The blood was still on his tongue and my hands became wet with it, but he went on working with his long tongue until all was clean. I am forgiven!

When I went to bed my dreams were as vivid as ever, and unsettling. I dream that a tall old man is bending over my bed. There is a faint light behind him, but I cannot see his face. He is telling me something very important, whispering, whispering. (I cannot now remember a word but at the time it was vital). He takes my hands; his own are hairy, like paws! He leans towards me and I think he will kiss me; instead he licks my throat with a long, rough tongue. I shudder from head to foot with revulsion ... and yet I want it to continue. I have no will to stop him.

I paused in writing to say a prayer. It seems, as I look back at my journal, that all I have recorded are sick ravings. Am I ill? Surely these dreams are not healthy – will I call evil upon myself, by writing them down?

22nd August

I can barely hold the pen to write. I am exhausted and my eyes cloud with pain.

Last night when I met the wolf he would not come to me, only looked over his shoulder and trotted away into the orchard. I followed. I know I should not have done so, but with him a strange condition of mind comes upon me; that I am conscious but bereft of my own will – or rather, my will is all to obey him. So I put on hide boots and a shawl and go with him. As we cross the pastures my feet (even through the boots) become soaked. The sky is thick with stars and their soft light turns mountains and forest to an uncanny, shimmering realm. I look around fearfully as we go, yet with my friend I feel safe. He is so strange; sad and in need of my care, yet so strong – all that fierceness coiled up in his red eyes!

A spell is on me. We turn east along the base of the ridge, which leads us higher and higher along a climbing deer track. There are spruce saplings around us. Then we cross a stream and enter the forest, passing a shepherd's hut as we climb the long valley. The slopes grow steeper. I am uneasy and out of breath. The ground between the great spruces is covered in thick black mould, full of fallen branches and trunks. Once I see two large shapes pass between the trees some distance away; bears. They watch us pass. My feet hurt, and I worry that we are going too far. I know I will not reach home again before dawn. Yet I cannot stop.

When dawn comes, we are deeper in the mountains than ever. We reach the top of a steep ridge just as the sun blazes on the silver limestone crags of the Carpathians. The chain of peaks rings us all around and they look as cold as snow. I am very tired now, cold and frightened. But whenever I falter, the wolf turns his bright eyes on me and forces me on. We are so far from anywhere!

Now we pass breath-taking narrow gorges and plunging waterfalls. I drink from streams, too tired to feel hungry. A mass of grey cloud comes down and soaks us in mist and rain. Animals watch us; wolves and foxes, lynx and wild pigs. They form a ring around us, as if the wolf draws them yet warns them away; as if he holds a magical power over them also.

The journey is confused and blurred. A mud path along a shadowy gorge, a grassy, open saddle with hazel groves, elders and blackberry bushes. We descend and climb a deep gulley, and the firs close in, thick and dark around us. The wolf leads me out of the forest onto a rough track, the long white brush of his tail swaying.

There is a steep, thinly forested ridge on one side, a deep valley with a fierce river on the other, and a long silver line of mountains beyond. Far along this track, my companion halts. I sink down exhausted. I had my eyes on the ground, but as I look up I see a castle, a great, towering pile with broken battlements and ancient towers above a precipice. I catch my breath in terror. The Szekely farmers whisper of a castle from which evil has been visited upon them and their ancestors. No one speaks its name. But I know – with the deep dream-knowledge that my friend gives me – that this is that place.

The wolf leads me into the undergrowth below the track, and here I see the timbers of some great box that has been broken up and left to rot. He is directing me; I know what to do. Lifting lengths of timber aside I see a pile of earth that is darker than the brown mould on which it lies. Mingled with this substance are thick patches of a lighter dust, a sort of ash.

I spread out my shawl and with my bare hands I scoop the ash into it. It is damp, mould-scented, all laced with cobwebs. The wolf watches intently, panting, his tongue lolling over his long teeth. I cannot stop until all the dust is gathered. I make a bundle of my shawl. As I do so, he goes up onto the track and picks up something small and white between his teeth. Delicately, like a cat carrying a kitten, he brings this item to me.

It is a handkerchief, lacy and delicate, such as an Englishwoman would have. The initials W.H. are embroidered on one corner. I use it to tie the top of the shawl. Then the wolf has me carry the bundle to the courtyard of the castle.

The great gateway and the high frowning walls sway across my sight. I am terrified; ghosts and dead leaves blow about the courtyard, black passages yawn into crypts. Surely the stone towers will come tumbling down and bury me. My companion shows me a niche in which to hide the bundle. Then I run away down the long, hard path.

Of the journey home I remember little. My feet were sore, and I was delirious from exhaustion and lack of food. The wolf must have led me safely back to the farm; my strongest impression was of the force of his will, which seemed loyal, single-minded, yet wholly pitiless.

It was afternoon when I reached the farm. I looked around for my friend but he was gone. I had not eaten for two days, and I was all in filthy rags. The shock of my father and the farmers when they saw me! They had been searching for me. And I could not explain where I had been, or why, for I don't know.

Somewhere I stepped out of reality and entered a nightmare.

When I could not and would not explain, my father dragged me to my room, closed the door and beat me with his belt. I deserved it, I know. Now I am locked in the room alone, without food, writing my journal to keep me from crying with pain.

I can hear my father arguing furiously with the farmer and his wife through the door. Oh God, they are telling us to leave! They say that their youngest son saw me feeding a great white wolf by the well, that the shepherd saw me walking through the forest with my pale companion. They say I am a witch, in league with the Devil, I will bring a curse upon them if I stay!

Because of me, my father will lose his good friends and be unable to complete his paintings. He will never forgive me. Tomorrow, they say, we must go. Oh God, help me. Soon it will all be over.

23rd August

I am leaving the farm, but not as my father thinks. My decision is made and my heart beats so hard I turn faint. In secret I have packed a very few belongings in a small bag – to which I shall add my journal, when the time comes – and I wait.

I was meant to leave tomorrow with my father. We could not arrange a conveyance to Bistritz until then, and there have been bad scenes today. When I came out of my room, the family made the *mano pantea* at me, a hand-sign against the evil eye, and my father grew furious with them and called them superstitious fools. The farmer, who can be very fearsome with his long black moustache, grew even angrier. They would have come to blows, had the farmer's wife and daughters not intervened. They want us gone and the atmosphere is uneasy. I came back to my room but my father followed and questioned me for hours about where I had gone for two days in my nightclothes, why was I seen with the wolf, and so on. He made me weep with fear, but I would not answer. Pride will not let me tell him even the little I know.

'Has some man dishonoured you? Some greasy shepherd, some gypsy?' he shouted at me. 'You have brought disgrace upon me! I should have known better than to trust you! Even Miklos will not have you now! What am I to do with you? What have I done to deserve so wild and disobedient a daughter?'

I felt a little sorry for him, for I cannot be the perfect daughter that he believes I should be. The fault is mine. But it cannot be helped.

At last he struck me across the face and left, locking me in. I am still trembling, exhausted from his questions and the injustice of them. But strangely I feel distant from all of it. No longer afraid of him, no longer distraught or ashamed – because I am going away. Father has lost me. Perhaps he has always feared this moment, and that is why he is so angry.

The door is locked, but I wait by the window for night to come.

All is quiet. A great silence lies on the world, as if it waits also.

He is coming! A long white shape in the darkness, speeding towards me. His eyes are two red stars. His great head rises up behind the glass, his tongue lolls over his long fangs, a strange blue-white mist shimmers all around him ... and I must open the window, and go wherever he leads.

26th August

I have come a long way since I last wrote.

When I left the farm, I took a bag containing only a few garments, a little food I stole from the kitchen, and my precious gifts from Madam Mina: my journal, dictionary, pens and ink. My companion led me again towards the forest. We had gone only a few hundred yards across the pastures when my father came running after me in his nightclothes, shouting so furiously at me he was almost screaming. I froze in horror. So enraged was he that his face was dark with blood even in the dim milky moonlight. He must have been spying on my window from his own room!

He catches my arm and orders me back to the house. I pull away and refuse to go. At that, he strikes me so hard that my head reels and I find myself lying on the grass, with the stars and forested steeps whirling around me. As I lie there, I see my pale friend growling at my father. My father begins shouting at the wolf, trying to frighten him away. But the wolf puts his head back and howls; and suddenly, from every direction, huge, woolly white sheep-dogs come running, fiercer than wolves, barking and snarling, their ears down and lips drawn back to reveal ferocious teeth.

I see my father's expression turn to one of terror. These dogs are trained to kill. He turns and tries to run, but they leap at him, catching his arms and legs in their great jaws. One jumps at his face. He screams. I wish I could forget that sound, so raw, harsh and despairing! Part of me longs to help him but part of me wants only to watch, cold and passionless – and the cold part wins.

I see Father fall down among the long white backs of the dogs. They rip and tear at his flesh. I glimpse his face and throat, a mass of blood. He stops moving yet they go on worrying at him, tearing at his limbs.

Then my companion goes quietly between the marauding dogs. I am afraid they will attack him, too, for wolves are their great enemy. Instead they step aside to let him through, as if he were their pack leader. His tongue lolls out to lap blood from my father's throat.

I cover my eyes.

The next I know, my wolf is beside me again, urging me away with him into the trees. I see motes of light moving by the farm gate, lamps and torches. We hurry away, leaving the dogs to gnaw at my father's body ... and although I am shocked, I feel only the faintest ache of grief, as if this had been meant to happen.

My friend leads me once more across the wild terrain towards the castle. The journey seems longer than before, if possible. I stumble after his wraith-like form along deer-tracks and gorges, as if in a horrible dream. He must be a werewolf, I think, a man trapped in wolf's form ... nothing is impossible.

Some hours into the next day, we reach the castle. In the courtyard, with the stone walls and towers frowning down upon us, we recover the bundle of ash, collected on our first journey, from its hiding place. I carry it as he leads me along a narrow, arched passage to a ancient door of iron-clad wood. He indicates, with muzzle and paws, that I should open this door. A small wooden cross has been roughly nailed to it, and a whitish substance used to seal the crack between door and wall; the wolf growls with his head lowered and ears back to tell me most eloquently that this must be removed. The door is unlocked. I open it and pick the stuff away; it is a kind of putty, with other, papery matter mixed in. I find a piece of fallen slate to scrape the substance away and to prise the cross from the door.

The putty has a smell of old, stale garlic. Someone has tried to seal the castle with wards against evil … to stop something going in, or coming out?

I discard the scraps and the cross at the far end of the passage, in a dank, mossy crevice where wall and flagstones meet. As soon as the door is clear, the wolf bounds over the threshold and into a low corridor. I feel intense tiredness creeping over me, and with it coldness and unease. I trust my friend, but this place feels bad. Ancient, full of loss and dark memories.

He leads me down into a deep, ruined chapel, where faint rays of daylight fall through the broken roof. The air is thick with the odours of mouldering earth, mixed with the charnel odour of decay, as if a thousand rats have died here. And I see rows of graves and great tombs. A crypt! All is still and heavy with dust, as if nothing has been disturbed for centuries. So desolate. My companion leaves me and slips between the tombs, jumping up to look inside some. He looks less like a living animal than ever; he is spectral, skeletal. A thin high whine issues from his throat, hurting my ears. I move like a sleepwalker through this death, this horror, until all of it overwhelms me and I sink down on the earth floor. All I want is to sleep. But the wolf takes my skirts between his front teeth and pulls at me. As I look up, I find myself beneath a great tomb with one word engraved upon it.

DRACULA

I cannot encompass how I feel. The name means nothing and yet is familiar; it produces in me a sense of breathtaking awe and terror, and this feeling is so vast it seems to pass outside me to take in all the ancient chapel, the steep walls of the castle, the precipice and beyond, all the dark wolf-infested forest …

My companion will not let me rest. He snaps and snarls at me, until I get up, alarmed. In his jaws he brings an ugly brass urn from somewhere, a squat bowl with a lid, and directs me to put the ash from the shawl into this receptacle and keep it safe. Then he digs frantically at the earth, and instructs me to fill my shawl instead with loose soil. None of this makes sense. It only seems imperative that I obey. My hands are black with the malodorous stuff, and the bundle is so heavy that I can barely lift it. At last I collapse, weeping with exhaustion.

Then the wolf leads me, dragging my burdens, up a spiral stair into the body of the castle. I don't think I could remember the way back. He brings me to a room and leaves me, and here I remain. Where has he gone? Will he return? Now I am lying on a couch in a large apartment that I imagine was once light and pleasant with tapestries and rich furnishings; but now all is moth-eaten and draped with dusty webs. It is growing dark again. The waning moon rises. I ate all my food on the journey, so the only nourishment I have had is a bottle of wine I found, fifty years old and as dark as blackberries. It was good, but has made me heavy-headed.

What will become of me? I will die of cold and hunger, but nothing seems to matter as I rest here in this dream-like haze.

I look across an expanse of flagstones shining in the moonlight. In front and to the side are vast latticed windows, the stone mullions as delicate as lace, the night sky and the forests below the precipice all silvered by this mystical light. The whole window expands in my vision, a great lacy veil of white and silver against which motes of dust glitter and dance. I feel hands stroking me. Soft voices laugh and sigh like glass bells.

'Sister,' they say. 'Sister, sweet sister.'

I am cold. So very cold.

Morning

I must make this record quickly. My hands tremble and tears blur my eyes, but grief will pass and I must move on.

I fell asleep as I wrote, I think. Or as the waking dream took over, pen and journal fell to the floor. I remember shaking violently with coldness. The chill of the stones was seeping through my whole body. I wanted to touch the phantom hands of those women, to grasp them or to push them away, I know not which – but there was nothing there. I was alone with ghosts. I began to sob in fear.

Suddenly my friend was with me again! He climbed upon my couch and lay down beside me. His eyes were very bright, dazzling like the setting sun, and his tongue was warm as it rasped at my hands. (It always felt cold before). I was too tired to think or to be afraid. As I slipped into a doze, I felt that he was actually lying on me, to keep me warm. I felt his tongue and teeth scraping gently at my throat. My whole body seemed to tingle and tighten with a strange breathless feeling – not unpleasant – and although my eyes came open I could not move. Then it seemed to me that the spectral wolf was actually a man, a tall figure in black with long pallid hands.

Yet this human figure is not upon me but very far away, and although he reaches out to me he cannot touch me. I remember a feeling of desolation, rage, the urge of the dead to clasp vivid red-blooded life. I see long, muddled visions of battles, armies, mountains, a strange cavern where flames leap from an abyss and turn the very walls to red and bronze. And again the two steel knives flashing down towards me. Death, limbo, Mina

Harker's sweet presence passing me by, oblivious to my need. Longing, bitter anger, and then a thrust of will so firm and resolute it seems physically to pierce me. And all of this comes from the solitary pale figure in black. I am filled, as I was by the tomb, with dread and awe. At last, breathing heavily from the weight on my chest, I fall into deep, black sleep.

When I woke – half-an-hour ago – it was day again, I was once more shaking with cold and the wolf, my dear companion whom I have come to love, lay dead beside me.

I was grief-stricken to find him so. I wept bitterly, with my arms round his dear furry neck. But my tears stopped very suddenly as I heard a voice: heard it inside my head, not so much the words as the *intent*. Now I understand this much:–

The spirit that animated the wolf has passed, for a time at least, into me. Thus, it was never the wolf, the shell, that I loved, but the spirit inside. This is the soul – if soul is the right word; perhaps I mean will, or essence – of the tall man whom I do not yet know, but whom I will surely come to know. If I do not fail him!

He needs me. He tells me that it is all my responsibility now to help him be resurrected, reclothed in his own flesh. He had entrusted himself, body and soul, to me; so I am the only one now who can help him. I must not fail him. If I want to see him, to touch him in the flesh, I *cannot* fail him.

I feel that I have met the other half of myself, my shadow, my soul-mate. I will do anything for him.

My father, my uncle and Miklos are nothing to me now. I leave my family and follow a rockier path, like a saint. He will be my guide. My Dark Companion.

Cat and the Cold Prince

The all-night café was squeezed between two factories that soared up and up into the night. Grids of windows hung along the endless breadth and height of their walls, shining bleakly into the dark rain. The metallic chug of machinery never ceased. Crushed yet indomitable, the small café seemed to be bracing itself between the walls of an abyss. Its windows spilled oily yellow light onto the wet street.

Aurus stood alone, observing. His arms were folded over his pale full-length raincoat, his long hair tucked up beneath the crown of a wide-brimmed hat. He watched the comings and goings at the little oasis of light and all the time, the rhythm of industry shook the very ground under his feet.

This was as good a place as any.

All night, every night, Cat served fried food and coffee to factory workers going on or off shift, to administrators seeking sanctuary from their desks. Always the same bleary faces, same bland clothes of denim or neutral acrylics. No visible expressions of difference. Soaked in the perfume of chips, burgers and kebabs, marinated in fluorescent light and deadened by the drone of manufacture, Cat slaved and watched, like a goddess turning on a spit.

She'd rarely seen the day but from the glimpses she'd caught, she had missed nothing. Under the heavy, oily skies of New Encomium, day no longer came.

Her childhood in a home for surplus infants was a half-forgotten blur. The café owner, Dika, had plucked her from there when she was thirteen or so, but as a pseudo-parent he did not even come close; barely came close to being an employer. He owned her; that was all. Surly and volatile, he stopped short of actual abuse. He kept his distance enough that she feared him only a little and, thankfully, hardly knew him at all.

Cat drifted through the hours. She cooked, served, and cleaned with the energy of youth. When exhaustion felled her, she slept in the pantry. If this was life, she found no reason to engage with it. She had dreams in which she was running and running, but these dreams terrified her. Beyond the café lay one soaring abyss of factories after another, to the end of the world. To her there was no concept of escape, only of being lost in a dreadful labyrinth.

Casual staff came and went, but Cat stayed. All she feared was losing what little she had.

Dika was bearable. Lording it over his little empire, he even made her laugh sometimes. One day a new customer came in from the rain. He was tall, and had a commanding presence that his beige raincoat failed to disguise. His face was long and hawkish with strong bones, his eyes a chilly grey. As he leaned over the counter to pay for his coffee, a silver symbol on a chain spilled out over his collar and caught the light. Cat glimpsed a stylised human shape with a lion's head.

Dika went mad, swearing at the man in a savage whisper and threatening to report him for breach of the Visible Expression of Difference laws. Customers stared. Cat edged away. The man only smiled, tucked the offending jewellery out of sight, and slipped two crisp red notes of high value into Dika's hand.

The effect on Dika was gloriously predictable; an instant switch from indignation to smooth, obsequious avarice.

Cat suppressed a smile, but the stranger caught her eye. 'That seems to have made a visible difference,' he said. Holding Dika's eyes like a stage hypnotist, he added softly, 'Tell me, do you have an unused room of any description?'

Aurus hardly registered her at first. The café owner, with his black moustache, olive skin and grease-stained apron, was a bundle of energy and business sense. The girl was always in the background, nondescript and virtually silent.

After a few visits, though, Aurus began to think her silence interesting. Usually she wore the face of a mannequin, but sometimes he saw her smirk at some private joke. Except for utterances such as, 'Onion salad?' or, 'Three-forty, please,' she never spoke. What did that mean?

Perhaps nothing. Just another vacuous being in a vacuous world. All the same, Aurus began to watch her.

Her name was Cat and she had a fine, slim figure beneath the white banality of her uniform. She was about seventeen, he guessed, or even a gauche twenty. Sleek blonde hair curved around a slender, pale, elfin face. Her long green eyes were shiny and watchful. The café lights and the oily heat seemed to baste her in a golden sheen of her own sweat.

Aurus stood shivering in the heat, hating this place. Hating the city. Hating everything.

On Friday evenings, Cat observed the trickle of strangers who slipped past the counter and vanished into the rear corridor. To an indifferent eye it looked as if they were heading for the washrooms. In ones and twos they came, drably dressed and making eye contact with no one. She counted thirty-three in all.

Dika had hired out the café basement to them and she assumed it was as good a place as any for clandestine activities. Renting out the room meant good money, and a big risk.

Naturally it was forbidden to ask who they were or what they were doing. Forbidden even to think it. As each Friday night wore on, Cat went about her duties and tried to pretend they weren't there; but all the time she was acutely aware of their presence. She could feel them, like grit on her skin. She sensed their presence in the spaces between the metallic, throbbing chorus of the factories. Sometimes, if she lingered in the corridor that led to the kitchen, she thought she heard faint voices, snatches of song or chanting. Then she would hurry past, averting her eyes from the closed door.

She had heard rumours that such things went on: underground religious or political groups, hiding away in basements. They might be arranging fake flowers for all she knew, since – for the sake of fairness – even the most innocuous group meetings were frowned upon. Every year for many decades the law had been extended. The discouragement of religious festivals had eventually become a ban, along with the proscription of any form of religious symbol or clothing. Affiliation to political parties had followed, and at last the sweeping harvests of all self-expression. No more shirts bearing the names of pop stars or football teams, no individual clothing of any kind. Clubs of all kinds were banned, since, however innocent their activities, they were by their nature exclusive and divisive. All to avoid even the slightest risk of causing offence to those of a different persuasion, there were now, officially, no persuasions at all.

There was only industry.

Cat had never tasted those far-off days of Difference. There couldn't be many still alive who had. She couldn't even visualise what it was that might have offended her or others. A brightly-coloured scarf? The wrong kind of silver pendant? Why?

Sometimes she had a vision of men and women in a factory yard, dancing naked around a bonfire with ivy in their hair, but that only made her smile. The reality couldn't even be guessed at. It was deep, dark and sinister, a mystery that whispered and rustled with terrifying energy.

The closed door drew her. It was narrow and nondescript, tucked in behind mops, brooms and coat hooks. As the weeks rolled on, she passed closer and closer to the door on her trips to the kitchen. She began accidentally to brush against it, trailing her fingertips across the off-white paintwork. Once or twice, it swung ajar.

The first time, she fled in guilt. The second, she looked quickly around to make sure no one was watching. Then she edged towards the gap.

She saw the stairs leading down, a light glowing from below. She heard the low mysterious murmur of voices. She forgot herself, forgot her duties; tasted a wild excitement that spiked her heart and her loins with heat.

The next moment, Dika caught her arm and threw her back against the wall.

'You don't ever go near that door again,' he breathed into her face. 'You don't even think about it. You know what happens if the authorities find out?'

'Y-yes,' she gasped, choking on his ripe breath. 'No.'

'They close us down. They throw us in prison. All of us.' He shook her for emphasis, glaring into her eyes. '*All* of us.'

'I would never say a word!'

'But if *they* catch you,' he pointed at the door, indicating his illegal patrons, 'it will be worse.'

'Worse than this?' she whispered. She looked up, feeling her body vibrate with the grinding heartbeat of machinery. She meant the café, New Encomium, their existence.

Dika gave her a last shove and stepped back, looking her up and down with exasperation. 'You don't know how lucky we are.' He tapped his two middle fingers on her temple. 'You're a good worker, but there's something missing up here.' His voice became gentle, even sincere. 'It's for your own good I tell you, Cat, to keep away from that door. Perhaps they collect stamps. Perhaps they beat each other with spiky whips. It's not our business. I'm trying to protect you. You understand?'

'Yes.'

'You will tell no one, because there's nothing to tell. Nobody here but us.'

When she came to take his empty coffee cup away, she always watched him with those glistening green, impassive eyes. Aurus held her gaze. He felt he knew her now, well enough to play with her. She was innocent and special.

'What do you dream about, Cat?' he asked.

That stopped her in her tracks. She showed only the barest trace of surprise. 'I don't dream,' she said.

'You must. Everyone does. Do you dream about silence? Green fields and forests? Birds in flight?'

'I don't know what those things are,' she said.

He touched her wrist. She jumped at the iciness of his fingers. 'Do you dream about me?'

Cat stood at the top of the basement stairs, like a high-diver poised on the brink of a cliff. Behind her lay the banal glow of the café and kitchen. Below her, dark fathomless waters.

She saw figures moving in slow formation – dancing? – all in black; tight leather shining softly, sooty lace frothing at wrists, pale skin shining though black chiffon. Some sinuous pale creature she couldn't identify wove among them. A fiery light from below painted them with orange and crimson. She saw them all pause and rotate, in perfect formation, to look up at her. In their centre towered Aurus. She saw thirty-two upturned faces shining in the hellish light, shining with hunger.

Behind her, the door closed. The metallic factory throb became muffled. Someone seized her arms from behind and she found a wild-eyed, red-haired woman grinning over her shoulder.

'No remarks about cats and curiosity, but we wondered how long it would take you,' said the woman. 'We took bets.'

Cat caught her breath, said nothing. Below, she saw Aurus's harshly carved face tilt upwards a little as he regarded her. He wore black leather trousers and waistcoat, and over them a black, loose-sleeved open robe. His hair was long, spilling down his back like raven wings.

'Medea, be careful with her,' he said.

The woman released her, whispering, 'Show respect to the Cold Prince.'

'Come down, Cat,' Aurus called gently. 'Come and join us.'

Cat moved among them as if in a trance as they passed her from one to another around the circle. She felt their long fingers and hard, painted fingernails on her skin, breathed the heavy incense of their perfume. They looked human but were not; she sensed it, tasted it. Arriving, they had looked ordinary, but here they were transformed; their faces sharp and pale, with elongated eyes, their hair wildly styled and rich with ebony, scarlet and purple. The faces were not all beautiful, but they were all exotic. The shimmer of luscious velvety fabrics was delicious and strangely exciting. Around each pale throat hung the same symbol, the shapely female figure with the head of a wild cat.

She no longer recognised the basement, with its concrete floor and stacks of crates and boxes. The group had changed it with lamps and incense, with their presence. It was a glowing space without boundaries. Circles with intersecting lines and strange symbols shimmered beneath her feet.

Cat was acutely conscious of her own plainness, her dull white uniform, the frying smell impregnated into her skin and clothes. Her mouth was dry.

Someone gave her a drink from a purple glass goblet. The liquid was syrupy and strong, burning her throat. Defiant, she drank it all. Soon the room began to swim and everything she looked at floated in a thick golden light and was edged with flaring rainbows. She groaned. She was drowning.

She came face to face with Aurus and he loomed over her, a god hewn out of marble with eyes of silver ice. His fingers moved over her face, leaving prints of coldness where they'd rested.

'You smell of meat,' he stated. 'We'll cleanse you.'

The group closed in upon her. Cat stood helpless as intrusive hands unzipped and took away her clothing; apron, tunic and trousers, shoes and socks, underwear. She stood naked among them, aware of what was happening yet detached from it. Drugged, dreamy, watching herself in amazement. Male and female hands brushed gently over her; tongues touched glossy, painted lips. She expected to feel teeth in her flesh.

Deep within her a tide of fear began to rise, only to break into harmless foam on the sea-wall of drugged acceptance.

A slender woman in black satin came through the crowd and on a golden chain she was leading a leopard. If not a leopard, then some similar creature, a big sleek fierce-looking feline. Cat had seen such things – in old, old films sometimes shown on the TV that Dika kept in the kitchen – but she had never imagined that such a being in reality would be so solid, so beautiful and terrifying.

Its fur was snow-white and marked with spots of cream and pale gold. Its eyes, too, were golden and as cold as Aurus's grey ones.

The woman had a finely-carved, hard yet tragic face, and wings of black hair. Over her perfect satin-sheathed body she wore a cape of fur, like the pelt of the creature she handled. She bent and unclipped the chain from its collar.

Waves of fear washed inside Cat, but failed to move her. She stood and waited as the leopard came to her, began to sniff at her. She smelled of beef and lamb and bacon, and they laid her like bait for its hunger …

The beast reared lightly and put its front paws on her shoulders. Magnified, she saw the gleam of its fangs, the redness of its lips and a blue-black, gleaming tongue. Its breath had a soft, sweet scent, like clean skin.

The creature began to lick. First her forehead, cheeks and neck. She winced, laughing with the peculiar tortured mirth of being tickled. The dark souls around her gasped, perhaps with wonder that she simply stood there, passive and fearless. The tongue lapped lower, scratching deliciously at her skin; hollow of her throat, both arms, all around and over her breasts, working down over her abdomen and into the cleft between her thighs.

The intense pleasure of its muscular delving shocked her. Her arms stiffened and her head fell back. She gasped and cried out. The audience sighed with her.

The leopard dropped to all fours and completed its careful washing, over thighs and knees and calves, down to the tips of her toes then moving over her buttocks to finish with her back. The tongue worked patiently until it had lapped up every drop of juice and sweat.

Cat stood shivering from the moisture drying on her body. There was a spattering of applause from the watchers. Medea and a skinny young man brought a black gown, slipped it over her shoulders, wrapped it around her and tied it with a cord. Through a glaze of unreality she saw the fur-clad woman clipping the chain onto the leopard's collar, then standing proud at Aurus's side. They could have been brother and sister.

The Cold Prince Aurus came forward, moving slowly through a haze of rainbows. 'Do you know who we are?' he asked.

'No,' said Cat.

'I think you do.'

'I really don't.'

His eyes pierced hers. His presence was intimidating, but she faced him squarely, refusing to be controlled.

'Perhaps now you know how it feels to enter the other-world for a time?' he said. 'The grind of industry and this bleak, hateful world turn to paper and are torn away – just through simple ecstasy.'

'So you come here to play-act,' she said, aware she was slurring her words. 'To dress up, take drugs and have sex. I've heard about things like this. Dika thinks I'm an idiot, but I listen and I hear more than he knows.'

'Do you disapprove?' His eyes turned colder.

'No. What you do is nothing to me.'

'Nothing? Play-acting?' He paused. 'Are you afraid of us?'

'Yes.'

'You don't look it. Your mouth proclaims innocence, yet your eyes tell a different story.' The Cold Prince was trying to stare her down. She didn't know how to answer, but she wouldn't look away. She saw fine lines of pain around his eyes. Eventually he said, 'If the ecstasy were intense enough, we could make it real.'

'Make what real?' she asked, but he turned away.

The souls began to sing, some of them clapping and humming a rhythm beneath the insistent melody. Cat had the weirdest feeling that this had all happened before. An image pressed just on the edge of her memory, impelling her instincts. As they began to dance, she danced with them, hips swaying, arms weaving over her head, ever more wildly until she turned dizzy and fell.

Aurus caught her and set her upright again.

'You do appreciate,' he said thinly, 'that now you have seen us, we cannot let you go?'

Cat awoke in darkness. Her head ached; she felt ghastly, hungover. There was cold concrete beneath her. When she tried to sit up, her head hit metal and she swore with pain.

Lamp-glow appeared and she saw a jumble of shapes that quickly resolved themselves. A woman was coming towards her, bearing a lamp. Cat saw the basement with its piled boxes; and then she saw that there were bars enclosing her in a six-foot square space.

They had meant it. They had put her in a cage.

Cat rose to her knees, squinting against the light. The woman, Aurus's sister, squatted down on long balletic legs and looked her in the eye.

'I'm Ginia,' she said. 'I am sorry, but we really do have to keep you here. You're part of us now.'

'Is there any water?'

'Of course.'

A bottle from the café came through the cage bars. She drank.

'You can't keep me. Dika will miss me. He'll come and let me out.'

Ginia only smiled. 'I'm sorry,' she said again, and rose to move away

'Who is Aurus?' said Cat, desperate to keep her there. 'Why do they call him the Cold Prince?'

'There is always a Cold Prince,' said the woman. 'And I am the Ice Queen.'

Cat knelt up, holding the bars of her cage. 'You're his sister?'

Ginia smiled. 'His wife.'

The words were a slap. Cat must have made some visible reaction, for the woman's smiled grew thinner. 'You're jealous. Did you think he wanted you? Did you think you could thaw him?'

'No,' Cat whispered. 'All I want is for you to let me go.'

'That's what we all want. Escape.' The Ice Queen moved away. 'I'll leave the lamp. Try to sleep where you're supposed to sleep.'

Cat glanced round and saw that there was a low flat couch in the cage, padded and upholstered in red fabric. A blanket was heaped on it. She must have fallen out.

Ginia said, 'I'll come again with breakfast – yours and his.'

'His?' Then Cat realised there was another cage joined to hers, and in it, the leopard. His curved back was pressed against the bars and she'd been sleeping so close to him that he could easily have reached through and swiped her with a paw.

She couldn't bring herself to lie on the couch again; it looked like a butcher's slab. Instead she crouched in the far corner of the cage, shivering and miserable. She glanced at the ceiling, at the stairs where she could sense her guard, Ginia, waiting in the darkness.

'Dika will come for me,' she mouthed to herself, but she must already have been missing for hours, and he must know where she was, and yet he had not come. Finally she realised.

'He's sold me,' she said out loud.

Cat put her head on her knees and came close to tears. Close, but couldn't actually cry. There was an empty pit inside her; knowing that even if she escaped, there was nothing to escape to.

Who has sold you?

The voice spoke inside her head, making her jump. She looked up and saw the leopard sitting up, gazing at her with intense, frosted-gold eyes.

'My – my boss,' she said hesitantly.

The head tilted and the eyes narrowed a little in reaction. The voice was definitely the leopard's. *You must feel betrayed. Do you?*

'Not really. Dika would take money for anything. It's only what I would have expected.'

Now we're both prisoners. Are you cold? You look cold and sad.

'I am.' She gave a faint brittle laugh. 'You?'

Just sad. My fur is warm. Come here, and I'll warm you.

'Eat me, more like. You look hungry. I'll bet I tasted nice earlier.'

She heard a rumbling purr of amusement. *You did.*

'Eat me, then.' She uncurled and moved to the side of the cage where the leopard sat. 'I don't care.'

He came to the bars and pressed close. She put her hands through and buried them in the soft fur of his flank. His scent was softly musky and comforting. 'I'm Cat,' she said.

I'm not.

'No, it's my name.'

I know. It was a joke, a very bad one. They call me Leonid. But I'm not an animal.

'You look like one. You feel like one.'

But I'm not. This isn't my true shape. Can't you tell?

Leonid turned his beautiful head and looked straight at her. Behind his eyes was an intelligent soul. Her mind reeled. Again she felt the press of memories that would not quite enter consciousness.

After a time she said, 'So these people aren't human, and you're not a cat.'

Any more than you are. You're one of us.

'Who is "us"?'

You don't yet remember?

'There's nothing to remember!' Frustration made her angry. 'I don't know what any of you are talking about!'

His whiskers shivered with a sigh. *We look human but we are ancient. We have been called elves, demons, faerie-folk, gods, Vaettir, Vaethyr, Aelyr, many other names. We're old beyond the earliest reach of history, princes of the unseen realms. There is no division between us and nature, and our energy is elemental; some of us can still change shape ... Cat, you are frowning. I am telling the truth.*

'But I can't believe it,' she said. 'Or part of me can't; the other part feels as if I already know everything you're saying.'

Leonid's tail flicked and his thoughts poured in faster. *Yes, that's how it was for me. Some of them – the most ancient – have always known what they are. Others, like us, lost our way and our memory, and we thought we were born fully human, surface dwellers ... but when they come and touch us and remind us, the light goes on inside and then you can never turn it off.*

Intense, suppressed fear radiated from him. He felt more trapped than she did. 'What happened to you, Leonid?' She spoke gently, caressing his warm neck.

I don't know. They swept me up and in the heat of the moment, I changed shape; to

175

please them, to please myself, to prove I could: and now I cannot change back. It happened a long time ago. Now I'm part of the rituals and I play the role.

'Rituals? Is that what they do here? What does it mean?'

If you will let me finish the story: once, the ancient ones lived alongside the surface dwellers and we passed freely in and out of the other-worlds as we desired. Over the centuries, as surface dwellers grew powerful, our freedom dwindled and somehow … It must have taken us unawares, as if the world spun a thick cage and closed around us, sealing us like pearls in an oyster. The world changed. New Encomium is our tomb. We must escape or die.

Strange feelings and images were budding inside her. That she felt paradoxically terrified and tranquil at the same time was not due to any drug. It was her nature, her gift. 'They can't escape,' she said sadly. 'No amount of dressing up and chanting will change that.'

They're not play-acting. They believe they can escape to another world through ritual.

'Magic?'

It would seem so, to surface dwellers.

'Do you believe it?'

The glittering eyes dulled. *I don't know. We must do what's required. Forgive me.*

'What are we?' She clung closer to him, only caring for his life, not her own. The knowledge came from a deep well inside her; not from anything she'd learned on Dika's TV. 'We're sacrifices, aren't we? Sacrifices.'

On the seventh day, Aurus visited the captive goddess. He found her in calm spirits, sitting cross-legged on her couch, bathed in lamplight that turned her luminous. Each night, a different member of the order had watched over her, and all reported that she'd been docile, calm and watchful throughout her imprisonment. She and Leonid had slept on the floor, hugging each other as best they could through the bars of the cage, the girl whispering into his fur.

'That is as it should be,' said Aurus.

He moved to the cage and called, 'Cat?'

Her eyes flew open, glistening pale green, gathering all available lamplight and beaming it back at him.

'It will be tonight,' he said. 'I don't ask your forgiveness. You must understand that you are an essential part of this and therefore there can be no way out. But there's no need to be afraid.'

She only stared back, unblinking. 'I'm not afraid, Cold Prince.'

When Cat woke again, the door of her cage stood open. Her couch had been moved and Leonid's cage was empty. The whole basement was bathed in a red-gold glow and she could not resist the lure of freedom.

As she stepped out, black-clad figures came out of nowhere to claim her. Her robe was taken; Medea and Ginia washed her with scented waters and left her standing there, naked. Chanting swelled, carrying her along, sweeping her into its rhythm. She saw swirls of magical symbols spiralling on the floor, and at the centre stood the couch, on fire with the light of lamps and candles.

She felt as she had when they had first drugged her; but this time she was clear-headed, in a trance of her own making. A strong and serpentine power moved within her.

Murmuring as they appeared out of the darkness, the ancient ones came to take her. Female hands held her firmly, turning and easing her backwards over the padded couch until she was lying on her back, a sacrifice on a satin altar.

Ginia led the leopard on a chain and he padded forward softly, eyes intent, whiskers scenting her. She did not realise what was meant to happen until the last moment, when he began to rub his silken cheeks along the insides of her thighs, to ply her with his tongue. She felt the briefest pang of shock, gone in an instant. There was nothing to fear; the ritual must take place; and because of that they were more than beasts, more than human.

As he mounted her he looked into her eyes. She saw the trapped soul within the beast, and loved him. *I'm sorry. Trust me.*

She thrust her hands into his fur and let the pleasure and the energy pour through her. They were transported in a fierce golden sphere of energy, god and goddess in union.

Through the fire she was dimly aware of the thundering of feet on the floor above them. Faint shouts of, 'Police! This is a Difference raid.' Visions of terror-frozen customers, of Dika pale and distraught, helpless as the Difference squad searched, kicking down doors until they found their way into the basement, uncovered the juicy red-handed evidence of illegal assembly ...

But it was all swirling, distant. Cat could only hear her own heartbeat, feel the slight weight of Leonid on her and the waves of pleasure building, piercing her. Her skin was burning. In her mind she felt Leonid's climax as well as her own and the ecstasy was intense, unbearable. Inside her, tension broke and she knew who she was; became *herself.* Fiery lights seared the air. They convulsed together and the world broke open. Green light spilled through a sparkling rent in the air.

The basement door shook. Police dogs bayed.

Aurus and the others were running, crowding through the portal. Leonid and Cat fell off the couch together, scrambled up and followed them.

Silence.

There was a flood of emerald light; the saturated green of trees, misty rain turning the forest to one green veil after another. They stood in a new world; an ancient world. The dew-soaked wildwood around them gleamed with blue light.

'We're home,' said Aurus.

Cat looked about for Leonid, couldn't find him. Then she saw something pale unfolding from the ground. A white leopard pelt lay discarded on the ground and a young man stood in front of her, naked and glistening as if new-born.

'Cat,' he said, smiling.

'This way,' said Aurus. No smile touched his face but an intense look of triumph sat on the haughty bones. Even Ginia's face had lost its hardness. He strode off and his followers ran after him, dancing and singing, hair flying like banners. Cat and Leonid walked after them.

Where the trees ended there was a steep hillside, a green landscape beyond, and in the far distance, a silver-blue city glittering. 'There is our destination, our home, the ancient towers of …'

'Are you mad?' said Cat.

Aurus turned to stare at her. 'Say on.'

'You escape one city, only to plunge straight back into another? You can do what you like, but I'm not going there.'

'You must.' He spoke kindly and sternly, expecting his will to be obeyed as always.

'Why must I?'

'You're part of us now, Cat. You've become our goddess, our muse. We can't let you go.'

'You have no choice,' she said.

The grey eyes shifted, thoughtful and implacable. 'Your ingratitude is amazing, considering that I have just rescued you.'

'We rescued *you*!' Cat exclaimed. 'You used us! And now you expect gratitude, subservience? Is your name Dika? I've lived all I need of that life. You have no power over me, Aurus, any of you. I can shed you all like a skin and simply run away.'

The Cold Prince continued to glare down upon her, but the look was impotent. 'Where to?'

'The wildwood looks inviting. I shall never set foot in a city again.'

Aurus had tears in his eyes. One fell, catching the light.

She stepped away, almost dancing as she went. The wet grass trailed over her feet, thrilling. The ancient ones watched, but no one tried to hold her. When Leonid began to follow her, she put a hand to his bare chest and stopped him.

'No,' she said sadly, 'I can only love you as you were. I don't know you in this shape.'

'I'm still the same.'

'No. Not without that. She pointed to the glorious white and cream bundle of the pelt. 'It's up to you.'

She felt her own skin turning to silk, her teeth lengthening, every sense sharp and sensuous. The power of her true self surged, sun-bright. Cat plunged into the virgin forest and ran, for the sheer pleasure of running, into the heart of the mystery.

Persephone's Chamber

Note: Fela's story later expanded into part of Grail of the Summer Stars.

I see a city of gleaming black stone that shines with jewel-colours; crimson, royal purple and blue. I see labyrinthine passages and rooms where you can lose yourself for days, months.

Lofty pillars. Balconies onto a crystal-clear night full of stars, great sparkling white galaxies like flowers. Statues of winged men looking down with timeless eyes. I want to stand on those balconies and taste the breeze and hear the stars sing and be washed in the light of the moon. There will be ringed planets, and below – the tops of feathery trees blowing gently. An undiscovered land full of streams, with birch trees in spring green, and oak and hazel – and their elemental guardians, slender birch-white ladies with soft hazel brown hair – and mossy banks folding into water.

And through this citadel walk graceful men and women with lovely elongated faces and calm, knowing eyes – with a glint of mischief – and they are perfect and know it and they are imperfect and know it. They have seen too much. They might wear robes of medieval tapestry or jeans and a shirt but you would never mistake them for human. It's so much more than beauty. Look at them once and you can't look away. These are Aetherials in their oldest city, Tyrynaia.

They have been building the citadel for thousands of years and it will never be finished. Upwards it spreads, and outwards, and down into the rock below. Their seat of power. Their home.

They take the names of gods, on occasion.

And sometimes they are heroic and help the world.

And sometimes they are malicious and turn it upside down.

Some might be vampires. It's hard to tell.

In the deepest depths of the citadel, a ceiling of rock hangs over an underground lake and here is Persephone's Chamber. She welcomes and cares for those who come, soul-sick with despair, seeking solace, rest and sleep. Here they need not speak, only sit on the black marble lip with their feet on the thick glass, and watch the lake and the luminous fish beneath, which is like a reflection of the sky far above. If you lie down in despair, Persephone will lie down with you.

–Diary of Faith Fox [From Elfland]

While she was alone, the dark maiden Persephone – who liked that name best of all those she was given – undertook her habitual purification of her domain. She swept the shiny-dark surface of the floor to clear any lingering energies. In the centre, she paid special attention to the ledges where her guests would sit in contemplation, as if gathered on benches framing a sunken pond. The ledge was worn smooth, and warm to the touch. She stepped down and knelt to polish the recessed slab of crystal: her clear window onto Meluis, the lake beneath.

Persephone paused, sensing the approach of a new visitor.

Someone was tumbling downwards through the streets, walkways and terraces, descending the long flights of steps that connected the city's many layers. Reduced to a pale soul-essence, the newcomer darted like a terrified cat between the legs of Aelyr citizens in her flight. No one noticed her. She was a ghostly streak against dark rock. Persephone sensed her name and the heat of her panic, but no other information.

The fleeing soul escaped the bustle of the upper layers and plunged onwards through channels of wet black rock, into lightless tunnels and caverns where few ever came. Deep into the city's secret heart she came, a ghostly streak against dark rock. Persephone noted, without surprise, that she had no idea how she'd come here. There was nothing in her mind but fear, and the terrible cold reek of water drawing her like gravity into the deepest subterranean caves of the underworld.

The dark maiden continued her work. She lit fresh candles in the niches all around the walls until the chamber danced with multiple shadows. She poured crimson wine into small golden cups.

Presently, without a sound, the newcomer arrived.

She was an indistinct, whitish shape the size of a lynx, sliding around the uneven walls of the cave to a recess far from the edge of the underground lake. Her golden eyes were feral. She shrank in on itself as if trying to vanish, while at the same time coiled ready to defend herself with lashing rage.

Persephone let her be. She never approached her guests until they were ready. She acknowledged the visitor with a gentle glance and turned back to her tasks.

Everyone who came here was broken, but each was broken in a different way.

The deepest chamber was a black obsidian cave, dappled with watery light from below. Fela slunk in, clinging to the contours of the cave-wall until she found a recess. There was almost nothing left of her. She pressed her elemental form into the angle where floor met wall, wishing herself invisible.

She had no idea where she was, still less how she'd found the place. A frantic flight through darkness. Before that – nothing. A confused mass of horror. A nightmare.

Whoever she'd been before – it was lost. Some appalling event had reduced her to a wisp of animal terror. All she knew was that her soul-essence had been severed from her body. That she was dead, and yet not dead.

Worse. Suspended in some strange half-death.

Hiding in this echoing black space that rippled with soft lights, with no conscious memory of how she'd found her way. Only a wordless, dream-like knowledge that she belonged here. This was the last refuge, a cave at the end of the world. There was nowhere else.

The source of the glow was an oblong hole in the cave floor, perhaps fifteen feet long, like a large sunken pond. The ever-moving light made the chamber seem full of water. She imagined she lay at the bottom of the sea, all breath and life crushed out by the water's weight.

Fela became aware of a figure moving around the chamber; a female of some Aelyr affiliation she didn't recognise. The woman had a lovely, ageless face with bright skin, thick black hair falling loose, a long soft tunic tied at the waist, an open robe of the same raven black worn over it. As she moved, the outer robe showed flashes of a coloured lining. Blood red.

That hue made Fela tremble. It was wrong. The dark maiden said nothing. She looked at Fela with grave, kind eyes of darkest purplish-brown – actually *saw* her, as no one during her nightmare flight had seen her.

The look communicated a firm message: '*You are safe here.*'

Fela dared not believe it.

The jade glow arising from the floor transfixed her. It spoke of something deep, mysterious, and ineffable. She didn't want to look, but had no choice. A mesh of soft blue-green radiance reflected from every surface, creating an overlapping, hypnotic rhythm.

After a time, the dark maiden spoke softly. 'I'm called Persephone. Welcome, Fela. No one will disturb you here. Speak or be silent, as you wish.'

Fela recalled her own name only when the woman spoke it. She didn't question how she knew; she was the guardian of the chamber, and therefore knew everything.

Fela tried to speak and was surprised when a faint rusty whisper came out. 'That light, where is it from?'

'From Meluis, the underground lake. It shines always.'

'Make it stop!'

The dark maiden blinked. 'I can't, but it won't harm you. Most find the light soothing.' She held out a hand. 'Come and see.'

Persephone's voice was steady and mellow, the sweetest voice Fela had ever heard. But her dread was stronger and she clung to the cave wall.

'No,' she whispered. 'No.'

With a grave look, the maiden nodded, and turned away.

Fela crouched where she was and waited. Pressed into her niche along the wall, she was as safe as she could hope to be. Slowly the fear sank back inside her. Still there but quieter now, like a steadily beating heart. As helpless as a wounded animal with no rational thoughts and no memories, she closed her eyes and slept, half-dreaming. Whispering her forgotten past to herself.

Aurata leads me into the citadel amid a laughing group of Felynx. I'm used to the soft waterways of the wetlands, to solitude and twilight, so I'm overwhelmed. The Felynx are creatures of the sun and the stars; the Tashralyr dwell in the dusky, damp forests. We are not enemies. We simply coexist, fiery sun and remote shadow. Yet ... who can resist the temptation of being cheered and celebrated for our speed, taken among the golden ones and celebrated, almost worshipped—if only for a year or two?

Aurata and her brothers, Mist and Rufus, are so beautiful. They seem to delight in my innocence, my wide-eyed stares at every new sight. Because I'm unused to holding a two-legged shape like theirs, I feel insubstantial, like a creature of rippling silk amid their golden solidity.

Aurata takes me through one vast hall after another. There seem to be no walls, only columns holding up ceilings of light and gauze. I'm dazzled. Dozens of beautiful wildcat masks turn to stare as we pass. I walk taller, reminding myself I am here to represent the Tahsralyr, and for that reason I feel proud. I move among the Felynx with all the grace I can gather, like a column of cool water sliding between them.

I find Mist at my shoulder – first congratulating me on my victory and then murmuring a warning. "Be careful of my brother and sister. They will play games with you. I'd urge you to flee the palace now, if you would – but if you stay, be wary."

Mist is different. He appears lonely. He has a paler complexion and darker hair than his siblings, as if there is more water than fire in his soul-essence. Does he have many lovers or none? He is a mystery. I shouldn't even contemplate the question.

His concern touches me. More than that: his kindness is a jewel in my heart that will stay forever.

Soon I discover what he means. Rufus is the most beautiful of the Felynx, but I'm afraid of him because I've heard tales. I fear that if he can't seduce me away from Aurata, he might try to lame me instead.

Then I drink too much spicy wine. Needing fresh air, I become lost in the endless halls of the palace and Rufus appears at my side, all smiles and flowing russet mane. He tries to kiss me, but when I push him away he only laughs. It's something else he wants. 'Come with me, swift Fela, to a view a sacred sight that few are privileged to see.'

'Please, my Lord Rufus, stop,' I whisper, daring to be impudent. 'From what I hear, half the population of Azantios is familiar with the sight.'

Rufus throws back his head in delight. 'I'm not referring to my personal attributes, as pleasurable as I'm sure you'd find them.' He puts his lips to my ear. 'I'm talking about the sacred heart of the Felynx.'

He guides me up secret, winding ways to a spire at the summit of the mountain. The topmost chamber is covered by a crystal dome, and in the centre, the Felixatus stands on a column the height of my chest.

I see spheres within spheres, with a web of metalwork securing the structure to a base that is carved with Felynx symbols. The mechanism shines so brightly that I can't look away.

Then I understand. The Felixatus shines with the soul-sparks of a million Felynx. They are falling into it like dust from the stars as I watch.

Rufus is talking, though I barely hear him. 'This is a place so sacred that the only ones allowed to set foot here are my parents and the Keeper, who as you see is absent. Consider yourself privileged, little swamp dweller. You're standing in the holy of holies.'

I am uneducated, but not stupid. I realise he's brought me here for the sake of mischief, just because he can. It pleases him to commit sacrilege. But he assumes he can control me, when in fact he can't.

I walk towards the Felixatus. The soul-light dazzles and mesmerises. I hear Rufus exclaim, 'No, don't touch it!' – too late.

The sacrilege has gone too far, even for him.

I lay my hands on the casing and at once I know.

Everything.

When Fela awoke, someone new was there. Panic jolted her and she sat up – the dream forgotten – still in her semi-feline form; not remembering, yet, that she'd ever had any other. From this low angle, the glowing pool was foreshortened to a green slot in the flat black floor. By its radiance, she saw a man lying along the far rim as if he'd fallen headlong. His arm was curled under his head, his face hidden. He lay so still that she thought, at first, that he was dead.

Then she saw a tremor in his shoulders. He was weeping.

For a long time, Persephone left him alone. She watched over him, but asked no questions. Fela remained where she was, observing. She quailed to see the man lying so close to the lip. It was like witnessing someone carelessly asleep on the very edge of a cliff, oblivious to the drop beneath.

A broken heart. That was his story, much later when he dragged himself upright and sat, head drooping, on the rock edge above the lake. His feet rested on a surface Fela couldn't see and he stared down into the water she dared not confront. Abandoned by some heartless lover, he'd come from the city above to nurse his misery in the darkness. Persephone tended gently to him as the words flowed from his throat in a torrent of grief.

As he told his story, another woman came. Her long fair hair was pulled back severely from her face, emphasising gaunt cheekbones, and the hollows and shadows around her haunted eyes. Her hands trembled as she reached out to Persephone, who took her in a firm embrace and said, 'Gentle heart, welcome, and rest as long as you need.'

Fela leaned forward to catch their conversation, relinquishing contact with the rock wall behind her.

'You're always here,' said the woman, tears creeping from her reddened eyes.

'Always,' Persephone agreed.

'I'm here too often.'

A slight smile. 'Are you?'

'When this heaviness of spirit comes over me, there is nowhere else to be.' She held up a hand at the chamber ceiling. 'They berate me for being unhappy – how dare I be sorrowful, in the very heart of our sacred domain? I can't make them understand. I don't even try, because this is my burden, not theirs. My shame.'

'No shame. Never feel that,' the dark maiden answered.

She held the woman's gaze, and Fela understood, as clearly as if Persephone had spoken aloud: this was a place where no one would be judged. Persephone took the woman's hand, and led her to sit beside the man.

Fela shivered. Her whole insubstantial body hurt. She lay down again, shaking, and then she felt Persephone's gaze on her, from across the chamber, like physical warmth. Simply holding her steady.

The fair Aelyr woman was silent while the man finished his tale. Then she began to speak, a rambling, anguished description of an unrelenting desire to kill herself. But she was Aelyr, she complained; one of the ancient elite race of immortals. She could not die. Not properly, at least; not finally.

'Is it so wrong, to want oblivion?' she said. 'I crave it, yet I fear it. I could take a knife to my own throat and bleed out my life – but my soul-essence would still be aware, wouldn't it? There might be no respite from consciousness at all. I don't want to continue indefinitely! I don't wish for one life after another. Nor do I want to fade into the Spiral, no longer myself yet still aware, part of some mass of energy that never rests. I dread it!'

'I've never met an Aetherial who admits to fearing his or her own existence,' put in the man. He sounded intrigued, now focussed on a problem other than his own. 'Most Aelyr long for the final dissolution.'

'Do they? Are you sure? Am I the only one who feels this terror?'

'To merge with the forces that created us! How could there be any more blissful form of being?' The man frowned. 'It's natural.'

'Then why am I afraid?'

'I don't know.'

Quivering, Fela murmured, 'You're *not* the only one who fears this. Being torn out of yourself and dropped into darkness … What could be more horrifying? Who would not be afraid?' She spoke too softly for them to hear. Only Persephone heard, and flashed a kindly glance her way.

Dappled green light played over the cave walls. The man and the woman talked and argued, their eyes reflecting blue-green fire from the lake. Fela listened. Meanwhile Persephone moved around the chamber, lighting fresh candles, bringing them golden cups full of red cordial, asking nothing of them.

'But what does it mean to exist forever?' the woman implored.

'What does it mean to exist without love?' the man countered. 'You're asking for an answer no one can give.'

'I know there's no answer.' Her voice was calmer, and she pressed the man's hand with her own. 'I can bear it, as long as we can bring our pain here, where no one judges us. Persephone's acceptance is everything.'

The man said, 'Good Lady Persephone, have you no advice? Won't you stop us wallowing in misery, and thrust us back onto the path of shining Aelyr perfection?'

'There are countless others to do that,' she answered wryly. 'This is a place where nothing is demanded of you. That's all.'

'There must be more.'

'Only if you need more.'

The man and woman drank from their golden cups in companionable silence. Presently they rose and left, hand in hand.

Fela drowsed.

Others came to contemplate Meluis, seating themselves on the rim, or reclining along it on one elbow. Some needed to talk; others were silent, staring into the limpid light. They sipped Persephone's red cordial and ate the fruits and small cakes she offered. Some stayed a long time. Days went by … or a single, beautiful evening moving in a never-ending circle.

Ultimately they left, one by one, leaving their burdens behind in the chamber.

With a start, Fela awoke properly. She had a lingering impression that many others had come to confess their fears and sorrows while she slept, but they were all gone now. Only the dark maiden remained.

Fela began to edge across the cave floor, which was smooth and cool beneath her outstretched form. She crawled flat on her stomach, thinking she'd feel safer like that, less likely to fall in. She felt as if her skin were stretching, cracking to reveal new flesh. It hurt. Anxiety rose but she pushed herself on, inch by inch, until her head crested the lip of the pool and she was looking down at a glass slab, and at the lapping waves beneath.

Through the thick clear layer of crystal she saw the body of water, a vast tank of aqueous light with no boundaries, no bottom. The surface glittered, washing against the underside of the glass. The first few feet were transparent, but further down the water turned opaque like cloudy emerald, hinting at unimaginable depths, unbearable weight.

Terror surged and choked her.

She imagined falling in, sinking forever through a fissure in the underworld into an ocean abyss, eternally drowning but never dying ... She jerked in a spasm of horror. Her form was changing, unfolding. She tried to scream. Only a rasp emerged.

Panic unravelled her. Knowing that, in her previous forgotten life, she'd been tricked, betrayed. Turning round and round in some desolate marshland, trapped, but no one there to help her. And then a powerful force, dragging her, pushing her down until water closed over her face. The last silvery bubbles of her breath were rushing up towards the surface. Murky green water swallowed her, sucking her down ...

Hands pushing her down.

Then the dark maiden was there, holding her. From a position high on the cave ceiling, she watched herself screaming in Persephone's arms.

Persephone held her as she gasped and sobbed. Fela thrashed as her feline-form changed, limbs straightening, fur turning to smooth skin, hair flowing from her head. All of her terror, confusion and pain flowed into Persephone and she took it, absorbing Fela's horror into the endless shadowy labyrinth of her being.

At last Fela lay still across her lap, exhausted. She was a slender, pale girl, all silver and pearly white within a cowl of shimmering mist. Still insubstantial. An orphan soul.

Finally she said, 'Someone killed me. They lured me to a marsh and drowned me. I was ... my old self was ... murdered.'

Persephone asked carefully, 'Do you remember why?'

'No.' The girl's face contracted in pain. 'I try, but there's nothing there. Sometimes a fleeting dream ...'

'Tell me.'

'I can't. I try, but it all slips away. I saw something I should not have seen, and for that ... they drowned me.'

'You died on the surface world, but Aelyr can't die – not truly. And so your soul-essence was drawn here, deep into the Spiral. You could have gone to the Mirror Pool, the place of rebirth – yet you came to me instead. That shows great determination.'

'Or despair. Blind instinct brought me to you. It wasn't conscious.'

'Well, that is how Aelyr find me. Fela, if you can't recall what happened, it doesn't matter. You can go forward into a new existence and leave the old one behind. Forgetting can be a mercy.'

Fela was quiet for a time, her thoughts burning. Then she said, 'No. I need the truth.' Her body tensed, and Persephone shared her vision – a flash of city spires, white and golden. Feeling herself in racing form, down on all fours in cheetah-shape, her long strides eating the ground, a soft roar in her ears – the cheers of a crowd? – then it was gone. Fela's memory was little more than a cobweb, or else too painful to face. 'I was … an athlete, I think. That's all I know. Whom did I offend?'

'Perhaps no one,' said Persephone.

'But I can't bear not knowing! Not just for my own sake. What if they do the same to someone else?'

'Is that your responsibility? They killed you.'

'And I can't turn away and pretend it doesn't matter. It does. I don't know why, but this is important. Not just to me, but … I don't know.' She pulled herself from Persephone's arms and knelt facing her. 'What should I do?' She laughed. 'No. I heard you tell the others that you never tell them what to do.'

'No, but I can suggest a choice.'

'Please.'

'Dear heart, this is a place of refuge, but you can't stay forever. Some decide they will, and I don't try to prevent them – but no one ever does. A stronger force always pulls them back to the upper world, back to life. But you have a choice.' Persephone pointed upwards, indicating the city above, the realms of the Spiral that lay around it. 'You may go out into the Spiral, find a rock or tree or hill in which to slumber until you're ready for rebirth. Then you will be drawn to the Mirror Pool, and begin your spiral journey outwards again, towards your next life.'

'And if I do that, I'll forget?'

'Yes. And that would be the easiest path.' Then she pointed down at the glass floor. 'However, if you want the hard and thorny path, a way to solve your mystery and resolve the wrong done to you, you can swim deep into the lake and leave through Meluis.'

She saw Fela shudder. 'Is that the only way?

Persephone nodded. 'The surest.'

'I used to love the water. Now it terrifies me. I'm afraid of drowning. Again.'

'You will not drown. They say Meluis joins all the waters of the Spiral. All the streams and lakes and seas flow into Meluis, even the Mirror Pool itself. It's not the water you need to fear, but what you'll find beyond. Are you ready to face your murderer again? To relearn the truths that were so painful your mind has wiped them out?'

Fela was quiet. Her silvery face was pinched by fear and doubt, all the rawness of the betrayal she'd endured. 'I must,' she said.

'Then you've made the choice,' said Persephone.

Fela noticed, as she knelt on the stone lip, that the lining of Persephone's robe had changed from the blood-red of death to bright spring green. Strange, but she felt no need to ask how or why.

Fela leaned down towards the glass slab and made herself look once more. She saw the ever-lapping bright water of Meluis, rich and clear as an emerald in sunlight. Fish slid through the shallows, their scales flashing with rainbows. Now and then a leviathan would surge up from the deeps and vanish again.

Others might find this soothing, but the idea of following those great fish into an unknown realm filled Fela with dread. She had died by drowning, and feared to do so a second time. Still, she held herself steady.

Now she saw her own reflection swimming up to meet her: a soft white shape, undulating and reforming in the depths. She reached down a hand and pressed her palm to the cold glass slab. Her twin soul reached up on the other side.

She rose to her feet and said, 'I'm ready. But how do I ...'

Persephone opened her hands. As if by some swift silent mechanism, undetectable to ordinary sight, the glass slab was gone. The turbid, cold scent of water flowed up to envelop them. The sound of its lapping filled the cave with sharp echoes.

No barrier lay between her and Meluis. The glistening surface was both repellent and inviting.

'How do you bear this?' Fela asked. 'Always being here, and people endlessly spilling their misery into you?'

Persephone lifted one shoulder. 'Pain exists in time, but my sanctuary is timeless. I'm always here, always the same. But if you come here again, in one year's time or in many, you may not remember this visit. And I ...' She smiled sadly. 'Much as I would wish to do so, Fela, I may not remember you either. So, take courage now.' She indicated Fela's ghost-self reflected in the water. 'Your *fylgia*, your shadow-soul, will be your guide.'

Fela took a last look at the guardian in all her dark splendour. Her arms were half-raised, palms open in blessing. Then, like a swimmer poised to race, Fela focussed her full attention on the waters of Meluis.

In Persephone's Chamber all fear dissolved. Raising her arms, she took a last breath and dived – unleashed herself like an arrow into the green-glass depths.

An Owl in Moonlight

Dedicated to Charlotte and Thomas Firth

The occasion of my sister Hetty's wedding to the Reverend William Musgrove was an amiable affair, thanks in large part to the abundance of champagne and sherry at the wedding breakfast. I say breakfast: in fact the affair began at noon and lasted well into the afternoon in our parents' spacious, if modestly appointed, drawing room.

My sister fairly glowed. Her new husband bore a beaming smile, and he made our aunts flush red with embarrassed yet delighted laughter at his jokes. Whoever guessed a reverend could be so – irreverent? I saw why Hetty had chosen him and I raised my glass to their happiness. Outside, a great red and white striped dirigible strained at its ropes, ready to carry them away to an undisclosed destination on their honeymoon. France, I hoped; anywhere dreamy and sunny and pleasing to them.

I, alas, was having a less comfortable time of it.

'Thomas, you are twenty-one years old!' Hetty said to me, teasing. 'It would so please mother and father if you were to find a respectable young lady of your liking. I want you to be as happy as I am, my dear. Truly, you deserve it.' And she kissed me sweetly on the cheek.

Now, I did not mind this from my beloved sister. However, from a flurry of aunts – both married and maiden – the endless refrain grew cloying.

'Thomas, you are twenty-one,' they said, some in stern tones, others with a wink. 'Are you still not yet courting? Surely the time is long overdue. There are so many sweet, respectable girls with whom you could settle down – but they won't wait forever.' This was said in a warning tone, as if young ladies, like plums, might over-ripen in the autumn and be eaten by wasps. 'The next time we hear wedding bells, they had better be pealing for you!'

And so it was that I edged through one tide of chattering relatives after another, until at last I washed up in a corner with Great-uncle Bartholomew.

This was the metaphorical fate worse than death at all family gatherings. Those poor victims inadvertently trapped with Great-uncle Bartholomew had been known to fake a swoon or a violent stomach ailment in order to escape his overbearing presence. But he who engaged the redoubtable uncle's attention throughout the duration of the gathering would later be lauded as a kind of quiet war hero, or a captain who'd bravely gone down with his ship for the sake of the many.

Today, I decided to be that hero. For Hetty's sake.

Bartholomew was a tall, coarse fellow, with a big face that suggested elements of dray-horse and ape in his ancestry. This animated visage was fleshy, full of lines, and blotched scarlet from champagne. His once-gingery hair was now mostly white, but still thick and curly, worn in long mutton-chop whiskers fashionable in his youth – although I doubted that so much unkempt hair had ever been 'fashionable' in the strict sense. His waistcoat strained over an impressive paunch.

Capturing me with enthusiasm, he arranged chairs so that I was literally caged in a corner between fireplace and bookshelves. He drew up his seat opposite, plump legs spread wide apart, passed me a glass of wine and leaned in with his bloodshot eyes gleaming.

A waft of alcohol-laden breath almost felled me, mitigated only by the fact that I had imbibed more liberally than is my usual habit. Especially at this hour of the day.

'Ah, dear boy. Nephew – name? Name?' He snapped his fingers, as if to jog his memory.

'Great-nephew, sir,' I replied. 'Thomas.'

'Thomas!' he said heartily, although I'm fairly certain he had only a fuzzy recollection, in this sprawling family, of whose son I was. No matter. 'For the love of heaven, call me Uncle! None of this 'Great' nonsense – I need no reminder of how deep into my dotage I am!'

'Surely not so old, sir,' I replied. He spoke over me as if I were someone to talk at, rather than to.

'Splendid wedding, eh? What a spread! Splendid! Now if I could only remember the bride's name …'

'Hetty,' said I. 'My sister.'

He was roaring with laughter or just … roaring. 'Hetty! Wonderful girl! So many weddings, they all blend into one long … wedding! Ha!' He took a big gulp of his drink – he was on brandy, I noticed, so I obligingly refilled his glass from a nearby decanter. Perhaps, if I were lucky, he would pass out.

He poked me in the chest with a plump finger. 'You'll be next, young man!'

Oh, not again. Perhaps I would be next, but at present I was too busy studying law to concern myself with romance.

'But Uncle, you are a bachelor, are you not?' I said this light-heartedly. He was a man of cheerful disposition, I'll grant him that. One only had to mention that the sky was blue, or that a particular door had a particular style of doorknob, and he would hold forth all day on the subject.

However, when I uttered my rather too intrusive remark, he went silent.

Astonishing. This never happened, to my knowledge. I rubbed my left ear, wondering if I had momentarily gone deaf. Then, after a pause of a good five seconds, he started up again.

'Indeed, young man, a confirmed bachelor all my days.' His voice went low and gruff. This surprised me, too, since his habit was to bellow. 'And I know what everyone thinks: what woman would have a garrulous, fat old fool like me? But I tell you, Thomas, I was once young and handsome, with a fine figure like a willow lath and the modest income of a cloth merchant's son-and-heir to my name. I could have had my pick of gentlewomen. It was not for want of opportunity, I assure you.'

'Why, then, did you deprive a lady of a fine husband?'

'Oh, I had my reasons. It's quite a story – and one I've never had the chance to tell. Damned annoying, that. I never get past the first few words and someone stops me in full flow, declaring they have some essential task to do or an important person to meet, or that dinner is served, or some such nonsense.'

I cleared my throat. I swallowed hard. 'I should like to hear your story, Uncle,' said I.

'True love, dear boy.' He leaned forward, hands braced on his knees, his face uncomfortably close to mine. 'Love was my undoing. I fell desperately, hopelessly in love with a woman who could never be mine. After her – no one else ever could or would compare. After her, all other women were shadows.'

'That's ... terribly sad,' I said in all sincerity. 'It's tragic.'

'She wasn't human, you see. She was one of the faerie folk. A goddess, in fact.'

This was the point at which, I surmised, my uncle's captive audience would suddenly remember a pressing engagement or an imminent repast. However, I had committed myself to listening and, to be honest, I was rather intrigued. Who doesn't like a good fairy tale?

'A goddess?'

'And possibly a madwoman.'

This addition was startling. He tapped me on the knee and sat back in his chair, apparently pleased to have shocked me.

'Mad?' I said.

'She was like no human woman I had ever met. More like a ghost, doomed to haunt the netherworld, incessantly seeking something she would never find. I tried to help her ... I offered myself to her service, like a knight swearing fealty to his queen ... and I wonder how many others she has driven to distraction over the centuries? I wonder ...'

As he went on, he spoke to the air above my head, absorbed in his narrative to the extent that he forgot I was there. I was glad of a little space to breathe. Now I was the one who sat forward, trying to catch his words over the general hubbub of the room.

Bartholomew walked across the meadows beneath the full moon, or rather wove his way from the local hostelry towards his father's house. All his drinking companions had scattered to their own homes along the lanes and now he was alone. The night was eerily bright to his bleary eyes. He barely felt the air's chill, but he drank in the cold air as if it were water to sober him.

Frost was forming on every leaf, twig and grass blade. He could see frost feathers growing into long spindly crystals as he went, the fields turning from grey to white until the whole world glittered.

Presently he noticed a small deer watching him from behind the trunk of an oak tree. Prettiest creature ever seen. A pure white doe.

Bartholomew moved very slowly so as not to frighten her away. The world spun slowly around him like a spider's web, or a tunnel made of gleaming gossamer. Dizzy, he staggered. When he regained his balance, there was no doe beneath the tree.

In her place was a young woman.

He saw at once that she was not human. She was all in white fur with flowing pale hair, her heart-shaped face as pale as the moon, an aura flaring around her like snowy flames.

She was more than beautiful. She was lovely enough to put the angels to shame.

Bartholomew's instinct was to run, but his legs turned to rubber and he tripped, sprawling clumsily at her feet ...

Feet? Was that an owl's claw peeping from beneath her hem?

He froze. Kindly she leaned down and helped him up, and the moment he looked into her shining eyes, he was lost. Hers forever.

The universe seemed out of kilter, like a sinister reflection of itself, doused in a blue-violet hue against which she shone like pure light. A dim purplish corridor stretched behind her and he knew, with strange trance-like certainty, that she was standing on the threshold to the Otherworld. And so was he.

'Will you help me?' she asked. Her expression was sorrowful. She twisted her delicate bare hands together, fingers interlaced.

He couldn't speak.

'Don't be afraid,' she said. 'I am Estel. They call me the Lady of Stars, because I came into existence with the stars, and I was all alone for great gulfs of time … But I did not know I was alone until the Earth formed and I saw creatures begin to move upon its surface and the forests growing and falling and growing again …'

'My lady,' he croaked.

He was overwhelmed by a desire to fall at her feet and cry with joy. Of course he'd read fairy tales, and ancient myths of gods and goddesses and the Otherworld. Nothing could have prepared him for the overwhelming reality of meeting this deity. None of those legends had touched the truth.

A doe. A simple girl in white. Yet she was the unknown goddess who came before all others. He did not need to be convinced. One look at her and he knew.

'I need your help,' she said again.

'My lady Estel, anything within my power I can do to help you, I shall do,' he answered.

'I'm searching for my lover. The dear true love of my soul.'

Her words gave him a jolt of disappointment – an irrational response, since he knew that she was far above him, too alien and magical ever to consider courtship from him, a mere commonplace human. This knowledge, however, did not dampen his longing to aid her.

There was such a thing as chivalry. An unconditional vow to help another out of pure love, with no hope of gain for oneself. He made this vow to himself on the spot, never to be broken.

'I – I have seen no one, my lady,' he said. 'I know these woods and meadows. I would have noticed a stranger. As for your consort, if he is a god who shines as you do – how could I possibly miss such a being?'

Estel dipped her head a little and clasped her hands in front of her. 'You do not understand …'

'Bartholomew,' he said as she paused, prompting him to give his name.

'I have been searching for thousands of years.'

'Thousands …?'

What response could he make to this? Her presence was so gossamer-delicate that he feared she would vanish like frost if he blinked. And yet here she stood in front of him, so real and commanding that the rest of the world faded to nothing around her.

'I've hunted everywhere. All through the human world and all through the Spiral.'

'The Spiral?'

'Some call it the Otherworld. Or the Land of Faerie, or the Aetherial realm. There exists more than the visible world, Bartholomew. There are many worlds, and I have sought my lover Kern in all of them.'

'My lady Estel, perhaps you should grieve for him, and cease your search.'

He thought this was quite a wise thing to say, but she looked unmoved.

Not angry, not upset. Simply determined, her eyes burning like silver fire with her unshakeable obsession.

'I have found parts of him,' she said. 'A strand of hair. Two small bones from his foot. Leaves from his cloak.'

She was, indeed, mad. An insane goddess!

'My lady, I don't ...' He tried to say that this was no evidence at all that she'd found anything of significance, but the words would not come out.

'Kern was lord of the forest, in the early days when Aetherials first took on living forms. I, who had always been alone, fell in love with him the first moment we met. And for centuries we were happy. But a male called Perseid, a cold prince from Sibeyla, the realm of snow, formed a desire for me. He tricked Kern away from me and tore him to pieces and scattered him all across the realms. What am I to do, but go looking for all the pieces? If I can make him whole again, he may return to life. And if he does not, at least he will be where he belongs again. With me.'

Bartholomew took in her words with a sense of wonder and despair. He recalled the story of Isis, who had gathered the scattered body parts of Osiris ... but there had only been a few: fourteen or forty or thereabouts, according to which version you read. Leaves, hair strands, bones? How many bones were in the human body? Did an elfin body contain the same number?

'This is an impossible task,' he said.

'Do not say "impossible" to me,' she answered coolly. 'I have searched for countless aeons. I'll go on until time itself ends. You have not even begun.'

'I wouldn't know where to ...'

'I keep being drawn to this place. I'm sure there is something here. If you would only help me, perhaps you will find the fragment of Kern that I cannot. Will you try?'

His heart gave him no choice.

'Of course. But how will I know?'

'Oh, you'll know. Every piece is guarded. Every piece is inscribed.'

She drew on the air with her finger, and the twinkling white image remained for a second before fading: a spiral shape.

'And did you undertake the quest?' I asked, pouring my uncle more brandy.

'Oh, yes, I searched!' he said fervently. 'I explored the forest for days until my clothes were damp rags. Miracle I didn't freeze to death! At first the ground was like iron, but then the frost thawed and the earth turned to mud. I ate berries from the bushes, autumn berries so wrinkled and sour even the birds had left them. Looking back, I would appear to have lost my mind, but I couldn't stop. I was under a spell. I had to undertake the hunt for her sake. I'd made a vow. The Lady of Stars held me in thrall.

'Just as I was beginning to despair, I saw something.

'I was on the bank of a stream, a tall steep bank with soil exposed where part of it had fallen away into the water: a tangle of tree roots and ivy. The object I spied was only a pebble, but it drew my eye because it was pale and smooth, while all the other stones were rough and grey. I plucked it out. My fingernails were already torn and full of dirt, so I cared nothing for the grime.

'I rubbed it clean with a handkerchief and there it lay; not a pebble but a little bone the precise size and shape of a small finger joint. And on it was engraved a tiny rune, a spiral.

'I enjoyed a full two seconds of elation before a – a *thing* flew at me. It was like a small dragon, but I cannot dignify it with that description. No, it was too hideous: a flying reptile with wings and fangs and poisonous yellow eyes. It was no earthly animal! Then I knew I had found something of value, for what was this, if not the object's guardian?

'The monster came straight for my face, clawing at my eyes. It hissed. Its breath scorched my cheeks. I fell backwards and dropped the bone, but it would not cease its attack. Its whirring wings and dagger claws forced me down towards the water's edge. However, I seized a fallen branch and defended myself, like Saint George fighting the dragon. I was no soldier – but for Estel's sake I became a knight that day … and at last I struck that devilish, hissing thing out of the air. It fell, and landed in the stream, and moved no more.'

I have of necessity condensed my uncle's account. The telling took three hours, and the battle between my uncle and the yellow-eyed demon-dragon was a veritable epic, with much interplay and climbing of trees, not to mention narrow brushes with death before he finally whacked the monster out of the sky.

'Then I went down the bank and waded into the current to retrieve the finger bone,' Bartholomew continued, somewhat breathless by now. 'Washed clean by the water, it was pure white, like a polished jewel. I have done it, I thought. I have found one little piece of her soulmate to give her hope! Alas …

'In due time I found my way back to the oak tree, but Estel was gone. I waited for hours, but she did not come back, not even when the moon rose again. Eventually I fell asleep, and was woken by my father and brother standing over me, scolding me for drinking too much ale and falling down insensible in a field in winter! To them, I had been gone for only one night. One night.'

I hardly dared suggest to my great-uncle that he might have dreamed the whole thing. In truth, it had been rather a fine tale, and I didn't want to break the magic. I thought it a shame that people did not listen more closely before dismissing him as a drunken old bore. For him – unless he was the most astonishingly accomplished liar ever born – these unearthly events had really happened.

'But where was Estel?' I asked.

'Gone,' he said with heavy sadness. 'Alas, I never saw my goddess again. Time and time again I went out under the full moon, looking for her, to no avail. But I never stopped trying. And I never gave up the search for pieces of her lover, Kern. I devoted my life to her, and for nothing, but I don't regret one single moment of it. Not a moment, young Thomas.'

His eyes half-closed. He looked exhausted and I thought he was near sleep.

There was a stir of movement around us, rousing him. The party was coming to its end. This meant that Hetty had already gone to change into her travelling attire, and that my encounter with Great-uncle Bartholomew could reach a natural conclusion.

'Thank you, dear boy,' he said, seizing my hand between his large, over-hot paws. 'Thank you for letting me tell my tale. I feel … unburdened.'

He took something from his pocket and pressed it into my hand. I looked. It was a small slip of ivory that might indeed be a finger bone, inscribed with a tiny spiral.

By the time I started for home – at present, my student lodgings – dusk was falling.

We had waved Hetty and William goodbye and good luck as their airship rose gracefully into the blue afternoon sky, propellers whirring. Hetty wept and laughed, wafting her handkerchief at us. The craft looked, I thought, like a giant red-striped humbug as it drifted and dwindled away. I felt a little strange as she disappeared over the horizon, floating happily towards her new life. I was glad for her, but also sad, oddly melancholy. She would always be my sister, but everything had changed. She was a married woman now, a clergyman's wife, and perhaps, before long, mother to my nephews and nieces. What an extraordinary thought!

Would I become the eccentric uncle, entertaining them with supernatural tales?

Would I, one day, be flying off into the sunset with my dear heart's companion at my side, my new wife, whom I have not yet even met?

And so I slipped away and made my way on foot along ten miles of cart-lanes that wound between hedges, through the woods and across open fields towards my lodgings in town. I could have stayed with mama and papa, but I wished to clear my head, rather than have them talking at me all evening. Although my desire to marry was unformed and hazy, I knew with absolute certainty that I did not want to turn into another Great-uncle Bartholomew in my old age: eccentric and lonely.

An owl watched me from an oak tree as I wandered along. The moon was caught in its branches. The great arching black sky seemed to be a face looking down, as if the night sky was in fact the visage of a goddess with the stars of the Milky Way braided into her hair.

This was a beautiful illusion, awe-inspiring and more than slightly alarming. My heart began to race and stumble. I swore I would never drink so much, nor walk alone at night, ever again. I felt the smooth shape of the finger bone in my pocket and rolled it between my thumb and forefinger, as if it were a talisman against danger.

I saw no doe, although it seemed to me that the owl took flight and brushed me with its wings – a flurry of pale, knife-edged feathers.

Then she stood before me.

A small, slender woman in white furs. She glowed. Like a dewy cobweb at dawn, like moonlight on snow, she shone with her own light.

Her sweet face was sombre, her eyes staring intently into mine. She was imperious and intimidating, yet vulnerable, soundlessly imploring me for help.

I fell to my knees.

'I've waited so long,' she said, her voice soft, sad, infinitely patient. She held out her hand to me, palm facing upwards. 'Did you find anything, anything at all to give me hope?'

Silent, I dropped the tiny cylinder of ivory into her hand.

She clasped it to her heart and closed her eyes, lips parted. 'There is an Aetherial legend that every bone of Kern's body is a stitch that holds the Earth and the Spiral together. If ever I found the whole of him, the two worlds would tear apart. Would I chance that, to have my beloved one with me again?'

I found my voice with difficulty. And I dropped my gaze, for I knew that if I looked at her for one moment longer, my fate would be that of Bartholomew – always to search, never to know peace.

'I think you would chance anything to find him, my lady Estel.'

'Ah well,' she said softly. 'It is only a tale.'

Ruins and Bright Towers

The rain was endless. It poured between the tall buildings on either side of the street as if falling into a bronze canyon, eerily half-lit by orange streetlights, dirty and dark yet shining like oil. This was where Sylvie always saw the girl.

Sylvie had lived all her life on this road and she knew every building: the vast derelict factory along one side, the other side crammed with big old terraced houses: separate households no longer but accommodation for the transient inhabitants of student digs, flats, the children's care home. Further along stood a pub, a row of shops and the shabby old community centre.

A low-level industrial hum made the air throb. It seemed to tremble up from the ground and into Sylvie's bones. Metallic, disturbing, just loud enough to be unpleasant. The factory was long-closed so it did not come from there, unless ghost workers still operated machines behind the darkened windows. Power lines, maybe. No one ever mentioned the noise. People must be so used to it that they didn't hear it any more. The sound, like the rain, was never-ending.

Sylvie was just fifteen. The girl, nicknamed Red, was a year younger. They knew each other only slightly. Other kids came and went from the home at all hours – she often crossed the road to avoid their attention – but Red was always alone. She was short, skinny, usually dressed in shabby jeans and a t-shirt, or a baggy sweater when it was really cold.

Sylvie saw her now on the edge of the pavement, arms wrapped around herself, rain beading like dew on her sweater. Her face in profile looked about twelve, upturned nose, pouty lips, no smile. Dusky brown skin implied mixed parentage; her hair was dyed crimson, hanging in long thick dreadlocks that were just starting to lose their colour and show black roots.

Red looked up and down the street. Nothing to see but slanting sheets of rain, and Sylvie standing a hundred yards away at the bottom of the steps that led up to her dad's flat. Sylvie raised a hand to wave a cautious 'hi.' Red looked away

A car came. Red got into it and was gone.

'How long's it take to walk to the bloody shops and back?'

Sylvie let herself into the hall of the tiny top-floor flat and stood dripping onto the lino. Her father was there waiting, with that grinning, joking yet snide manner he had. He held a can of strong cider in one hand, a joint in the other.

She said nothing. What sort of mood was he in? If good, he would laugh a lot at nothing, as if tickled by some private comedy show in his head. Bad: there would be self-pity, followed by blame and yelling. Sometimes worse.

'You got my stuff, Syl?'

She handed him a six-pack of cider, went to put away a pint of milk and some dented cans of beans in the tiny kitchen. How did the sink get so full of dirty dishes, when he hardly ate anything? Perhaps it was her own negligence. He would blame her, in any case. She stared indifferently at the mess.

'Why don't you put a damn coat on when you go out? Don't want my little girl getting cold. You going to mop up that puddle you've dripped on the floor?'

And he went back into the living room to watch football, or one of the noisy quiz shows he liked. A good mood, then. He'd forgotten that he'd sold her coat at the community centre sale two weeks ago – along with her only weatherproof boots, and some books she'd failed to hide from him – and kept the money instead of giving it to the organisers like he was supposed to.

Sylvie went into her bedroom and shut the door. She got a towel and began to squeeze the water out of her hair. Her hair, once brown, had turned pure white when she was nine. That was the year her mother had left home. She'd been taunted at school – both about the greying hair and the slut mother – but she rarely went to school these days, so it didn't matter.

She pushed off her trainers using her toes; her socks were wet underneath. She pulled them off too, but there were no clean dry ones so she sat barefoot, cross-legged on the mattress that was her bed.

The flat, although cramped, had an echoey feel. No carpets. No curtains in the front room, since her dad had accidentally set them alight a few years ago. Her room had ancient, thin curtains with cartoon characters on them: trains with grinning faces. The curtains didn't meet in the middle, so streetlight painted her room orange. Outside the rain roared and the industrial hum throbbed without respite, causing the building and even the bones of her skull to vibrate.

She picked up a paperback novel and began to read, holding it one-handed while working at her hair with the other hand.

The Storm Lord by Tanith Lee.

Actually it was half a book. She had no tape to stick the torn halves back together. The cover was bent and tattered, the pages crinkled, but she loved the cover: in lurid shades of green and orange and purple, the mysterious otherworldly figures of a warrior and a goddess rode an alien beast towards their destiny.

Sylvie read with slow, careful attention. She entirely forgot her father and the rainy wasteland outside. She lost herself in the world of the Vis, where Dortharians ruled savagely over the pale, passive Lowlanders of the Shadowless Plains. The Vis lords *'moved with a special, almost a specific arrogance which pronounced them alien to this landscape far more than did their black hair and black-bronze burnish of their skin ... for they were Dortharians, dragons, and they carried a High King in their midst.'*

A brutal world, but there was something in their brutality that spoke to her. The High King Rehdon, roused to unbearable lust by the mystical phases of the Red Moon, chose a Lowland woman, Ashne'e, to lie with him. There was no question of her saying no.

'She seemed carved from white crystal, translucent eyes, like discs of yellow amber, open wide on his, the tawny cloud of hair fixed as frozen vapour ... "Tonight you lie with me," Rehdon said.'

Sylvie paused, biting the tip of her thumb. This portrayal of sex distressed her. The image of powerful men forcing themselves onto subjects who dared not refuse made her shudder with confusion. Disturbing, yet the scene filled her with nebulous excitement.

No wicked act in *The Storm Lord* went unpunished, however. *'Plains women, it was rumoured, knew strange arts. Knew, too, how to stare in at a soul stripped naked by the pleasure spasms of the flesh.'*

Rehdon the High King was not going to survive his night with Ashne'e. By morning he was dead, and the temple girl was carrying his son: Raldnor, the rejected child of mixed Vis and Lowland blood, who would grow to be a tall beautiful man with dark skin and pale hair, the fascinating tormented hero.

'Pleasure spasms of the flesh,' Sylvie read softly aloud to herself.

Her dad's fist banged on the door, making her jump.

'Oy, princess! You ever going to make supper? There's fucking beans but no fucking bread!'

She jumped to her feet as he barged into the room. The one time she'd tried to put a bolt on her side, he'd smashed it off with a hammer, then swung a hammer-blow at her head that broke her left middle finger as she put up her hand to protect herself. He hadn't taken her to hospital, so the finger had set crooked. The woodwork around the door was still splintered. It would never be mended.

'I had enough to buy bread or cider, not both,' she said. Her voice was flat and quiet. She dropped her head to one side, letting the straggly white hair cover her face.

Bad mood now. He started moaning on about her utter uselessness while she moved mechanically to find a last, ice-crusted pizza in the freezer, to heat it, cut it in half and arrange it on two plates with warmed-up beans.

They sat side by side on the sofa to eat, telly blaring. Father still smoking his spliff. The smell made her feel sick. He pushed the beans around his plate with a look of disgust on his face. Then he said, 'This is shit,' and let the full plate slide off his knee to land in a splattered mess on the floor.

Sylvie pushed a chair against the inside of the door. She settled down on her mattress with her book and a can of his cider: she'd left him snoring. With luck he wouldn't wake until morning. She had left her own full plate on a side-table, just in case, because if he decided he was hungry after all and there was nothing left, she would bear the consequences.

Most likely the congealed food would still be there tomorrow.

He never actually meant to hurt her when he threw things or lashed out, but the rooms were small and she wasn't always quick enough to evade him. Then he'd squash her against his thin chest and soft beer belly, overcome with emotion, his tears dripping into her hair, protesting that he was, 'Sorry, sorry, sorry, Syl, my poor little girl.'

One thing he didn't do was interfere with her body. She'd heard about that from the care home girls. Dads, step-dads, uncles, cousins, even teachers: pawing, sticking their fingers where their fingers had no right to be, doing god knows what else as if their flesh-and-blood children were blow-up dolls. She'd heard the kids speak casually about this horror as if it was only to be expected – as impassive as the Lowland women in the story.

'The Lowland girl lay like a corpse beneath him, while her hair seemed to set the pillow alight.'

At least her dad didn't do that to her. She considered herself lucky.

He didn't do much of anything, except drink.

Sylvie read for most of the night. She recoiled at the scene where Raldnor – he was meant to be the hero, after all, yet he … he was in love with the white-haired Lowland girl, Anici – 'She was all whiteness … and all of her framed by hair like blown and nacreous tinsel.' – yet despite Anici's innocence and fear, the Red Moon possessed him and he raped her.

Sylvie put down the book and hugged her knees. Her eyes were sightless. Something formless moved inside her … fear and fascination. Her head whirled with vivid images.

The young, reluctant, shrinking girl, overpowered by a man who was supposed to love her … Raldnor's agonising regret, which came too late. Then his callous visit to a prostitute, supposedly to spare Anici from his lust … were men really like this in real life, even the good ones?

Sylvie found her place, bookmarked with an old scrap of paper that bore her mother's handwriting. The story was horrifying yet she could not stop turning the pages.

And then, Anici's encounter with the new Storm Lord – Raldnor's half-brother, the dark and twisted Amrek – who sent his men to kidnap her for his pleasure. The moment the Storm Lord touched Anici, she died of sheer terror.

'Under the dull bleeding of the incense braziers, she lay like a white inverted shadow, stretching out from his blackness on the floor. He bent over her and found that she was dead.'

And Raldnor was not there to save her because he'd gone to visit a brothel.

He was tormented with guilt forever afterwards. And so he should be, Sylvie thought. Yet she still felt for him in his pain. And for Anici too, the wide-eyed victim of these mighty, terrible men.

It was all wrong. But that was the power of the story. All the horror and injustice and catastrophic mistakes – they were what made her care, made her read compulsively until she finally fell asleep near dawn.

She'd only got the book because of Red. The sale in the community centre had been a fund-raiser for the children's home. Some of the kids were there helping out and Red had been standing behind a table piled with old paperback books.

Sylvie and her dad had no money to spend. They were there to be nosey, see what they could steal, her dad also to commit fraud for beer money. As she approached the book table, she saw Red take a paperback off the pile and slip it into a carrier bag. But there was another care home kid nearby, a skinny older boy, and he saw what Red had done. He grabbed the book out of her bag and held it in the air, taunting her. Angry, she jumped up to take it back, but he was too tall. He ripped the book in half and flung it down. Both halves fell at Sylvie's feet.

No one said anything. The boy sauntered away. Red's face was expressionless. Sylvie picked up both halves of the book and took them home.

Nine o'clock in the morning, and Red was on the street near the children's home. She wasn't on her way to school, though. She was blatantly just arriving back from somewhere. A few yards away Sylvie saw the blue car, and four men standing around it, Red talking to them.

One of the men was white; gaunt, stubbly and cold-eyed. Two were dark-skinned, Asian-looking. The fourth she couldn't tell; he had his back to her, a baseball cap hiding his hair, but he looked short, stocky and middle-aged. The two dark men held her attention. Young and confident, with broad smiles, thick black hair and shining eyes.

They made her think of the Vis, the Dortharians in the story. Dragon Lords, like Raldnor. Frightening yet attractive, full of raw power like panthers. One of them touched Red on the shoulder as she walked away, and Sylvie felt a tiny pang of jealousy.

'What you staring at?' Red said, giving Sylvie a quick hard glance as she passed.

'Who are those men?'

The car pulled away. The street was empty. Nothing moved but the drizzle, and half a dozen pigeons taking sudden flight from the factory roof opposite. Sylvie felt she and Red were the only two people left alive in the world.

'No one. Just some friends.'

She sniffed. She looked grey with tiredness, and slurred her words. Her eyes were as red as her hair.

'Are you supposed to be out with them?'

'What are you, my care worker?' A small sneer. 'Mind your own fucking business, yeah?'

'Okay. Sorry.'

'What d'you want, anyway?'

'To give you this.' Sylvie held out the half-book, the front section with the lurid orange and green cover. 'You wanted to read it, didn't you? I saw you take it in the community centre, before that idiot grabbed it off you. I've got the other half. I'll give it you as soon as I've finished.'

Red stared at the cover, as if trying to remember why it was important. She said softly, 'Is it any good?'

'Yes, brilliant.'

'Go on, then.' She took the gift and made for the concrete steps up to the front door. Sylvie looked longingly after her: she didn't want to go back to her father, but she had nowhere else to go. She called after the retreating back, cloaked by long scarlet dreadlocks,

'Are you all right?'

'Yeah, fine. Thanks for the book.'

Her mother's drinking was the reason her parents had split up: ironic, considering that her dad drank even more. There had been screaming arguments, broken furniture, accusations about other men. One day, just after Sylvie's ninth birthday, she came home from school and her mother wasn't there anymore.

Sylvie hadn't seen her since.

As a child, she must have been upset and cried, but she didn't remember that. All she remembered was a kind of numbness gathering around her until she didn't feel anything, except the emotions she drew second-hand from characters in books.

'Outside the snow sugared the world with its levelling pallor.'

She liked that line. That was how she felt. Everything quite cold, controlled and still inside her. Level.

She was onto the second part of the torn-in-half book now and there was a new character: Astaris, a red-haired Vis woman, a princess. *'Pricelessly*

204

rare,' one of the characters told Raldnor, who by a strange chain of events would become a guard in the service of his enemy, the High King Amrek. *'A mane the colour of rubies.'*

Pricelessly rare – as if Astaris had value only as an exquisite work of art, not as a human being.

Astaris was to marry Amrek. She was self-contained and completely enigmatic – until she and Raldnor set eyes upon each other. No, not the first time they saw each other … but the first time they were accidentally alone together. But even before they met, they touched each other's minds and they both knew.

'Her hair was the precise colour of blood … and she was in his skull like flame and he in hers … The longing came swift and devouring and fed on itself in each of them.'

Sylvie wondered how that would feel … to meet your soulmate and simply *know* there could be no one else in all the world. But in the world of the Vis, you did not fall in love with the High King's future bride without dire consequences.

Betrayed, Raldnor and Astaris had to flee for their lives, each thinking the other dead.

'She lived within herself, and no part of her reached out to commune with others …'

I'm kind of like that, thought Sylvie. So is Red, I think.

She read on in a feverish rush, wanting the story to go on forever, yet wanting to finish so that her friend could read it too and then they would have something to talk about. Something magical.

'Is Red your real name?'

'It is now.'

She and Red walked through the rainy streets together, aimless, but farther afield than Sylvie usually went on her own. The city thrummed and shook, but its relentless pulse seemed muted. 'You got any friends at the home? How long have you lived there?'

'You ask a lot of questions, don't you? I've been there about a hundred years and they all hate me, but I don't care anymore. Okay?'

'You're not the only one who gets bullied, you know,' said Sylvie. 'I'm dead scared of those kids, too. And I got hell at school. First because my mum walked out, then because my hair turned white – they'd yank strands of it right out of my head and call me 'grandma' – then because everyone knows my father's an alky, then because I liked schoolwork and I was good at reading, then because – I don't know. They didn't even need a reason. I know how you feel.'

'You don't know anything about me,' said Red.

Sylvie shrugged. 'I know you love books. And I know you've got no friends, same as me. But I like you, even though you're rude and miserable. I like you anyway.'

'Fuck off,' said Red.

Most of their conversations went like this. Fragments here and there, skipping between one thing and another. They were both finding their way.

Buildings towered around them, staring down with blank windows. Weeds struggled out of the tarmac. They walked down to the canal and along the towpath. Deserted red factories stood all along the far bank and some ancient narrow boats were moored there, bobbing against the slimy green brickwork. People lived in them.

Looking at the canal, Sylvie said, '*The sky had turned black, and spears of pallid light flickered beyond the river; rain began to fall in huge molten drops, and the river boiled.*'

'That's from *The Storm Lord*, right?'

'Sometimes when I see things, I think how Tanith Lee would describe them. Makes the world a bit more romantic and less sordid.'

Red grinned. Sylvie hardly ever saw her smile, so she was pleased.

'You know a lot of big words, don't you? Don't tell me how it finishes.'

'I wasn't going to.'

'By the way.' Red took a scrap of paper from her jeans pocket and pushed it into Sylvie's hand. 'You left your bookmark in it. There's an address on it, so I thought you might need it.'

'Thanks.'

Pause. 'Is that where your mum lives now?'

'No. I don't know where she lives. But she wrote the note, and she left hardly anything else behind, so that's why I kept it. Stupid, really.'

'At least you know who your parents are. That's more than I do.'

'Yeah, and I sometimes wish I didn't,' said Sylvie. 'Ever feel like you're stuck, like really trapped, and life will just go on and on and on exactly the same until you drop dead?'

'I just feel like I wish it would stop fucking raining.'

'I understand why my dad drinks. I steal his cider sometimes. It gives me a bad head, but I could get used to it. You got any guilty secrets?'

'Like what?'

'Those men.'

She thought Red was going to clam up again. She was quiet for a while as they walked. Plastic bags drifted across the canal, carried by the wet breeze. Sylvie saw a narrow road leading up between the factories and a street name, Wharfside Lane, but it might as well have been another country. Then Red looked at Sylvie with a strange glow in her eyes. 'They're all right. They give me stuff. Presents, sometimes. All the drink you want, and other stuff that makes you feel amazing, like you're flying.'

'But what do they want in return?' No answer. 'Do you really think you ought to …'

'What? Like you said, there's nothing else to do.'

'That's why I read stories. I can go into another world …' She decided to change tack. 'You enjoying the book?' Red nodded. 'What do you like best about it?'

'All the sex,' Red answered with a smirk.

Sylvie rolled her eyes. 'What else?'

'I like Astaris. I like the way she's so cool and just doesn't mind about anything. When Amrek the Storm Lord gets mad because she takes no notice of him, he tells her that even her beauty will get boring and then he'll kill her. And all she does is smile. Yes, I like that.'

'*She lived within herself, and no part of her reached out to commune with others,*' Sylvie quoted and Red laughed, understanding.

Sylvie felt a little thrill of conspiracy.

'You *are* Astaris,' she said. 'The dark skin, the blood-red hair. You're her.' She pulled at her own damp, pale hair with a colourless hand. 'And me, I must be Anici.'

'So Raldnor should be along to rescue us any day, right?'

'*Anici bent over him and touched his shoulder. He got up in the darkness, and she stood waiting, the wind washing through her silver hair. The white moon shone behind her; he saw the shadow of her small bones beneath her skin. As he approached her, she raised her arms, and long cracks appeared in her body, like ink lines on alabaster. Then she crumbled all at once into gilded ashes, and the ashes blew away across the moon, leaving only darkness to wake him.*'

'Oy, princess!' Her father was yelling at the door. 'Go down the shop for me cider, will you?'

Sylvie started up on her mattress in panic. She'd been asleep, dreaming. Red had the second portion of the book now so she found herself dreaming about the characters instead; dead Anici haunting Raldnor, about the enigmatic Astaris with her blood-red hair, about Amrek's soldiers slaughtering pale Lowlanders there in the street outside her window, the gutters running with blood and rain.

'Dad, I can't. They know I'm not eighteen, they won't serve me anymore!'

'Don't talk crap, Syl, they don't care who they serve. Get us a half-bottle of the cheap vodka while you're at it.'

'It's dark. It's raining.'

She sat huddled, waiting for him to burst in and yell at her.

'What're you doing in there?' he said through the door. 'You got a boy in there, you little slut?' Then he gave a sort of exasperated guffaw and shuffled away. She waited a few moments, clenching her teeth in anger. Eventually she got up, as resigned and passive as Anici herself, and went to do his bidding.

She and Red spent the whole afternoon together next day. Her father was still sleeping off the previous night; no adult seemed to care that they wandered the streets and stole chocolate from the newsagent and walked along the canal where it wasn't safe and never went to school. No one cares that we exist, Sylvie thought, but maybe we can look out for each other.

She was impatient for Red to finish *The Storm Lord*. As it was, they talked idly about which part she'd reached, and why each character did what he or she did.

Mad, tormented Amrek had set about slaughtering every single Lowlander in the world out of fear and rage. A Lowlander – Ashne'e – had killed his father, he believed. Another Lowlander – Raldnor – had stolen Astaris. Now in savage vengeance he lashed out, intending genocide on their whole race.

'*The storm gods of Dorthar that directed Amrek in his holy war – they would no longer brook the scum of the snake goddess.*'

And Raldnor – now possessed by that very goddess – had to stop him by gathering an army of his own, but it was a long, terrible struggle and anyway, what was it all for when he believed Astaris to be dead?

But Anackire, the snake-goddess – She and Red agreed that was their favourite part, the gigantic statue hidden in a long-forgotten temple underground.

'*And then the soaring whiteness of the giantess with her whirling golden tail. Anackire, the Lady of Snakes …She towered. She soared. Her flesh was a white mountain, her snake's tail a river of fire in spate.*'

Their talk stopped. All thoughts of the book vanished.

The blue car was there again, a few yards along from the kids' home, the same four men leaning against the bodywork with arms folded. Red tensed like a bird about to take flight. Sylvie couldn't tell if she was spellbound by fear or excitement. Maybe both.

At once all Red's attention was fixed on them, as if her companion had ceased to exist.

Sylvie resented this. Of course the men were infinitely more exciting than a dull, bookish girlfriend, but she hated them for that. She wanted to tell Red to ignore them, tell them to fuck right off with their sly smiles and lazy, knowing eyes. If she and Red were Anici and Astaris, the men were Dortharians: dark and powerful and able to take whatever they wanted. A touch from them and you would die of fear.

Yet she tingled with curiosity. Truth was, she was jealous of Red with her

knowing smiles and her secret world. She wanted to taste this forbidden …
whatever it was. The closest she'd ever come to 'partying' was a stolen can
of strong white cider in her bedroom. And Red was the only friend she'd
ever had, because people around here were so closed-in and hostile, too
busy armouring themselves from the hostility of everyone else in the world
to risk a kind word.

Ignoring the pallid man and the creepy middle-aged one, Sylvie could
only look at the two panthers. She thought about Dortharian dragon lords
with their dangerous, erotic beauty. She remembered the glow in Red's eyes
as she said, *'They give me stuff. Presents, sometimes. All the drink you want, and
other stuff that makes you feel amazing, like you're flying.'*

Helpless, she watched Red walk to the men and give herself into their
hands. Then one of them, all shadowy languorous beauty, looked at her and
called out, 'Hey, what's your name?'

'Sylvie.'

'You want to come and party with your friend, Sylvie?'

'You disgusting little slut.'

Daylight blinded her. Her father's face was an inch from hers, red with
fury, his sour breath smothering her. She rolled away, retching. Her head
throbbed in time to the metallic pulse of the city, steel hammers beating her
brain. The previous night – a blank. She didn't even remember how she'd
got home. Sore everywhere.

And her father had a fistful of ten-pound notes, and was shaking them in
her face.

'Yer gone all night. Roll back in at eight, stoned out of yer head, reeking
of god-knows-what, and this in your pocket. I know where you've been!
Whoring, just like your mother! Exactly like your fucking mother. Apple
doesn't fall far, does it?'

He took the money and left, slamming the door.

Sylvie lay still for a long time, thinking of nothing. She only moved when
her bladder was bursting and her mouth so dry she couldn't swallow. By
then her dad had gone out. Pub. Bookies. Shops, for more booze. Her night
of shame was a bonanza for him.

There was no hot water. Once she'd washed in cold and put on her other
pair of jeans and a fresh sweatshirt, she let herself out and walked down the
street to the kid's home.

She stood looking up at the windows. Nothing stirred inside. The rain
grew heavier and she began to shiver.

'Red?' she called. No answer. She didn't know which room her friend
slept in, and she daren't shout too loud in case some of the bigger boys
heard.

The hell she daren't. She marched up the steps and pounded on the front door, but no one came, not even an adult. Eventually she retreated and walked away, feeling deflated and stupid.

There was a woman on the other side of the road, staring at her. A stranger with long thick hair, very pale: blonde or even pure white. A floating dress with handkerchief points, the colour of mist, like white muslin in shadow, as if the garment were partly made of rain and moving gently on a breeze. An apparition, not of this world. Eyes rimmed with black, like an Egyptian goddess. Such intense eyes. Terrifying, challenging, chiding, full of fierce warmth. Staring, staring, staring into her.

White pigeons rose up from the pavement in a whirring flock. They spiralled around the woman in a flurry of wings and when they vanished, so had she.

Sylvie stood looking down at her father. He lay flat-out on the sofa, one hand trailing on the filthy floor, mouth open, drooling. There was a nearly-empty bottle of whisky lying among the cigarette ends, roaches and cider cans. The front room was a stifling, fetid cave.

His eyes were open a slit, gleaming. He seemed to be looking at her, but his breathing was off. He wasn't so much snoring as groaning. *Ahhhhh* ... he groaned, as if to say, *help me.*

Was he asleep or in some kind of coma? His skin looked yellow and, despite being so thin, his belly was grossly swollen. Perhaps he'd had a fit. Perhaps he was dying.

'I'm sorry, Dad,' she said softly, without emotion. 'I can't look after you anymore.'

No response.

'Dad, I'm leaving now.'

The street was a red brick chasm, the road surface iron-grey and boiling with rain, the sky swollen with a sickly orange glow. She felt a sharp chill in the air. On a corner where a side-road joined the main street, a gang of boys from the care home stood around, aimless and menacing. They were sniggering at something on a smart phone, but as she passed they all looked up and stared.

'Oy, blondie!' one of them yelled at her. It was the scrawny boy who'd taken the book from Red and torn it in half. 'Whitey! Hey, granny! Grandma, where's your walking stick?'

Usually she scurried past them as fast as she could, hiding her face behind a veil of white hair. Today, though, she stopped, turned, marched across the road.

'Give me your phone,' she said.

The scrawny boy gave a horrible mocking laugh. 'You what?'

She smelled the smoke and sweat that clung to them. Sensed them clustering around their prey, excited.

But she wasn't scared. How did she look to them? She felt that she suddenly wore the face of Anackire, savage and terrifying with fire for eyes and writhing snakes for hair. She showed her teeth and their confidence wavered.

'I said, *give me the fucking phone.*'

The blue car was already there. Red was on her way towards it, arms folded, head bowed, faded-scarlet hair draping her khaki sweatshirt.

'The rain beat down. Her fabulous hair seemed full of fires.'

Sylvie remembered almost nothing of the previous night, except little flashes that kept stabbing like pins through her eyes. The men no longer looked enticing or even interesting to her. The sight of them made her nearly sick.

And yet Red was going to them again, as passive and insouciant as Astaris. She felt dismayed and helpless, but most of all she was furious.

'Red,' she called, running to catch her up. 'Red, don't go with them. Please.'

Red glared at her with hard eyes. 'What's your problem? You had fun, didn't you?'

Sylvie shook her head. 'Maybe the first half-hour. But the stuff they made us do … That wasn't fun.'

'You get used to it. It's not that bad.'

'Yes, it is!'

'Thing is, you can't start and then stop,' Red answered in a harsh whisper. She held up a clenched fist. 'They get you like *this*. You're a coward. If you can't take it, go back to your dad.'

The men were all leaning on the car, waiting. Smiling their contemptuous, predatory smiles.

Red started towards them again. Sylvie grabbed her wrist, hard.

'I've left my dad.'

'So?'

She showed Red the stolen phone. 'He's sick. I've called an ambulance. But I've got to get away from here, and so have you. If you don't come with me *now*, I'll call the police.'

Red started breathing very fast, her eyes widening.

'You call the police, those guys will kill us.'

Sylvie stared her down and hissed, *'I. Don't. Care.'*

'Hey,' called one of the men. 'You little sluts coming with us, or what?'

'Raldnor isn't on his way to save us. We have to save ourselves.' Sylvie dug her nails in and jerked Red's arm as hard as she could. 'Run,' she snarled.

They ran.

Sidestreets, footpaths, the unlit spaces beneath a railway bridge – the labyrinth swallowed them. Wasteland and weeds streaked past in a blur, gleaming dully from the strange orange glow of the sky. The rain was bitterly cold. It stung like needles. Sylvie's wet hair whipped around her face, but she hardly noticed the discomfort of her sore lungs or the penetrating cold. She ran and ran with a kind of insane glee. Red laughed too, in between gasps, as if they were fleeing the scene of some outrageous prank.

The men intercepted them on the canal towpath.

The car was already there – they must have squeezed it down some alleyway – headlights shining on the muddy path. The two white guys were by the car on their right, the two dark ones ten yards away on their left, all four grinning like jackals. Sylvie and Red were trapped in between.

In front of them the canal lay like a slow black snake.

She thought of Raldnor plunging into the river Okris, trying to escape Amrek's soldiers after he and Astaris had been found out. *'Sluggish and very cold beneath … When he lifted his head for air, he rose against a stone wall, viscous with muddy weeds …'*

Sylvie seized Red's arm. Together they rushed forward and leapt.

The water was a black, icy shock. She floundered. Dark turbid water as thick as oil, full of floating detritus: plastic bags and bottles and stuff better not to know what it was.

'I can't sw–'

Red was sinking, panicking, thrashing to keep her face in the air. Sylvie grabbed the collar of her sweatshirt, held her head clear, and dragged her through the sewer murk of the canal. Water kept splashing into her face. Floating objects collided with her as she swam, awkward and one-handed, fighting to keep Red's face clear of the surface.

On the other side she reached a moored narrow boat, got hold of a rope that was trailing in the water, and helped Red to scramble onto the back of the vessel. It rocked under their slight weight as they found their balance. From there, they pulled themselves up three feet of slimy brick wall and onto firm ground. They paused, shivering, sobbing, coughing.

The men stood on the far bank, silhouetted against the car headlights. Just standing there, like four stick men in a cartoon, rigid with frustrated anger.

One of them called out, 'We'll hunt you down, you little bitches.'

Red cackled. Sylvie had never heard her laugh so loud before, with such abandon. Then she yelled at the top of her voice.

'Fuck off!'

And Sylvie gave them the finger; the crooked middle finger that had healed wrong after her father broke it.

Lights came on inside the narrow boat. By the time the grumbling occupant emerged, the men had slouched back to their car and dissolved into the gloom, while Sylvie and Red were a hundred yards clear, running hand in hand along the narrow Wharfside Lane.

Above them, the rain turned into snow and came down in white swirls.

'I've got summat to tell you,' said Red. They were walking fast now, out of breath. Soaked, frozen, but too full of adrenaline to feel the cold. The world was turning soft and white around them. Snow muffled the harsh pulse of the city until she couldn't hear it anymore; the silence was unnerving.

'Yeah?'

'I'm a girl.'

'Duh.' Sylvie laughed. 'Me too. So what?'

'Well, cos I was born a boy.'

'Oh,' said Sylvie. The universe shifted. 'Oh, right.'

'Is that a problem?' Red's voice had a flat, belligerent edge.

'That's why you got bullied in the home?'

'Yeah.' Red sniffed. 'Pretty much. I was born the wrong sex. They said I was a boy but I always knew I was a girl. You want to see my dick and have a good laugh, like they did?'

'Don't be daft.' Pause. 'I'm sorry that happened to you.'

'I don't want sympathy. Like you said – if it wasn't that, would've been something else. We were all as bad as each other in different ways. Just wanted you to know.'

'Thanks.' They went on in silence. Sylvie took Red's hand. 'I don't mind. We're still who we are. You're Astaris, I'm Anici.'

'You're crazy,' said Red.

'*There was a light, indeterminate, white moth snow blowing on the wind, melting colourlessly on the pavements of the city ...*' Sylvie remembered descriptions of snow from the story. '*Snow flamed on the wind. The wind was on fire with snow. When the snow stopped, the Plains lay in unbroken whiteness under an exhausted purple sky.*' That was exactly how the city seemed to her now. '*Over the city a snow moon burned like a lamp of blazing ice.*'

There was no moon, only lights shining from the windows of a house, and a soft lamp over its closed front door. Everything was covered with feathery, yellow-tinted whiteness.

They stood opposite the house, a high narrow Victorian villa with steps up to the entrance. *67, Wharfside Lane.*

That was the address her mother had scribbled on the scrap of paper. Sylvie had always known what it meant, even though, at the age of nine, she hadn't properly understood.

She understood well enough now. Knew, too, that her otherwise useless mother had left her this tiny lifeline on purpose. Just in case.

Light poured out of the windows but didn't reach the shadows where they stood on the opposite side of the road. Red, until now brisk and defiant, shrank into herself with nerves.

'Are you sure? There's no sign on the door.'

'Of course there isn't. People who've run away from being abused and beaten up don't want their boyfriends or whoever to *find* them. They're not going to put a sign on the door saying, "Women's Refuge, find your terrified wife here!" are they?'

In a small voice Red asked, 'Did your mum come here?'

'No idea. She just left me the address.'

'What are we going to say to them?'

Sylvie thought about *The Storm Lord*: the part where the passive Lowland slave girls rose up and slaughtered their Vis overlords. *'Their hair striped with hot blood, killing and killing, without thought or hesitation, like machines with eyes of blanched steel.'*

Out loud she said, 'Did you finish the book?'

'No. It's back at the home. You'll have to tell me how it ended.'

'If you don't mind spoilers.'

'I don't care. Tell me.'

There isn't time, Sylvie thought. And it was so brutal all the way through. Amrek was evil, but Raldnor was nearly as bad. His own armies brought as much violence and death, until he woke the goddess herself and she destroyed Dorthar with a massive earthquake. Anackire, the great goddess with her golden snake-tail, rising up out of her hidden temple to tower above Dorthar as the city fell.

'Now the foaming water had lifted her a little and was thrusting her up against the roof of the cave. Her golden head grazed the granite above …Now the land slid and fell away. Out of the chasm emerged the massive milk-white torso with its burning eyes and hair … She crested the hills and rose incredibly into the pitch-black sky, a towering moon of ice and flame … Anackire soared and blazed, crushing them with the eight maledictions of her serpent arms. They had seen nemesis. Their world was ended. The goddess shone like a meteor in the black air, then sank, as the wave relinquished her, into the torn mirror of the lake.'

Anackire had taken her revenge. Then the mad possession left Raldnor and he became human again …

Sylvie saw a remembered glimpse of the woman with the floating ghost-grey dress and intense kohl-rimmed eyes, the white pigeons fluttering around her. *You know what you have to do*, the eyes told her.

'The birds are always an omen,' said Sylvie.

'What?'

'There's too much. I'll just tell you the important bit.' Sylvie's teeth chattered with cold as she spoke.

'Raldnor kills Amrek and becomes the Storm Lord?'

'Too obvious. First he had to go and rescue Astaris.'

'I'm frozen,' said Red. 'You gonna stand here all night?'

'No,' said Sylvie, looking at the brightly-lit house. The door was locked – of course – but light spilled out all around its edges. 'There'll be people exactly like us in there. When we go in, I want to tell them what I'm telling you. I never expected the story to have a happy ending, but it did. When Raldnor found Astaris, he didn't care about becoming the Storm Lord. All they cared about was each other, so they ran away together and disappeared.'

'They did?' Red looked sideways at her from under lowered eyelids.

'Love meant more than power. Come on.'

Sylvie knew she would be too nervous to say a word when the door opened. But she imagined opening her arms to the spiralling snow and sharing her revelation with anyone who would listen.

Astaris and Raldnor escaped. We escaped.

So can you.

Other Titles by Freda Warrington

A TASTE OF BLOOD WINE
A DANCE IN BLOOD VELVET
THE DARK BLOOD OF POPPIES
THE DARK ARTS OF BLOOD
ELFLAND
MIDSUMMER NIGHT
GRAIL OF THE SUMMER STARS
THE COURT OF THE MIDNIGHT KING
DRACULA THE UNDEAD
THE AMBER CITADEL
THE SAPPHIRE THRONE
THE OBSIDIAN TOWER
DARK CATHEDRAL
PAGAN MOON
THE RAINBOW GATE
SORROW'S LIGHT
A BLACKBIRD IN SILVER
A BLACKBIRD IN DARKNESS
A BLACKBIRD IN AMBER
A BLACKBIRD IN TWILIGHT
A BLACKBIRD IN SILVER DARKNESS (OMNIBUS)
A BLACKBIRD IN AMBER TWILIGHT (OMNIBUS)
DARKER THAN THE STORM

For further information: **www.fredawarrington.com**

About the Author

Freda Warrington was born in Leicester, England, and began writing stories as soon as she could hold a pen. The beautiful ancient landscape of Charnwood Forest, Leicestershire, where she grew up, became a major source of inspiration.

She studied at art college and worked in medical illustration and graphic design for a number of years. However, her first love was always fantasy fiction, and in 1986 her first novel *A Blackbird in Silver* was published. More novels followed, including *A Taste of Blood Wine*, *The Amber Citadel*, *Dark Cathedral* and *Dracula the Undead* – a sequel to Dracula that won the Dracula Society's Best Gothic Novel Award in 1997.

So far she has had twenty-one novels published, varying from sword n' sorcery and epic fantasy to contemporary fantasy, supernatural, and alternative history.

Her novel *Elfland* (Tor US) won the Romantic Times Award for Best Fantasy Novel of 2009. *Midsummer Night*, the second in the *Aetherial Tales* series, was listed by the American Library Association among their Top Ten SF/ Fantasy Novels of 2010.

Titan Books are republishing her vampire series – *A Taste of Blood Wine*, *A Dance in Blood Velvet*, *The Dark Blood of Poppies*, and a brand new novel *The Dark Arts of Blood* (2015) – with gorgeous new covers. The first three were originally published in the 1990s, long before the recent explosion of vampire fiction! (So – no teenagers, no kick-ass super-heroines, no werewolves ... but a dark, gothic romance for grown-ups, set in the decadent glamour of the 1920s.)

A long fascination with King Richard III led her to write *The Court of the Midnight King*, an alternative history/ fantasy take on Richard III's story. First published by Simon & Schuster in 2003, the novel was re-issued – both in Kindle format and in paperback – in 2014 in order to celebrate the astonishing discovery of the King's remains and his reinterment in Leicester.

Freda lives in Leicestershire with her husband Mike and her widowed mother, where she also enjoys crafts such as stained glass and beadwork, all things Gothic, yoga, walking, Arabian horses, conventions and travel.

Copyright Details

Other Telos Horror Titles

GRAHAM MASTERTON
THE DJINN
RULES OF DUEL (WITH WILLIAM S BURROUGHS)
THE WELLS OF HELL

HELEN MCCABE
1: PIPER
2: THE PIERCING
3: THE CODEX

DAVID J HOWE
TALESPINNING
TALES FROM THE WEEKEND (Editor)
A superb science fiction/fantasy/horror anthology containing
contributions from **David J Howe, Paul Lewis, Steve Lockley, Simon
Morden, Justina L A Robson, Darren Shan, Sam Stone** and **Freda
Warrington.**

RAVEN DANE
ABSINTHE AND ARSENIC
DEATH'S DARK WINGS
1: CYRUS DARIAN AND THE TECHNOMICRON
2: CYRUS SARIAN AND THE GHASTLY HORDE
3: CYRUS DARIAN AND THE DRAGON

SIMON CLARK
THE FALL
HUMPTY'S BONES

STEPHEN LAWS
SPECTRE

PAUL FINCH
TERROR TALES OF CORNWALL
chilling tales by Mark Morris, Ray Cluley, Reggie Oliver, Sarah Singleton,
Mark Samuels, Thana Niveau and other award-winning masters and
mistresses of the macabre.

SAM STONE

THE VAMPIRE GENE SERIES
Horror, thriller, time-travel series.
1: KILLING KISS
2: FUTILE FLAME
3: DEMON DANCE
4: HATEFUL HEART
5: SILENT SAND
6: JADED JEWEL

KAT LIGHTFOOT MYSTERIES
Steampunk, horror, adventure series
1: ZOMBIES AT TIFFANY'S
2: KAT ON A HOT TIN AIRSHIP
3: WHAT'S DEAD PUSSYKAT
4: KAT OF GREEN TENTACLES
5: KAT AND THE PENDULUM
6: AND THEN THERE WAS KAT (Forthcoming)

JINX CHRONICLES
Hi-tech science fiction fantasy series
1: JINX TOWN
2: JINX MAGIC
3: JINX BOUND (Forthcoming)

THE DARKNESS WITHIN
Science Fiction Horror Short Novel

COLLECTIONS
ZOMBIES IN NEW YORK
CTHULHU AND OTHER MONSTERS